MURDER IN PURGATORY

A Lyon County Mystery

GK JURRENS

1/11/2025
TUCSON, AZ

UpLife
Press

eBook ISBN: 978-1-952165-19-1
Paperback ISBN: 978-1-952165-18-4
Hardcover ISBN: 978-1-952165-20-7
v.2200711_1532
r.010524
GKJurrens.com

See Appendix A for the Cast of Major Characters

Also, please write and post a brief review on Amazon. Or email your thoughts to
gjurrens@yahoo.com.
I read every single review with gratitude. Thank you.

And feel free to browse or subscribe at GKJurrens.com
for announcements and giveaways.

I

Wednesday
April 4, 1934
South of George, Iowa

LYON COUNTY SHERIFF BILLY RHETT KERSHAW DRILLED HIMSELF for the millionth time. *How in tarnation can I have both nightmares and insomnia at the same time?* He had not slept well for a single night in the last sixteen years.

As he pursued an erratic driver down Lyon County Route 14, the vivid image of his murdered deputy last year—bloodied and disrobed—haunted him. Without warning. Again. Plain as day, in his mind's eye, he visualized the almost-unrecognizable, nearly naked corpse of Deputy Roddy Braddock found last summer on this very stretch of dusty road. Nor could he purge the memory—or the feeling—of twenty-year-old Roddy's pregnant wife beating on his chest with both of her tiny fists. He remembered her fury when he delivered the news of the kid's murder. *Worst part of the job, right there. I can still feel those little hands hammerin' on me.*

A foot-deep rut tried to hurl him off the road. A new rattle clattered underneath his police cruiser and interrupted his waking nightmare. The new sound and vibration wasn't all that obvious, but he feared a mechanical failure, one of a whole collection of fears. *Strange for a guy everybody thinks is fearless. If they only knew.*

Billy vaguely noticed the landscape flying by in a blur. *The last dadgum thing I need right now is a broken axle or snapped leaf spring.*

He needed to stop the careening truck, still two hundred yards ahead of him. *This idiot's gonna kill somebody, maybe himself. Why does everything happen in this part of the county?*

Not only was this where they found Roddy's body, he and some deputized citizens battled a bunch of brutal mobsters on Chief Dan's farm last year, five miles south. *Deputized citizens... now the best friends I got.*

Billy took some small comfort that the fancy flashing light on his left fender and that troublesome siren on the other side both worked today. *New-fangled contraptions decide for themselves when they wanna work. But I sure don't need no farm truck jumpin' out of a blind field road about now.*

This battle-hardened police cruiser, though only two years old, had already been through more than older cop cars. Big and little dents, several bullet holes, and a few scorch marks remained from that altercation during last summer's monster black blizzard. *Yup, that was one helluva storm, in more ways than one.* He secretly admitted those "decorations" added a certain... authenticity to his cruiser, and to his boring job profile in otherwise sleepy Lyon County.

He wasn't *only* an elected official. He and his deputies cleaned up last June by kicking that bunch of big-city bootleggers from out east right straight through the gates of Hell. *Served 'em right.* And with the election coming up in November, a few reminders couldn't hurt.

Billy surprised himself at how much he wanted folks to re-elect him. Being sheriff was more than a job he'd settled into. *There ain't a helluva lot else, with Alice gone 'n all.* He'd lost his young wife to the Spanish influenza sixteen years ago last month.

Right now, though, he'd better focus on his driving. The steering wheel jerked with brutal resolve under his two-fisted grip as the front tires and wheels reacted to the punishing ruts and bumps. The half-frozen ground of this notorious roadway offered no lenience—none at all.

He didn't recognize the old stake-side truck ahead of him. *Now why in thee hell would some stranger be racing through my county at breakneck speeds? What don't I know here? No crimes reported.* But since when were criminals known for their logic? *Maybe he ain't no criminal.* But speeders who fled lawful pursuit, while rare, *were* law breakers, *and* such opportunities gave Billy a sense of official purpose. Truth be told, his job was downright boring most of the time. Now he worried whether the county budget could afford costly mechanical repairs to his cruiser - one-third of their "new" law enforcement fleet.

But he could *not* let this law breaker escape. Despite the dry freeze on the ground, the idiot's truck disappeared now and then into a dust cloud as he kicked up powdery road dirt. Made Billy more than a little nervous whenever he drove into one of those clouds without much idea what he was heading into.

To say the fleeing truck was operating in a crazy manner didn't do justice to what Billy was able to see ahead of him. *Fool must be drunk!* And as if to prove his theory, the driver's front-end dived into a rut that threw him into the west-side ditch. Kicked up dead grass, dirt clods and chunks of debris behind him. Some were parts from his truck. Not a deep ditch, but it was deep enough to roll the truck over twice. No, almost three times, at a blazing fifty miles-an-hour, before it settled onto its driver's side in the adjacent field.

As Billy slowed—he didn't need to brake much as the rough road clawed down his speed on its own—he wrestled the wheel to his right. His two passenger-side wheels descended into the shoulder-slash-ditch. Now, steam rolled out from under his hood. *Must a popped a hose. At least I caught this sumbitch.* His siren took its time winding down. He stepped out of his cruiser and surveyed the scene with deliberation. Just like his deputy, Dwight Spooner, taught him.

The truck had tossed its driver clear. Billy spotted him ten yards away from the truck at the edge of the field. No doubt he'd been thrown out during one of the initial rolls as the truck was farther away from the road. Billy wore his holster low on his right hip with a leather lanyard that secured its bottom to his thigh. Like the pictures he'd seen of Old West lawmen. Not taking any chances, he unsnapped his revolver's retaining loop over its hammer as he approached the driver. Confirmed he was nobody he knew. *Scruffy-lookin' fella, aint'cha?* He had come to rest on his back with one arm bent way back and underneath him—obviously snapped up near the shoulder socket.

Unconscious and unresponsive, lots of blood had already flowed down into his already matted hair. More blood from the center of his forehead had dribbled into his eyes and down onto both temples. He had left the truck through the windshield.

Must a snagged his carotid based on the pool of blood that's drainin' from that gash on the side of his neck. Ain't pumpin' or spurtin', though. Billy'd bet a whole dollar at that point there'd be no pulse.

Could be the old boy hit one of these rocks after the truck tossed him out, too. And something had punctured his left eyeball—looked like its juice leaked out and left it sagging. His other eyeball? All blood-red. *Jeez, mister. Tore you up some, for sure.*

FIRST THINGS FIRST. STANDING AT THE FELLOW'S SIDE, BILLY nudged his foot with his own boot. Nothing. Kneeled down. No pulse. *Yup, darn fool got himself killed, alright. Damn.*

He relaxed a little. Checked all the pockets for identification. Nothing but a tin of chaw with a sticker on the back from Boy's Town General Store. The old boy's shirt was torn and had ridden up. Billy spotted a small but strange tattoo—and only one, as far as he could tell —below his belt line and on his right hip: ♍. He was no fan of tattoos.

And that's when a whole lot of nasty body odor assaulted him. He reeled on his haunches from bowels and bladder set free of the gift of life, as they say. *Cripe sake, mister, ever take a bath?*

The old boy's fingers looked busted up, all gnarled. Could be what they call arthritis, or more likely, old breaks. Or both. Then Billy saw the ring—just one ring. Looked like a wedding ring, but it had been biting into that old boy's finger for a long time. He clearly never took it off. Looked like the only way to get it off now was with a hacksaw. A dull gray thing, ugly, with a slight gold tint, like maybe it was valuable once, or still was if cleaned up and polished. He lifted the old man's gnarled hand just enough to get a closer look. The tiny engravings around the ring's main feature—a bony skull—were too worn to make out. *What in thee hell? What's your story, old son, and what in Sam Hill are you doin' tearin' around God's green acre like a lunatic?*

Billy wrinkled his nose and drew in a sharp breath through his clenched teeth as his knees creaked when he stood. He imagined a thousand possibilities as he shoved back the brim of his favorite black Stetson to scratch his forehead. Fingertips came away greasy.

After staring at the corpse for a good long while, wondering, he noted the time in his ever-present pocket notebook with a stubby little pencil. Half-past eleven in the AM. Jotted down notes on the body's position, a sketch of the unusual tattoo, and the locations of the victim's visible wounds. He scratched out another sketch of the ring, listed the chewing tobacco can, its sticker, even wrote a note on the nature of the old duffer's rank odors.

But Billy registered surprise that he didn't find any evidence of alcohol consumption given his erratic driving. He also noted the truck's location relative to the body. *Not a bad crime scene diagram, cowboy. Too bad this one includes a body.* He immediately scolded himself for being insensitive. That passed.

Based on his proximity to Silas Hummel's farm, he knew he was about four miles south of George on 14, west side. Recorded it all according to the procedures he and Dwight established last Fall. Those procedures were based on his deputy's experience as a homicide detective with the Minneapolis Police Department before the war.

Billy turned away from the corpse and approached the overturned truck in the fallow field. Half-frozen weeds crunched underfoot. That didn't stop dust tendrils from escaping up around his ankles. *Cripes, it's dry.*

He stopped, watched the clouds of vapor from his breath rise straight up—almost no wind. Another note. Steam rose from the truck too, still resting on its driver's side with the radiator pointing back toward the road, like that's where it wanted to be. Stunk of gasoline, but no smoke or flames.

As he got closer and walked all the way around the wreck to get a general sense, Billy noticed some peculiar things. He'd learn more after one of the mechanics from Bairns Motors in George gave her a good once-over. No license plates, front or rear. No registration tag on the steering column. Some blood there, and on the wheel. All the bed's stake sides were busted off, scattered closer to the road. But bits of straw and smears of manure clung to cracks and gaps between the warped planks that made up the truck's bed, which was now more vertical than horizontal. *Like a farm truck. But this shit don't stink like any hog or cattle or horse or even turkey dung I ever smelled before.* This was different.

Plus, he spotted some greasy white stuff smeared here and there on the truck's bed.

Before he wrote down those tidbits, he scratched the back of his chilly neck. *Shoulda worn a jacket and a scarf.*

Somethin' about this whole deal stinks to high Heaven. Billy wrinkled his nose at the strange stench of this many unanswered questions.

What in thee hell?

2

T hursday
April 5, 1934
Rock Rapids, Iowa

SHERIFF BILLY MADE A FEW PHONE CALLS FROM HIS DESK AT THE
Law Enforcement Center. No crimes had been reported nor any trucks
stolen. But then, at that moment, everything stopped. Outside of him,
anyway. Inside, it all raged.

Mid-afternoon doldrums clawed at Billy's conscience the worst.
Especially days like today. He sat frozen in an endless time loop—
sixteen years ago. He battled memories of his dead brothers-in-arms
killed by the enemy, but especially every kid he slaughtered with his
own hands. Those memories squeezed him, every hour of every day,
but right now, more than usual. Each bloody accident or crime scene
made them worse. *Why did Dwight and I survive and they all died? How
can I live with that?*

Every single face—their empty eyes, their mouths hung open in...
surprise... at that, their final moment. Because of him. Each remained

etched behind his own eyelids, seared into his nightmares—awake *and* asleep. Like a branding iron burns into hair and flesh on the rump of a steer.

The endless images of their shredded bodies rushed him, coupled with the stench of their rot from too long left in the mud. The agony of their silent screams. And the fresh ones—that coppery smell of wet meat... and those expressions of... surprise.

Billy relived these endless moments in full color, full motion, and three dimensions. On top of all that, the remembered stench and the screams drove him to distraction. But the non-stop ringing pounded in his ears. Like now. All part of God's reminder: thou shalt not kill.

Sometimes that deafening ringing stung him worse than anything else. No doubt from a week of non-stop artillery barrages raining down on them in the Argonne Forest. He even got a tattoo, of sorts, from an up-close powder burn in front of his left ear, thanks to a Mauser Gewehr 98 rifle's muzzle. He felt that sixteen-year-old stippling—courtesy of a teen-age Nazi—with his index finger. Everything that he still heard in that ear now came to him thick, like through a pillow.

On days like today, he drowned in images of hundreds of German troops and bayonets and eyes dying, inches away—some innocent like he used to be, some murderous. *We did what we had to do, didn't we, cowboy? We survived. Me and Dwight. But all the rest? I'm a good cop, if nothin' else. Gonna find out what happened to that old boy in the truck, aren't we? Yessir, I can do this.*

A haze of dust motes hung in the silent squad room around him in the LEC that fronted on Main Street. Calling it a squad room was a hilarious euphemism. The entire two-room LEC looked more like a medium-size general store with knee-to-ceiling glass facing Main.

Four desks, a couple of bolt-in holding cells in the back, along with a glassed-in office next to the cells for private stuff, which is also where their part-time science guy worked. Old Doc Gustavsen was also the county's as-needed medical guy—general practitioner, coroner, cheerleader on tough cases, whatever. He wasn't around much. Doc Gus also worked the emergency room at the hospital in Spencer.

Lyon County did just fine with a sheriff and two deputies. Most days. Young Jimmy Lenert loved cruising. He'd drive around the county looking for trouble. Dwight Spooner, however, was Billy's age, with similar mileage. His time at the Minneapolis Police Department Metro Division as a decorated detective ended with the war.

After Dwight returned from France in 1918, he shared Billy's night-mare-induced insomnia. They'd both earned their sleeplessness clawing their way into and out of the same bloody fox holes—hundreds of them—in and around the Argonne. After France, Dwight left MPD for unspecified reasons to become a beat cop in the small city of Worthington, Minnesota, for fifteen years.

Then last summer, Billy asked his friend for help with some mobbed-up bootleggers that had invaded Lyon County. Dwight would never refuse a brother-in-arms. He came to work for Billy, who now looked up with just his eyes.

He'd been at his desk all night. It showed. *Morning already? Shit.* Saw Dwight coming through the front door and thought, *Ole Deputy Dawg's runnin' from somethin'. Poor guy.*

❧ 3 ❧

F riday
April 6, 1934

DWIGHT SPOONER SAUNTERED INTO THE LYON COUNTY LAW
Enforcement Center from the morning shadows out on Main. And
there sat Billy, his boss, a living corpse, except for the rubbing. *No
doubt Billy's reliving the horrors of the Argonne. Again. Poor guy. Looks like
hell.*

"Hey, boss. Doing okay?" He waited three long beats before Billy
responded.

"Oh, ah, mornin', Dwight. I'm good. You?"

"Man, you look like crap. You here all night again? How's the arm?
You're rubbing it again."

During one of the running battles with some nasty Chicago mutts
almost a year ago now, Billy's right arm took just a single brutal blow
from an Irish psychopath. The animal wielded a bat with razor blade
chips sticking out of it. Just that one blow is all it took.

"Well, some days 'r better 'n others. Doc tells me floatin' bone fragments in there grind on each other. Can't do much at all over my head anymore, but it's fine." Billy rubbed his arm above the elbow once more. "Doc keeps telling me we need to do somethin'. How was your day off? You sleeping yet, brother?"

"Uh... the county permit office says a circus is coming to town. Already here, in fact. A real gypsy outfit, by the sound of it. They wanna set up at the fairgrounds east of town. City says no, but can't find a legal reason. Ideas?"

"Don't we have a lawyer for such stuff? A circus, eh? When's the last time we had one a them come to town?" Dwight knew his boss didn't expect an answer, him not being from these parts. He moved down from Minnesota last summer, during... the troubles.

"All they need is a temporary business permit, and the county attorney says we have no legal grounds not to grant 'em one given the charter of the county fairgrounds."

"Dwight, you got any experience with this sort of outfit from your days in Minneapolis?"

"Yeah, some. They're different folks who keep to themselves, except during business hours. They don't mix well with everyday folk, is my experience. Some are shady, but most are okay, I guess— the shows we had up there, anyway." He nodded over his left shoulder in the general direction of Minnesota. "Would be smart to monitor 'em, though." Dwight wrinkled his nose and added more syrup to his words than he was feeling. Some things were better left unsaid.

"How long they wanna stay?"

"Mavis over at Permits says the maximum - a week. Rolled in late yesterday. Their head honcho knows we'd be hard-pressed to keep 'em out. I guess they called ahead. Nothing else in April, for sure. County Fair isn't til July. Still too cold for tractor meets, too. Fact is, they're already set up over there."

"Well, we should wander over, introduce ourselves, ask if they need anything, welcome 'em to town." The sheriff winked.

"Aw, Billy, I do believe you are just a young boy at heart who always wished he'd run away with the circus. Either that or you're hoping for a glimpse of some of them hoochie-koochie girls from the sideshow, eh, brother?" Dwight winked back and smiled. Looked like a perfect time for a distraction, anyway. And maybe there was some dirt to plow.

Billy turned serious. "Well, we also got this fatal accident down south of George. Nobody I know. After Doc Gus collected the corpse on Wednesday, he took it over to the hospital in Spencer. I owe him a call to see if he learned anything. We can ask the circus people if they're missin' anybody."

Billy shared the specifics of what he saw at the scene. As they wound up that discussion and prepared to head over to the fairgrounds, a crowd of six uppity-dressed women burst through the Law Enforcement Center's front door.

❧ 4 ❧

🙥🙥🙥

The obvious leader of this posse aimed the blunt end of her voice at Billy like she kissed a bullhorn with her wrinkled lips. "Sheriff, we need to report a crime!"

Billy groaned inside but smiled on the outside. Old Laticia was a looker in her day. Now? "Um, well, c'mon in, y'all. Deputy, scare up a few more chairs for these nice ladies, if ya please. But while he's doin' that, is anybody in any danger right this moment?" Billy's first concern was public safety, even considering the source. While Dwight gathered all the chairs in the squad room, the ring leader plopped down first in the chair already in front of Billy's desk. She started speaking again before her bony butt even hit the chair.

"We're *all* in danger, Sheriff, *imminent* danger—of losing our souls."

Billy's expression of mild urgency—as required by his station— developed into one of tolerant skepticism. He didn't wait for the rest of the ladies to be seated before he dropped into the swivel chair behind his desk. Picked up a pencil, poised it over a tablet's fresh page. "Alrighty. First, your full name, please?" He knew who she was. Lived right across the street from the LEC. One of those rabble-rousing

13

church ladies from First B. They always stirred up one ruckus or another—she and the rest of her Lyon County Civic League, including some members from down George way.

"You know who I am, Billy. What're you playing at?"

"It's for the official complaint, Laticia. Now please state your full name, for the record." *If she 'n her gaggle are gonna muddle up my morning, she'll play by my rules, dag-nabbit.*

❧

"Fine." She fussed with the lap material of her fancy dress. Tugged on the hems of her gloves as she flexed her fingers while she decided just how much nonsense she'd allow this *agnostic* to get away with. "Laticia Portia Morgenstern, complainant. Satisfied? Now can we get on with it, please? We are *terrified*."

❧

Amidst a hubbub of scraping sounds and the shuffling of stiff fabrics, Dwight gathered three chairs from the other desks. With two more chairs used for interviewing complainants and suspects, he seated the five ladies. He remained standing. They appeared pissed— all except one younger lady, a girl whose head remained bowed. She looked no one in the eye. Not yet.

Billy said, "Okay, Laticia. Thanks. And who are you other lovely ladies?" As they each introduced themselves, only one name stuck in Dwight's mind: the attractive girl with the downcast eyes who wasn't wearing a ring—Justina Ringwall.

Billy recorded everyone's name in his notebook before he allowed anyone to say anything else, even though Laticia seemed the only person who was allowed to speak for this group.

"Alright, then. Very good. Now, Laticia, would ya kindly state the nature of the crime you're reporting, please?"

"Sheriff, I am shocked you're not already aware of the travesty taking place just west of here at the fairgrounds. You are allowing our fair community to be *invaded* by a cauldron of iniquity. That, that *circus* looks like they're here to stay, and it's a downright crime they are here at all! We need to understand what you are doing about it. What do you have to say for yourself, *Sheriff?*" She spat out the last word as if Satan himself had already set her tongue aflame.

Dwight felt some pity for Billy, but this little dance amused him. With the election coming up, he could not afford to alienate a single voter, what with Rock Rapids mayor, Harold Deemers himself, running against him. The man was a menace, but the ladies all loved his folksy Will Rogers humor and his Clark Gable demeanor—the hair, the voice, the mustache, the money, everything. Might be a genuine threat. He didn't know jack-shit about law enforcement, but delivered a helluva good law-and-order speech to anybody who would listen. It's like he needed *sheriff* on his resume en route to some higher office.

"Laticia, I understand your concern. I do. But you're talkin' to the wrong guy. I enforce the laws, I don't make 'em. The county attorney, Clint Grossman, says there ain't no legal grounds to keep that bunch out. Besides, they're just folks gettin' by, and only here for a week. They ain't breakin' no laws."

"Sheriff, need I remind you how we warned you Zach Mutter's speakeasy down in George last year would be trouble, and you ignored us? Next thing, you're in there with a couple of federal ruffians shooting up the place, killing Zach, and sending Rafe Plunkett to prison, not that he didn't have it coming. Remember that?"

"Of course, I do, Laticia, and—"

"*And* now you're failing all over again. You haven't learned your lesson, have you?" She wagged her right index finger at Billy from inside her spotless white glove like she was scolding a neighborhood child from atop her pristine pedestal of righteousness. Awhile back, Billy had told Dwight she never had any children of her own.

"Laticia, I was just going over there to make darn sure that—"

"Billy, you've done some good for the county, what with ousting those big-city bootleggers last summer, but the righteous must remain vigilant. I'm sure you don't want the Lyon County Civic League endorsing Harold for Sheriff come November, do you?" Laticia's animations caused her well-powdered forehead and sharp nose to glisten, not to mention setting her adequate bosom to dancing. Not that there was much there to see, but her brassiere worked overtime as she flourished.

"Ladies, I hear you. Let me see what I can do. Fair enough?"

"Thank you, Billy. That's all we ask. Now go get those... *monsters* out of our community. We'll be watching, Sheriff." And with a whirl-wind of taffeta and parasols, the Lyon County church-lady posse blew on out of the LEC.

Dwight spotted the girl, Justina, looking over her shoulder. She met his eye, as she was the last to leave. His heart flipped as her lips parted, just a little.

After they all left, Billy looked at Dwight, shrugged, and said, "So let's go look Satan's helpers in the eye. See if we can still save Lyon County from getting sucked through the very gates a Hell. Okay, Deputy?"

※ 5 ※

T he Lyon County Sheriff's department descended upon the small circus-slash-carnival called Perlatelli's Oddities and Wonders. Their logo above the main gate was a huge brown eye with the turquoise letters *POW!* in its center.

A lanky roustabout past his prime introduced himself to Billy and Dwight at the gate. He offered no last name. Explained that one of his jobs was security for the circus lot.

"Nice to meet ya, Jed." Billy offered his right hand. Jed took a couple of beats to spit a cheek full of tobacco juice off to the side before he shook it. Dwight held back a giant step.

Billy consulted a copy of the show's permit he clutched in his left hand. He continued. "We'd like to talk to Antonia Perlatelli. Sorta welcome y'all to Lyon County."

"Well, ah, sure. I guess Madame wouldn't mind." He pronounced it *m'DAHM*.

"Madame?" Billy mimicked the guard's pronunciation, but it came across sounding phony from within his nasal drawl.

"Yeah, that's what we call the boss. Madame Perlatelli. Some folks have trouble with her last name, ya see? And we got more 'n a few foreigners workin' the show."

Billy's cop sense kicked in. Jed wasn't unfriendly, but was uncomfortable talking to lawmen. His body language screamed it. Billy glanced over at Dwight, who picked this up too.

Jed hesitated, as if still wrestling with escorting these outsiders onto *his* lot, before he wheeled in his tracks after an awkward few seconds and limped away. "This way to the back lot, gents," and led them off past a row of animal cages perpendicular to the show's midway, toward an area marked, *Authorized Entry Only*. Dwight and Billy looked at each other, both sniffing the air.

Jed unhooked a droopy chain that guarded a narrow entrance between two temporary fence-ends. Allowed them to pass. Re-hung the chain behind them, hooking the last link onto a nail. Both cops noticed the lax security across the entire lot. No surprise. They were only here for the week.

Thirty yards later, after weaving through various wagons and trailers scattered helter-skelter, they stopped at the base of a set of steps that led up to an ornately painted wagon. The sign above the door on its rear read, *Office*. A noisy generator thumped away nearby, spewing diesel fumes heavy enough that the air tasted and smelled of greasy soot.

Jed limped up the steps—must be a peg leg—knocked on the door, and after hearing a muffled response, he cracked it open. Said a few words, left it cracked, turned and trundled down the steps again to stand beside the cops. The door swung wide with a flourish, and there stood the boss, Madame Antonia Perlatelli.

Although neither knew what to expect, Madame's appearance startled both Billy and Dwight. Jed slithered away without another word as if he dared not remain too long in *Madame's* presence.

She was young and attractive. No, she was stunning. With a name that sounded Italian, Billy and Dwight expected dark hair and an olive complexion. Her appearance left their jaws hanging slack. They stared at her swirls of brilliant blonde hair and a full-body compliment of magnificent body art on creamy bronze skin. At least the ample portion of her hour-glass shape they could see, despite the chill in the air. Colorful tattoos extended from her bare shoulders to her wrists. They covered every square inch. From her slender but muscular legs where they emerged from a *very* skimpy pair of shorts down to her ankles, even from high on her neck down to her winsome cleavage and down to her bare midriff had all been some ink master's canvas. No tattoos on her perfect face, however, a face that enchanted both men, nor on her hands. She looked nothing like the boss lady of a rough gypsy circus. Not that they would know.

Madame's pouty lips complimented her high cheekbones. A sharp Roman nose divided her gigantic green eyes—both dark *and* luminous. She wore at least one exotic ring on every finger, bracelets on both wrists, and a multi-threaded necklace that hung halfway to her pierced navel. *A ring through her navel?* That navel was also surrounded by intricate geometric designs of blue-green, red and yellow. Looked like a staring eye. The effect was startling.

Her short rust-red nails punctuated the end of each finger and matched the color of a wide flapper-style headband that covered her forehead. Her silk-white hair was long, but gathered in two loose buns low at the rear of her neck on each side—an active woman's hair. This casual style allowed two enormous silver hoop earrings to be in full view under each of her lobes.

She floated down the stairs in some sort of practical athletic shoes. She looked every bit the part of a working gypsy girl, but not a hardball show executive.

The young woman glided to a stop in front of Sheriff Billy, who wore no uniform—only his gold badge over the right breast of his western-style checkered shirt. She stared at his official black Stetson perched atop his straw-colored hair. Next, he was in for at least one more shock from this exotic woman. Dwight remained a strategic distance away.

In a husky half-whisper, Madame Perlatelli projected her voice like a stage performer, which startled Billy as it pierced his expectations of this tall young woman.

"Gentlemen." She seemed amused as she cast a magnetic gaze, first upon the sheriff and second, at Dwight. Both men appeared... *unsettled.* She continued, "I apologize for my appearance. Normally I cover my body art when meeting members of a community for the first time. Some find it... cómo se dice... *unsettling*."

Billy thought, *Interesting she used that word. Almost as if....*"Um, right, ah, no worries, ma'am."

"Sheriff, would you do me the courtesy of addressing me as Madame?"

"Oh, ah, sure. Doesn't that mean you're married, like in eye-talian, or somethin'? I mean, just for the record. Isn't that—?" Billy's verbal stumbling advertised his discomfort, not with women in general, but specifically with *this* woman. He couldn't explain it, nor would he try. She smelled like fresh morning coffee on a campfire in the woods. *Jeez! Where did **that** come from?*

"Yes, Sheriff. Or something. My heritage is from the Basque region in the north of Spain, near the southern border of France. I speak many languages, but as a matter of convenience, I speak the English and the Spanish. Few understand the Basque. Mi esposo—husband—who was Italiano, no longer wanders this plane of existence."

"He's dead? You're a widow?" He didn't like how that came out, as if this was a pleasant surprise. *Jeez, Billy!*

Dwight said, "Sheriff, don't you have a couple of questions for *Madame?*" Billy heard the unmistakable derision in Dwight's voice. He turned to his senior deputy to give him a chance to collect his own wits. Dwight *was* in uniform and had hooked his thumbs in his equipment belt. The fingers of his right hand curved back to hover near the butt of his service weapon. Professional power posturing.

"Yes, of course." Now sounding official, trying not to stare at those incredible tattooed legs, or that cleavage, or that pierced navel, he raised his eyes to look into hers. She watched with obvious amusement. He cleared his throat. "Madame, I'm sure you're no stranger to small towns and—"

She interrupted with that husky whisper. "You are here to inform me that some of your citizens do not welcome us here. And that we can expect some who believe we are a bad influence, or even evil. I suspect you've received at least one visit from a handful of your people who have demanded that you—how you say—*kick us out,* no?"

"Well, uh—"

"I see by the plaque on your chest su nombré es Billy, yes?" She pronounced it BEE-lee, and followed that with a coy smile. "May I call you Billy?"

"Sí. I mean, yes."

"Well, Billy, está bien. We are no strangers to those who understand us. But we *are* different. We... stand apart. And we are performers. We expect this. But we are also a business. Please accept these four passes to all of our performances, for you, your deputy, and your wives—good for the entire week we are here. Por favór." As if by magic, the passes appeared in her hand a moment before she slid them into Billy's left shirt pocket after she unbuttoned its flap with her delicate fingers. After she inserted the tickets, she patted his pocket with her left hand.

"Oh, neither of us is married, Madame."

"*Muy* bien, Billy. Now, if you will excuse me, I must attend to business." (BEEZ-noos). "We open mañana. I am hopeful you will find our parade through your village entertaining."

"Just one more thing... Madame. There was a single vehicle accident about fifteen miles from here, someone not from around these parts. An older gentleman with long hair and beard. He had no identification. Drove a stake-side truck. He one a yours?"

"I do not believe so, Billy. Adios, mis amigos." She pecked him on the cheek. Billy did not pull away. Instead, he leaned into it. A little. Just like that, she spun and glided up the steps. He admired the "body art" that covered most of Madame's backside, too. Looked like some might be religious. She closed the door without a sound. Billy stared up at the door.

A helluva thing.

6

"**H**ey, pardner, you okay over there?" The entire spectacle amused *and* concerned Dwight, though he was glad his boss and friend benefitted from an amusing distraction.

"Huh? Jeez, Dwight, what the hell was *that?*"

"Show people, brother. Be careful. That there is the head of the snake."

"You don't like... show people, do ya?"

"So BEE-lee, what are you gonna tell the church ladies about the parade through our *village* mañana, *Sheriff?*" He mimicked the way church lady Laticia Morgenstern had said that last word earlier.

"Oh, boy."

BILLY LED THE WAY THROUGH THE LEC'S FRONT DOOR AFTER THEIR return from the fairgrounds. Wandered over to his desk, plopped into his chair, and motioned Dwight to his guest chair. Tossed his Stetson onto the floor-standing rack behind him without looking. He'd hit the mark, like always. Rubbed his forehead with worry, then his sore arm. Unconsciously.

"Have a seat, pardner. I'm scratchin' my head over this truck rollover on Wednesday. I could use another pair of eyes." He'd been trying to tackle this mystery solo, which was foolhardy, especially considering Dwight's experience. A matter of pride now to be swallowed.

"Well, at the MPD, we'd focus on what the evidence shows us. What's that?"

With a one-hand flourish, Billy whipped open the small notebook he had retrieved from his hip pocket before he sat down. He'd read his notes from the scene so many times, he didn't need to refer to them now as he rattled them off.

"The old guy was most definitely a stranger to these parts. Was drivin' crazy, but nothin' says he was drinkin'. No sign a drugs either. No license plates or vehicle registration. Old guy was wearin' a weird ring with a skull on it, and he sported just one small tattoo." He showed Dwight what he had sketched in his notebook. "And all the old boy had in his pockets was a can a chaw with a Boy's Town sticker on the back. Oh, and I won't never forget the strange shit stink comin' from the truck's bed. Ain't like any manure I ever been around before. And when I touched the edge of the truck's bed, I came away with some greasy white stuff on my fingers. What's that all add up to, other than zilch?"

"Hang on there, boss. This tells us more than nothing. For example, *because* he's a stranger says he's away from his home turf. Another good question to add to our list is *why?* Next, erratic driving—erratic, but not drinking or drugging? Says maybe the guy had mental issues. Or he was hallucinating. Might influence how we investigate this. And the ring? I bet somebody knows what it stands for. Maybe another good clue. And the Boy's Town sticker? I'll bet dollars to donuts your lady friend's show worked Boy's Town. I'll run it down."

Dwight was on a roll. "A vehicle with no plates says he was looking to conceal his identity or the ownership of the truck. Plus, the only strangers we've seen around here are from the show over at the fairgrounds. He likely drove a circus truck, but running like crazy *away* from the circus? To me, says he was running scared. Something or someone within the show scared the shit out of him. Finding out who or what might help us understand *why* he got himself killed. This was *not* just a fatal vehicle accident. I'd ask your lady friend some very tough questions, boss."

"Dwight, she *ain't* my lady friend. Although that peck on the cheek she gave me was mighty nice." Wink.

"Smelled good too, even six feet away. Now, speaking of odors, that exotic dung we passed today in those animal cages, that our new acquaintance Jed hustled us on by? I'm betting you caught that big cat or monkey stink like I did, boss. I saw your eyes. Same as in that truck, maybe? Confirmation that your lady fr... that *Madame* lied to us? If true, they call *that* obstruction. We could bring her in."

"Whoa! Let's reign that in some, cowboy. We might get there pretty quick, but I'd like to sniff around a little more first. That's a great crime scene analysis though, *Detective*. We gotta get inside that darn show somehow. Get somebody to open up. Can't believe they're that close-mouthed over there!"

"Billy, I've come across their type before. I'd bet anything they're hiding a lot more than what we're investigating. And I guarantee there's a *lot* off-kilter inside that crowd. They're acting guilty because they are. Guaranteed."

"You might be right, Dwight, but I don't wanna kick that hornet's nest before we score some honey. They'd only close ranks more'n they already have. We need solid evidence."

Dwight wasn't happy. "You're the boss, but we're stalled unless we shake something loose."

"I know, pardner. I know."

❦

Billy's phone rang. He hoisted it off his desk, plucked the earpiece off the hook, held the mouthpiece in front of him. "Sheriff Billy Kershaw here."

"Sheriff, Doc Gustavsen here. Something mighty strange happened last night, Billy. Somebody broke into the morgue over here at the hospital. Grabbed your rollover victim's personal effects, such as they were: a can of chewing tobacco and a ring."

"The hell, you say! Everybody okay over there, Doc?"

"Well, yes. We're a little shaken, though. Nobody's ever done anything like this before. Like I said, mighty strange. Had to press a bone saw into service to get that darn ring off the old boy's finger, too."

"Huh. This case just got a heap more interesting. I'll send Jimmy over." Click.

Dwight looked on, having heard only Billy's side of the conversation. "What?"

7

T he Hardt Home Place
Six Miles South of George, Iowa

SOPHIE GREW UP A TOWN GIRL. BUT A YEAR EARLIER, SHE MARRIED A poor farmer and penniless inventor named Jacob Hardt. Now, a few of Jake's inventions were paying off, at last.

This past winter over at the hospital in Spencer, Doc Gustavsen delivered her son, Leo. Doc said afterward that complications almost killed both mother and child.

Since she was eight, when polio had struck her, Sophie had lived with partial paralysis of her right hand and left foot. The virus also atrophied and curved her spinal column which caused its own set of complications. But she never let her handicaps stand in her way. Quite the contrary, Sophie claimed they only strengthened her. Nobody doubted that. She was a force of nature. Early on, the shock of moving from town to the farm almost broke her. But she not only adapted, she now loved the life of a farm wife with her sweet Jake and little Leo.

Today was a day for good moods.

. . .

"JAKE, I CAN'T TELL YOU HOW MUCH IT MEANS TO HAVE A PUMP right here in the kitchen. This is, well, a true blessing! I don't have to carry water any more. And now, with this new electrified refrigeration appliance, well, this is better than living in town!"

"Ya know, since Chief hired me, it's downright spooky what a man can do with a regular paycheck." He cut loose with one of those infamous Hardt smirks. "Sorry it took this long to get some of the stuff you deserved from the start, Soph."

"Well, now, with little Leo and the start of our own family, we are truly blessed." She looked down at the squirming bundle in her arms. Baby Leo was now four months old. *And he not only stinks to high Heaven, again, he's soaked clean through. Praise the Lord, the plumbing works!*

"Well, you scared Hell right out a me, Soph."

"Jake!" His insistence on the use of profanity never ceased to annoy her. Just a little. She smiled.

"Sorry. You scared me. I thought I lost you *and* Leo—" A lump in his throat cut him short as he remembered, again, her difficult delivery.

At that moment, his live-in cousin and farm hand Walt Weller joined them in the kitchen after kicking off his boots in the mudroom behind them. Walked straight up to Sophie sitting at the table next to Jake and pecked her on the cheek. Tweaked little Leo's nose, while his other arm rested on Jake's right shoulder. Jake smiled up at his rowdy cousin, who said, "How's my godson doing today, Soph? Can I watch you breast-feed the little shaver?"

"Walt!" But she knew he was only joking, not that she cared who witnessed that treasured intimacy between mother and child. But to say it out loud cheapened its beauty somehow.

"Jake, the snow fence along the driveway is all repaired."

"Walt, I gotta ask you, cuz. You had a great thing going with the casino up in Fort Tate. The tribe loved your work spotting grifters and managing the floor for 'em. Why'd you give that up?"

"Hey, from the get-go I told 'em it was only temporary because I had to get back here to help raise my godson. Even though Sophie won't let me watch her breastfeed."

That was Walt. Sophie just smiled. It was good to have him back. *He is so good for Jake.* Last summer, criminals burned their barn and killed some of their livestock because Walt had crossed some dangerous people. His real reason for taking the good-paying casino job at the Lakota reservation up in North Dakota? That allowed him to help pay for the barn's rebuild and replace Jake's hog that was killed.

Just then, the excitable Edie Everniss burst into the kitchen. "Hello, everyone! Hi, Walt. Welcome back! Have you all heard the news?"

❦

EDIE WAS SOPHIE'S LONG-TIME FRIEND FROM TOWN WHO NOW LIVED at Chief Dan Rustywire's place. Besides being one of Chief's few friends, Jake worked at Red Chief Dirigibles, Inc.—at his farm.

Edie had taken sanctuary at Chief Dan's place four miles farther south on County 14 last summer to escape her abusive ex-husband. The First Baptist church ladies in George accused her of living in sin, a *divorcee* living with an *Indian*, no less. Chief slept in the barn, as was his habit, and Edie slept in the big house. They were friends. Chief had a big heart. But she was a pariah to these pious town ladies—had been since the previous June. Didn't bother her one wit. She thought it was funny.

Walt said, "Edie, hi! Didn't hear you drive up."

"Oh, I broke down out in the driveway and hiked in. Lots of steam, or smoke, or whatever, coming out from under the hood of Chief's old truck." As if breaking down and hiking in was the most normal thing in the world.

"So, that's your big news? That's not news. That truck is always breaking down."

"Silly, a circus is in town! Well, up at the county fairgrounds in Rock Rapids. An old friend visited me earlier today with the news. I couldn't wait to come over here. Isn't it *wonderful?*"

Sophie loved seeing her oldest and best friend animated, but she worried. "That *is* exciting news, Edie. An old friend, you say?" The furrow in Sophie's brow that accompanied her coy grin could not be mistaken for anything other than worry. Edie and several of her *old friends* had become addicted to a rogue batch of liquor mixed with drugs last summer. It almost killed her. She'd battled her addiction ever since.

Edie's face lit up at her best friend's concern. "Oh, my, Sophie, dear. Not to worry. This is just Dorothy Jones. She was never part of *that* crowd. That's where I draw the line. Hey, are we going to the circus, or what?"

8

***

Deputy Dwight Spooner found himself helpless. He leveraged his official capacity at the Hall of Records to research the young church lady who had caught his eye. When she visited the Law Enforcement Center as part of Laticia Morgenstern's delegation of Lyon County church ladies, he thought he must have caught her eye too. Something about her, something undefinable, but compelling. He just *had* to know more about her.

Normally, he wouldn't consider associating with... a *church lady*. Aw, who was he kidding? There was no *normal* with women for him. He'd been a loner since the war. No explaining that, but now, he wondered if things might be different.

He found the unexpected. Justina Ringwall grew up in the middle of a large and troubled family in George, with three brothers and two sisters. Like him. Her dad drank. Mom was the pious one. Dad left, leaving Justina's mother to raise six kids by herself. Rough.

He'd call her. Yup, that's what he'd do. As a follow up on the circus investigation. Unofficially, of course.

Nothing wrong with that, is there?

9

J ed cringed.

Why had Madame called him to her wagon? She *never* did that. Something had happened. He was in trouble. He spit before climbing the steps to her wagon with some difficulty. The darn peg leg always had to follow his left.

He knocked. Heard her soft but sharp voice inside, "Entrar." Her crisp whisper sent a shiver all the way down his spine, every time. His gut lurched. Being this close to her, well, was always dangerous. He opened the door, stepped in, closed the door, and stood there. Awkward.

She sat behind her desk in tight trousers that left *nothing* to his imagination with one thigh-high leather boot hoisted on top of an open drawer to her left. "Please to sit, Jed." She motioned to the stool in front of her tiny desk with a short riding crop looped around her right wrist.

He did as he was told without saying a word. Dragged his ragged and dusty fedora from his head, and gripped it with both hands between his knees. He dared not gaze into her eyes. Instead, he stared at his hat with only an occasional glance cast in her general direction. Then only at her elegant fingers that had set aside the riding crop. They now worked over a poppet on the desktop. *That poppet, that was one of Garth's!* By all that is holy, he feared what she'd say next.

"Jed, you must now tell me the truth." Sounded like *zee troot.* "This effigy, does it not look very much like you, dear Jed?"

Did she call me 'dear?' If I were a Christian... Jesus, Mary 'n Joseph! He could feel his face flushing to the color of a pickled beet. He realized he had to say something.

"Madame, I'm not sure. Is that one of... *his?*"

They all acknowledged Garth Nitstone for his spells, especially his vengeance curses. A mean son-of-a-bitch, that one. Some say he had genuine power.

"Sí, and I believe that is no surprise to you. Tell me of the curse. Now."

"Madame, please—"

She snatched the riding crop once more and slammed the flat of its head on her desk. The loud slap caused Jed to jump off the stool. It toppled behind him. He almost lost his balance. Dropped his hat. To buy time, he wheeled around, picked up the stool. Turned to face her again. With eyes wide and a visible tremor, he stood there, frozen, speechless.

Finally, he cast tearful eyes toward this powerful woman, this beautiful, strong woman. The words came slowly at first. Then, they tumbled out faster and faster until they slurred into one another from his now-parched throat. "Madame, he... humiliated me. He said, er, awful things. I threatened him. He told me he would curse me. A death curse. By the looks a that poppet, he done that. I'm thinkin' it's been startin' to work. Dunno. That's all I know."

He sniffled like a schoolboy who'd had the back of his hands swatted with a ruler. Wiped his nose on his sleeve, then on his thumb knuckle.

"Jed, I do not mean to be cruel, but I must know, you see. One more matter. What is that you hang around your neck with the leather strap?"

The sudden look of shock and shame eclipsed his reaction to their earlier dialogue. He backed up a step, squinted, jerked his head from side to side as if it were an involuntary reaction. "Madame, no—"

"Jed, you tell me this instant. You must tell me."

He started sputtering an almost inaudible chant.

"Jed?"

"Well, um, it's, um," he spit it out, now louder than he intended in a tumble of words, "it's a nine-charm bag, is all."

As the show's general manager, it fell upon Madame to clean out Garth Nitstone's personal effects after his death. He kept most of that in an old sea chest. She knew that was a family heirloom.

Madame wore a distinctive rust-red nail polish she conjured from alkanet root, olive oil, henna, and beeswax. She was also well-versed in the art of casting spells for healing, for facilitating emotional well-being. And yes, for some influencing, as well. It shocked her to find a small wide-mouth bottle in Garth's chest that contained toenail clippings stained with her unique color.

She also discovered a lock of silver-blonde hair that matched hers. Someone was casting a charm in her direction. For what purpose, she could guess. She always thought Jed's crush on her was harmless, even adorable, and that he tried hard to hide it. But if this was what she suspected, it went too far. Despite having made her feelings crystalline clear, he had persisted. And now, this. It had to stop.

Madame retrieved Garth's jar from a pocket in her tunic and tossed it onto her desk with a small clatter. The tiny collection of intimate artifacts was in full view through the transparent walls of the little bottle. It lay on its side between them as it rolled to a stop. Jed now cowered like a dog about to be beaten.

"Madame—"

"Jed, what sort of spell did Garth cast for you? Now you must be honest with me."

THE POOR MAN JUST STOOD THERE. HER HEART HURT FOR HIM. HE pressed his palms together under his chin, as if to pray. His hat dangled between the heels of his hands. Raised his eyes and risked looking into hers, but could only do so for a second before peering at the little bottle laying there, like a reckless accusation. "Madame, I have potent feelings for you. I just thought—"

"Oh, Jed. Haven't I made myself clear? I am most flattered, but this must stop. I am your boss. Now if you wish to stay with the show—"

The poor man blubbered, shook his head violently side-to-side, shaking loose a short string of foamy spittle from the left corner of his mouth. "I'm sorry. I'm sorry. I'll do anything. Don't cast me out. Just being here in the show is enough. I realize that now. Madame, please."

"Give me the bag."

He looked as if she was about to tear out his heart. Shook his head again, but at last, he relinquished. Instead of slipping the stout thong from which the small leather bag hung over his head, he reached under his shirt. Grabbed the bag in his now white-knuckled fist, and jerked downward—not in anger, but with passion. It took two tries. The thong snapped. He stepped forward and laid the pouch on her desk, but was slow to release it.

"Gracias, Jed. Now please return to your duties."

"Thank you, Madame. Thank you." He risked one more longing stare at her, then at the bag, inhaled her scent which permeated the wagon's interior, and turned to leave. Stumbled on a wrinkle in an ancient throw rug. He recovered with an embarrassed sideways glance over his shoulder at the floor next to the door, and left.

AFTER THE DOOR CLOSED BEHIND HIM, SHE MUTTERED TO HERSELF, *Santa Madre de Dios....*

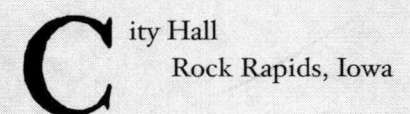

10

C ity Hall
Rock Rapids, Iowa

HAROLD DEEMERS TOOK GREAT PRIDE IN HIS IMPECCABLE appearance. Nobody in town dressed as well. Nobody else had that kind of money, or cared as much about their appearance.

But right now, he thought little about that. He slumped in his grand executive chair with his enormous desk behind him. Both were the property of his expansive estate. Feeling sorry for himself, with his elbows on his knees, he peered out of the vast array of windows that overlooked Fifth Street three floors below. Nobody down there.

Anyone who imagines being the mayor of a small town is easy has no idea what it's like. Provincial attitudes trump rational reasoning. Constituents assume I have power that I don't. Now, this gypsy circus and a dead body show up. The most influential locals are in a lather, and nobody knows what the hell is going on. I need to grab the reins before things get out of control.

· · ·

ALL MAYOR DEEMERS EVER WANTED WAS TO SERVE. THE PUBLIC. AT least that's what he told anyone interested enough to ask, or to listen. When he was six, he pretended to be the general of an invincible army on the grounds of his parents' manicured lawn. His lust for influence ignited and burned brightly then, as it had ever since. But it was not just egoism. He imagined his political leadership could change the world, or at least a piece of it. To his advantage, of course.

What happened in the next several days, however, might very well launch or end his career before it ever got off the ground. Beyond that of a small-town mayor, that is.

He needed serious help. Again.

❧ II ❧

F ri   Friday
            April 6, 1934
            Lyon County Fairgrounds, Rock Rapids, Iowa

THEY CALLS ME BABBO THE MANIMAL. NEVER HAD NO REAL NAME AS I *can remember. They calls freaks like me pinheads. But that ain't the fancy doctor name for what I got born with.*

I like hangin' out with the rousters instead a the other freaks or them performers—they's too full a themselves, except fer Lilith, a course. She looks up to me. That's sayin' somethin' cuz I be just four feet tall. Madame measured me, 'n it's printed on me billing with me picture. I done slouched a might.

Lilith is a little person, ya see. Not a oddity like me, and not a dwarf, mind ya, but a perfect little beauty. Sings 'n dances 'n plays the fiddle in the midget show under the big top. With her daddy, Tom Smalley.

I got almost nothin' in common with most a the other freaks. They all think I got nothin' upstairs, and that's okay by me. I just ain't never had no real schoolin', is all. Plus, I work the gaff pretty good.

Tonight, gonna hang out down at the back lot where a few a the rousters hunker down in the bunk tent. Like most every night, we be playin' cards and cuttin' up jackpots—sharin' lies 'n tall tales—about other shows we done worked all over. Stuff the rubes'd never understand. We won't start til later tonight after a tough set-up that done took longer 'n usual today. The ground, just damn hard, and a big wind done kicked up. That sure pissed off the boss canvasman, ole Cogholdt. But most everything pisses off that fancy pants. He also be the ringmaster.

The rousters, they a bunch a boys alright, but they let me join in even though I win a lot. They still nice to ole Babbo. A tiny head don't mean a tiny brain.

Twenty years ago, I think, me mum popped me out with a small noggin, which is still just the size of a grapefruit—more like a pointy squash. Folks laugh at me huge forehead, me big hooked nose and no hair anywhere 'cept a tiny patch where most men go bald. Folks wonder 'bout that. I be growin' a pony tail, cuz I can. They be shavin' me everywhere else for the shows. I like that okay.

Madame features me as one a her star oddities. Says the word oddity is only fer the chumps that pay fer the sideshow. And she always spots me right next to the big top, right at the top a the midway. "Prime spot, Babbo," she says. Madame Perlatelli's Oddities and Wonders be more oddities than wonders now, anyway.

The big top only seats maybe thirty chumps in all. I got more'n that oglin' at me in the sides on a good day. They even lets me in the ring sometimes if the crowds ain't makin' enough noise. Madame says they laugh cuz I be a good performer, too. But I ain't snooty, or full a me self. Madame ain't a bad sort, and she smells real good, but she be one tough nutter, alright. Gotta be fer the show, especially bein' a woman 'n all.

Sometimes they dress me up like a girl. Messes with the chumps, ya see. Babbo don't care none.

Some calls the show Madame's Purgatory. Some a them whinin' types—'specially them performers, 'specially cocky Cogholdt. Not me. Hell, this be way better 'n me last gig with the big show everybody's heard of. We don't say the name. They done treat me like a animal.

Madame's gig is way better, but ain't as showy. I still draw in the chumps. Folks come in to me tent to meet me now, like a real boy. Instead a bein' in a Ten-in-One Freak Show, Madame spots me in me own Single-O—just me in me own tent. Madame even lets me be my own pitchman. Chumps ask me questions and I answer 'em. Most 'r okay—curious-like, cuz they never done talked to no freak before, ya see. I be nineteen now, I think, and never happier, but I miss me mum. Never had no daddy comin'up.

Madame treats her freaks good as long as we draw the chumps. I play me fiddle now cuz I want to. Still pretty good. The chumps 'n the rubes—that be the payin' customers—they okay in most towns, but some of 'em be downright mean. They think a dime buys 'em a right. I guess I get that.

Besides, people be scared a what they don't understand, or what don't fit inside their kind a normal. Still hurts, ya know? Some 'er meaner 'n others.

That's okay. I got plans. Big plans. Right here in this here town.

12

"If ya please, ma'am. We put this up in yer window, and ya get a free ticket to the circus at the fairgrounds. Includes all the performances in the big top when we open after the parade tomorrow. Okay by you?"

Shopkeepers told Deputy Dwight Spooner that was their standard pitch. He guessed nobody refused something for nothing. Especially these days. Show bills went up all over town.

Not to give anything away, or to scare the townies, the only show folk spreading the word were the roustabouts who looked plain enough and friendly enough. They did come across somewhat rough and dressed a little funny by local standards. Also hired a few local kids and a handful of adults with motorcars to plaster bills elsewhere in the county.

Since he couldn't be everywhere at once, Dwight first cruised Main Street in Rock Rapids and visited a few shop owners when he saw a show bill in their window. "Were they okay?" Everyone knew what he meant.

"Yep, no problem at all. Even gave me two free passes!"

Suckers. "Glad to hear it. Holler if you need to."

"Thanks, Deputy."

He cruised down to George and all the way over to Sibley, Ashton, and even down to Boyden and Hull in the southern reaches of the county. Had to hand it to *m'DAHM's* folks. They sure got around.

Most folks seemed excited. Billy told him it had been years since a circus bothered coming to their little corner of the state. He guessed folks needed a distraction, and a circus was sure to be that.

Neither he nor Billy had spotted any concrete connection between that so-called accident down south of George on Wednesday and the circus. But Dwight's nose twitched, and he would not trust those show folks. They weren't talking.

After that security guy hustled them off the lot this morning, and Billy got all gushy over that gypsy tramp, he wondered whether his old friend could be objective. Sure, she'd boil the varnish off a shiny railing with those eyes and her... equipment, but all the more reason to maintain some distance. Something very weird there.

Too bad Billy hadn't found a more normal girl. Like Justina. Dwight thought about her—all the time, now. Peaches and cream, that girl. Wholesome. And soft.

Get a grip, soldier. She's too young.

Or is she?

13

Friday
Late Night
April 6, 1934
Lyon County Fairgrounds, Rock Rapids, Iowa

*I DON'T MIND FOLKS CALLIN' ME BABBO. JUST DON'T LIKE THE MANIMAL
part, ya see? Ain't part a my name. Just how I'm billed.*

*I talks ta me self all a the time. Keeps me company, ya see? Sometimes, I be
the only one who listens, 'n that's okay by me.*

*We done finished the set-up today. Well, yesterday, now. The bunk tent be
shakin' and creakin' cuz a them prairie winds kickin' up. I warn't in no mood fer
the standard rouster bullshit tonight—this dark mornin'—or fer them accusin'
me a card-sharkin'. Ya see, every one a them boys got serious tells. I ain't blind
with these big eyes. Bless 'em all.*

*Plus, I be dog-tired from the set-up. Everybody helps. Even the freaks 'n most
performers. The rousters, they like that. Madame, she don't give 'em no choice.*

*I like walkin' the midway tonight, like most midnights, me favorite place in
the whole world, 'specially in the dark. Settles me sight, but it don't do much to*

stomp down me stinkin' thinkin'. Dead quiet out here now, except fer a buckin' wind.

Babbo likes the oily diesel soot in the air, even though the generators be quiet now. And me big nose picks up the sweet-hangin' stink a cheap cotton candy. They don't clean them machines but once every long while, ya see. Or the fryers 'n their rotten grease. They spills that into the dirt at the grab joints. Another day or two, this here dirt'll ripen up like old grease too. Nothin' like it!

Like on the lot in every town, we done set up the strings a colored lights today. Me long arms sure be achin' tonight. We hammered the bases a fifty-odd coal-oil torches into the ground—well, the rousters did—but they all dark and cold now. Not like when the marks stroll and nibble and sass the barkers durin' show hours. They all think they're smart 'til they walk away with empty pockets 'n don't know how they got that way.

After a couple a show days, I love the stink a the tromped-down and puked-on prairie weeds. No place like the midway anywhere, no matter where we set up. And no place sadder right after a tear-down, ya see?

This here midway popped up on this lot today like one a them fancy greetin' cards that pop up when ya open 'em. Like magic. Only a couple a dozen feet wide 'n maybe fifty yards long, she runs from the big top 'n sideshows back yonder, to the animal menagerie up ahead at the other end—by the show's gate—where I be headed. Like the last town, only different dirt 'n dust.

I stare hard at them dark game booths and grab joints ta me left. They all feel real sinister tonight. That's a word Madame use a lot—sinister. The Ferris Wheel, Merry-Go-Round, Circle Swing and Roll-O-Coaster off ta me right crouch like bone piles a gloomy Goliaths. Like in the Bible. Plenty a room between 'em fer long lines a chumps that don't show up no more.

None a the midway cheers up ole Babbo tonight. An omen? Another word Madame uses. She be real smart. So's Sister Shipton. She be odd too. Sees stuff nobody else sees. Sometimes, Sister scares ole Babbo. Like yesterday. Said some-body got the hex. Said, "Be careful, Babbo dearie. All of us now. The grim be upon us." She calls me dearie. That's nice. She be nice.

Ah, breathe in them animals! Some folks confuse the animal menagerie down here with the freak menagerie up by the big top. Turnin' left off the midway to visit the row a cages that're home to the family pets.

Madame calls the show her family, and we all sorta feels like that, even with all the squabblin' between the tribes. Makes fer lively run-ins. Folks believe in different stuff, some fer rituals 'n curses 'n remedies fer all kinds a reasons. But mostly cuz a where they from, which be all over, 'n who or what they pray to. But we all show people—family. Altogether, nothin' like it—anywhere.

Show's animals be like pets—not like the big shows with them rings a fire, and whips. The trained dogs be everybody's favorites here, and the show's most important act. We don't got no elephants no more, and no real aerialists—only them's on the Russian Swing.

But I 'specially love King here, this tired ole lion 'n his moltin' mane, and ole ManEater yonder. That be our scrawny tiger who mostly sleeps. They don't leave their cages no more hardly at all, except once in a while. Jed, their trainer, he takes King fer a walk on his leash. An' ManEater ain't up for walkin' no more at all. The rubes still love oglin' at 'em. Pretendin' they brave by gettin' real close to the bars. Some holler at 'em. Them cats don't mind.

Like ole cat row 'round here, ya see? I ain't gettin' no younger myself. Jed too. He used to train and run a string a elephants fer one a the big shows, 'til one of 'em tromped on his leg. Lost that leg, poor fella. Now's a peg leg, but gots a shoe-shape at the end of it. Real nice, but says he gets real sore walkin' on it.

Two old chimps—Tit 'n Tat—they a couple. Tit always nags Tat. They nice, but they stink like rotten jackal dung, bless their chatterin' little hearts. Always chatterin'. And spittin', but they don't bite nobody. No teeth, no more. Their eyes 'r dartin' tonight, like always. Showin' lots a white in the slivered moon, but they dead quiet, like they waitin' fer sumpin' to happen.

They all love ole Babbo. I bring 'em treats. They always hungry. I smuggle 'em pockets full a greasy scraps from the chow tent where they only put out two skimpy meals a day, now. Me trousers always stinks like old lard. They be ragged-cut above the knees to show off me soccer-ball knee caps. I always got big-ass grease stains outside a all a me pockets. Nobody says nothin' though. These here animals be my best friends in the whole wide world, except for Lilith, a course.

Now, one in the mornin' on this here windy night, after a real hard setup, Babbo be tired. Done give out all me scraps. That wind be whistlin' through the cages and flappin' loose canvas. But me still thinks about makin' one more trip back up the ole midway before hittin' me rack in the bunk tent. Midway's a sleepin', along with ManEater and King. Tit 'n Tat ain't sleepin', just quiet as the grave. The hangin' strings a lights—dark 'n cold—wrapped in ropes a tinsel made a tin scraps we laced on twine, they rattle and tinkle hard fer the wind. Reminds me the show is sleepin' like I ain't never gonna. The show just be waitin' on the next herd a marks to tromp on through.

I always imagine this be my midway, now gettin' more 'n more beat-up and old and ragged and faded. Like comfy old shoes, ya see? Like me.

Them winds means warm weather's a comin' fer the show season. Madame got us an early start. Hope we don't suffer another blow-down this year. Nothin' scarier 'n a monster prairie wind when ya live under canvas or in wagons. 'Specially fer these poor animals. King be half blind—took a piece a straw right through his left eye a couple a summers ago. That kind a wind sucks air right out a yer lungs so's ya can't breathe good, even when it ain't blowin' dirt 'n grit. Or straw.

Sure, this here carnival still pretends to be a classy outfit. Harder now. Ain't much, no more, but it's still the life, ain't it? It's home. Beats bein' thrown out a every town I ever visited without the show, don't it? Done that a few times. Besides, a big tip jar fills up after every Single-O. Even pity money's better 'n starvin' or diggin' ditches fer pennies 'n gettin' beat up regular. What would Babbo do outside a the show, anyway? Play me fiddle on a street corner, and take beatin's instead a cash fer tips? Nope, not Babbo. Like I said, a tiny head don't mean a tiny brain. And I got plans.

What's that, now? A clatter behind ManEater's wagon? But the ole boy ain't budged. It ain't him. His nose still be nuzzled into his favorite stuffed animal, the ole elephant I done give him. His snorin' is still buzzin' 'n rumblin' over the whistlin' wind, but there be that noise again. Odd. Like a scrapin' screech now 'n again. That screech lights up me big ears real good.

I come 'round the back corner a ManEater's cage that be weld-mounted on his travel wagon, just like King's. And just then, lightnin' hammers the top a me head, drivin' me down... down. And there ain't a damn cloud in the sky. Figures. The black night, lit only by that moon sliver up yonder be gettin' a whole lot blacker.

Jus'. Like. That.

14

———

"Hello?"

"Good morning, Miss Ringwall, this is Deputy Dwight Spooner. We met at the Law Enforcement Center yesterday."

"I remember. Is something wrong?"

"What? Oh, ah, no, I'm following up with you on the, ah, circus investigation."

"Oh, I see. Deputy—"

"I'm Dwight."

"Okay, Dwight. I'm Justina. I'm sorry. Laticia is a very passionate woman."

"What? No, it's fine. Passion is good."

"Pardon me?"

"I mean, I respect that. Passion. Shows depth of emotion, you know?"

"Dwight, did you have questions for me? Because I'm not sure—"

"Yeah, no, I, well, would you like to get a cup of coffee with me sometime? I mean, I could drive down to George, or—"

"No!"

Dwight's heart sank. "No?"

"I mean, yes, that would be lovely, but not in George. Some of the other ladies here might not understand, what with George being such a small town. Do you understand?"

"Of course. Given—"

"Exactly."

"When do you think you might be in town, then?" Dwight indulged in the smallest grin.

"Maybe... later this afternoon? Around three?

"Meet me at the Main Street diner?"

"Great. It's a date. For coffee, that is."

Dwight showed up at the diner thirty minutes early. Justina showed up fifteen minutes early. She said, "Am I late?"

He jumped up. Might have even left the floor. Walked around the small square table with the rounded corners and slid her chair out for her. Slid it in again under her as she sat down. The *scraaaape* turned a few heads. One old farmer in bibs sitting at the counter smiled, turned back to his coffee and pie to mind his own business.

"Naw, you're early too. I was nearby...." His embarrassed expression and jittery body language left no doubt. "You look lovely, Justina."

He sat down across from her. The waitress came to take their order —too soon. Before she reached the table, Dwight popped his head up, sent her a subtle sideways nod. She wheeled around with her own nod and a grin. He wondered if anyone around them imagined the two of them looked odd together. After all, he was at least twenty years older than her. He didn't care. Neither did she, it seemed.

"Dwight, I hope you didn't think it embarrassed me to be seen with you. People talking can get awkward."

"About you seeing a cop while all this murder stuff is going on, or that I'm more than a few years older than you."

"Honestly? Both. And once this circus affair settles out, well, I'd like to see more of you. Is that okay?"

"Okay? You kidding? That'd be great, Justina."

She reached over and grabbed both his folded hands on the table with both of hers, and smiled. "Nothing would make me happier."

Deep down, Deputy Dwight Spooner wondered, *What in the world am I getting myself into here?*

❧ 15 ❧

S aturday
April 7, 1934

❦

SILAS HUMMEL SAT AT THE DESK IN HIS STUDY GROWN STUFFY WITH closed windows and air baked dry from wood stove heat. He surveyed the stacks of his farm journals and romance novels that belonged to his long-deceased wife. They littered every horizontal surface. Each book reeked of its own memories. A thick layer of fine dust blanketed everything. Rays from a gauzy sun penetrated the closed blinds with slanted shafts of golden haze.

The old farmer asked the operator to connect him to the Lyon County Law Enforcement Center in Rock Rapids.

"Sheriff, this here is Silas Hummel. Saw you was out this way Wednesday chasing the truck that rolled, and the other one what followed you. The fella who rolled is dead, isn't he?"

"Yes, Silas. Now if there's nothin' else—"

"Billy, you remember the last time I called you? About finding your deputy out this way last winter?" He could only imagine the painful memory he dredged up for the sheriff.

He wondered if Billy had hung up on him. Then, after a long silence, Billy responded, "Why are you doin' this, Mr. Hummel?"

"I *am* sorry, Billy. I'd rather not, but I found another. Body, that is. In almost the same spot. Five miles south of George on County 14. In the west-side ditch. A half-mile north of where that truck rolled. And you are just not gonna believe this. I suggest you high-tail it out here fast as you can. This is, well, ugly."

Another long silence. Did the sheriff wonder if this was some cruel joke? "Silas, say no more. Party line. You wait for me out there. You understand?"

The strident tone accompanied by the sudden crack in Sheriff Billy's voice startled him. *The poor man has been through a lot.* Folks had told Silas stories of the Great War, not that Billy'd ever talked about it himself, but stories got around. And losing his young wife while over there? Plus, that nasty affair last summer with those Irish mobsters? Billy was one of the good ones, but a man can only take so much. Now this. Yep, he'd drive back out there to meet Sheriff Billy, alright. But it was a damn good question how he'd react to *this.*

The sheriff blurted at the last moment, "Wait. Silas, don't hang up. Did ya say another fella *followed* me Wednesday?"

"Yup. Came racin' by as fast as you did. About half-a-mile back, even before the dust settled from you and the ole truck ahead a ya."

"Did ya notice what kind of vehicle it was, Silas?"

"Well, I seem to recall a truck, not a car. Yep, an open truck, sorta like the one that you chased. Didn't think too much about it, though."

"Thanks, Silas. I'll be there straightaway."

BILLY'S SHOCK AT ANOTHER BODY DISCOVERED JUST TWO DAYS AFTER the first one left him wondering if Silas wasn't reporting the truck accident's aftermath he'd witnessed on Wednesday. But that made no sense. He'd said *another* body. And now he found out that somebody chased *him* while he chased the old boy that got himself killed under mysterious circumstances?

Billy rubbed his right arm. Sore as Hell itself today.

Was there a serial killer loose in his county?

❧ 16 ❦

❧❦❧

Deputy Jimmy Lenert remembered his fellow deputy, Roddy Braddock, murdered last year by an Irish mob enforcer. Roddy thought he should have started with the department as a detective, not a lowly deputy.

He and Roddy started as rookies together, just a month apart. They both learned the job from Billy. But Roddy snooped around, looking for trouble, never assumed anybody's innocence. That's what got him killed. *Wherever you are, Roddy, I hope you took your big nose with ya, partner.*

Losing a fellow deputy would be traumatic for any peace officer. Both he and Roddy were only twenty, new to the job, and they didn't know what they didn't know, which was a lot. But Roddy always assumed he had it all under control. Jimmy still stayed in touch with Roddy's wife, Sarah.

He recalled how he felt at the time....

. . .

JIMMY AND RODDY WERE TWO PEAS IN A POD, SHINY NEW LYON County deputies, who both worshipped Sheriff Billy Rhett Kershaw. A year and a winter out of high school, they burst with righteous indignation at every injustice. They would make right all that was wrong with the world. By solving one tiny crime at a time. After all, with their attitudes, how could it be otherwise? Plus, they were invincible.

Jimmy was satisfied shadowing Sheriff Kershaw around the county for thirty days of training. They made conversation with Marvin over at the general store in George, and with Mr. Barnes at the Feed and Seed in Rock Rapids. They talked with anyone who had a problem, or just craved conversation.

Roddy, though, who started a month later, looked for trouble. His nose enabled him to spot anyone with anything to hide. Got him into more trouble than not. Sheriff Billy had to get him out of one jam or another at least once a week, where Roddy had accused somebody of wrongdoing—unjustly. But that only made him hungrier to be a better cop. He was on his way.

And then, one cold January day last year, they found his body in a ditch out on old County 14 south of George. Almost exactly where they just found the body of a circus freak.

Jimmy worried about Sheriff Billy. Hell, he worried about himself, too. A good thing Dwight Spooner was on the job. At least he had homicide experience.

Shit! Roddy would have loved this, bless his nosy heart. But I am not going to end up in a ditch. Like him!

This was all hands on deck. Billy, Dwight and Jimmy processed the ditch where somebody dumped the odd little man's body. Billy found it strange that they were investigating the death of a circus freak in his county hours before the circus would joyously parade through his town. The whole situation had an awful stink to it.

Worse, that weasel Lionel Johns, the Lyon County News reporter, beat them to the scene somehow. No doubt the rotten fruit of party line gossip. Small county. And no sense asking Lionel to give up a source. Lionel took photographs and snooped around.

"C'mon, Lionel. Give us a chance to work the scene, okay? Now back away."

"Sure thing, Sheriff. Just doin' my job."

"Well, do it somewhere else for a while."

"Got a statement for me? Anything? Is this a circus murder?"

"Confound it, Lionel, I'll give ya somethin' when I can. Fair enough?"

"You got it, Billy. Didn't mean any harm. Weird, though, huh? I mean, just look at this guy." He nodded toward the gnarled corpse, obviously from the circus.

৩৯৯

REALIZING HANGING AROUND WOULD BE A WASTE OF TIME, JOHNS took off. He needed to develop his sensational photographs. The man *guaranteed him* the front page of the Lyon County News—above the fold—for any sordid news having to do with the circus. Even if he had to *extrapolate the narrative*. After all, he had a job to do.

Besides, he was investing in his future.

❧ 18 ❧

❦

Sophie Hardt's husband Jake, and his rough cousin Walt, were princes among men in her book. They loved taking care of little Leo and toted him everywhere on the farm. Called him their *farmer-in-training*, even though he wasn't even a half-year old yet.

She hated leaving her baby, but even their neighbor, Chief Dan Rustywire, had adopted little Leo as his *papoose*. And Dan's fiancée, although neither he nor Edie would use that word—not yet, anyway— was Sophie's best and oldest friend in the world. She also loved little Leo as if he were her own.

No, Sophie need not worry about Leo getting enough loving attention. He was a community project. Anyway, it was Edie's fault for dragging her to that darn circus.

So with its new radiator hose installed, the two of them drove Chief's truck to Rock Rapids to catch the parade. Sophie brought her old foot stool for getting in and out of that farm truck. Even had a rope attached to it. She'd use that to pull it in after her. Jake had made that for her.

They arrived early to make sure they had a place to park. The town was crazy with people from all over the county. She guessed news of the circus traveled by word of mouth like wildfire. That's how small communities worked.

Some homeowners a few blocks off Main rented parking space on their lawns for a nickel. But the girls were lucky enough to find a place for free right on Third Avenue.

According to the flyers and the newspaper, the parade would start at one o'clock on Tama Street near the fairground's entrance. It would then turn left on Main, another left on Adams, and left again on Fifth Street past City Hall to loop back to the fairgrounds.

They invited everyone to become part of the parade and to follow it for free admission. Most everyone at the parade did precisely that. Who could refuse something for nothing? For everyone else, it would cost a nickel at the gate.

The parade was shorter than most expected, led by a pair of clowns in their floppy footwear, who tossed hard candies to the kids lining the gutters and boardwalks. The clowns criss-crossed the street and blew goofy whistles. Kids scurried to retrieve the candies, some hoarding them and following the clowns to score even more. Adults pointed and laughed.

A two-horse team pulled each of six wagons. Every horse wore a colorful yard-long feather plume on its head and a kaleidoscopic skirt rimmed with a rainbow of sequins and streamers.

A five-piece band blurted out *The Man on the Flying Trapeze* with their brass instruments. An ironic choice of songs, since this circus no longer featured a true aerial act. The drummer kept an absurd cadence.

Two of the lead wagons contained wild animals. The colorfully painted canvas sides were unfurled low enough to cast them in shadow and to prevent a satisfying peek. But they were raised just enough to expose the feet and legs of the big cats inside. The pictures on the awnings advertised "King of the Beasts" on both sides of the first wagon, and "Man-Eating Tiger" on the second.

The smaller third wagon with its lowered awnings pictured "Wild Apes of Borneo" with a cautionary sign that warned, "Danger!" These *dangerous* animals chattered away, making sounds few from Lyon County had ever heard—sounds from some faraway jungle. Somehow, those sounds seemed amplified, larger than life, but coming from apes? Some were dubious, but also curious enough to get a better look later at the fairgrounds.

Parade-goers saw little of the fourth wagon's interior. It was obscured behind the canvas sidewalls that advertised Madame Perlatelli's Oddities and Wonders with wild and exaggerated images painted in a menagerie of primary colors. The sideshow wagon featured huge paintings of bizarre and deformed creatures—both alive and artifacts on display in the show's Dime Museum. A scaled arm slithered out from under the canvas side curtain to wave or point at parade-goers now and then. Or they'd get a flash of huge luminous eyes between the flaps. Many in the crowd issued an audible gasp and whispered to their neighbor at such sights. Some heard an ominous growl now and then.

The fifth wagon was an elevated stage upon which performers offered a hint of acts pictured on the sides of the wagon-stage beneath them. A juggler juggled. A pretty girl on a swing swayed. And a handsome brute commanded a dog to perform clever tricks. They occupied the stage with much fanfare as heralded by the band on the parade's sixth and final wagon.

The bandwagon comprised another small stage upon which the band played non-stop. All danced and turned as they played. Even the drummer with his snare strapped to his waist whirled to face audiences on both sides of the street. These were seasoned musicians who knew how to engage an audience.

A devastatingly handsome gentleman in a top hat who appeared to be the ringmaster occupied an elevated platform surrounded by a railing at the rear of the bandwagon. His handheld megaphone looked like a yard-long funnel with his mouth inches from the small end. He beckoned everyone at the parade to follow him to the big show. It was as if he appealed personally to every person within the sound of his booming voice, a hypnotic voice—the pied piper of the circus. He prevailed even over the boisterous band who played with enthusiasm.

Every girl and woman fell in love with this beautiful man and his beautiful voice in his beautiful red and black bowtie, tails, and thigh-high black leather boots with huge cuffs at their tops—like a dashing pirate. They all wondered if he was a moving picture star.

The men shrugged and followed the parade for the promise of free admission. Almost to a man, their women had dragged them away from unfinished chores for this ridiculous spectacle. There were a few, however, who'd heard rumors of a kootch show they'd read about in one of those big-city magazines at the dentist's office, or at the barber shop. Most had never seen a girlie show. And, of course, everyone wanted to get a good long look at some freaks, maybe even get their fortune told.

What could it hurt?

19

D wight met Justina at the diner in Rock Rapids after she drove up from George.

Once they settled in with their coffee and pie, she asked how he felt about "those heathens at the circus."

"Well, I've had run-ins with show folk before up in Minneapolis."

"You can't trust them, can you, Dwight? I'm tickled pink we have that in common."

"They attract people who are running from something. That's for sure, but—"

"And they bring all their sins with them, too. I'm just scared with all of that close by, but you'll protect me, won't you, Dwight?" She raised her eyes to meet his. That coy little smile melted his heart and stiffened his... resolve.

"Ah, sure, that's my job." He grinned.

"Is that the only reason?" She reached across the table to cover his hand with hers.

"Look, I like you, Justina. Wanna go get some ice cream down the street at Percy's?" His stomach fluttered, but now with an inkling of uneasiness—a cop's uneasiness. She hated show people even more than he did. He guessed that wasn't bad, but what was she basing *her* feelings on?

"I'd love it!" That smile again.

Is she just echoing the sentiments of that old church lady, or does she really feel that way about circus folks?

And... what else? Something.

20

H arold Deemers grew up in Rock Rapids. The only time he had lived away from home was the four years he spent at Princeton, where he acquired his degree in Public Policy with a minor in Psychology.

He and his family always had their eye on the governor's mansion in Des Moines—Terrace Hill. Frederick Hubbell was one of his heroes as a former governor and patriarch of Iowa. That was his near-term aim, although most governors, like Hubbell, were attorneys. Harold didn't have time for such finery. He had bigger plans and had to move fast to achieve them.

The mayor stood at the large span of windows in his third floor office at City Hall, looking down at Fifth. He liked this town well enough, but had gained a more sophisticated palate during his time in Princeton, with summers at the Jersey shore and weekends in nearby Newark.

"Mr. Mayor, Laticia Morgenstern is here to see you. She does not have an appointment."

Harold knew Laticia hovered just out of sight next to Velma's desk in his outer office, like always. He said with gusto, "Mrs. Morgenstern needs no appointment, Velma. Please show her in."

He remained standing, but now in front of his desk. Shot his fancy French cuffs to make sure his diamond links were both visible. Tugged down on his vest. But he did not bother to retrieve his suit coat from the back of the generous executive chair between his desk and the window wall he cherished.

Mayor Deemers preferred to present the countenance of a hard-working public servant—in silhouette, no less. For effect, he snatched up the sheave of papers that had been collecting dust on his desk for the past week. Pretended to read the top page, leaning his posterior on the front of his desk, ever the busy city executive. The perfect image. He timed setting the impressive fistful of pages back on his desk just as Laticia passed into his sanctum.

"Laticia! How nice of you to grace me with your presence." The grin that could melt icebergs in the Arctic did not have the desired effect, which put him off his game. Without saying a word, this church lady marched right up to him. Then, and only then, did she speak, and they were not the genteel words the mayor always hoped for.

"Harold, when are you planning to rename our fair city?"

"Come again, Laticia?"

"My committee and I wish to learn when you will rename the city. To 'Den of Iniquity' or 'Gomorrah' or 'Homicide Town,' because that's the kind of town you clearly wish to administer."

"Laticia—"

"Mister Mayor, my committee and I pleaded with your sheriff to keep that *circus* from invading our fair city. He failed. Now we have two dead bodies on our hands, and at least one of them is doubtless a murder. This is already galloping out of control."

"Let me assure you, Laticia—"

"The civic league does not want assurances, Harold. We want action, and—"

"Laticia, I am going to interrupt you in order to update you on recent developments, dear. Now please have a seat and listen to what I have to say. Can you do that for me?"

That settled her down, at least until she fired her next salvo. She seated herself with reluctance in a comfortable chair across a coffee table from the mayor. He sat opposite on a small sofa, his elbows on his knees—his most earnest pose to demonstrate how serious he was taking this matter.

"There were no legal means to prevent this circus from coming to town, and believe you me, we had our county and city attorneys delve into the matter. Even prior to their arrival late Thursday, before the county issued a permit, it was our intent to get them to move on.

"I've personally communicated with the managing editor of the Lyon County News. And lacking legal means, we will administer this situation like they do in bigger cities where they have experience in such sordid affairs."

"What does that all mean, Harold?"

The Morgensterns lived across the street from the Deemers when Harold was growing up. They still did. After his parents passed, Harold, ever the bachelor, remained in their family's home place. Their small in-town estate neighbored the Law Enforcement Center just across an alley. Harold now preferred to call that alley a side street.

Twenty years his senior, Laticia had always been the neighborhood matriarch, and Harold was always one of the well-mannered neighborhood boys. She could not shed the mantle of that relationship, even now. And he would not insist she call him *Mister Mayor*. He needed her vote, and her influence, especially when he made a run for Des Moines.

"Laticia, if we can't try this circus in a court of law, we will try them in the court of public opinion. The *News* has assured me we are of the same mind, and they will miss no opportunity to cast aspersions on anything to do with the circus. Our citizens will respond. They will boycott this circus, these... *people*," he only broke for a breath in mid-sentence, making it awkward for any interruption, "will have no alternative but to move on of their own volition.

"Further, you may or may not know that the owner of the circus has appealed to Sheriff Kershaw—*she* wants to leave town as soon as possible. Their business is already drying up, thanks to our well-lubricated rumor mill."

He took a deep breath and awaited Laticia's response. She rewarded him with a slow-blooming smirk that acknowledged the

Machiavellian nature of his scheme. "I knew this meeting needed to be just the two of us for a reason, Harold. That is brilliant. That means the circus is leaving town." Not a question.

The mayor squirmed in his chair, adjusted the crease in his trousers, straightened his tie, and shot his monogrammed cuffs—again. "Well, no. Sheriff Kershaw says they can't leave until they can investigate these deaths."

"What?"

"I'm doing what I can, Laticia, but once again, Billy has the power of the legal system supporting his decision. There are several suspects within the show. He cannot allow them to leave his jurisdiction, because this is where the crime or crimes were committed.

"Oh, for the love of all that's holy, Harold, what are we to do?"

"We will continue to press our strategy with fervor—to try the circus in the court of public opinion. That is a powerful force, Laticia, and the reason I am in my office on Saturday afternoon instead of pruning my roses. And that is why poor Velma is out there on the phone instead of at home baking her Saturday pot roast for her family. At the very least, we apply public pressure to ensure the sheriff concludes his investigation as soon as possible. Then, he can release the circus, and they can get the hell out of *our town*."

"Harold, does this have anything to do with you running for sheriff against Billy this November?" Her expression betrayed her conflict. She was caught between her desire to see this circus expelled from *her* town, and supporting this well-behaved neighborhood boy in pursuit of his obvious aspirations. He was learning the rules of the game exceptionally well. "And why would you go from being mayor to sheriff, anyway?"

"Two words, my dear Laticia, *Des* and *Moines*."

She gasped with pleasure. "The governor's mansion. Of course. You need the law-and-order vote. Brilliant! Well, let's see how you handle your city before we get you into Hubbell's House, shall we, Mr. Mayor?"

"Indeed, my dear Mrs. Morgenstern. Indeed." They exchanged conspiratorial smiles.

But his smile blossomed for a reason different from what this old woman assumed. He still needed her.

Mission accomplished. Now if I can just keep a lid on that other matter.

❧ 21 ❧

T he back lot teemed with activity after the parade. Mireia and Bartolo, otherwise known as the Flying Busquetas, directed four rousters on the careful relocation of their precious Russian Swing from parade wagon to big top.

Not far away, Linus hustled two of his Magnificent Hounds from their parade wagon to his tent to settle them down before the evening performance in a few hours.

Other performers prepped as well. Jugglers practiced. Cinder the Flame Eater replenished her act's supplies and arranged them precisely on the small cart she'd wheel into the ring with her.

The hubbub always made Jed Strain feel like he was part of something important—larger than himself. The circus was all he'd ever known. He loved the life even though it had crippled him.

But it was his own damn fault. He lost focus—just for a moment—working Jumbo Lucy, the biggest elephant he'd ever trained. She got grumpy from being hobbled. They get that way. Should have known. Proud beasts. Got to get inside their heads. Otherwise, you're done. Jed missed one of Lucy's moods that fateful day.

Working on her rear-leg stand, she came down wrong. Jed dived out, tried to get out of the way. But she still came down on the lower part of his right leg. Crushed it, and it had to come off. He rode a peg leg ever since. Wasn't Lucy's fault. The show let him go. A one-legged pachyderm trainer doesn't look good in the ring. He understood.

Madame Perlatelli took him in to work her big cats. They were tired, like him. Not much to do. She also made him head of her little show's security. Madame—a great woman. More than most would ever know. Even if she didn't feel the same. For now. He had a plan. There was nothing he wouldn't do for her. Nobody messed with Madame. He made sure of it.

And nobody had a finer collection of Madame memorabilia than him. His most treasured items? Her toenail clippings and several locks of her hair. He relished the moments before he collected those treasures. Often dreamed of those erotic snippets of time lying on his belly. He'd watched under the canvas of her tent while she clipped those lovely nails and trimmed her hair. He imagined the two of them were alone. They were. Just not together—nothing but dirt, canvas and six feet separating them.

Some day, m'boy! Some day!

Enough day-dreaming. I need to manage the stragglers from the parade.

22

"**S**heriff, what are you doing to solve these crimes? We need to get these heathens out of my town!" The mayor seethed with faux anger and real impatience.

Billy looked with longing through the big office windows at his cruiser down on the far side of Fifth. He did not appreciate being summoned to City Hall, much less to the mayor's office on a Saturday afternoon. This would be the last time.

This popinjay played politics. He didn't. And there sat that pompous church lady, Laticia Morgenstern. Unlike both of them, he remained standing at the center of the room, as if he'd been called to the principal's office. A hazy sun drifting in through the enormous West windows lit up the dust particles in the air they breathed.

"Mr. Mayor, this is an active investigation, and we do not discuss it with civilians. No offense, Laticia." He swiveled an apologetic glance at her, but turned it into an official dead-eye stare.

The mayor pounced on this. "Sheriff, we are in a crisis here, and—"

Laticia took her turn. "Billy, I'm acting as the mayor's consultant in this matter. Get on with it, for pity's sake!"

This was a no-win scenario, and Billy knew it. Clever. *Sumbitch!* Well, maybe it wasn't. *Let 'em chew on this.*

"Fine, if I had my way, I'd throw this damn show outta *your* town right now. *And* the lady who runs that outfit would like nothin' better. But are you prepared to risk an obstruction of justice charge on your record as the law-and-order candidate for sheriff, Mr. Mayor?

"We don't just let murderers go free. Now you can advise and consult all you want, Laticia, but as much as you'd like, not you or any other citizen in this town gets to make up your own laws. Do you understand that? And do you understand I have no choice here?"

He knew there could only be one right answer from the mayor. And as much as he hated painting an important constituent into a corner, this was getting out of hand. Before they could craft their response, he continued, "And by the way, this is *my* town, too. Now, why don't you let me do the job y'all elected me to do? If you'll excuse me...."

Billy chewed off a big risk, but to hell with these games. He took his time to do an about-face, thumbs still hooked in his gear belt, and walked out of the office at a deliberate pace. He gave them every opportunity to stop him. They did not.

HE NEEDED TO TAKE ANOTHER RUN AT THE SNAKE LADY, MADAME Perlatelli. He could already imagine her haunting scent, and the sight of all that smooth olive skin under all those tattoos. And—

Jeez, Billy, get your head out a yer ass!

23

"Jed, I don't give a damn if she's busy. This here is a murder investigation. Now get the hell out a my way, or I'll take you in right now for obstruction. You read me, mister?" Billy pushed his way past the show's security guy trying to block his path to the back lot. Maybe he shoved on the center of the guy's chest too hard because he almost fell backwards off his gimp leg.

Billy unhooked the chain between him and the back lot. Left it dangling and hustled off. Jed tried to keep up. Billy kept one eye peeled toward this guy in case he favored stupidity over wisdom.

It was as if she knew he was coming. As Billy approached her wagon, she floated down her stairs. Met him at their base.

"Billy, I hope you enjoyed our little parade. It is very nice—"

"Madame Perlatelli, you lied to me."

"Perdona?"

"You said the victim of that fatal vehicle accident was not one of your crew. How do you explain evidence that places that old gent in Boy's Town, Nebraska, one of the last places you played? And how do you explain the lion, tiger and monkey shit in the bed of that truck? A sharp lady like you, and you don't notice one of your trucks is missing? Why'd you lie to me, young lady?"

"Billy, I—"

"And before you tell me another lie, know that I *will* arrest you and lock you up for obstruction of justice in a murder investigation. Because the death of one of your freaks less than forty-eight hours after this other *accident* is clearly related. Next, I expect some answers about the violent death of your Babbo the Animal, or whatever. Now, what's it gonna be? Jail or talk? And Jed, you take a step back right now, mister, or I'm drawin' you down. *Now!*"

Billy never took his eyes off Madame, but made it clear he was about to pull his revolver. After a small nod from Madame, Jed stepped back, almost stumbling. Again.

"Well?"

MADAME SHIFTED FROM ONE FOOT TO THE OTHER AND BACK, clenching and unclenching her fists as if this was a fight-or-flight moment. She looked over at Jed and said, "We're okay here, Jed. Please make sure no *other* unwelcome guests invade us, if you please." He also looked ready for a fight, but slumped at the admonishment and limped away.

"Sheriff, let us speak in private." She turned and led the way up the stairs and opened the door on the rear of her wagon. Billy stood at the bottom of the stairs until she turned and stood in the doorway. He wasn't sure if this was a good idea, but he needed progress on these two make-or-break cases. Kept his hand on the butt of his service weapon. Wasn't sure why.

The inside of that wagon was indeed a working office, but the interior seemed more spacious than its appearance from outside. Warmth radiated from a tiny pot-belly stove in the front corner opposite her small desk close to the front wall. Next to it sat a bucket of coal. Madame didn't seat herself behind her desk. Instead, she nestled into a tiny sofa along the wagon's right side and to the rear, close to the door. She patted one of the copious cushions next to her as she peered up at him expectantly.

No way in hell am I sitting that close to her!

Billy kept his wide stance just inside the door, which he closed behind him to keep the heat in. "No thanks. Now, what are you gonna say that'll keep you out a one a my cells at the Law Enforcement Center up the street?"

"Sheriff, running a show like this? It is, how you say... complicated. Many of my, ah, crew, as you call them, expect me to protect them. Little else keeps them from wandering off to another show who *will* protect them."

"Madame, we're *way* past you worryin' about losin' yer folks, here. I'm investigatin' one, and possibly two, murders. Unless you have somethin' relevant to tell me...." He reached to the rear of his belt to retrieve his handcuffs and held them out, like an invitation.

"That won't be necessary, Billy. But please, sit." She patted the cushion next to her once more.

"Talk. Now." He kept his distance.

"Very well. The man in the accident stole one of our trucks. His name is Garth Nitstone. Of late, he suffered, ah, how you say, a mental breakup."

"A mental breakdown?"

"Sí. He took the strong drink and also used the drugs. We are a family. We tried to help. But—"

"See, now, there ya go lyin' to me again, lady. No sign of drink or drugs at the scene or in the body. We did one a them autopsies."

"No, Billy, I do not lie. Garth's terrible problems began when he took the oath to *stop* the drink and the drugs. He is clean and sober for weeks now. But the demons, they visit him at night. You understand?"

Billy understood. He fought his own battle with alcohol. "So why lie to me, Madame?"

"The dead cannot speak for themselves, Billy. We must speak for them, no? Garth is family. And what would we do for family? You have the family, Billy?"

She seemed sincere. He almost admired her for her supportive attitude of a drunken addict within her own show family. *Weird that she still speaks of this guy in the present tense.*

"Look, Madame, I am an officer of the law. You must not lie to me, or hold back information. Do you understand?"

"You have lost someone, no? Su esposa, perhaps?"

"Now, what can you tell me about Babbo?"

"I know little. Babbo was... loved. It is such a loss. I know not why anyone...." A sudden fit of sadness seemed to grip this beautiful young woman, to the edge of tears. She seemed, what, vulnerable? Wait, this was no helpless little girl. This was a hard-nosed businesswoman in a rough-and-tumble business. *Goddammit, she's playin' me!*

"Okay, lady, cut the crap. Why was this kid killed and dumped in my county?"

The tears dried up, and she looked up at Billy with what appeared to be newfound respect. She nodded, shrugged and said, "Sheriff, everyone loved Babbo. He was even a favorite of our most, ah, capable men, the roustabouts. They protected him as he was, um, vulnerable in many ways. I truly do not know who would do such a thing to dear little Babbo.

"You must understand something about show people, Billy. Most have chosen this life because they are private people. Most have had problems with the law in the past. They do not talk to outsiders. That is not my doing. But I respect their wishes. Some are decent acts or strong backs who either used to be with the big shows or they are just in love with this life."

She swept her arms to engulf the wagon's interior. "If they add value to my show, they stay. If not, they are gone. Listen to me, Sheriff, even though we are just a tiny carnival, I provide jobs. They will not talk with you, but I will inquire for you. That is all I can promise. Is that not fair?"

Billy wasn't sure how much of this he would swallow, but at least this was something.

"That's all I'm asking." As if to reinforce the sincerity of his words, he secured the handcuffs dangling from his right fist back onto his gear belt.

"Now, won't you sit, Billy?"

"I think not. But I will be back. Afternoon, Madame."

A real hard case. Could she kill? Would she?

❧ 24 ❧

❧

Sheriff Billy sat tapping the end of a pencil on his cluttered desktop in the LEC. The afternoon shadows lengthened on the dark side of his blue enamel coffee mug, a Mason jar full of pencils, and various stacks of paper. Some peeked out of folders, begging to be filed. The room grew darker, and his mind swirled around his meeting with *the snake lady*—the head of the snake —Madame.

He lingered on how she invited him to snuggle up against her in her warm and cozy wagon. Three times, was it? How she could turn on the tears and look utterly helpless. Then that hard edge, just like that, with a nod of respect when he called her on her antics.

Despite all of that, and those crazy tattoos, he couldn't get those incredible legs out of his mind. Or that perfect face. Or her cleavage. Or....

Hot dang, Billy, get your shit together, son! She's a damn suspect! And what would Alice think?

In that instant, guilt ripped through him. He risked a sip of the strong farm brew they call yard mud from his mug, but could not swallow.

Sumbitch!

※

DWIGHT WANDERED IN THROUGH THE SIDE DOOR FROM THE ALLEY between the LEC and the eight-foot hedge that encompassed Mayor Deemers house and yard—more like a small estate—the biggest house in town. Hell, biggest in the county. He plopped down in the chair by Billy's desk. The guest chair in front of his desk, not the suspect chair beside it. Dwight rarely sat at his own desk.

"You're thinking about that snake lady, aren't ya, boss?" He knew Billy had gone to see her after a rough meeting with the mayor. Small town.

"Mr. Truck Driver now has a name, Dwight: Garth Nitstone. She says he suffered a mental breakdown. Convenient. That would explain his crazy drivin', but not why he was runnin' away from the show in what she claims was a stolen truck. Accordin' to the snake lady, he didn't have no problems with others in the show. Not sure I believe that. Nobody's talkin' either, besides her."

"She lied to us before. Seems to do it really well too, doesn't she?"

"Yeah, yeah. When you're right.... Pisses me off that every little detail has to come so hard from that outfit."

Dwight knew it was hard for Billy to swallow his pride. He always looked for the best in people.

"Show people, boss."

※

"DWIGHT, I'M GONNA CALL OUR BUDDY LANG EUBANKS." BILLY smiled at the memory of that dapper little federal agent and his pencil-sharpening fetish. And the weird tea blends he carried around in his vest pocket in little envelopes. "Let's see if we can find out anything about *m'DAHM's* little show and this Nitstone character. I doubt they'll have anything on our second vic, but—"

"Oh, yeah, Agent Eubanks. You talk to Lang since he helped us out last summer?"

"We chew the fat once in a while. The ATF always has him on some assignment somewhere. Heard he's in Omaha these days workin' with the FBI. Every time he calls, he thanks me again for the part we played in squashin' that bootleggin' ring before it went national. He's got a lot a contacts. He might could pull up somethin'."

Dwight wrinkled his brow. "I'll bet they don't have squat. Nobody better at being ghosts than show people."

"Well, we gotta do somethin'! Or they're gonna run me out a town on a rail. And they might not wait til the election."

25

eanwhile, outside the big top, rousters pushed back
twilight shadows by lighting dozens of coal-oil torches
that lined the midway. Generators powered not only the
rides, but the strings of twinkling lights strung aloft between and in
front of the small tents. They served as booths for carny games and
places to spend a nickel for a confection.

The crowd meandered the midway, exploring the wondrous fare for
sale, games to be played, and the Dime Museum. That was up near the
big top and promised bizarre exhibitions. But the freak shows
garnered the most attention. Edie wasn't interested. She wanted to
meet the seer called Sister Shipton.

When she had mentioned her to Chief Dan, her friend and protector, he said that's what they call shamans—seers—in his tribe up North
Dakota way. They saw and felt things nobody else could. That
intrigued Edie, but she didn't want to go alone. With reluctance,
Sophie agreed to accompany her.

. . .

As soon as they arrived at the show's gate, they could hear the band spurring on acts performing inside that large tent at the far end of the midway called the big top. The tattooed ticket taker told them where they could find "the fortune teller."

They wandered the length of the midway toward that colorful tent ahead of them that towered above the rides to their left and concessions to their right. Their destination was an exhausting walk away for Sophie. It took them almost fifteen minutes to hike the length of the midway, including rest stops, even though it was no more than fifty yards long.

A very unassuming little tent stood all by itself off to their right less than thirty feet from the big top. Three small painted signs on a single post hammered into the ground out front advertised, "Fortune Teller," and "Tarot," and "Palms Read." The girls stared at the tent, which was itself a work of art, if not somewhat crude in its ornamentation.

Only six, or maybe eight feet square, someone had painted the peaked top with multi-colored designs that swirled and confused. Distorted pictures of nature adorned its canvas walls: trees, cats, butterflies. This little tent's pastel hues didn't scream for attention, like all the other tents and banners splashed with gaudy primary colors and bold caricatures. No, this little tent created its own pastel oasis, serene amidst the din. An unassuming hemp rope held open the canvas flap offset to the right of center on the tent's front wall.

Sophie and Edie stood out in front, at least ten feet distant. They could just make out the shadowed back of a hooded figure seated in an overstuffed armchair, the kind you might find in someone's front room at home. The girls stood in silence, just looking at each other, then at the tent.

A wispy but nasal voice from inside pierced the cacophony consuming them and said, "Please come in, ladies."

Edie and Sophie wide-eyed at each other. Twilight had already descended into dusk. If not for the perpetual dust haze, stars might already be visible. Long gauzy shadows resolved into more crisp shapes now thrown around them by nearby torches. Their sooty smoke and golden glow lent a campy flair to the evening that seemed festive except within their tiny bubble of sincerity.

"Please, ladies, do come in." The voice elevated in pitch as she spoke. It seemed to ring, clear as a bell, over the otherwise raucous carny noise, like it separated them from all of the clanging and buzzing and ringing.

Edie whispered, "How did she know we were standing here?" Neither had uttered a sound on the otherwise noisy midway. Edie sounded eager.

Sophie shifted her weight as if to leave before committing to this madcap adventure. Ever the skeptic, Sophie scanned for a mirror or other reflective surface. "A good guess?" She didn't sound very convincing.

Edie grabbed Sophie's arm to prevent her from stumbling on the uneven ground—or from her trying to escape. Just like when they both lived in George, and Edie walked Sophie home. Ever since she was a child, after polio afflicted Sophie, she had managed her handicaps just fine, but sometimes a helping hand was welcome. Like now.

Upon entering the tiny tent, the overpowering odor caught them both by surprise. The hooded figure whispered, "You are most welcome here. I trust the incense does not displease you. It helps."

Their silent stances suggested they weren't sure where to sit in the darkness. The hooded voice interrupted their thoughts. "I am sorry to say I only offer one chair. It is a small space, as you can see. If one of you could wait just outside, we won't be but a moment. Our relationship builds on trust, does it not?"

Before anything else could happen, a long and crooked finger appeared from under the cloak and pointed at Edie. The faceless voice floated out toward them once more. "May I suggest you and I chat first, young lady? We have much to discuss, but I will not keep you long."

The gnarled hand appeared in its entirety, reached out, and squeezed Sophie's own twisted and flattened half-fist hanging by her side as she stood close to the seated apparition. But then she released it even before Sophie could react. "Thank you, dearie." The hood swiveled toward Edie. "And your name, my sweet?"

Just like that, Sophie became an outsider. She picked her steps to wait outside. That's what she wanted, wasn't it? But now she also wanted to be part of whatever would happen next inside that silly little tent. That surprised her. And that hand. It felt like hers. Sort of. Warm and sympathetic, but twisted, and somewhat dysfunctional. Then she realized that hand felt like polio! It was no accident that the woman squeezed her own polio-crippled hand, which was a longer reach for her than to her good hand. *Golly, what am I getting myself into here?*

Only a couple of minutes later, Edie came rushing out. "Sophie, Sophie, you must come meet Sister. She is wonderful."

"Why? What did she say?"

"Well, she says that's between her and me, but you're going to just love her. Do you know she's only nineteen? And she says she already knows you as a kindred spirit. I'm not sure what that means, but please go talk to her, okay? Okay?"

"Edie, golly, settle down. Yes, of course, if that's what you want. Did you pay her already?"

"Well, that's the darnedest thing. She wouldn't take my dime. Something's strange here. Just go talk to her, for Pete's sake!"

Sophie turned. Edie's hand hovered near her friend's right elbow, expecting her to stumble, but she made her way in just fine. Plopped down into the chair across from this *sister* without uttering a word.

With no preamble, the hooded voice said, "I already feel like a sister to you, Sophie. Is it okay if I call you Sophie? Edie shared your name with me."

"Well, ah, yes, of course. You suffer from polio, like me."

"Polio, yes, but I do not suffer. Not from polio. Neither do you. Like me, it makes you stronger. Dearie, you do not need a seer. You see just fine. You are the strongest person you know. Your husband loves you like life itself. But why do I waste our time telling you things you already know? What you might not yet know is how invaluable you will become to a dear friend. No, not to Edie—you've already done that, haven't you?"

There was something about that voice, and her certainty. "A man worries about many others, much more than himself, especially you. And my intuition tells me it has to do with our little traveling band of performers and oddities, like me, at least partially. I seem to know things. Just don't ask me how, because *that* I do not know."

"Are you talking about helping the sheriff with the murder investigation?"

"Very possibly. My sight is somewhat limited. But I do know some things. Is that helpful? Because, dearie, I now grow very weary."

"Yes. Thank you... Sister." Sophie couldn't explain how she felt at that moment, but she reached across the tiny round table that seemed more for leaning upon than anything. There was nothing on that table, except an unlit candle with three curled wicks. A pair of frightening hands, spindly hands with misshapen fingers, fully visible for the first time, appeared from within the folds of Sister's robes. They closed around Sophie's now-extended hands on either side of that candle. Both women held each other.

Even though Sophie could see nothing but shadow under that floppy hood, she imagined she was gazing into penetrating eyes. She had yet to see anything of Sister other than those incredible hands.

Then the moment passed. Sister withdrew and seemed to shrink and sag even further into her stuffed armchair. Her hooded face dropped to her chest. Sophie suspected that's also where she slept. It would be in the forties tonight. As she rose, leaning on the table for support, Sophie heard Sister mutter, "Please drop the flap as you leave, dearie."

Sophie did as instructed. She noticed the painted words "Closed" and "Private" were now visible on the outside of the unfettered flap. And that was that.

Sophie needed to talk to Billy.

26

After the ladies left, Sister felt like an empty husk. She had had a horrible feeling, and today she learned someone murdered little Babbo. Dear Babbo.

There was evil afoot. Loyalties notwithstanding, she could not stand idly by—even if she were able to stand. Fortunately, she made money for Madame, who even tasked a roustabout named Josh to help her as needed.

Josh shared his last name with no one.

But now she felt she could trust no one in the show, and that left her vulnerable. That is why she solicited outside help, as bold and unprecedented a move as that was. She took this terrible risk. There would be a cost.

Poor Babbo.

As always, she tried to unfold herself, without success. The weather would not allow her to sleep here tonight. She'd need someone to carry her to her wagon. Sister retrieved the whistle hanging on a lanyard around her elongated neck with some difficulty. She blew into it with the thin rope-like lips that slashed at an angle across her sunken face, and hoped someone who knew what it meant would hear. With luck, that would be Josh.

While she waited, she fingered her second most prized possession—a wire bronze pendant shaped like an eyebrow, with a single tear flowing down from its turquoise eyeball inset.

She whispered, *Ha"u-Wil'uk.*

27

❧ ❧

T rue to the promise of the ringmaster on the parade wagon, the rousters at the gate who worked with Jed admitted all who followed the wagons to the fairgrounds. But anyone who wanted to watch the opening extravaganza inside the big top had to pay a nickel a head. More wanted in than the tent could accommodate. Hearing the music and excitement coming from within would see the rest returning for later performances.

Lyon County had never witnessed such showmanship. Not in recent years, anyway. Those turned away from the packed big top wandered the midway to play games, enjoy rides and eat food that would cause dietary distress later. Even though they had just opened, foot traffic already pulverized the dusty brown grass underfoot on the midway.

Noise and lights festooning the Ferris wheel and the calliope music of the carousel competed with the grab joints offering pretzels, deep-fried butter, chocolate-covered bacon, mini-doughnuts and cotton candy. Barkers drew in the chumps to play ring toss, shoot at targets with guns that propelled weighted corks, and duck-fishing in livestock tanks with winning numbers painted on their bottoms.

MEANWHILE, INSIDE THE BIG TOP, THE BRASS ENSEMBLE HAD MOVED from their parade wagon to the small bandstand next to the back lot entrance to the big top. That's where the acts entered the single dirt-ring inside. Folks sat on the collapsible wooden bleachers that surrounded the ring on three sides. Customers entered through a break in the bleachers on the midway side. Everyone knew the show was about to begin as the music built to a crescendo. Then it just stopped. The audience fell silent in response. All heads turned toward the ring.

Unlike playground swings, a Russian swing has steel bars instead of ropes, and its swinging platform can rotate three-hundred-sixty degrees around the horizontal bar from which it is suspended. Two acrobats stood on the heavy swing's platform which was anchored at one end of the dirt ring. They pumped back and forth until they swung in a high arc. From there, these aerialists seemed to defy gravity, letting go of the swing and returning to it in mid-air after some feat of athleticism and grace. None of the local folks had ever seen anything like it. The aerialists's terrifying courage drew round after round of applause.

No sooner had they completed their act than the juggler and flame eater entered the ring together. Not only were their respective skills impressive, their joint choreography was worthy of the finest stage performance. Flames shot a dozen feet through the center of airborne juggling pins. Two clowns danced around and between them, providing comic and dramatic relief with faux fights and feats of tumbling through goofy antics cleverly choreographed.

The audience feasted their eyes and ears. Each time one of the acts did something spectacular or funny or horrific, the band pressed and highlighted it. The drummer's rim shots punctuated moments of contrived terror like a rifle's reports. The music ebbed and flowed between major and minor keys with the performers' movements as they delighted and amazed the awe-struck audience.

Throughout the performance, the smell of popcorn mingled with the sharp fumes from the flame eater's combusted fuel and that of the coal-oil spotlight. Even the dust kicked up from the action in the ring and dead grass not yet completely trampled insinuated a cocktail of pungent prairie odors to the revelry.

The band's sometimes raucous sound effects, with cowbells, cymbals, bass drum and snare drum, plus the clowns' ridiculous slide whistles and honking bulb horns seemed deafening in the enclosed space. But it all contributed to a cacophony of delight and amazement.

Every eye followed each momentary focus of the performance as highlighted with the brilliant coal-oil spotlight that swiveled to draw the eye to its focal point. Perhaps it was the happy clown pummeling the sad clown with a huge bowling pin. Or huge flames shooting from the mouth of the skinny little gal in dirty white tights.

The lightning movement in the ring kept everyone guessing where they should look so as not to miss a moment of this macabre madness, this feast for the senses. Those in the front row felt the heat of Cinder's flames. Some leaned back, sheltering their faces with their arms, thinking they would otherwise be broiled alive. But then momentary fear once again transformed into grateful applause and whistles of appreciation.

The handsome but unusual ringmaster called out each act. Although his face was painted to appear skeletal, his top hat and waistcoat presented the illusion of a cultured Victorian gentleman. His voice rang loud and true. The man was a born showman.

At last, the headliner act, Linus and His Magnificent Hounds, entered the ring with much fanfare. Just when the audience didn't think the band could get any louder, it did. The hounds howled on command.

Hounds? More like pooches with illusions of grandeur. But their marvelous training outshone their diminutive stature. Nobody understood superb animal training better than farmers who herded unruly livestock.

The big top performance lasted less than thirty minutes as the band pounded out their finale while all the performers took a final bow. But the audience didn't seem to mind the brevity of this performance. Much happened in that short half-hour. They'd spend weeks thinking back at all they had seen and heard and smelled and tasted. Many would return to relive what they missed the first time. It seemed everyone felt thoroughly entertained.

28

Sunday
April 8, 1934

CLAYTON MOORE FANCIED HIMSELF AN IMPORTANT MEMBER OF THE community. After all, everyone in Rock Rapids depended on him. Especially on a day like today. While all those do-gooders went to church to make themselves feel better, he'd be sweeping up confetti and streamers and shoveling horse dung. This was *his* town, and Hell would freeze over before anybody could say his town looked or smelled like road apples.

Everyone overlooked sanitation until he didn't do his job, like the slacker before him. Yep, Clay had his work cut out for him after that circus parade yesterday.

The scum-bastards left one helluva mess to clean up. Oughta be a law.

Maybe he'd bring that up to his old high school buddy.

Maybe Harry can do somethin'. Yeah, maybe I can get some changes made around here. Harry'll help!

He and the mayor did favors for each other. Always had. Besides, dirty streets wouldn't look good for Mayor Harold Deemers, and Clay Moore could *not* allow that. Harry was *his* mayor. Nothing he wouldn't do for that great man.

Clay had always protected Mayor Deemers, his geeky friend at RRHS, and covered up for him when he drove a motorcar drunk and killed his girlfriend. That's how he remembered it, anyway. Yeah, he'd gotten Harry drunk, but still.... Clay took the blame since he didn't really care about anything back then. It was all about friends and loyalty. Plus, it added to his reputation as a bad boy. Besides, Harry had always helped him with his homework.

They'd been on- and off-again friends ever since high school, but always behind the scenes. Harry explained, "Us politicians gotta project a certain image, Clay. I'm sure you understand. And the better we protect that image, the more I'll be able to do for you down the line. You certainly understand the importance of that, don't you, Clay?" Yep, he did.

Almost two decades later, after serving four years at Fort Madison and several drunk and disorderly convictions, Clay couldn't get a job. He wanted to be a deputy, and Harry—with utmost secrecy through a friend of a friend—arranged an interview for Clay with Sheriff Kershaw. The only thing Harry asked was that Clay not use his name as a reference. Clay thought that odd, until Harry explained, "This sheriff hates politicians, and it would only hurt you." Good tip. That damn Billy Rhett Kershaw hates everybody. He remembered that interview like it was yesterday, not two years ago....

BILLY ASKED, "SO, CLAY, WHY YOU WANNA BE A COP?"

"Well, Sheriff, I suppose like anybody, we gotta keep the streets safe from anybody not like us." When Billy asked him about that, Clay said, "You know...." Circled his own face with a forefinger and winked.

"Okay. Hmmm. Let me ask ya this. What if you was asked to testify in court to keep a black man out a jail if your evidence proved he did not do the crime. Could you do that, Clay?"

Clay chuckled. "Uh, hey, Sheriff, is this a trick question?"

And that's when Billy said, " Look, Clay, this ain't gonna be a good fit. You have the desire to be a cop, which is great, but your reputation precedes ya, son. Your convictions hurt ya. Them's a no-no for a cop. And you'd hate the job. You really would. I'm just bein' honest with ya here, Clay. You understand?"

Clay remembers saying he understood, but he didn't.

When Clay told Harry about the interview in a very private meeting, the mayor didn't press the matter further. Instead, he secured the sanitation job for Clay. Said it was part of his *Second Chance Outreach Program,* whatever that was. Told him it was a stepping stone, and that he'd take care of him. The mayor—a great man.

But that freak of a sheriff? Some day....

29

Senior Supervisory Agent Milford Langford Eubanks fussed with his tie. It refused to behave where it crept out from under his impeccable worsted wool vest. He stared out of the north-facing window of the East Omaha ATF field office that overlooked the east-west bend of the Missouri River. The brown water swirled with sediment en route to the Gulf of Mexico and New Orleans via the Mighty Muddy.

The junior agent behind him—one Samuel Ellis—stared at his own shoes as the silence swirled around them. He stood at attention, staring at his boss's slender back, awaiting the rest of the tongue-lashing sure to follow. The kid thought, *who keeps their desk this organized? This is downright... fastidious.*

He shivered at the drop of sweat that now dribbled down the center of his back under his starched-stiff shirt. Had to be ninety degrees in the small office. He'd been standing there for ten minutes. His own wool suit coat irritated him where it touched the base of his neck. Was it wool or horse hair, for crying out loud! He resisted scratching. Didn't even dare squirm.

Agent Eubanks spoke over his shoulder as he continued fussing with his tie. "Agent Ellis, might you surmise the source of my displeasure?"

"Sir, I was convinced he possessed a stash of automatic firearms—"

"Young man, you went with your gut. I respect that. What I cannot abide, however, is recklessly endangering your life by charging into an unknown scene with no plan and without backup. I trust this will never happen again." Not a question. He wheeled around to look the junior agent in the eye and smiled.

This was not what Sam expected. "Um, no, sir. It will not."

"That will be all, Agent Ellis." The junior agent hesitated before making his hasty escape under a wrinkled brow as he issued a silent sigh of relief.

❧

THE TELEPHONE ON AGENT EUBANKS' DESK STARTLED BOTH HIM AND the young man retreating from his office. Seating himself before answering, Lang's face lit up when he heard that nasal cowboy accent.

"Sheriff Kershaw, it is a delight to receive your call. And your timing is impeccable. I require a diversion. How may I be of assistance? Are you still nursing that arm? Surely this is not merely a social call. "

"Howdy, Lang. Always good of ya to grace me with yer Georgia drawl and a batch a questions, my friend. Mighta known you'd be in there on a Sunday. Still bustin' the young agents' chops?"

It was as if the country sheriff surveilled his office. Uncanny. "Billy, I must introduce you to a few other federal agents to run your errands. But after last summer, you can call this errand boy any time you need a favor."

"Funny you should say that, pardner. We got a little circus-slash-carnival and a couple a murders down this way that I could use some G-man eyes on, my friend. You game for a little fishin' expedition?"

"Well, to business. Name the circus and your victims, if you please." Lang knew that whenever Billy called, an interesting time was in the offing. He smiled at the memories of the previous year, when Billy deputized several locals. They battled a small army of ruthless Irish mobsters and won—with a little federal help. Courageous folks in Lyon County, Iowa.

After they discussed the sparse specifics, Lang committed to looking at this post haste, especially since he had no challenging cases running at the moment. He was due to return to his native Atlanta, but there was no rush. The bureau granted him a great deal of latitude based on his record of finding and closing significant cases.

Plus, he had grown to love the people out here in the Midwest.

❧ 30 ❧

❧

They packed into the small sanctuary. Throughout the sermon at the First Baptist Church on Harms Street in George, Sophie envisioned those twisted hands. Sister Shipton's voice tried to hide her desperation, but the more Sophie thought about it, hers was a lonely cry for help.

She and Jake held hands through much of Pastor Hildebrand's sermon on brotherly love. Cousin Walt cradled little Leo. He insisted, all the while bouncing him on his lap. Leo slept. The three most precious men in her life surrounded her.

On the ride home, Walt and Jake bantered on about the roast and vegetables slow-cooking in the oven of the old wood stove they called Blackie. Lately, they'd taken to keeping the fire at a slow burn with some chunks of store-bought coal. Walt said, "Boy, oh boy, I can almost smell that pork bakin' away! Sophie, you're one fine cook. Jake, you're a lucky man."

"Don't I know it, cuz. Soph, did you have a good time with Edie at the circus last night? Why the heck did she ask you to go with her? Didn't think you went in for that sort a monkey business. I worried sick about you, what with that poor circus fella's body they found yesterday afternoon 'n all. I had half a mind to keep you home." Jake fidgeted with the heater knob on the sedan's dashboard.

"*Keep me home?* Mister, do you remember who you're talking to?"

Walt's belly laugh from the back seat startled little Leo. He fussed, but settled right back down with Walt's gentle bouncing. He said in jest, "How long you been married to this woman, Jake? She puts her mind to something, you best jump back, cuz."

"Soph, what's going on with you and that circus? I see that look in your eye." Jake's genuine look of concern warmed the cockles of her heart. She squinted at his concern, but he looked straight ahead while he drove. And she wondered why she was already deeply committed to getting even more involved after what, a two-minute conversation with some circus performer last night? No, Sister was now a new friend. And that meant something.

She told the boys about their experience the night before, and how she felt this young woman at the show needed her help, and maybe *only her help.* Told them Sister was a polio victim too, and that she'd be driving up to Rock Rapids again that afternoon.

"You're a good woman, Soph." Jake took one hand off the wheel, just for a moment, without taking his eyes off the always-treacherous County 14. He squeezed Sophie's good hand. Neither Walt nor Jake said another word the rest of the way home. Leo slept.

SOPHIE KNEW SHE NEEDED TO TAKE HER RELATIONSHIP WITH SISTER Shipton further. But she would need to get this done without Edie, who just wouldn't understand. Or, if she did, it would do her no good to get snagged into the ripping emotion of a homicide investigation. Besides, while Sophie tucked the danger factor of getting more involved into a neat little corner of her mind, it remained.

Despite the risk, Sophie *needed* to help this young woman who seemed snared in what might be a life-threatening situation. She couldn't explain why *she* needed to do this. Billy said the rule in the show was that nobody talked to outsiders. Ever. Could Sister be taking a big risk?

She would share none of these feelings with Jake or Walt. Their response would be swift and unmistakable.

With the three boys safely tucked away at the farm south of George, and their promise to cover her evening chores, Sophie's sedan whisked her up to Rock Rapids.

She needed to talk to Billy.

This was already a long Sunday—too long.

❦

It delighted Sophie that her husband, Jake, worked for their friend and neighbor, Chief Dan Rustywire, at Red Chief Dirigibles, Inc. He was a good friend. They had landed a small but lucrative defense contract, and for the first time in his life, Jake collected a regular paycheck. Farming alone was always a gamble, especially these days.

With his extra income, Jake even bought Sophie a used sedan from Henry, her father, at Bairn's Motors in George. Jake insisted on paying full retail even though Henry wanted to shoot him a deal—a family discount, he called it. Jake wouldn't accept that. But the best part? No more step-stool to get in and out of the farm truck.

Besides, Sophie celebrated her newfound freedom with a vehicle she could drive without robbing the farm of Jake's truck. He and cousin Walt needed that truck for farm operations. And the boys had been wonderful about her spending a little time off the farm with her friend, Edie.

. . .

Sophie needed to update Billy after the previous evening's meeting with Sister Shipton. Even though it was Sunday, he would either be at the Law Enforcement Center or in his small apartment above it. When she came through the LEC's front door, Dwight's smile met hers, but she quickly shifted to all business.

"Where is he?" She liked Dwight, but he could be a little, well, big city.

"Where else? The man has no life other than this." He swept his arms to take in the LEC's interior.

"Oh, and you do, Dwight?" She smirked and winked.

"Yeah, yeah. I'll go get him for you." He popped up from his desk with more energy than she had felt in her entire life. This was the first time she ever saw him *sitting* at his own desk.

As stoic as she pretended to be, getting around was a major chore. Her bum hip burned like the blazes today, especially after the long drive to and from church, then all the way to Rock Rapids from the farm. She gravity-plopped into the guest chair in front of Billy's desk and waited. Reached her left hand across to massage her right hip that had already taken a lifetime of abuse compensating for her bum left foot. She'd wobble as she walked.

Sophie wrinkled her nose at the burnt-dry coffee in a pot nestled on top of the small wood stove behind and to her right.

Men!

The place gave off the town version of the stench in her farm's mudroom, but not as pungent, and less musty, but more... metallic. She guessed that was the gun oil. The place reeked of it.

Dwight reappeared through the alley door with Billy in tow a few minutes later. She had heard them clomping down the exterior steps from his apartment upstairs. The sheriff wore a plaid shirt that was yet to be buttoned over his sleeveless white undershirt. As disheveled as he was—including his thick straw-colored mop of "bed hair," he still cut a handsome figure. Had he splashed on some Aqua Velva?

Adorable.

. . .

BILLY COULD NOT DISGUISE HOW PLEASED HE WAS TO SEE SOPHIE. She thought his crush on her was cute, even though he was two decades her senior. As did dear hubby, Jake. But not the reason for the crush. She bore a remarkable resemblance to his deceased wife, Alice, who would now be almost her mother's age if she had not passed sixteen years ago. *That must have been a love affair for the ages. Poor guy.*

"Sophie, I'm always glad to see ya, but it's Sunday afternoon. You okay?"

"Hi, Billy. Late night?" She smiled. "Yes, I'm fine. How's your investigation going?"

"You mean the circus murders?"

She raised her eyebrows, then dropped one of them as she cocked her head, still holding his gaze. "How many investigations are you running, Sheriff?" She waited for him to shrug and chuckle before she continued. "Yes, and does that mean you're now classifying *both* deaths as murders?"

঺৵৩

"SOPH, WHY ARE YOU HERE?" BILLY WAS PATIENT, BUT THIS WAS official.

Dwight watched this apparent dalliance between his boss and another man's young wife. Within moments, she grew very serious, not being one to trifle with. Still, she was a civilian.

"Look, boys, I'm betting you're running into roadblocks looking into the murder of one or both of the victims you found close to our place down on Route 14."

"As a matter of fact—"

Dwight interrupted him. He felt his experience while with Minneapolis Homicide would serve them well enough, even here. "Billy, at the MPD, we never shared the details of an active investigation with civilians," he glanced over toward their guest with one cheek puckered, "no offense, Sophie."

"None taken, Dwight. I get it. If you don't want my help, I'd understand. And honestly, I'd be relieved." She planted her hands on the chair's arms, as if to leave.

Billy said, "Now hold on a minute, you two. Remember who wears the big badge here? Mind if I get a word in edge-wise?"

"Sorry, boss."

"Soph, we *are* findin' these show folk stubborn as a herd a constipated mules. Nobody talks, and when we ask, they get downright ornery." He swiveled his let-there-be-no-doubt gaze toward Dwight. "What's the harm in listenin' to what Sophie's got?"

"You're the boss, Billy. I guess it's a different set of rules down here. I'll get there. Besides, as of last summer, Sophie, you're a brother-in-arms, as they say. You held up pretty darn good under fire."

❧

She shot him an appreciative nod as she envisioned, for the thousandth time, the shoot-out at Chief's farm last summer. These two and her circle of friends, along with a small army of federal agents, put that mob of Chicago bootleggers and most of their mercenaries in their place—six feet under. That brought a grimace to her face, which Dwight mis-read. "Sophie—"

"No, Dwight, it's fine. That's a rough memory." Both Billy and Dwight understood that. They had lost friends. They also struggled with their own hell-scapes from the war. She now understood that—all too well. *All that blood... and the senseless—*

Billy brought them back. "Alright. Sophie, we just identified that scruffy old fella that crashed himself dead down your way last Wednesday. The circus boss lady first told us he warn't one a hers. But then said he was. There's some suspicious stuff around that whole deal. Got anything more'n we do about that?"

"Not sure yet. Alright, you told me what I needed to hear. You can't get anyone inside the circus to talk with you. I believe I can. Would that help you boys?"

"*What?*"

32

S ophie's question stunned both *boys*, who stared at each other, then back at her. They'd been turned away on every official visit to the fairgrounds over the last few days. With no actual evidence, they had no recourse to be more forceful, either. And Madame's promise to inquire on their behalf hadn't yielded anything yet. Now Sophie Hardt, of all people, claimed to have an inside source.

Billy was the first to come to his senses, like it took him some time to parse the meaning of her statement.

"How—?"

"Edie and I met someone at the circus last night. She says she'll talk to me. She said, and I quote, 'I know things,' and when I asked, 'Are you talking about helping the sheriff with the murder investigation?' she told me, 'Possibly. My sight is somewhat limited. But I do know some things.' She not only seemed willing, Billy, I'm betting she is *eager* to help. I just don't know why. Yet."

Billy said, "Well, that's great, Soph! We might have to deputize you —again." He offered her a warm smile, but she did not return it. Instead, she slantwise glanced over at Dwight. Then back at Billy.

"How about you give me the rest of what you have. Then, when I get a chance to talk with Sister again—"

"Sister?"

"Yes, that's what she calls herself. She's the show's seer, and—"

Dwight pounced on this like a wolf onto a three-legged lamb culled from the flock. "Wait. You're telling us that your source is a *fortune teller?* Is she getting her information from beyond the veil of death or some such bullshit?"

"Dwight Spooner! Now you watch your language, if you please! I sense this is personal for her. Something's happened, and she is angered or saddened by it, or both. And I imagine it has everything to do with current events. Now if you don't want my help, say it right now, mister, and I'll go tend to my little Leo. You can take your cynical attitude to the unemployment office when your boss loses his job because you can't do yours hobbled with that attitude. Are you an investigator, young man, or are you a petulant child who can't keep his tongue?"

Billy smiled at the handsome dressing down by a *civilian* two decades younger than both of them. *Sometimes it takes a strong woman, don't it, Billy Rhett, no matter her age? Dear God 'n little sonny Jesus, she looks and sounds like my Alice!* Billy had used poor Dwight's same exact words with the mayor and Laticia Morgenstern about involving civilians, but this was different.

He said, "Sophie, we do want your help. And let me just say that I, for one, wouldn't want to be at the business end a one a those beat-downs. Dwight's just had some unfortunate experience with show people in the past. I'm sure he don't mean nothin' by it." Dwight received another one of his let-there-be-no-doubt stares before Billy continued.

Sophie squirmed in Billy's chair as if she needed to adjust not only her physical position around that cussed hip, but also her emotional state after getting all fired up like that. She glared at Dwight, then focused on Billy's sincere tone.

"Now here's what we got: two corpses in Doc Gus's morgue over in Spencer, and almost nothin' to show for it. We're gettin' a lot a pressure to make progress on this investigation. Only problem is, we're not investigatin'. Most everything starts and ends with that doggone show, and nobody's talkin'.

"We been callin' victim number one Truck Driver. Looked like an old bum with a tiny tattoo, is all. He wasn't carryin' no ID on his person or in his truck. Nothin'. Like that was intentional. Sometimes, what you *don't* see is just as important as what you *do*. Dwight taught me that."

He glanced over at his deputy who was still licking his wounds.

"We now know he's from the show. Name's Garth Nitstone. But that's about all we know about that feller. I was chasin' him at the time. He was drivin' real crazy, like he was drunk. But I didn't smell no booze on him or in what was left of his truck. I caught a whiff a some weird-smellin' sh—, ah, manure residue 'n bits a straw in the bed of his truck. We're thinking exotic animal poop. Found some greasy white gunk at the edge of the truck bed too.

"Only physical evidence I found in the old boy's pocket was a tin a chewin' tobacco with a sticker on the back from the Boy's Town General Store. We called over to Boy's Town in Nebraska, and they confirmed our little circus played there before they come here by way a Sioux City. It's a sure bet our scruffy Mr. Truck Driver was our first victim and was runnin' from m'DAHM's show."

Sophie scratched her cheek. "m'DAHM?"

"Yup. She insists on bein' called that. The head lady over to the show—m'DAHM Antonia Perlatelli. Plus, this truck driver was wearin' this creepy little ring. Looked like he never took it off, even if he could. Just a human skull on its crown with some faded writin' around it. Oh, and he had this little tattoo on his right butt cheek. Looked like this..." Billy scratched a diagram on a page of his notebook to draw ℳ, tore it out, and gave it to Sophie.

"Now, Doc Gus over to the hospital in Spencer is still scratching his head over the cause of Mr. TD's—Nitstone's—crazy drivin'. No booze in his system, and he can't seem to find any drugs or signs a drug use. But he says if he knew better what to look for, he might find somethin'. Otherwise, bupkiss on number one, except he's part of POW's crew."

"POW?"

"Yeah, sorry. Perlatelli's Oddities and Wonders." Sounded funny coming out of Billy's mouth. Brought back memories of prisoners of war, or P.O.W.s.

Downright ignorant namin' a show that. Don't translate to American too good. Foreigners.

Sophie absorbed all of this, and said, "Well, that's some good detective work there, boys." Dwight still stung from Sophie's scolding, but he softened when she threw him a hundred-watt grin. He nodded his gratitude. She said, "So what about victim number two?"

"Dwight?" The sheriff gave him the nod and sat back in his hardwood swivel chair. Shifted his position to relieve his numb tailbone.

"Yeah, this one's odd, and I choose that word on purpose. First, Silas Hummel found him not too far from your place, Sophie, and not that far from where Billy ran Nitstone to ground just two days earlier. Now that right there is either one helluva coincidence, or—"

"We had heard that."

"But when Billy and I went down to the dump site—the ditch where someone threw out number two's body—there was no doubt where *he* came from."

"You found some ID?"

"You might say that. He was an adult male, about forty-nine inches tall, with an abnormally small head. And the only hair visible was a pony tale on the upper rear *point* of his cranium—his tiny little brain pan. And he had long, spindly fingers."

"Oh, my."

33

The first thing that occurred to Sophie were Sister's long, spindly fingers that she had held in her own hands the previous evening. But she said nothing about that. Not just yet. Besides, she didn't want to light Dwight's fuse again.

"So he was one of the circus freaks. Golly, I hate that word!"

Dwight said, "Yup, he was. On our last visit to the show yesterday after its opening, we noticed a banner on one of the sideshow tents right next to the big top. Advertised a freak—for lack of a better term, mind you—called Babbo the Manimal. Seems like he was a big deal in Madame's show, one of her featured *oddities*.

"Even though losing one of her featured acts must affect her income, she still refuses to talk to us. The public isn't allowed in the show's back lot where we tried to question her. After we told her about finding the, um, freak's body and described it, she was visibly shocked. She almost passed out. Then she just disappeared between the bunch of wagons back there. Left us standing there with our thumbs hooked in our belts. Ten minutes later, when Billy and I walked back up the midway, they were already breaking down our second victim's tent."

Sophie absorbed all of this, but something gnawed at the edge of her consciousness. "Where was this tent located?"

"Right next to the big top. Your fortune teller's much smaller tent was nearby just on the opposite side of the midway, set back a ways." Dwight stared at Sophie, awaiting a reaction. This was not lost on her. She felt both like a fellow investigator and now a suspect being interrogated. But she refused to take the bait.

Billy took over after Dwight fell silent. "Doc Gus says the cause of death was something called blunt force trauma, from several blows to the top and back of his tiny noggin. In plain old English, somebody beat his brains in with somethin' real heavy, Doc's guessin'. Plus, somebody made real sure this kid was dead with evidence of at least a dozen more blows to his back and sides before they moved and tossed the corpse. That's all we got.

Maybe it was time to level with the boys. Her first meeting alone with the fortune teller after Edie had introduced her with such enthusiasm challenged Sophie's rock solid foundation in logic and objectivity. She wasn't sure what she thought about this bizarre little woman. Her sincerity compelled Sophie to listen hard to her every utterance. Like it was holy writ.

"Boys, Sister suffers unbelievable pain. Her dark little tent was barely big enough for the two of us sitting across from each other with nothing between us other than a tiny round table. No crystal ball, no cards, just a candle. Her every word choice was, well, efficient, as if she had planned what she wanted to say to me, what I needed to hear. Her face was in complete shadow, and by the lay of her floppy hood, it seemed odd-shaped, like maybe her head is larger on one side than the other. The only part of her I saw in the darkness were her hands. Billy, she had long, spindly fingers."

Billy admitted to himself his affection for little Sophie Hardt might affect his judgment. But he was not about to miss a word of Sophie's mesmerizing description of the first meaningful meeting any of them had with any of the show people. She had terrific instincts. Not that he understood all that mushy stuff, but he respected it.

DESPITE SOPHIE'S EARLIER SCOLDING, DWIGHT GLARED AT BILLY from the second guest chair next to Sophie's. He dripped with cynicism that advertised his skeptical attitude toward all show people. The otherwise objective deputy muttered, "Sounds like you're in love, Soph."

"Put a lid on it, Dwight. What else, Sophie?"

"I believe she might know what happened to your second victim."

❧ 34 ❧

A half-hour later, Sophie limped up the midway, ignoring the barkers who tried to draw her in. She admitted to herself the smoky smells from the greasy food vendors along the way distracted her, even appealed to her. In the last six months since having Leo, her weight had crept up fifteen pounds. She kept moving over the irregular ground, eyes down and ahead, with focus. She lived with a constant fear of falling.

At Sister's tent once again, the flap was open and she could see the back of her hood, the same as the previous night. But in full daylight, everything appeared differently.

"Hello, Sophie. That is you, is it not? Please come in."

"How did you know—" Sophie entered the little tent and approached the chair opposite Sister.

"I'm sorry. I don't mean to be mysterious or anything. It's just that, well, I know things. Please sit down. Your hip bothers you."

"How—"

"No magic. I know that walk. I read people. Remember? Please close the flap before you sit. No one will disturb us then, dearie."

As the tent darkened with the flap closed, Sophie said, "Sister, are you taking a risk talking with me?"

A spindly finger appeared from the folds of her floppy sleeve and pointed. "If you please...."

Sophie could see well enough from the light leaking under the tent walls, where they didn't quite hug the hardpan dirt. Sister gestured. Sophie picked up the box of wooden matches from the table, took out a match, struck it on the box's side grit, and lit all three wicks of the fat candle. It was a well-made piece. Each wick popped a flame as soon as the match came close. It emitted an exotic odor. She set the matchbox down and with a nod from the hooded figure across from her, dropped the spent match to the ground. She plopped into the chair across from this young lady, who seemed wise beyond her nineteen years.

For the first time, she could see some of Sister's features in the glow of the undulating flames. It was as if her skin had never seen the sun—more gray than white, as far as she could tell in the flickering light. Her left eye appeared much higher than her right, and they were both... luminous. Amber? Or was that just the candle's reflected glow? And that long, crooked nose—almost like another finger—cast her slanted slash of a mouth in its shadow. Sophie tried not to appear shocked. A wave of pity overwhelmed her to tears.

Sister croaked, "My unusual features do shock at first, I know. But I am not to be pitied, any more than you are to be pitied."

Oh, golly! Is she reading my mind?

"Sophie, I'm just reading your expression. Now you need to know a few things, dearie. A few of my friends have agreed to meet with you, but you must be discreet. They risk everything. Much you will not understand, and you must know that is alright. You must fill in the blanks with your own intellect. Do not push too hard. Do you understand?"

This simple farm wife, cast into the role of reluctant amateur sleuth, scrunched her forehead. She clenched her bad hand with her good one under the table, and wondered, *What in Heaven's name have I gotten myself into here, Lord?*

Not sure why, but she whispered, "Well, I think I understand. I'll try. Why don't you start by telling me why everyone is petrified to speak to outsiders?" Sister's voice still sounded... haunted. *Those almost-lips! How on earth does she drink without dribbling?*

"It may be impossible for outsiders to understand, but there is much contention within our little troupe of troubled souls; however, many also feel blessed. This keeps us together and safe—a tight-knit group. We depend on each other, as we must. In general, we may joke about the *canvas wall,* but violating that unspoken rule is... awkward. Very awkward.

Many have not fared well outside the show and do not wish to be cast out, or worse. A very different set of rules exists out there for folks like us. You might think what I am about to share with you seems chaotic and dysfunctional. But it works for us—that is, it *has* worked. Now, people are dying, and there is a greater evil to be uprooted and defeated. Balance must be restored. But it will not be easy."

"A greater evil, Sister?"

"Some within the show have upset our social and ethical balance. There are those within the family who worship dark forces. Some would call it black magic. Strong beliefs and bizarre experiences cause some to act against their better nature. The balance within the show has tipped too far in their favor. And I sense that is only part of our current tribulations."

Sophie struggled to follow this strange monologue. She had never heard such talk. But she chose to just listen without comment or judgment. For now. She fought back wave after wave of doubt, riddled with skepticism. She waited for Sister to continue in that voice that sounded both strained and smooth.

"Others follow a lighter path that would be clear to your Indian friend. You and Edie have such a friend, do you not?"

"Um, well, yes. Our friend, Chief Dan."

"Chief Dan would understand why we call our groups within the show *tribes.* Our tribe that treads the path of light Chief Dan might think of as practitioners of the nature religions—respecters of earth, air, water, fire and ether. Your Christian friends might call such practices paganism because they worship and respect *all* of creation—without humanizing one deity. Your face tells me you are a Christian,

Sophie, and that is wonderful. Unlike others of us who have been subjected to unfortunate persecution, I do not judge. But all of this is important for you to understand."

"Sister, how should I think of these, um, tribes?"

"There are those who practice secret occult rituals. Others practice what the ancients called the faery crafte. Christians of old labelled it witchcraft."

"I thought witchcraft *was* dark and occult and evil."

"Oh, on the contrary, my dear. Sixteenth-century Christianity demonized all witchcraft for their own purposes, motivated by a plague of profit and influence. There is good and bad in any human endeavor. For our purposes here, we have our occult tribe and our faery tribe. Dark and light. Both are necessary."

"Okay, Sister, but I'm way out of my comfort zone here. Just please tell me what this has to do with our murder investigation."

"You are already listening with an open mind, even though you struggle. Very good, dearie. You'll understand in a short while, at least as much as I do. Now, we have the occults. They practice secret rituals. They're avid practitioners in the art of influence. And then we have the faeries, for lack of a better label. They use their craft for healing mind and body. But that's only half of the entire troupe's ebb and flow."

"Okay. I'm trying real hard to absorb all of this."

"Yes, to an outsider, I'm sure it's a lot. There is conflict between these two tribes. There is also conflict between four major work factions within our troupe: performers, freaks, labor and management.

"Our performers will tell you they don't much care for freaks because they're not 'normal' and possess no skills other than they're different.

"Likewise, freaks don't care for performers because they view them as arrogant and full of themselves.

"And the roustabouts, or rousters, which is our labor—our muscle —they know the show could not move, get set up or be torn down to move without them. They view their jobs as the most important of all.

"Madame, of course, is management. We all try to please her, but few succeed. She motivates us to *be* more, to *do* more.

"You see, Sophie? We are a troupe of conflict, and it all works *because* of it, not in spite of it. Without understanding this, your investigation will go nowhere."

"Golly, that's a lot of conflict that needs a lot of understanding."

"But all of this also creates a cohesive bond that should explain why we don't talk to outsiders. It is all too easy for anyone outside the show to misunderstand—or worse, to judge—especially officers of the law."

Once more, Sophie sought to understand. "And now that you've shared all of this with me, why *me*? And how does this relate to discovering who killed Mr. Babbo?"

At the mention of that name, a sudden shudder visibly shook Sister. Sophie heard her gasp as if punched in the stomach. Sophie jolted back and looked around with fear in her eyes. Had some outside threat invaded their little space? No, a battle raged within this strange creature, hunched before her in hooded shadow. The silence that followed lasted a minute or more while Sister collected herself. The shuddering subsided. Sophie waited. Then, once again, she leaned forward to listen hard, and it *was* hard, almost overwhelming.

Sister said, "My apologies. You will learn the truth of what happened by uncovering clues and motives, Sophie. As I said when we met last evening, I know things, but my sight is not complete. We will discover the truth together. Why you? Because, dearie, you and I are kindred souls. I possess a gift of sight, and you possess a gift of open-minded intellect. Know it or not, you are an empath, dearie. I see we trust each other—deeply—as we must. We will help your friend, the sheriff, discover what happened to Garth, who hated Babbo."

"Garth?" Even though Sophie had heard Billy speak the name, she wanted Sister's point of view.

"Garth Nitstone, a rouster who was steeped in dark magic. And I need your help in discovering who murdered my brother, dear Babbo."

Sophie's jaw dropped and stayed there under wide eyes.

"What did you just say, Sister?"

35

S ophie had been leaning into Sister's every word, but now she leaned back as far as she was able in the uncomfortable chair, bracing herself against the rickety little table, absorbing this shocking new insight. "Your... *brother?* Mr. Babbo is your brother?"

"He is just Babbo. Yes, he is—was—my twin brother. I do not believe even he knew that. Our mother cast us in different directions very early, but I knew. Later, I made sure I worked the same shows as little Babbo, to keep an eye on him, and to protect him if I were able. Three days ago, I sensed something in his future. I warned him, but to no avail. Someone... murdered him... anyway. It would seem we are slaves to destiny, despite our gifts... and our burdens."

It was Sophie's turn to collect herself. As she processed this new insight, and Sister's profound grief, she too came to the brink of tears. As an only child, she could only imagine this pitiable soul's sense of profound loss. But she also saw this as a unique opportunity to move the investigation forward, to seek justice. For Babbo, and maybe for someone named Garth.

Yes, she would jump at the chance to help the grieving girl hunched in front of her. It was the Christian thing to do. She asked, "Can you tell me anything that might help me understand Babbo's state of mind before he was... attacked?"

"Babbo was unique, and not just physically. Unlike me and my many birth defects, shortly *after* birth, he developed a condition called microcephaly. That means a small skull, or more accurately, a skull that never developed like most other babies. But he was not a stupid boy. Given his condition, that made him extraordinary. Most pinheads suffer from mental deficiencies. Quite the contrary, Babbo was brilliant."

"Pinhead, Sister?"

"That's what some people call folks like Babbo. Even though he was a freak, rousters considered him a friend. They otherwise avoid socializing with freaks or performers. But Babbo played cards with them almost every night. He even slept in their bunk tent with them. They loved him. Protected him.

"Rousters are a rough bunch with very tough jobs. The only rouster who didn't like Babbo was Garth. He and a few other rousters practiced the dark magic. Babbo never liked that and wasn't afraid to say it. In fact, Babbo didn't go in for any of that spiritual stuff, light or dark. He believed in what he could see, touch, hear, and smell. His sense of taste never developed. He would eat anything, bless his little heart.

"Also, you should know that he was in love with a performer— another taboo. He and Lilith Smalley could not get enough of each other. Her father was livid when he found out his precious young Lilith had fallen for a freak. Our little show's version of Romeo and Juliet, you might say."

"Oh, my...."

"Further, Madame Perlatelli saw the friction that Babbo caused between performers, freaks, and rousters. While she appreciated the revenue Babbo brought in, and he was one of her favorites, she did not appreciate the show's balance being upset. I believe she viewed Babbo as a contributor to that imbalance."

· · ·

S<small>ISTER CONTINUED WITH A WEARY UNDERTONE IN HER VOICE THAT</small> now croaked, "For your insight, dearie, here's what Babbo told me a while back. In his own words—about his history with another show. We do not speak its name." She closed her eyes, lowered her head.

When Sophie heard the voice that issued from underneath Sister's cowled hood, her eyes widened once more, and her jaw hung slack, again. A different voice, a masculine voice, projected more forcefully than Sophie imagined possible from Sister's frail little frame. She imagined she was listening to Babbo himself....

'Madame still borrows me out to other shows sometimes, ya see. Over there, they put me in a cage with straw. Real clean straw. Tell me to squat and grunt while the front man pitches the gaff, like they catched me in a gorilla hunt down in Africa. Hell, I be born in New Jersey to me mum, a performer. She'd call me her special little angel before she done gone to Heaven.

"Fer the finale a that side in that big show, I play me fiddle. Proves to the chumps I ain't just an ape, ya see. I was pretty good, even with me arms hangin' to m'knees. That makes playin' harder, ya see, even with the long bow they gimme fer me fiddle. Sometimes when yer hungry, ya do things, ya see? It's fun. Like a real performer.'

Then Sister passed out. Sophie blew out the candle and let her sleep. Dropped the flap.

So much to think about.

36

Sister slept.

The sun surrendered to the western horizon in a dusty haze as Sophie stumbled out onto an uncaring midway. Mrs. Sophie Hardt—Iowa farm wife thrust into the role of homicide investigator—wasn't sure what to do next.

After the gypsy fortune teller collapsed in her tent from exhaustion, it was understood that Sophie would visit Sister again the next day. She made her way past all the noise and stale smells to her car parked on the now-flattened grass outside the gate. She was barely conscious of anything but that disembodied male voice that had drifted from Sister's throat as if she were possessed. By her deceased... *twin brother?* That voice now lived inside of Sophie's consciousness, haunting her. *"Proves to the chumps I ain't just an ape, ya see. I was pretty good, even with me arms hangin' to m'knees."*

Just Babbo. Little Babbo.

She needed to talk to Billy. Dwight too. They had left Deputy Jimmy Lenert in the dark on this whole circus thing, by design, and that was okay with her. Her sedan found its way to the Law Enforcement Center, and she wobbled in as if in a daze. The lights were already on.

⌘

"SOPHIE! YOU ALRIGHT? LOOK LIKE YOU SEEN A GHOST." BILLY hoisted himself out of his desk chair, hurried across the room, and grabbed her elbow. Guided her to his guest chair. Helped her get seated. Grabbed her a glass of water from the pitcher atop the filing cabinet closest to his desk. Set it in front of her. She didn't seem to notice. He dragged the guest chair from Jimmy's desk to sit beside her at an angle (the "suspect chair" *beside* his desk was bolted to the floor). She stunk of candle smoke, and something else. His look of concern deepened as her silence continued. She had yet to utter a word. He waited, staring with worry.

Finally, she pivoted her gaze to meet his. Despite the early Spring temperature outside and a residual chill in the LEC, her forehead glistened. Looked like she had just finished her chores in record time. Despite her fragile back, she slumped in the hard chair. She croaked, "Billy, I'm not sure I can do this." Didn't help that it had already been her longest Sunday *ever.* And she still needed to drive home fifteen miles distant. In the dark.

With profound concern, Billy jerked into an aggressive stance as he stood and looked down at the top of her forehead, ready for action. Instinct shot his right hand to the butt of his service weapon. After a moment, his left hand landed with a heavier touch than he intended on her right shoulder. "What on Earth happened? Did somebody hurt you, Soph? Who was it?" He gave her shoulder a little shake and squeeze.

⌘

"NO, NO, BILLY, NOTHING LIKE THAT. PLEASE, SIT DOWN." SHE softly beat her flat fist on her chest several times, on the verge of tears. She swallowed her doubt in a throat so dry, it could only *try* to swallow, as if it meant to disobey. Her good hand rubbed her left thigh as if she could think of nothing better to do with it.

Where to start? She realized how shaken she must appear to Billy. That had not been her intent. Yes, she had grown more confused and concerned during her twenty-minute interview with Sister, especially the lengthy emotion-laden silences.

Dwight was nowhere to be seen. She didn't need to deal with his drama right now, anyway. *That voice. All that conflict. Yet Sister had said, 'It works for us, that is, it has worked. Now, people are dying, and there is a greater evil to be uprooted and defeated. Balance must be restored. But it will not be easy.'*

Sophie had entered some vast reality radically different from her own. She couldn't imagine people lived like that—chose to live like that. But that assumed they *had* a choice.

Billy sat back down with tense deliberation. He was a coiled spring. She needed to give him a task to settle him. And herself. "Billy, I'm never out this late—alone. Please call Jake. Tell him I'm here and will be home before bedtime. He and Walt and little Leo should eat supper without me. Make sure he doesn't panic, okay? Then I'll share what I learned over at the circus."

She drew in a deep breath and let it out, still recovering herself.

🦋 37 🦋

Billy returned from the telephone with even more nervous energy. "Soph, Jake sounded concerned. Because I did, I guess, a little. Now, what the heck happened over to the circus?"

"Well, it's so different. It's hard to imagine. They got all kinds of craziness going on over there. Trying to sort it all out. Lots of suspicions. I can't quite...." She pointed at her left temple with her index finger and held it there. She tried to swallow. Took a sip of the warm water.

"Sophie, tell me what you heard. Was it all from that fortune teller?"

"Billy, Sister prefers to be thought of as a seer. She's arranged for me to meet with a few folks. First, I'll meet with her again tomorrow. For now, let me see...."

Sophie collected her thoughts. "They have performers, freaks and manual laborers they call roustabouts. And management, Madame Perlatelli, stands apart from all of them, but also watches out for all of them. None of these groups like each other much, with a few exceptions. Victim number two, Babbo, is a freak that most of the roustabouts liked and watched out for. Also, Babbo was in love with a performer, which upset her father, Tom Smalley. And it turns out victim number one—somebody named Garth Nitstone—and Babbo did not get along. Plus, Babbo was Sister's twin brother, Billy." She waited.

"Thee hell, you say! Holy sh—, ah, that's... Jeez. Explains why she's helping us, I guess. You were right, Sophie. You said it was personal for this... sister."

"That's her name, Billy. Her name is Sister. She's my gifted friend who also happens to be a freak. Sort of like me." Surprised herself how defensive she sounded as she grasped her helpless permanently flat-fisted right hand with her left, and tucked her bum left foot under Billy's guest chair.

"Sophie—"

"There's friction between two spiritual groups with opposing beliefs. They practice rituals and such. Not sure how much focus to put on that, but Sister seemed to think it was important. They call one group *occultists*—sounds like very negative and secretive stuff. Maybe even devil or demon worship, but what do I know? The other group they call faeries. Not like in fairy tales, but like old-time witchcraft. Sister claims they're more worshippers of nature, like the Indians. She said Chief Dan would understand.

"She hinted these two groups go at each other from time to time. But Babbo didn't go in for any of that stuff. Garth was into the occult. Not sure how or what that means, though. We didn't get much into this tribal stuff, as she called it. I'm thinking there might be plenty of motives to go around for both murders, especially from these occultists. Sister also spoke of what she calls a *greater evil*. Scary stuff, Billy."

"Mrs. Hardt, I do believe you are bustin' this case wide open. Now, where do we go next, *Detective*?" Billy started to relax, even grinned. All Sophie could muster was a tired smirk, almost like she was doing all of this under protest. But those amber eyes, one higher than the other, that awful nose over a crooked mouth, and that haunted voice— two *different* voices—coming from somewhere inside that floppy hood....

"Well, I guess tomorrow Sister tells me more. She's lining up a few interviews for me. I'll report back."

"Damn it, I'm going with you—"

"*No*, Billy! Do *not* destroy the trust that's already taken a lot out of me to get going. Golly, I didn't know this would be so... taxing."

"I sure hope your new friend knows eventually I'm gonna have to haul a few folks in for further questioning. This is an excellent start, Sophie. Okay, you got this!" He reached over and patted her shoulder with as light a touch as he had in him.

"I don't know, Billy. When I was close to Sister, I felt... not sure I know. I felt, joined with her, almost... sort of unhinged. She's, ah, there are no words. Maybe... powerful?" Sophie stopped talking. Dizzy....

"Sophie, breathe! You are huffin' like a quarter horse that just done run a full mile flat out."

38

M onday,
       April 9, 1934

NOT AGAINST HER BETTER JUDGEMENT, BUT BECAUSE OF IT, AND despite her doubt, Sophie found herself back in Sister's little multi-colored tent for the third time in three days. Testing Jake's patience at her venturing out on her own "all the time," she reminded him of how important this had become to her. She just wished Sister's tent was closer to the front gate and to her car.

The candle was already lit. Its three wicks flickered from a breeze that mere canvas could not deny. Sister invited Sophie in—sight unseen —again. She hunched close to the small flames for their heat against Northwest Iowa's April chill.

Sophie found this second interview with Sister less taxing, as if they had eased into a more comfortable give-and-take, which was a lot less exhausting. Maybe it was because she was more receptive, more open, and she felt less like resisting.

Also, shocking revelations now came more easily to this small-town girl from Sister. *She reads me like a paperback book, and that makes it easier for both of us, doesn't it? My word! Yesterday, that idea would have frightened me.*

 SISTER MUTTERED, *"HA"U-WIL'UK"* TO herself and then said, "Sophie, it's time to talk about who might have wanted to go beyond rituals or benign curses, and why. Here's what I can tell you, dearie. Some battles between good and evil rage behind closed doors, or tent flaps, even as we speak. First, let's get you up to speed on curses."

Sophie's skeptical look of disbelief, tempered with an expression of reluctant acceptance, told Sister where she needed to start.

"The Bible mentions curses in various forms no less than two-hundred-and-thirty times. They are cast through ill-wishing, negative judgments of others, negative thoughts about one's self, or unhealthy relationships and sexual activities. Words and intent possess power, Sophie. As an example, as you well know, it is all too easy to wound someone with an unkind word or hateful phrase.

"Curses, possession and demons exist even within the practice of Christianity. Deliverance ministers and exorcists who have the gift of discernment, for example, can determine whether a person has been cursed and is afflicted by a demon. There are likely to be signs of mental or emotional breakdown, repeated and chronic illness, infertility and miscarriages, financial problems, or a tendency to have accidents.

"It's a mysterious wide world out there, Sophie. To believe only what you've been personally exposed to can leave you vulnerable to larger truths, or at least to what other folks take on faith. Beliefs are the most powerful force inside any of us. It shapes who we are and how we react to the world around us. You should keep all this in mind as you interview the folks I suspect are most likely to be helpful.

"Garth practiced dark magic. Some say he placed a death curse on Babbo—which isn't illegal. But some suspected it backfired on him, which could not have happened without him self-validating his own ritualistic magic—his beliefs. It is said that the person who makes a curse ultimately suffers the effects of it. He who practices the dark arts is most vulnerable, because he already believes."

Sophie's eyes had widened and stayed that way. She did a lot of that lately. "Do you accept this stuff, Sister?"

"It doesn't matter what you or I accept, Sophie, only what the killer or killers and their victims believe. You see that, don't you, dearie?"

"Yes, I suppose I do."

"Outside of Christianity, you should also remember curses are considered part of a system of justice. Practitioners invoke powerful evil spirits. The Greeks and Romans used curses as a part of their daily lives to gain advantage in business, politics, sports, and love. The Egyptians wrote curses on magical papyri, a practice adopted by Greeks and Romans.

"In cases of possession and exorcism performed by the Catholic Church, for example, cursed objects are dangerous and must be destroyed."

Sophie did not say that her family always considered those Catholics practiced heresy within Christianity by considering all this symbolic stuff literally, but now....

"I know this is a lot for you, Sophie, but this sets the stage for your investigation. For less extreme cases, the effects of—or belief in—a curse can be removed by a number of actions. For example, prayer, attendance at church, reading the Bible, repentance, renunciation, placing crucifixes and religious objects in the home, and attending to a virtuous life. I sense even you expect to earn crowns in Heaven because of the type of life you live on Earth, do you not, Sophie?"

"Well, yes I do," Sophie astounded herself. She *could* see how these beliefs could become a motive for murder, or for becoming a victim.

Sister continued, as if lecturing a student. "It is said numerous remedies against cursing exist. Amulets protect against or deflect curses, whether or not a person has specific knowledge about them. The early Greeks and Romans wore certain carved semiprecious and precious gems as rings and necklaces to ward off curses. Even today, some practitioners wear a crucifix. Why? Who is to say?"

It seemed to Sophie that Sister almost subconsciously fingered an amulet she wore on a necklace around her own neck. She pretended not to notice.

"It is *assumed* in many cultures that one will be cursed by one's enemies for any reason. Spells and charms—like magical words, mantras, phrases, chants and incantations—are expected to invoke the protection and intervention of benevolent spirits. An individual who has been cursed sometimes visits another witch or sorcerer to break the curse and perhaps to curse the curser. Such are the powers of the human mind.

"Sophie, you must understand that even if you do not trust in such things, many within our tribes do. And buried within those beliefs, you will discover what you seek—clues and motives and the truth of what happened, or what is yet to happen. You understand. I know you do."

"I do, but—"

Sister said, "I suggest you start your investigation by chatting with Crocodile Man. CM is a good person, but he sometimes shakes and shivers from his anger. Those who know him understand the ordeal he suffered sometimes reveals his jagged edge. And the bigoted Garth Nitstone had always hated him. Not because CM was a freak, and a *made* freak at that, but because he married interracially. From there, you will find patterns that will offer you what we seek."

Sister slumped. That was all. Sophie gathered her momentum to rise and leave. A soft sound that could have been a quiet chuckle came from the shadows. She paused. Sister whimpered, "You must think us all mad. Remember, like you, we live the life granted to us. Blessings be upon you, Sophie. Many thanks.

"Now go."

Go, indeed!

❧ 39 ❧

❦

Sophie's heart wept.

She found it hard to remember Sister was a little nineteen-year-old deformed dwarf. And she had just lost the closest person to her in the world, or the *only* person close to her. And now, she was part of this little woman-girl's world, seeking justice. She stumbled and almost fell as misty eyes clouded her vision under the weight of her task.

Outside, twilight threatened to smother her. A leathery little roustabout grabbed her arm, startling her.

"Hello, Miss Sophie. I'm Josh. Sister says yer heart is true."

"Hello, Josh. What else did Sister say?" His eyes said there was more.

Somewhat more bold than shy, he grumbled, "That we wasn't to run no cons on ya, and that if you was to fall down, ya might not get up."

"Cons?"

"Yeh, miss, confidence games—pig-in-a-poke, the badger, razzle-dazzle—slick ways to bilk ya out a yer money. What some do for extra cash. Hard times, miss."

"Oh, my."

"Not to worry. Sister watches out for ya. Worth a lot. I'm to take ya to CM's tent. Is that a'right with ya, miss?" She looked into a huge pair of doe eyes in the middle of a face wrinkled before its time. Josh's grip was powerful. His were soft eyes in a hard face six inches below her own and shone from within a cloud of pungent body odor.

"Thank you, Josh. I'd be in your debt."

"Ya just find out who killed my friend." His accent was hard to place. Irish? Since she was talking with a roustabout, she said, "Garth?"

He sneered. "Not that blaggard. No friend o' mine, that one. You find out about little Babbo, miss. And I'll be in *your* debt, a sure."

Those kind eyes hardened. They began darting about like he expected trouble. He ushered her around to the backside of Sister's tent, out of sight of the midway. As if he feared someone would see them together. This also startled Sophie, but she understood. Madame.

"What can you tell me about CM, Josh?" She asked as Josh led her over the rough ground of the back lot's periphery—rougher than the midway.

"He's a good man who's been through a mighty ordeal. They say he was a riverboat captain for a time in a place called New Guinea. Fell in love with everything local. Wanted ta be a part of what a few of his mates down there called a *rite of passage,* or some such. Every one a them little flaps in his skin is another deep cut. Took nigh onto a week. The whole process turned him a little crazy, I'm a thinkin'. Flipped a switch somewhere in his brain. Maybe a crocodile mind, now. Not sure.

"Miss, some things don't get explained. Ever. Hard ta make a livin' outside a the shows that scarred up. Joined Madame's show down Louisiana way. Met Tara 'n Tamra. They hit it off right out a the chute. A month later, they married."

"The *three* of them married?" *This just keeps getting more and more bizarre. Remember—circus folk, Sophie!*

"Yes, miss. TnT is the show's two-headed girl. Kinda like Siamese twins, but with only one body from the shoulders down. A miracle they survived birth. But they got a special diet, and the two a them talk a lot with Madame. Ya know, girl talk—CM's okay, but there's a lot he don't understand about TnT. They're real nice, most of the time, but gotta be more than a might confusing. They both love him ta death.

"Tare's the more romantic one, a sure. But Tam, that lass, she thinks too hard. Watch out. Sometimes, I think she gets a little jealous a Tare. But they're all good people, as far's ole Josh knows."

Ole Josh? This kid can't be twenty years old. Nice enough, though. And just like that, Josh placed a firm but not-ungentle grip on Sophie's right arm. Continued to lead them away from the obvious beaten path over even rougher ground. Within thirty seconds, they arrived at an unassuming tent of dirty brown canvas much larger than Sister's.

"Miss Sophie, you don't go sayin' nothin' to Madame about this, like Sister says."

She said nothing in response to his solemn expression, but offered him a serious nod. Decided she'd have to meet this Madame at some point, though. He released her arm, placed a supportive hand on the middle of her back, and said, "I'm a thankin' ya, miss." And in a louder voice toward the tent now in front of them, "Hey, CM, ya made freak. Brought you a visitor from Sister. Ya play nice now, ya hear?" Josh raised the flap in front of her and held it. He winked with a good-natured nod of encouragement.

From inside the tent, a booming voice startled her. "You said your piece, Josh. Now clear out, ya little shit!"

Oh, my!

The gruff rumble from inside caused Sophie's eyes to widen, like she was about to step into a wild animal's cage, unarmed.

🦎 40 🦎

❦

"Well, lady, you comin' in or not?"

Talk about bluster! She picked her steps over the rough ground. Once inside, Josh dropped the flap behind her. The next step found her on an area rug. Of sorts. Smoothed out the lumpy ground underneath. Somewhat.

A muscular naked back with broad shoulders greeted her. Was he reading something? Peering into a mirror? He was black, almost blue. Sophie had never known any negroes. But what she found most remarkable was the slender diamond-shaped, what? Thick skin flaps that looked like reptilian scales? Symmetrical patterns of hundreds, thousands, of these flap-scales swept up from his lower spine toward each shoulder, leaving a small v-shaped area close to the back of his neck unmarred. All but the top of his very normal negro head—handsome, even—was shaved clean. Up top he had hair, but it was close-cropped.

Sophie said, "Ah, Mr. Crocodile Man—"

Still seated on a swivel stool, he spun around fast. Startled Sophie for the third time in the last ten minutes. She stumbled backward with eyes like saucers and waved her arms in search of balance. The huge man jumped up, rushed at her with lightning speed and agility. He caught both of her arms to prevent her from falling. Guided her with sudden tenderness to the lumpy double bed three paces to her left. This all happened so fast, Sophie thought she was being attacked. At first. She soft-fell like a rag doll the last six inches down onto the bed with a squeak in this freak's tent.

Golly! She drew in a sharp breath to scream when the huge man stood up and said with surprising gentleness, "Are you alright, miss?"

Oh, for heaven's sake, Sophie! "Yes, I thank you for your help, Mr.—"

"Just CM, ma'am. Sorry if I startled you. Happens sometimes." He growled, like he was frustrated with himself. He pounded the sides of his thighs with both fists several times as a snarl sculpted his striking face. He visibly shook. She saw that his own lack of impulse control frustrated him. Something else, too. She tried to catalogue the entire effect in her mind, but failed.

Those piercing black eyes!

"Sometimes, I'm scared of this... *thing* I've become. And I ain't *only* talkin' about this." He aimed the ends of both arms toward his chest, open palms facing upward, fingers spread wide and pointed inward toward his body. He drew them downward with clumsy deliberation. Almost every square inch was scarred with thumbnail-size flaps of skin meant to look like the scales of a crocodile's hide. At least what was visible of his naked upper torso, bare calves and the tops of his feet.

Now, sitting on this man's bed, she stared at his navel—at eye level. *My goodness. Those muscles! And all that, um....* "CM, I'm Sophie. Won't you sit down, please? Do you know why I'm here?"

He seated himself next to her at a respectful distance from her on the bed. "Josh, the little shit, says Sister sent you. Good enough for me. About Garth and Babbo, right?"

"You don't much like Josh, do you, CM?"

"Aw, ain't nothin'. He's a rouster, I'm a freak. Worse, I'm a just *made* freak."

"Well, Sister tells me freaks and, ah, rousters don't get along, except for Babbo. Right?"

"Yeah. Babbo, he was a natural freak. I ain't even that. Sure, I could do other stuff for a living, Miss Sophie. Cover up all this," he rubbed the tiny scars on both his shoulders with a light touch by crossing his arms, "but I couldn't be close to TnT then."

"Yes, your wife. Wives?"

"Yeah, most non-show folk can't understand—don't even try. State of New York even says I'm a bigamist. But what if my girls tried to marry two men? Or is she just supposed to always be alone?"

That growl again, only softer.

"And our marriage ain't legal in a lot of states, more 'n half of 'em, because TnT's white, and I'm just a darkie. Or didn't you notice, Miss Sophie?" He smirked as a residual growl escaped his throat. She noticed the chords in his neck pulsed.

Sophie smiled and surprised herself. She reached over, placed her good hand on his scarred right hand that rested on his thigh. Then she removed it lest he misunderstand. She liked this man. "Humor, CM? Um, I don't understand your lifestyle. I don't need to. Just tell me. Who would want to hurt Babbo? I have to ask this. Would you want to hurt Babbo?"

Oops.

CM started clenching and unclenching his fists again. He launched off the bed, which made it shake under Sophie, and he paced in a small circle at high speed. "Lady, Sister vouches for you. That's got weight. The only thing Babbo and I got in common was some gambling debts. You're gonna find out, anyway. I owed Babbo some money. Not a lot. He was a freak, and hid behind that simple face of his, and in a girl's dress they'd sometimes put on him for the gaff. Truth is, he was a damn card shark. The rousters all got it. But they let the little guy win, didn't they? Stupid me. I learned too late he'd read any player's tells like nobody I ever seen. Even on the Ramu River down in New Guinea. Almost like he saw my cards through my eyes, not his. Some said he cheated. But nobody ever called him on it, or caught him. He was just that good."

CM scrunched his nose as if the memory of repeatedly being beaten at cards by Babbo were stinky recollections he'd rather forget.

"So what happened to Babbo, CM?" She leaned back on the lumpy bed as his lightning pace brought his clenching and unclenching fists that he swung like wrecking balls dangerously close to her face. After a few minutes, he sat down again, as if against his will. Started rubbing his thighs through the coarse cloth of his dungarees. She wanted to ask him why he was so scantily clad, but that would not move the investigation forward. By the crust on his leathered and cracked feet, looked like that's all he ever wore despite the chill in the late Spring air.

Is that all he ever wears?

She now feared offending him further, and where that might lead. The man's fuse almost didn't exist. She awaited with the patience of Job. He assembled his thoughts with some obvious difficulty as he wrinkled his brow, squinted his piercing eyes, and jerked his head from side to side—almost like spasms.

"Miss, I keep wondering if there's some nasty connection between Babbo and Garth. That bastard was the only rouster Babbo couldn't abide because he practiced them rituals. I heard Garth owed Babbo money, too. Never accused him of cheatin', but I dunno. I don't think nobody'd kill over *that*." CM struggled with some emotion, as if deciding whether to speak more ill of the dead. Then....

"Somebody said Garth cast a death curse on little Babbo. Not that I cotton to that, but if you believe in that sorta stuff, dunno. What they call, um, self-fulfilling prophecy? Josh told me little Babbo laughed at that curse when it got back to him, laughed at Garth to his face. You can imagine how too-full-of-himself Garth reacted to *that*. Fancied himself the damn shaman of the occultists hereabouts. He damn well knew if you don't believe in curses and incantations and rituals, they got no hold on you. Babbo knew that too. The kid even joked about it. Pissed off ole Garth."

It tempted Sophie to scold CM for his profanity—like she would if he were Jake or Walt. But that was not her place here, nor would it be productive. So she stuffed her admonishment. Instead, she said, "CM, who else might have had issues either with Garth or Babbo?" Since Garth was already dead the Wednesday prior to Babbo's murder late Friday night or early Saturday morning, Garth had the perfect alibi. When CM only looked at his feet, not saying anything, she tried another tack. "How about this? Who would want Garth dead, and how would they go about killing him without leaving a mark?"

"Look, Miss Sophie. I'm the wrong person to ask. But some would say Garth kept at this death curse thing against Babbo. They say he even made a show of rituals to threaten his own little demons for not doing his bidding. All bullshit to me. But when the little freak turned it into a joke, believers would say Garth's own curse kicked him in the ass. Made him crazy. Runnin' mad from his own demons. You should talk to Milo. Another believer. He's one a our clowns. And he could tell ya whether that damn curse could drive Garth to his own ruin. Could be Garth drove *himself* to his own grave in one a Madame's trucks. Other than that, I got nothin' else for ya."

"Okay, that's just fine. Now what about Babbo? Who wished him ill enough to kill him?"

"Miss Sophie, all I can tell ya is most folks either loved or pitied little Babbo. I didn't like him much, and I got sick a losin' to him at cards. I just steered clear a the little faker. He made like this dumb little pinhead, but he was sharp as a tack. And Josh mentioned he was, well, secretive a lot. Miss Sophie, we're all takin' a risk talkin' to you. I'm sure Sister told you. But we all love our little Sister. One person you should talk to about Babbo you can't."

"Madame?" Sophie chose not to betray Sister's confidence about Babbo being her brother. Not her place. At the mention of Madame's name, however, she saw CM visibly shudder.

"Yeah, Madame was maybe closer to Babbo than anyone, except for Sister. Not sure what's there, but if anyone would know what happened to Babbo, it would be Sister or Madame for sure."

"I'll have to think about that. Anyone else?"

"Sorry. Oh, here's my TnT. Hey, love!"

When the loves of his life entered the tent, the transformation that gushed over CM was remarkable, even before Sophie saw them herself.

41

S ophie sensed a swirl of fabric and smelled something exotic. Didn't recognize the scent. It was overwhelming but not unpleasant to her sensitive nose. That said something.

She stood up from this couple's bed as fast as she was able—took a few tries—feeling awkward. Guilty? But that was silly. Saw her—them —and started to throw up—just a little. From... shock? She found it almost impossible to process what she was seeing. They were... beautiful, almost identical. And they were looking her over, too. As if *she* were the oddity.

Sophie swallowed and blurted, "Hello. I'm Sophie, a friend of Sister's."

"Yes, she sent word you'd be visiting."

Sophie guessed that was the more bold Tamra that spoke from what Sister and Josh had told her. Tamra was the one on, well, her left —the "rightmost head?" This was almost... too much. A two-headed girl? She watched CM first kiss one, then the other. They held hands. He turned to stand beside her—them—so they all faced Sophie. He squeezed the loves of his life around her waist.

"Oh, Lord, this is ridiculous." She stared at them, not knowing what to say next.

CM raised his voice, now with a dangerous edge. He snarled, *"Excuse me?"*

Sophie realized what she had said, and how it sounded. "Oh, no! I mean, I don't have any idea how to talk with you, so I don't come across sounding like—"

Tamra interrupted. "A rube? A chump? Too late."

Realizing he had jumped to the wrong conclusion and suddenly sounding contrite, CM jumped in. "Oh, ah, Miss Sophie, that's what we call all outsiders. No offense." He tossed a stern look at Tamra. Tara lowered her eyes, no doubt embarrassed by her twin sister's brash manner, and her husband's hair-trigger.

Sophie smiled, and said, "Yes, Tamra. It *is* Tamra, isn't it? I don't want to sound like a rube," She chuckled, *"or a chump!"*

Tamra smiled at Sophie's grit. Tara looked relieved, biting her lip with her left index finger guiding the way as she observed her sister out of the corner of her right eye. Tamra continued, "Fair enough, Sophie. We're used to this awkwardness, but most of the time it turns right into condescension, or worse, judging. But not you. That's refreshing. Yes, I'm Tamra—Tam. This is my sister, Tara—Tare. Please address us as individuals. We're not fond of being addressed together as TnT. That's... demeaning. *Unless* it's CM who calls us that. That's *his* special pet name for us—for more than one reason, I might add." Her devilish smile said what her lips only hinted. Did CM just blush? No, that wasn't possible, was it?

"We're conjoined twins, and we're both in love with this big freak." Tam looked up into CM's ebony eyes and Tare followed suit with a slight nod and a silent giggle. CM's eyes focused on his bare feet. "But since both of us go everywhere together, we both agreed to marry this brute. And we don't regret it for a second. Do we, sis? Make sense to you, Miss Rube? I'm kidding, Sophie."

Tam smiled. Tare stifled a guffaw. And Sophie laughed out loud, earning both their respect and a playful poke on the shoulder. Maybe even their friendship? Sophie took a clumsy step forward and grasped both of their hands. "I am very pleased to meet the two of you. This rube continues to be pleasantly surprised as I meet show folk."

Tam said, "CM, I like her." Tare said, "Me too!" She reinforced her opinion with a brilliant smile.

"Thanks, girls. Sister asked me to help her find out what happened to Babbo. Do you ladies have anything to add?"

Tam turned to CM. "You tell her about that asshole Garth, babe? And the money you owe Babbo?"

"Yeah, we talked all that out, baby."

"And Lilith?"

"Ah, not yet."

Sophie anticipated yet another nugget. "Lilith? One of the little people, right? Sister mentioned her."

Tare jumped in, startling Tam. "Ooh, Tam, can I tell her about Lilith and Babbo?" Tam nodded, but said, "Go for it, sis, but try not to shout in my ear, okay, sweetie?"

"Deal!" She said it too loudly. "Sorry." She swiveled her innocent gaze, eager to contribute. Her head was at a perpetual angle to her left, where Tam's head sat more erect atop her neck. Tare also seemed less mobile than Tam, like she had a stiffer neck.

With Tare's eyes wide, rolled up and to the right, she said, "Sophie, you must understand that Babbo and Lilith were so in love. That might seem strange to an outsider—a pinhead and a midget. Yeah, their relationship baffled many of us, too. You know—a freak and a performer. It was clear their love went beyond any *physical* attraction. When you meet Lilith, you'll understand. She is this perfect peaches-and-cream beauty, even though she's not even three feet tall. Babbo, on the other hand, was about as awkward physically as you might imagine. But their love, oh, Miss Sophie, those two gazed into each other's eyes like they were the only two people in the whole wide world." Tare lost herself in the romantic dream of every young girl.

Sophie loved this feel-good story, but she squinted. "That's lovely, Tare, but—"

"Why is this relevant right now? Because Lilith's father *hated* their relationship. *Hated Babbo*. First, Lilith's father is an arrogant *performer.* He thinks us freaks are sub-human, and aren't worthy of his or Lilith's respect or friendship, much less their love. I would put *nothing* past Tom Smalley. That's Lilith's father and only living parent. The two of them are one of the show's major attractions, and they're paid well. A few of the rousters are pretty loyal to them. Jump to your own conclusions. That's about all I know. Anything else, Tam?"

"Nope. Good job, sis." They nuzzled each other. Sophie thought that was awfully cute. Almost normal.

Golly, a lot has changed in the past few days! For me, anyway.

Almost as an afterthought, CM added, "Might be nothing, but a couple of folks mentioned a small group a them local church ladies been comin' around. 'Ministering,' they call it—even during setup last Friday. Mighta crossed paths with Babbo 'n others. Could tell right off they're phonies, just wantin' people to believe what they believe, like they keep score or somethin'—don't care none about us, what's important to us. Two, in particular—an older biddy and a cute young thing glued to the older one's hip. We're used to them do-gooder types. Kicked up a ruckus. Jed threw their ignorant asses out."

Sophie considered that, and said, "One more thing. Does this tattoo mean anything to you?" She handed the page over from Billy's notebook with the sketch on it.

CM looked at it. He muttered, "Hmmm, Virgo. Astrological sign. Can mean a desire to find purpose, maybe a dark purpose, or some such rot. Lots of 'em around. Don't mean nothin'." He handed the page back to Sophie.

"Alright, then. If you think of anything else, please tell Sister, and I'll hear about it. What would happen if I talked with Madame about all of this?"

Six eyes, suddenly wide, gave her the answer without a single word uttered. She added, "Never mind. I understand. Thank you, all. Now I must go."

CM said, "Sophie, you're good people, even if you are a rube. That little shit, Josh, is waiting for you outside."

"I can see you like Josh, CM, even though he's a roustabout. Do me a small favor. Just call him Josh, instead of... that little, um, you know?"

He said, "Sophie, you are *such* a rube!" They all chuckled,

Even though Sophie was only twenty-five, this trio looked young to her, but with CM, it was hard to tell. She stepped forward. Offered him a brief hug—which was both awkward and a bit stimulating as she embraced the bare skin of his muscular shoulders and the odd texture that covered them. Then she did the same with the girls. They added to her confusion and delight by each pecking her on opposite cheeks—at the same time.

Oh, golly!

❧ 42 ❧

❧

"**A**lmost invisible, isn't he?"

The stranger distracted Billy from his gaze at a lineman twenty feet up on a power pole across from the fairgrounds in Rock Rapids. Took a moment to realize this short newcomer referred to the lineman. He shared Billy's gaze up at the young man with spikes on his boots. They dug into the wooden pole to which he was strapped by a stout leather belt.

The stranger continued. "I'm fascinated by how he can scurry up and down a pole and work up there."

Billy stared down at this young man who was almost a foot shorter than himself.

"Sorry. I'm Sam Ellis. I work for—"

"You work for Lang Eubanks, am I right, Agent?"

"Yes, Sheriff. How did you—?"

"You got that same squeaky tightness as my ole buddy, Lang. Plus, that vested wool suit, sincere-stripe tie and spatted Oxfords? My friend, you *scream* federal agent. No offense, Sam. Nice to meet ya." He grinned and held out his hand. Took Agent Ellis a few beats and a scoff before he responded with a grin of his own.

"One a yours, I'm guessing." Billy swung his gaze back up toward the top of the pole.

"Pardon me?"

"The invisible man up there on that pole overlooking the main gate to Madame Perlatelli's Oddities and Wonders. One a yours, Agent Ellis?"

Ellis chuckled under his breath, looked down, and scratched the back of his neck, which shoved his charcoal fedora farther down onto his forehead. Gave him the appearance of boyish mischief. "I should have known. Yeah, that's Agent Murray Cline. Fancies himself a chameleon, a master of disguise. He's been watching the comings and goings through that show's gate for the last couple of hours. Either from the base of that pole, or from up there." Agent Ellis offered a dismissive wave toward the general direction of the pole.

"Well, we got a few dozen local busy bodies coulda given ya more information with a lot less abuse to Murray's young body."

"How'd you guess?"

"No guess. Look, Agent Ellis, the rules in a small town like Rock Rapids are a lot different than in a bigger city like Des Moines or Kansas City or Omaha. We got three city employees. One for sanitation, one for electrification, one for municipal buildings, and that fella ain't none of 'em.

"Now, we're workin' on buildin' trust with these show folk. It's slow sloggin' and an obvious surveillance operation ain't gonna move that along. Only set us back. Besides, I don't cotton to you runnin' an operation in my town without my foreknowledge. Now you get his butt out a there, if ya please. Okay, pardner?

❧

His boss, Senior Agent Lang Eubanks at the federal agency responsible for Alcohol, Tobacco and Firearms had warned him about this sheriff. Said he was *larger than life, and while he might sound country, he is all business, very sharp and trustworthy.* Sam observed he was downright likable, too. When he wasn't mildly pissed off.

"Sheriff, Agent Eubanks says you're trying to solve a couple of murders down here. Sent me to help."

"That's mighty nice of ole Lang. And just call me Billy."

"Alright, Billy. I'm Sam." He could sense the sheriff's appraising eyes looking him over as he eyed his agent up on the power pole.

"So you got a lot of experience investigatin' homicides, do ya, son?"

"Well, no, but——"

"Lemme guess. You're gonna help me get information on this little circus we're lookin' at, cuz you feds got resources we hicks don't have, am I right?"

"Yes, exactly. Wait, not that you're hicks or anything, but——"

"Kid, I'm shinin' you on. I appreciate the help. This little show's a tough nut to crack. But so's you know, one of my deputies—Dwight Spooner's his name—was a homicide detective in Minneapolis for a long time. Appreciate you checkin' the attitude."

"Attitude? I'm——"

"We're small town, through 'n through. That means we operate differently, cuz we gotta. And we're workin' real good right now with a civilian who's earned the trust of a few folks inside this circus, so we treat her like one of us. Name's Sophie Hardt. She's *my* chameleon, and she's makin' gen-u-wine progress. Okay, pardner?"

"Of course, Sheriff—Billy—and if you let me finish without interruption, I have information for you. Okay, *pardner?*"

The sheriff chuckled. Sam could tell he was embarrassed at coming on too strong.

"Say, Billy? Agent Eubanks has nothing but praise for you and your methods. I'm only here to help. Nothing more. And I will follow your lead. Fair enough?"

"Fair enough, Sam. Let's walk back to my office. Only a couple a blocks."

AGENT CLINE HAD BEEN WATCHING THIS LITTLE DANCE FROM NEAR the top of his pole, but couldn't hear them. Saw Sam point an index finger skyward and twirl one circle, and one circle only. Message received.

Wrap it up. *Now*.

🌿 43 🌿

Seated around Billy's desk at the Law Enforcement Center, Sam said, "So this little circus at your fairgrounds features quite the storied history. Because they travel a great deal, and members of that show have run-ins with local law enforcement, our sister agency at the DOJ, the FBI, has a dossier on them. Nothing major, but they've been reported here and there. As a result, we've dug into a few backgrounds. You're dealing with more than a few troublemakers over there."

THE SHERIFF POURED TWO MUGS OF COFFEE—SOPHIE'S RECIPE— from the pot on a constant boil atop the wood stove six feet away. She called it yard mud. He'd treat this city kid to real farm coffee. Both he and Sam grew more casual as they got to know each other. Sam took one sip, winced, and said, "Real smooth, Billy." They both chuckled at the obvious lie.

Billy couldn't explain what he felt inside at that moment, but he wanted—*needed*—more information about the show's boss more than anything. "Tell me what you have on Antonia Perlatelli."

Sam set his mug on the edge of the desk in front of him like it was poison, but in ready reach for his next cautious sip. "She's one tough cookie, Billy. She has a long record with the local cops where she grew up—a big city in the north of Spain called Pamplona. Small stuff. Survived as a street kid, later a prostitute, and con man—woman, that is. Started traveling with a Romani gypsy outfit in her late teens. Their culture revolves largely around entertainment and scams, plus more than a little superstition. Some even say witchcraft.

"After that, it gets rather sketchy until she showed up over here in Louisiana about six years ago. Hooked up with a few shows before she pulled her own troupe together about five years ago—a remarkable feat for a newly arrived immigrant. She ends each season's route with most of her show in Gibsonton, Florida, like an increasing number of other circus folk these days. They call the place Gibtown or Showtown, located south of Tampa. It's becoming a place where unusual circus folk go to feel safe. They say that town is *freak-friendly*. Plus, the winters are warm and cheap for those with meager means."

"So where do they normally operate during their season, and why are they in my county?"

"Last few seasons, they've worked their way north and west through Louisiana, Texas, Oklahoma, Nebraska, and a few larger cities farther east, like Kansas City, and St Louis. Later in the season, Nashville, Atlanta, and Tampa. But they almost always set up near the outskirts of medium to large cities. Never communities as small as this. *Why* are they in *your* town? That's a mystery. Times were tough for this show and all the traveling shows during the last several years, especially the smaller ones. Now, even more than before. They need to play bigger markets just to meet their expenses. Rock Rapids and Lyon County does not fit their profile."

"What others in this show do you have info about, Sam?"

"Quite a collection of international misfits and sociopaths, but that is pretty normal for folks who call the road their home these days, especially these smaller freak shows."

Billy winced at that characterization but wasn't sure why.

"So there's a suspected pedophile, a brawler, a reckless gambler and philanderer, plus a few others with records. A couple of B&Es in towns where this show appears, along with a bunch of minor cons that only popped for us because local authorities in several states reported them. But nothing that raised the stakes to homicide."

"Who's the pedophile? I hate creeps who prey on kids."

"A clown named Fenton Grant. Goes by the name of Happy. We've come close to an arrest on more than one occasion—in two different states—but no joy,"

"And the brawler?"

"A real whack job who's what they call a *made freak*—somebody who wasn't born that way, but did it to himself. Or allowed someone to do it to him. He's a character they call Crocodile Man. Given name is Charles Macklin. A real globe trotter—part of a subculture they call themselves Irish Travelers. Rather like Irish gypsies.

"Macklin left his native Ireland as a teenager. He next popped up in Papua, New Guinea where they say he killed a man for cheating at cards. Disappeared into the bush for a few years before he emigrated to the states. We lost track of him again until he got arrested and thrown into jail in New York. Beat four men to a pulp, none of whom pressed charges, but the locals had contacted us for info before they released him. That's how this guy popped for us. He had already joined Antonia Perlatelli's outfit by that time and was married to one of her other freaks. Be real careful not to piss this guy off, Billy. Like I said, he's a real whack job.

"Other than some small-time stuff, those are the highlights from a federal perspective. Except that there have been a dozen reports of unusual mishaps wherever this show tours, but nothing substantive. We've written off most of these as locals who hate circus people, and report crap that happens but likely has nothing to do with them. Nothing sticks."

"Like what, Sam?"

"Aw, don't waste your energy, Billy. People claim to have been cursed —things go wrong after they pissed somebody off in this outfit. Or chickens go missing after seeing some character skulking around their barnyard. Or mysterious weather follows this show around. Crap like that."

"Mysterious weather? Good gravy! Okay, I get the picture. Well, I'll be sure not to cross swords with this alligator fella."

"Crocodile Man."

"Right."

"Oh, there's this interesting character named Tommy Smalley. He's an ambitious little fellow—a midget—who has a weak spot for gambling and taller women. These vices have gotten him into precarious scrapes in the past, doing favors in return for paying off his debts. Normally, this wouldn't be of interest at a federal level, except for his ties to more than one interstate gambling ring. The Smalleys come from the Vaudeville tradition of the last decade. There was some mystery surrounding the death of his wife in late 'twenty-nine."

Billy said, "Now that's interesting. This civilian I mentioned—name's Sophie Hardt—has gotten an inside source to talk to her. She says that one of our murder victims—this Babbo—was head-over-heels in love with Smalley's daughter. Because Babbo was older than her, and because he was a freak, Smalley went bonkers over that relationship. I'm thinkin' possible motive. But I got the sense that the daughter is an innocent here. Looks like ole Tommy has kept her in a protective bubble. No surprise after losin' her mother."

"Hmmm... that tracks. We have nothing on the daughter. I guess that's as good a working theory as any, Sheriff."

"It's just Billy. And we got work to do, Agent Ellis."

✺ 44 ✺

Jake Hardt supported his wife's desire to follow this thing through, but Sophie could tell his patience wore thin. She acknowledged she was making genuine progress on the case, and if she were honest with herself, she'd become obsessed. Sister had gotten to her, and Sophie appreciated some of these show folks, people like she'd never met before, who believed things she never suspected existed. She'd make it up to Jake.

SOPHIE AND MILO VLADINOV, ONE OF THE SHOW'S CLOWNS, MET IN Sister's tent late Monday afternoon, as agreed—for privacy—and at Milo's insistence, far from the back lot. Besides, the circus had become a ghost town. Bad press and rumors of a "circus killer on the loose" had locals cowering in their homes.

Josh had carried Sister to her wagon, like he did on cold nights. The flap on her little tent now hung closed, and the candle's triple wicks already burned and flickered. Sophie sat in Sister's lumpy but comfy chair, and Milo, the bad-boy clown, occupied the less comfortable chair she herself sat in earlier in the day. He perched on it sideways, hunched over, playing with his chin in one hand, and the other bounced with nervous energy along with his right leg. His eyes never stopped scouring his field of vision, though there was nothing at all to scour.

Milo said, "Sister, she say your heart is true, that you care not about tribes. That you only seek truth. We talk." He pronounced the word *is* as *eece* and *truth* as *troot*.

"Yes, thank you, Mr. Vladinov."

He slumped further, bounced his leg harder, and whispered, "I am just Milo." Pronounced it MEE-loh, as if with raw sadness. Or was it self-loathing?

"So you leave your, ah, clown paint on even when you're not performing, Milo?" She circle-waggled her finger toward his face.

"They call it grease paint, Miss Sophie. And I wear none now."

Meece So-FEE?

Wait, what did he just say about no paint on his face?

"I'm confused, Milo."

"This white face and red lips? Tattoos." He grinned. No, he leered., as if daring her to challenge his judgment.

She looked down at the candle's glow to disguise her incredulity. Each moment was a novel experience with these people. "Oh, your clown face is now a permanent part of you."

"Da. It draw attention away from terrible scarring." With a circular motion, he pointed his own index finger toward the left side of his face that he presented to the candlelight, "and save time before each show."

This further confounded Sophie. She tried hard not to furrow her brow and cock her head. Even though she spotted no scarring at all, she found no reason to quiz this poor fellow about that. They had bigger fish to fry. She said, "Not noticeable, Milo. Thanks for chatting with me."

"Da, well, Sister, she say you okay, but Madame, she not need hear about this." He tapped the table with his middle knuckle to emphasize each of his last five words. And then he added, "And not nobody else, too."

"Whatever you say, Milo. Sister wants me to find out what happened to poor Babbo. That's all. Tell me something about that, okay?"

"Da. I not know much. Jus' that you should look at Happy. He not like Babbo much."

"Happy Grant? Why is that?"

"Happy, he like the young ones. Make Babbo plenty mad."

Oh, my goodness. Where is this going? At least he's talking.

She'd have to be careful if Milo meant what she thought. "So why would that cause Happy and Babbo to hate each other?"

"Well, Lilith—she is both young and little. Plus, Happy not like freaks. Much hate there. You talk to Happy. Old trouble there, too."

"Okay, Milo. I will. What else can you tell me?"

"Rousters, they like Babbo okay. Others not like him. Tom Smalley would just as soon see him gone, too."

Sophie said, "Because he doesn't like freaks." Sister's words. Not a question. She felt incredibly uncomfortable saying that word—freaks.

"Da. You understand, Miss Sophie. Like me, they performers, not freaks." He offered her a broad but creepy smile, wildly accentuated by the blood-red lip tattoo that covered most of his face below that hawkish nose. That tattoo winged out toward the middle of both sunken cheeks, just below his high cheekbones. To Sophie's eye, he looked downright... skeletal. She found his naked upper torso un-nerving, almost entirely tattooed in white, almost as if Milo bathed in permanent grease paint.

Sister told her he always performed in nothing but a tiny floppy hat that covered his shaved head, his white tights, and slender athletic shoes. They looked like ballet shoes. She'd seen pictures.

But more than all of that, the intensity in this man's eyes burned into anything in front of them. And he twitched. A lot. This was one scary clown.

Yes, he would be a formidable villain playing against Happy Grant, hero clown and potential pedophile—with *old trouble*.

45

The girl remembered that night like it was still happening. It had burned into her brain and now lived behind her eyelids....

THAT HAD BEEN A NICE NIGHT FOR A WALK, EVEN THOUGH THE wind still swirled up prairie dust with a vengeance. She tugged down on her scarf's tails and tied them tight under her chin with a double knot. She squinted against the airborne grit, but it didn't matter.

Though dark under only a sliver of a hazy moon, the midway tinkled and flapped as tinsel and canvas communed with gusts that tried to clear the air, but failed. She looked for him along the way, but knew where he would be—at the animal menagerie.

He loves those beasts like he loves the midway—and me. Little old me. His heart is so big.

As the main gate rose in front of her, she swung to her left, but something told her to stop. An unrecognizable noise. The lot had a rhythm of sights, sounds and odors. This noise didn't fit that rhythm.

At all. The last grab joint on her left, the first one customers encountered as they entered the show's main gate, offered her protection. Not sure why, but she kneeled and waited. That noise again. Then she spotted a figure too tall and slender to be Babbo. She didn't recognize him. He lurked behind King's cage. *There is Babbo! Oh! God, no!*

IT WOULDN'T BE UNTIL DAYS LATER THAT SHE WOULD RECALL THE horrific events that followed.

It was just as well.

Her life changed forever.

46

"So, is it true?"

Billy and Dwight sat across from each other in the LEC, with Billy's desk between them. It was late, and this didn't seem official. Might be as close as these two came to a friendly chat, just between two guys off the clock, though neither punched one.

Dwight thought it odd that Billy never invited him up to his apartment. But he never invited Billy over to the small bungalow he rented either. This was the same one that Billy lived in before he moved into the apartment upstairs to be even closer to the job. Sort of bothered him that neither he nor his boss had much of a personal life. Dwight knew what Billy was asking. He wasn't eager to have this conversation, even though Billy was the closest thing he had to a friend.

"Yeah, Billy, it's true. Justina and I have seen each other a couple of times now."

"You. And a church lady. What am I missing here, brother?"

It surprised Dwight that he felt defensive. "Billy, she's a nice girl, even though she hangs out with that old bat."

"You like her." Not a question. Just a friend making a casual observation, and listening. Dwight settled down. He said, "Yeah, although she has some real powerful feelings about circus people, among other stuff."

"Unlike you."

"Well, I've been listening to Sophie, or at least trying to. Sounds like there sure are some characters over there, but maybe some of them are okay. I don't know, Billy. Just a lot of folks willing to get all riled up, maybe a little too quick, ya know?"

"This girl's opinions bother ya, D?"

"Maybe. She's damn cute, and yeah, maybe a little young...."

"What's her family like?"

This now sounded like an interrogation, but probably because neither he nor Billy practiced much talking like anybody other than cops. *Yeah, that's it. He's just making conversation.*

"She came up rough. The church stuff is a way to smooth out some of that. Big family, a drunk for a dad who just left, and her mom raised six kids all by herself with no money. She doesn't talk much about that, but I can tell she gets out of the house as much as she can. Spends a lot of time at the church, volunteering over at Laticia's place, the civic league, stuff like that. Not surprising she echoes a lot of the old gal's ideas. But something else too, Billy. Sometimes Justina gets a real hard edge, real defensive, like more than the religious stuff. As if she's really pissed about something. But I can't put my finger on it. Then she smoothes right out again and is, well, downright lovable. Jeez, did I just say all of that?"

"Go with your gut, D. You got a good nose. And if this works out, I'm happy for ya, man."

Dwight was about to give as good as he got. Not without risk. "Thanks, boss. Hey, what's the deal with you and that snake lady? You thinkin'—"

"Madame *Purgatory?* Well, one look at her—"

Just mentioning her and Billy got fidgety. Started tapping that pencil on his desk pad faster, chewing his lip. There was no doubt. "Yeah, sure. But—"

Billy pasted on a flat expression. "She came up rough, too, D. Made her own way. Hard on the outside, for sure, but... the woman's complicated. Some good in there. Cares about her people. Just hard to be objective—"

"Objective? Shit, Billy, you melt every time you're close enough to sniff her."

"Never met anyone like her, is all."

"Strange brew, that one, but are you—"

"Too dangerous. Besides, right now, she's smack dab in the middle of this whole confounded mess."

Time to back off. Billy's eyes were on their way to becoming tired slits. Dwight hoisted himself out of his chair, headed for the stove with his mug.

"So, you want any more of this shitty coffee, boss? I'm buyin'."

47

The following morning, Sophie dropped in to the LEC for a moment on her way to see Sister yet again. She didn't bother sitting down.

"Billy, not sure this is any of my business, but I'm concerned about Dwight, both as a friend and his ability to deal with these circus people. Do you know what happened to him? Why he thinks all these people are guilty until proven innocent?"

"Not sure, Soph. But I can tell you he's comin' around, because of you. He's listenin'. Now his bluster is, well, smoothin' out some, at least in his conversations with me. He's a proud man. Give him time."

"Okay, Billy. I just want to make sure we're looking at this entire case with everybody's point of view given fair consideration. That's all."

She couldn't help but still wonder about Dwight.

48

Billy had just received Agent Lang Eubanks' complete report on Madame's show. It supplemented Sam's verbal briefing. The biggest surprise was how much of the show's track record the feds were aware of. No surprise, their finances were a mess.

But what concerned Billy most were the number of known offenders living and working under Madame's protection, *and* how they could afford to keep touring at all. They left a dismal wake of infractions, including unpaid debts, violent altercations in local drinking establishments, missing property, and a fistful of unsolved crimes.

More than a few were federal because the presumed offenders crossed state lines regularly, bringing their bad habits with them. Now, Billy needed to figure out what to do with all of this.

Foremost, he had two murders to solve, and was reluctant to drain an entire swamp to get that done.

ONCE MORE, SOPHIE SAT IN FRONT OF BILLY'S DESK AT THE LAW Enforcement Center. Dwight stood to the left side of Billy's desk in a defensive posture. Sophie shared with the boys what she had learned from her interviews. The unmistakable smirk pasted on Dwight's face broadcast to Billy that Dwight still lacked objectivity toward show people. Sophie pretended not to notice.

Dwight crossed his arms over his chest, his stance wide. He said, "So this crocodile guy has serious anger issues. And the villainous clown is unstable." Dwight uncrossed his arms long enough to reinforce his words with a rotating index finger aimed at the right side of his own skull. "And this *happy* clown is a pedophile with a record, besides all this black magic shit? Good Lord, Sophie." He swung toward the sheriff. "Billy, no wonder this zoo of criminals and crazies didn't want to talk to us!"

"Yeah, but they *are talkin'*—to Soph, brother."

❦

SOPHIE SAW DWIGHT WAS—WHAT?—JEALOUS THAT SHE WAS MAKING progress where they had failed? He could rise above this. But something had happened to poor Dwight. She'd find out.

Billy said he now had enough to bring Madame into the LEC for questioning. Get her away from her show and her over-protective head of security. Said he needed to get her alone on *his* turf.

Could he make that happen without an unpleasant altercation?

I have a feeling....

❧ 49 ❧

❧

Billy caught Madame by the big cat cages—the animal menagerie, such as it was. She wasn't *yelling* at some big guy moving a piece of heavy equipment, but she wasn't happy, either. He got the sense that a hissing whisper from Madame didn't need volume to slice deep. She wore those same damn shorts. Couldn't take his eyes off her.

Get your crap collected, Billy. She's a murder suspect, and the ringleader of a bunch of criminals 'n crazies.

She spotted him watching, ten yards away. In the very next second, she dismissed her minion with a careless wave, and a brilliant face erased her anger, like she was thrilled to see him again. Or she was putting on airs. Either way... that smile. Those eyes. Her.... *Shit!*

"*BEE-lee!*"

"Madame, we need to talk."

"Absolutamente. If you will follow me—"

"Nope. Sorry. This time, we talk at my place. Please follow me to my car."

She didn't seem shocked. Just... disappointed? Too bad. She just stood there. He clutched her arm, led her toward the gate. Out of nowhere, Jed appeared. He gripped a pitch fork in both hands. Held it out, like a warrior holds a spear.

Two things happened in rapid succession. First, Billy drew his service revolver and pointed it with a stiff arm at Jed's chest, still five yards away. Second, Madame screamed. Caught both men dead in their tracks. She spoke in a soft voice after that.

"Jed, thank you. Please to put that down and step back. The sheriff just wants to ask me some questions at his office. Billy, please to put that pistola away. I am going with you. Shall we?" She did not pull away from his grip on her right forearm. Rather, she placed her own left hand on top of his. With affection?

Billy and Madame strolled together toward the gate and into the parking lot. Both men did as they were told.

Billy's right hand still didn't wander too far from his holster.

❧ 50 ❧

❧

Somewhere in his past, Sheriff Billy Rhett Kershaw learned a good interrogation began by establishing *rapport*. He just called it getting to know somebody. They sat across from each other in what Billy called the fish tank, a glass-enclosed office that doubled as their part-time medical examiner's office.

"So, Madame, why you? Here? What's your history?"

She crossed *those legs* and looked relaxed with her hands folded in her lap. "Well, Billy, I grew up in Pamplona, Spain, just a hundred kilometers from the Pyrenees Mountains and the French border. They host a wonderful week each summer called the *Encierro* during the festival of *San Fermín*. The *Running of the Bulls* each day is quite exciting. Of those who run in front of the Torrestrella fighting bulls on Santo Domingo street, some are gored, but most just lead the bulls toward the ring where they fight with the matadors."

As much as he hated to admit it, Billy found this fascinating, never having traveled much. He asked, "So did you ever run with them bulls, Madame?"

"There has never been a law against women running with the bulls.

The entire affair is more like a party than an official event with rules. It is a question of tradition. In Pamplona, a man ran to show his love for a woman.

"Did someone run for you?" He really was curious.

"No. I was too young, and different than I am now. You understand? The San Fermín festival keeps the rich tourists flowing through the already crowded city every July. The city becomes engorged with more young men than girls. Your Mardi Gras? A civilized garden party by comparison. The streets of the city can be cruel, Billy, but during la festivál, they can also be generous. I grew up on those streets."

"Your family?"

"No. I have always been on my own. But for a week each summer I feasted on magnificent scraps. I hid in alleys in areas not popular with las touristas. But I would also sneak into the alleys off Calle Santo Domingo during the early morning hours when the drunks slept.

"One morning, a group of seven or eight boys must have been returning to their hotel from an all-night party. They spotted me with my head down in a barrel to retrieve almost an entire sandwich. I had let my guard down, seeking this treasure. They pounced on me like a wolf pack. I hear them talking as each took their turn on me. I was helpless. They were strong. And too many. One awaiting his turn said, 'even if she weren't a street scrap, everyone knows the authorities will do nothing. They like the money we bring to their city. Especially during El Encierro. Let's show this little wench the best time she's ever going to have, eh, monsieurs?'

"You see, I just kept thinking about that sandwich, *and* what a powerful weapon a penis was. At that moment, I realized I too possessed a powerful weapon. To this day, I thank those boys for arming me with the most powerful weapons known to man—the vagina of a beautiful woman and the skills to wield it."

❧ 51 ❧

Billy blushed.

Who was establishing rapport with whom here? He had never heard a woman talk about such things, or met anybody with this kind of experience. Did he pity her? *Or was this more bullshit?*

*Good Lord, who **is** this woman?*

She continued after displaying her own impressive blush, like she had just shared more than she intended. Now a wild animal in a cage, she stood. Started pacing. "A few years later, I moved around, Billy. Pamplona no longer served my purposes. You understand? I traveled with new friends, a troupe of gypsies. They taught me their trade. Now, the traveling show, she is in my blood. The show is my life. Now tell me about your loss. Someone very dear to you, no? A young wife, perhaps?" She stopped pacing, close in front of him. She looked down into Billy's eyes, searching. She stopped short of cradling his head in her hands.

His hackles made him gruff. He was tempted to tell her to sit her ass back down, but he didn't really care. Besides, he liked how she moved, like a cat. Not like her half-dead ones, but a young tigress, prowling. A predator. But....

Enough of this rapport crap. He'd already learned more about this woman than he thought wise. "We're not here to talk about me, lady. Listen, you want to move on. The town's leadership wants the same. Right now, the only way that can happen is if we work together to solve these murders, and I might overlook all the other shenanigans you're covering up. Now, are we gonna work together on this, or do you want to watch your show sit here and go broke? Or did that already happen? You've lied to me once about our first victim. Do not make that mistake again. Are we clear?"

She jumped between looking pissed, amused and impressed, as if she couldn't believe this mere mortal could resist her formidable charms. Finally, she plopped down most ungracefully, spread her legs, elbows on knees, chin in her hands. She appeared resigned to her fate. They were alone in the LEC. By design.

"Okay, Billy," (it still came out BEE-lee), "we do need to continue our Spring route. Yes, my show is always under the edge, with the money, but who isn't these days? Sometimes I feel like the mayor of a Hooverville. Many of my people travel with us at their own expense and in their own vehicles. Most of these acts supply their own animal feed, food for themselves, and gasoline. To be truthful with you, I have little or no control over them. Señor Billy, even though we are a little show, I provide jobs. Often, it is to those who can work no place else. Now, I am already in jeopardy of not making the nut for the entire season."

"The nut?"

"Si. That is the show's basic operating expenses. We must make money above our expenses. Otherwise, in my case, four dozen good people may starve."

"So let's see if we can't get you back on the road and solve both our problems. Okay?" He hated to admit it to himself, but he admired this amazing woman.

"Bien, Billy. When were you going to tell me about the spy you sent into my family?"

And here we go again!

"Spy? C'mon, lady, I got two dead bodies and at least one murderer on the loose. Your crew stonewalled me from the get-go. What the hell did you expect? One a your folks feared for her life and made a friend from my community. Conversations took place. What problem has that created for you?"

It looked like she wanted to unload on him, but only wrung her hands and said, "So what has your investigation revealed?"

"That's not how this works. I ask the questions, and hopefully, we get to some answers. Now, who do you suspect of foul play? I'll listen with an open mind, as long as you don't bullshit me. Okay, young lady?"

She raised an eyebrow. "Fine. What is it you wish to ask me?"

"I won't claim to understand how your little society over there works, but I'll assume it does, and a lot a the credit for that goes to you. I'm guessin' there's very little that happens over there that you don't keep tabs on. You have your, what, different groups who believe in different things? And you got some tension between the acts, the labor and the, ah, freaks, right?"

"Si. That is the skin of it."

"So who would want to hurt this Nitstone, and why?"

"Garth was, how you say, a forceful personality, on the outside. But inside, he was a frightened niño. He demanded and received attention. He practiced the rituals. Some believed. He believed. I believe he was a victim of his own fear."

"You know, until Sophie talked with your Sister and a few others, I would have said that was a load a crap. But I'm inclined to be open-minded about that. For now. Let's talk about the other fella. Babbo."

"Babbo was my friend. I am sick about this, this, *tragedia!* To do such a thing to poor little Babbo—"

"Well, let's talk about poor little Babbo. I hear he was quite the card shark, and took advantage of more than a few of your crew. Like your crocodile man owed him a heap a money. What do you know about that?"

"Yes, Babbo was not as simple a man as he pretended. That was his act. He was a clever boy. And more than a few of my family were indebted to him. That is how they made him feel significativo... meaningful. No reason to beat someone to death. The only person who truly hated Babbo was Garth. He made the joke about Garth's beliefs. But since Garth preceded Babbo in death...."

"Yeah, I wondered about that."

"Billy, I just don't know who would do this. And about this, I am most sincere."

"Well, hell's bells, lady, what are we goin' to do?"

She spoke her next reluctant words with care. "Is it possible someone from outside my show did this terrible thing? There is no shortage of, how you say, animosidad, toward my show, is there not? Especially toward those who are not like them? My freaks? Is that not possible?"

Billy had considered that, but wasn't ready to admit that to this carny. "We're considering all possibilities. For now, is there anything else? Tell me about your two clowns—Milo and Happy."

"Billy, you cannot suspect either of them capable of such violence."

"See, now there ya go again. My sources tell me I should. Why shouldn't I?"

"Milo is no angel. No one in my show is, if I am honest with you. But a murderer? I am sorry. No es posible."

"What can you tell me about him, Madame?" She looked pleased that he didn't call her *lady* or *young lady* again, but the more respectful *Madame*. And she smiled that the sheriff seemed interested in learning more about her family instead of passing judgement on strangers.

"Milo Vladinov was once one of my roustabouts. He held a very physical job with the show—a laborer who also performed other duties for us. Four seasons ago, poor Milo suffered a rather serious head injury while erecting the big top with all the show's other roustabouts. That day, the big canvas came down in a high wind with no warning. Milo fell on a wooden stake. He struck the back of his cabeza," she patted the back of her head, "and has not been the same since. The poor man is suspicious of everyone, and sometimes his behavior can be, well, unusual."

"You mean like tattooing on his clown make-up? For life?"

Madame shrugged, but also squirmed in her chair. She even *squirmed* with allure. *Focus, Billy. Jeez-Louise.*

"Isn't that unusual behavior, even for a career clown?" He raised his eyebrows and peered at her over the top of his cheaters. He had recently taken to wearing those dime store glasses, especially when he tried to read in dim light.

Madame flushed and said, "Yes, well, Milo takes his job seriously. He is unusual, but he is no killer. See here, Billy. I told you I will work with you. But you will need to show me some trust. I wish to find who committed these crimes as much as you. Milo has had problems, even with the law, as have many of my little troupe. That does not mean he or they are killers. Most of my troupe exhibits what you would call *unusual behavior*, including Milo. Why is this important?"

Billy was ready to test their mutual trust. "We found white grease paint on Nitstone's truck. Isn't that what you call that white stuff clowns paint on their faces?"

Madame thought for a moment before she said, "Milo does not use the grease paint. Tattoos, you remember?" Then she stopped speaking, rubbed her chin, shifted in her chair. "But Happy Grant uses the paint. And there is no love lost between those two. Many often access our trucks within the show. I do not believe that is a helpful clue."

"Okay, tell me about this other clown—the happy one."

He'd compare what Madame told her with what he'd ask Sophie to learn.

52

Before Sophie made her escape from the LEC earlier, Billy had said, "Hey, you've made great progress, Soph, but we need more info on both clowns. They're pointing fingers at each other, and right now, that's about all we have. We need you to dig deeper with this fortune teller."

"Billy, everything we've learned from her, she's *offered* to me, and that's been key to this entire investigation thus far. It's what she's *volunteered*. I'm concerned if I interrogate her, she'll clam up, and we'll be stuck again."

"I understand, Soph. But we're under a whole heap a pressure to get this case done. Just try, okay?"

"Sister, thanks for seeing me again. You've been a tremendous help. I thought I'd share with you what I heard from Milo before I talk to Happy Grant. Milo is pointing the finger at Happy, that he likes 'the young ones.' He suggests that Happy could have done harm to Babbo because Babbo went after him first, assuming he had somehow violated Lilith's sensibilities."

"Stop. Sophie, remember I asked you to fill in the gaps with your own intellect? Remember, I told you my sight is limited, and that I would share with you whatever that sight provided? This violates our agreement."

"But—"

"Such things are for *you* to discover. You said you understood."

"Look, Sister, if you know something here, and you're not telling me, if someone gets hurt, that's going to fall on your shoulders."

"Please leave." Her head sagged to her chest.

The little woman-girl would say no more. Had Sophie just ruined her chance to move this investigation forward, losing her new friend in the process? She prayed she hadn't.

 **53**

F riday
April, 13, 1934

THE SHADOWY FIGURE HAD REACHED ANOTHER BREAKING POINT. The electrified midway lights still burned with a pulsing glow, fueled by the thumping generator, which would shut down at eleven PM. The roustabouts had already doused the coal-oil torches that lined the midway when the show closed at ten. And the rubes had all gone home a half-hour ago.

Now, twenty feet away, behind the big top, there was that monster who couldn't or wouldn't control his impulses. Again. On today of all days. The bastard was on top of the boy's back.

The kid obviously had this idea, like others, of just wanting to run away and join the circus. Too bad his new friend turned out to be a predator. This kid couldn't be more than fourteen or fifteen. Looked like a street urchin—skinny, hungry, away from home for a while now. He was likely willing to do about anything for some chow, maybe a shot at joining the show.

Happy Grant. Yeah, the only people he made happy were himself and his clueless audiences. Strangers bought his act—hook, line and sinker. Mr. Goodie Two-Shoes.

After calling the sheriff's office from the wall phone in the nearby county maintenance garage office, he figured he had maybe five or six minutes before they found the clown. Took him two to hoof it back from the phone. Grabbed a bowling pin from inside the big top, the one that Happy used in his act. Rushed forward with it raised high over his left shoulder. Clobbered the pervert over the head, but not too hard. Just wanted to weaken him. He needed an advantage. A sickening crack, even though it wasn't that heavy. Had he hit the asshole's noggin too hard? Nope. He still squirmed. Okay, then.

The kid was in shock, but he rolled over in the weed-infested dirt to pull up his knickers and wipe away muddy tears with his sleeve. He helped the kid up who still sobbed and shivered. Said, "Keep your mouth shut, kid. Now beat it. Don't come back." After a grim nod of gratitude and more sniffling, he scurried off. Good for him.

Once the kid was out of sight, he pulled the bandana down from his face, grabbed Happy's shoulder, rolled him over—face up. Straddled his chest. Still had on his fuckin' grease paint. Other than that, he wore his dandy street clothes, more or less. Probably felt the kid preferred a clown's face to his real-world leer.

Clamped Happy's throat in his right hand so he'd stay put and quiet. With his teeth, he pulled the cork out of a small vial he held in his left hand. Snarled down at the piece of shit and said, "Reap what ya sow, asshole."

Dumped the entire contents of the vial—a watery yellowish syrup —down Happy's throat, and clamped his hand over that pasty mouth. Shoved the cork—still in his teeth—back into the vial. It disappeared into a threadbare vest pocket.

He held him there with a calloused hand still clamped over his vile lips, listening to his choked gurgling. Then footsteps approached. Muffled voices drew near. He whispered into the clown's sweaty ear, "Your own monsters are gonna kill you, Happy, unless you kill them first!" Picked up the bowling pin. Used it like a cane to get up off the prick's chest before laying it back down beside him.

The figure disappeared through a hidden slit in the big top's canvas as he saw the reflected light of an electric lantern coming around the big tent's curved wall. He looked back just long enough to spot the clown shaking his head as if to clear it and hoisting himself off the ground.

So long, sucker.

❧ 54 ❧

Ten minutes earlier, Deputy Dwight Spooner had answered the phone at the LEC. A panicked male voice screeched, "Help! He's got a kid under him. Holding him face down. Not sure what he's doing to him, but it's something awful! I'm scared! That clown is crazy! At the fairgrounds. Behind the big top. Hurry!" Click.

Shit! Damn show people.

Billy slept in his apartment upstairs. He'd had a long day. Wouldn't bother him. Dwight knew that Deputy Jimmy Lenert was cruising toward the end of his second overtime shift, already headed back to the LEC. Dwight rushed outside into the April chill. Hopped into his cruiser at the edge of the boardwalk, slammed the door harder than he intended. Didn't catch. Slammed it again. Started the engine before calling Jimmy on one of the modern car radios they received last Winter from their federal friend, Lang Eubanks, who has access to all the latest toys. "Jimmy, you read?"

"Yeah, Dwight. What's up?"

The doggone thing actually worked! "Someone's attacking a kid at the fairgrounds behind the big top. Where are you?"

"Three minutes away. I'll meet you there."

"Roger. Put the pedal down, Jimmy! In case this isn't a hoax." He threw the bulky microphone down onto the seat next to him, skidded through a dusty U-turn and roared up Main toward the circus lot.

By the time he rolled up to the show's main gate, Jimmy was already skidding to a stop behind him in a swirl of dust. Together, they charged on foot up the center of the deserted midway. The equipment on their belts jangled, which only fueled their urgency. A few show folk were still closing down for the night, turned their heads to stare. They ignored them. Strings of dim lights still swung in the gentle breeze.

Within a minute, they reached the circular big top's entrance at the far end of the deserted midway.

Jimmy said, "Which way?"

"You go left, I go right." Neither broke stride as they separated.

Dwight got eyes on him first, thirty paces away. Clownface was just getting up off his knees, shaking his head. Still had his dick hanging out. Looked like he was drunk or something. He staggered before steadying up. Then he spotted Dwight coming toward him with his electric lantern shining in his face. No sign of any kid.

The man issued a guttural scream, almost feral. The clown came at him. Had the look of a wild animal. Dwight hollered at him to stop. The man kept coming, now waving a large weapon of some sort above his head. His intentions were unmistakable. Dwight held firm to the lantern in his left hand, drew his service weapon with his right. "I said, STOP, asshole, or I *will* shoot." Dwight then noticed the guy had what looked like nothing more than an oversized bowling pin in his right hand, raised over his head, like he intended to use it as a club. His left hand clawed at the air in front of him.

"Stop, goddammit!"

The clown continued to scream like a madman. Dwight had never heard a sound quite like that. Must be shredding his vocal chords with that screeching howl. And his face! The man's stagger suggested he was impaired. Dwight slipped his gun back into its holster and grabbed the nightstick from his left hip with a smooth cross-body grip. Raised it to defend himself, and to set up for a counter blow. The next two seconds would change three lives. Forever. It happened with the guy only six feet away.

Blam!

Someone had shot the clown. In the back? He jerked, but kept coming.

Blam! Blam!

He went down like a loose pile of wet spaghetti after the third shot with his head at Dwight's feet—*on* his feet. Dwight recovered from the unexpected chain of events that burned through his mind at that moment. And there stood Jimmy at the edge of the lantern's dim pool of light. He still stood locked in his two-hand shooting stance. Eyes wide, hands shaking, Jimmy screeched, "Is he dead? *Is he dead?*"

"Jimmy, lower your weapon.... Deputy! Lower your weapon now. It's over. Jimmy, *do you hear me?*"

"Ah, yeah, right. Sure. Okay, Dwight. You okay?"

"Yeah, Jimmy, I'm fine. You got him. Crazy son-of-a-bitch. We're done. Now I need you to walk around and see if you can spot the kid this guy allegedly attacked. Jimmy, *can you do that for me?*"

"Oh, sure. Yeah. No problem, Dwight." But his sing-song response told Dwight that Jimmy was anything *but* okay.

"Jimmy, holster your weapon first. Do that now, alright, son?" The young deputy looked down at the white-knuckled fist that gripped his thirty-eight, as if somebody else's hand held somebody else's weapon at the end of his own arm. Still pointed toward the clown and Dwight.

If he'd have missed, **I'd** *be dead!*

After a long beat, he did as he was ordered. Took a couple of tries to find his holster.

"Okay, Dwight, I'll see if I can find that kid." With the stink of cordite already drifting toward Dwight on the breeze, Jimmy wandered off in a daze. But Dwight's experience told him that was better than the kid staring at the human being whose life he'd ended.

Jimmy's first shooting—a fatal shooting, no less. He'd remember this day until his own heart stopped. Rough stuff. To this day, Dwight still saw the faces of the German kids he'd shot or stabbed with his bayonet in the Argonne Forest sixteen years earlier. From that moment on, they had become a permanent part of who he was—is.

Would be the same for Jimmy.

Damn it!

Dwight wondered if they had just bagged their killer. The guy sure was crazy enough. And a child molester, to boot. He pulled out his notebook to process the scene, and started by noting the time of the anonymous telephone call. He reckoned it took him only about five or six minutes for him and Jimmy to arrive at the big top's entrance. And less than thirty seconds to sight the clown. *Where did the witness call from? And where the hell is he?*

While Dwight jotted down more notes by the light of his bulky lantern, which was awkward, a small crowd of show people gathered. Had to tell them more than once to stay back. They kept drifting closer to the body. Then the head of the snake herself slithered up in some sort of gown, demanding to know what had happened.

"Look, lady, I'll ask the questions, Who is this guy?" He nodded toward the body, lying on his side. Her sudden gasp told Dwight she knew who he was.

"Dios mío, this is Happy Grant, our star clown, Diputado. What has happened here?"

"He has a history of pedophilia. Is that correct?"

"Ped—?"

"Molesting children, Madame."

"Oh, my, of this I do not know."

And that's the moment Dwight spotted something he hadn't noticed earlier—a small pool of puke right under the body's nose and mouth.

Very weird.

❧ 55 ❧

After sparring with Madame, Dwight paced like a madman. He'd seen this before. Circus and carny characters bred lawlessness. If he weren't a law enforcement officer, he might well become the leader of a lynch mob from town. He'd lead the mayor and church ladies himself. These people didn't deserve to be anywhere except prison, maybe even Death Row. And now one of them had turned young Deputy Jimmy Lenert into a killer. Something had to be done.

Jimmy shot the clown at ten-forty PM. Since then, Dwight had hovered over the scene until Jimmy hustled back to the LEC to wake up Billy and to call in Doc Gustavsen. Doc rode in the front seat of the Spencer hospital's only ambulance to the fairgrounds.

They had grabbed a few roustabouts who gathered at the scene behind the big top to disassemble the show's main gate—a people gate. They drove their three cruisers up the center of the midway to the body. Lit up the area with their headlights. The assembly of show folk grumbled about a *full-scale invasion* of their lot. After one of their own was shot by local cops, anger festered. This might get real ugly real fast.

They heard shouts of "Predictable. Cops shoot first, ask questions later!" And "Clown killers!" And "Kill anyone who ain't local, right?"

⚜

FORTUNATELY, BILLY ARRIVED ON THE SCENE TO COOL DWIGHT OFF while Madame settled down her folks. Billy noticed she wore some sort of colorful silk robe. He imagined what might—or might not—be under that robe.

C'mon, soldier, focus!

Ten minutes earlier, he had thrown on some trousers and a shirt that remained only half buttoned even now. Didn't even bother with a badge. Hell, everybody recognized who he was and what he represented. Not that anyone around here respected that much. Except Madame, he hoped.

From Jimmy's earlier update after waking him up, he worried that his senior deputy might do something stupid, given his attitude toward show people. Now on scene and seeing Dwight's demeanor first-hand, he flew right into him.

"Dag-nabbit it, Dwight. Take your hand off the butt a your piece, and stop lookin' like you're itchin' to shoot somebody. This ain't helpin'."

"Goddammit, Billy. One of them tried to kill me tonight! What do you expect?"

"I expect you to do your job, Deputy. Jimmy's a mess too, but right now, we need him back on crowd control and the two of us interviewin' bystanders."

Dwight took a deep breath, then another in quick succession, and nodded. Billy could have predicted that nobody would talk, but they tried anyway. They got the impression from a few less angry folks that the kid who the clown had allegedly attacked was not part of the show's troupe.

That kid had vanished, if there ever *was* a kid. Nobody admitted to calling in the alleged attack either. Jed, the show's head of security, looked fit to be tied. He was not in control of his own lot and was a hungry cat on the prowl.

Billy grabbed Madame by the arm and hustled her off to the side. In a soft voice, he said, "Madame, somethin' mighty fishy is goin' on here. Some guy anonymously calls in an attack, like he's watchin' it happen. But there ain't no phone anywhere around here." Billy nodded toward the clown's body, now covered up with a canvas tarpaulin retrieved by a rouster. "Supposedly, this guy attacks a kid, but there ain't no kid around, although the clown's, ah, equipment was hangin' out. His clothes bein' a mess 'n all supports that somethin' was goin' on before my deputies arrived. And this Happy Grant, or whatever the hell his real name was, has a history of criminal behavior toward kids. Now we got three bodies since y'all arrived in town less than two weeks ago? Help me out here, or you ain't never leavin', lady."

After yelling at Dwight for his unprofessionalism, Billy's own unproductive anger had bubbled to the surface. He was mad at himself for that. His left eye twitched, and he was holding onto Madame's bare arm with a grip that was tighter than he intended. She shook free, and by her expression, she was building a wall between them. He hadn't seen her angry yet, but that was about to change.

"You look here, *Sheriff*. One of your deputies comes onto my lot and shoots one of my performers with little or no evidence of wrongdoing? I believe you need to work with me instead of accusing me and my *family*. Now can you do that? Or shall we destroy the trust we already share?" Her wrinkled brow and tight lips broadcast her own anger.

Shit! She was right. *Good Lord, she's a beauty. Even angry and just out a bed.* Billy dropped his head, looked at his dusty boots. After a triple beat, he said, "You're right, a course. I apologize, Madame. This guy charged my deputy like a madman, wielding a club. Turned my other deputy, not much more 'n a boy, into a killer. Had to shoot this guy cuz they feared for their lives. What would cause this guy to behave like that? Was that normal for him?"

"Like a madman, you say?" Her face transformed from anger to doubt, then to disbelief. "That is not *at all* like Happy. Despite his, ah, unusual affections, he is—was—a gentle soul, muy simpatico. He truly earned his name. This is very strange."

Yet another surprise. She sashayed over to the body, lifted a corner of the tarp near the clown's head, saw something in the shadows that caused her to jerk away, something she hadn't noticed earlier. Dropped the tarp and arose more quickly than he would have believed possible.

Billy saw she chose not to voice what she was thinking when she said, "I have some thoughts on this matter, but I need to make some inquiries. Billy, I will work with you on this. But you must give me a little time—a few hours. But now, I need to talk to my people again before their anger gets out of hand. I suggest you do the same."

Without another word, she wheeled around, her robe flowing behind her. Reminded him of a peacock strutting. He glimpsed one of those magnificent tattooed legs before it disappeared into the folds of that robe. Was it purple? Hard to say in the dim reflections of three police cruisers' headlights some distance away, and her partially in silhouette. A pair of fuzzy slippers kicked up small swirls of dust.

She looks good in silk 'n fluff, soldier. Better 'n boots 'n sweaty tunics, fer sure. Oughta be illegal!

56

L ate morning the next day, Doc Gus called Billy at the LEC. He confirmed that Happy Grant had indeed been engaged in sexual activity prior to his demise. Upon hearing the details of Doc's initial analysis of the physical evidence, which indicated some injury to the boy that was attacked, bile bubbled up into Billy's throat and disgust seeped into every corner of his consciousness.

More relevant to the clown's violent behavior toward his deputies, though, was what Doc concluded from his erratic behavior—uncharacteristic, according to his boss. "The symptoms presented might indicate nightshade poisoning. Their alkaloids—atropine and scopolamine—were the major active substances of the ointments of witches, of medieval "anesthetics", *and* of modern poisons."

"What the hell does all that mean, Doc? In good ole American, if ya please! Would it explain why this supposedly happy and gentle guy would assault Dwight?"

"Well, not by itself. But didn't you say your Sophie found occult practices prevalent in that community of performers?"

"Yeah. Some real weird sh—, ah, stuff."

"Well, this could be consistent with those practices, Billy, some quite ancient in their origins. I scoured the literature on this nightshade plant, which wasn't much. I called a colleague in Des Moines for more. She reminded me that in centuries past, females who were often labeled witches were the healers, midwives, gardeners and gatherers of herbs and berries. In this role, women developed an intimate knowledge of medicinal properties of plants, including the mind-altering properties of some of them. These women were early neuropharmacologists.

"Case in point, Billy, nightshade often shows up in the literature for witchcraft and occultism. Depending on the dosage and delivery mechanism, nightshade is used for everything from an aphrodisiac to an anesthetic to a deadly poison. In a medium dose-range, the predominant symptoms are hallucinations and illusions. The literature also suggests the use of nightshades in fortune-telling and religious rituals as well."

Billy's mind ran wild. "Fortune-telling? Oh—"

"While the use of nightshade would explain hallucinatory and even highly suggestible behavior, I found something else in the victim's throat. This substance suggests he was poisoned to incite violent behavior—a syrupy substance, some of which he vomited back up after ingestion, which might indicate a massive dose. I suspect someone drugged him with nightshade and something else. Perhaps a powerful stimulant. Combined with the nightshade alkaloids, that could explain his violent and uncharacteristic behavior. No telling what threat *he* perceived when Dwight surprised him with a bright light in his eyes. I'll see what I can find by testing his blood, but some of these substances prove elusive."

"Find out what you can, Doc. This guy's weird behavior, and the timing of the anonymous call reporting the victim's attack on a young boy? Suspicious. If somebody dosed this clown *after* he attacked a kid, we got another homicide on our hands. Could be raw anger, even revenge. Goes to motive. And the sumbitch who poisoned the clown used one of my deputies to execute the pervert. I am *pissed!*"

Billy had given Jimmy the day off to recover from the shooting, having stayed up all night processing the scene and interviewing hostile bystanders. But he called Jimmy at home to let him know what he'd learned from Doc Gus. The poor kid was still groggy and shaken. But he needed to know his actions were justified. The clown could have killed Dwight in his addled state.

Then Billy sat down with Dwight to more fully debrief.

"Jeez, Billy. Crazy stuff, but makes perfect sense. Means we got a serial killer on our hands. Crafty son-of-a-bitch too, using us to do his dirty work."

"Dwight, I know how you feel about show folk, but I need us to be as clear-headed as we can about this case."

"No worries, Billy. I'll reel it in." Dwight smiled as he acknowledged some prejudice launched by unfortunate history. He'd never been willing to talk about it. That had not changed.

"Good. If we assume Happy Grant's attacker is the same person who killed our other two vics, Happy can't be our serial, even though he was an earlier suspect. And victim number one, Garth Nitstone, couldn't have killed number two—Babbo—because he was dead before Babbo bit the dust. Jeez-Louise, what the hell have we got? Nothin'? Shit."

"Hold on, Billy. Our anonymous caller was male. And we now know our killer knows his way around poisons, or potions, or whatever this was. *And* that could explain your first victim's erratic behavior, too. Crazy self-destructive driving and running like a madman *away* from the circus. He was doubtless paranoid in the extreme about someone in the show. Is paranoia also a symptom of this, what, *signature poison?*"

"I'll ask Doc, but that wouldn't surprise me. That's a damn fine set of observations, though, Dwight. That would point to the same M.O. for victims one and three! You're right, Deputy, we don't got nothin'. We got somethin'! Okay, last night, when I questioned Madame..." Dwight's eyes lit up and grinned at Billy. He had seen him hovering over the snake lady in her silk robe with the slit up the side. Billy spotted that leer.

"Okay, knock it off, Deputy. The thing is, her face got all wrinkly when I told her how Grant was acting just before Jimmy.... Well, it was like a flash bulb triggered and blistered. Said she needed to talk with some of her folks. She knows somethin', like maybe who might use that sorta potion. She's itchin' to get out a Dodge. Maybe she's finally gettin' helpful. I'll quiz her on that.

"Meanwhile, you call Sophie. I want her to have another chat with that fortune-teller. Get Soph up to speed on this nightshade stuff. See if she can find out more than we might get from the snake lady."

"You sure *you* can be clear-headed around that silky piece of work, boss?" Now Dwight was just having some fun, and Billy knew it.

"All I can promise, *Deputy*, is that I'll get the goods before I sniff the perfume. Fair 'nuff?" He was having fun, too. What with all the pressure coming down from City Hall and Laticia Morgenstern's Civic League, his first loyalty had to be solving these murders. Especially now that a third body had dropped.

But a little break in the unbelievable tension proved a healthy tonic.

✳ 57 ✳

❧

After Dwight briefed Sophie on the Grant shooting over the phone, he asked her to talk with Sister again on Billy's behalf.

Sister's tent on the midway sat empty. Sophie risked a solitary hike to the back lot, unescorted, to find her wagon. She had been back there often enough with Josh that nobody challenged her. She stopped at CM's tent, knocked on the post at its entry. Tam and Tare stood inside, kibitzing with each other over something-or-other. While they seemed pleased to see Sophie, they sounded disappointed that she needed to keep moving, but provided her directions to Sister's wagon. They said they understood.

Unlike her ornate tent, Sister's wagon appeared unassuming. Bland, even. Like she didn't want to draw any attention. Clumsy in her climb up the five steps to the door at the rear, Sophie envisioned this wagon a prison. Sister only escaped if someone carried her. She knocked. From inside, she heard a quiet response.

"Enter if you must." Sophie did so. With reluctance.

This was the first time Sophie had seen Sister not concealed by her robe. She entered and closed the door behind her, looked up from her feet and froze at the sight and the smell.

Sister looked unconcerned, not surprised. It would have been hard to miss the note of cynical shame in her voice. "Sophie, you now see before you the little freak unadorned and in all her glory."

The wagon might have belonged to someone with no interest in the real world—no decorations and only raw wood walls never adorned with paint. A small shelf bolted to the wall planking to her right well below Sophie's waist level held a recessed wash bowl covered by a thin towel. A used wash rag hung on a hook nearby, still dripping. Another hook on the adjacent wall, three feet from the floor planking, held what looked like Sister's robe. More clothes dangled out of the open maw of a small chest on the other side of the washbowl. A single bed four feet long and the wheelchair in which Sister slumped completed the interior furnishings.

She wheeled her chair toward Sophie to offer her visitor a better look. Even performed an almost-adroit 360-degree maneuver—practiced but slow in its painful execution. Both of the chair's large wooden wheels squeaked. The two smaller wheels in front chattered.

"Maybe you think Madame might make more money by giving me my own Single-O in the sides, hmmm? Sophie, what do you see?" Obviously, Sister still stung from their last encounter when Sophie pushed harder than she should have.

Sophie collected herself, limped over to Sister's bed, and plopped down on it. "Is this pity I'm hearing, Sister? Am I surprised, even shocked at my first complete look at my new friend? Of course. That does not surprise you. But what *does* surprise *me* is the courage you show every time you make your way out of this safe little space. I am surprised you do not wallow in self-pity every minute of every day. That you have risen above all of that, and are concerned enough about the well-being of others to seek truth and justice for your brother, and others, despite the risks. *That* tells me you have the kind of courage and strength possessed by very few people on this earth.

"What was it we discussed when we first met? I said 'You suffer from polio, like me.' And *you* said 'Polio, yes, but I do not suffer. Not from polio. Neither do you, dearie. Like me, it strengthens you.' What's changed in just a few days, Sister? After that, I thought, 'She has to be one of the strongest women ever.'"

As Sophie spoke, Sister turned her chair from an angle where she was staring at the only photo on the wall to face Sophie head on. She lowered her misshapen head that sat atop a ropy neck that was too long. It was hard not to stare, so Sophie stopped trying.

She reached out for the young woman's hands, like they had at the end of their second encounter. Sister responded, slowly at first, then with resignation. Sophie then explored her every feature, not with abhorrence, but with sincere interest, with admiration. After a full minute of holding hands and examining Sister's countenance from head to toe, she said, "This isn't all polio, is it?"

"No, Sophie. Most of my unique appearance was caused either by birth defects or prolonged abuse, both before and after Babbo and I were born. Some was caused by chronic malnutrition while we were still in the womb. We looked up at poverty. After we were born, our living conditions further complicated our health.

"My mother, failing to have us destroyed at birth, as suggested by her friends—we never knew our father—Mother grew to resent us for the extra time and expense our care required. That resentment was likely the root of most of the beatings and the ridicule. Babbo didn't yet comprehend. I thought that was all normal. But early on, at least, we had each other.

"Then, a friend of my mother's, who had been a performer, bought Babbo and took him away. He was too young to remember. Called him 'the useful freak, a potential money-maker.' Not me, though, because I was just a 'waste of space.' He told Mother, 'Do yourself a favor. Just dump *it* in an alley somewhere.' I remember it all, even though I wasn't even two years old. That's when my gift started manifesting itself.

"By the time I was four, I had mastered an impressive vocabulary. Within a year after that, I became a novelty at the many parties my mother frequented. I started reading people. Mother collected the nickels. I possessed a knack for reading body language. And I was a meticulous listener. People took me into their confidence. It was fun. I was *not* a waste. After all, where's the risk in confiding in a deformed pile of useless flesh who would be dead soon, anyway?

"They'd say, 'she's so clever. Isn't that interesting? How does she do that?' Sophie, something inside of me said I *was* worthwhile, and if others didn't perceive that, I'd leverage that advantage at every turn."

"How old were you when you first started working as a seer?"

"When I was eight, my mother sold me to a carny in New Jersey. For a 'good price,' she told me. By then, it was clear I'd last at least a few more years, and I drew in the marks. I not only could read people, I was a freak too, and a child freak at that. I was a real bargain—a triple threat—the buyer told me.

"He taught me the business and said as long as I brought in the marks, he'd keep me alive. I learned the gaff, how to make my oddities work for me, what worked, what didn't. Taught myself how to read, and discovered I could absorb a tremendous amount of information, and retain it. Dear Josh still brings me books, most of which I imagine he steals. Some he returns after I finish them. I believe I am blessed— or cursed—with what is called an eidetic memory. I remember most everything I see, hear and read.

"I also remember everything I've ever felt. That is the most difficult of all. I also see things others don't, and not with my eyes. Comes in flashes, and never complete. I can't explain it."

Upon hearing all of this, Sophie realized her mouth hung open. "So, Sister, even with your troubled childhood and tribulations since then, though you are physically, um, disadvantaged, you are blessed with so many gifts. Most people would be envious if they got to know you. You do realize that, don't you?"

Sophie still held Sister's hands in her own. They had grown clammy. She leaned over, looking into those lop-sided eyes that had seen so much. She squeezed those spindly fingers with gentle affection.

"You're right, of course. I am sorry for my behavior in my tent earlier. I know you hunger for information. Like I said, I will share whatever I am able. My sense tells me neither of the Smalleys are your killer. Tom, Lilith's father, is an arrogant ass, but he's too much of a coward to incite someone to kill. Anything other than that would be nothing more than guessing or opinion on my part.

"You need evidence, Sophie. I would not be surprised if Lilith couldn't provide you or the sheriff with some insight. But do not pressure her. That is very important, Sophie. I cannot say why. Let her come to you."

"Thank you... my friend."

This could be it!

58

Billy reflected.

Sophie said earlier more than one clue pointed to Crocodile Man as a suspect in Garth Nitstone's death. She could tell Sister didn't agree, but he knew potions from his time in New Guinea, even though they discovered no evidence to suggest a potion caused Nitstone's death. Yet.

Ultimately, CM's alibi ruled him out. Same for Tamra and Tara. They had no contact with Nitstone the day of his death. *And* they had solid alibis for the night of Babbo's murder.

Milo's tent sat next to theirs. Despite his own problems, Milo and his bunkmate admitted hearing them arguing late that Friday night, and then, as usual, the noisy make-up sex lasted until well past Babbo's time-of-death window.

Other suspects with weaker alibis demanded Billy's attention.

BESIDES, BILLY HAD GROWN SYMPATHETIC TO THE PLIGHT OF THESE three freaks—he still hated that word, maybe more than they did themselves. The state of New York still astounded him. They considered CM a bigamist, at least according to CM.

And forget the freak part—their marriage was still illegal in twenty-nine states that ban interracial marriages. They consider Negroes something less than full-fledged humans across more than half of America.

Billy was more than pleased they had alibis. He had grown quite fond of all three of them. If he was honest with himself, even *he* used to think all freaks weren't worth knowing, and that was now a source of personal shame. Funny how perspectives change.

He saw a lot of himself in this angry young man, and wrestled with his self-image as a result.

"DEPUTY SPOONER—"

"C'mon, Doc, don't you think it's time you just call me Dwight? How long have you been our on-call medical examiner now?"

"Of course, Dwight. If the sheriff is about, have him listen to this, too."

"Sure. Hang on." Dwight pressed the mouthpiece of the phone against his chest and said, "Hey, Billy, Doc's got something for us."

He waited for Billy to cross from his own desk and held the earpiece facing straight up between their ears. Dwight said, "Okay, Doc, we're both here."

"Yes, well, I found something interesting as I was examining Mr. Grant's remains. I didn't spot it under his grease paint earlier. I understand that's what they call a clown's face paint. But when I cleaned him up, I discerned a rather distinctive bruise on the right side of his forehead."

Billy said, "But Doc, I thought he was struck from behind."

"Yes, Billy, he was, but this was a second blow. In addition to abrasions on the back of his head, I would conclude he was attacked from behind. He fell to the ground, and either turned face up on his own, or his attacker turned him over. He was then punched on the right side of his forehead. From that, we might conclude his attacker was left-handed, and strong."

Billy said, "That's good, Doc. Anything else?"

"Yes, there most certainly is something else. Do you recall someone broke into our morgue the day after we brought your truck rollover victim in? And that they stole that ring I removed from Mr. Nitstone's finger?"

Billy said, "Yeah, so why is that relevant now, Doc?"

"Do you remember the dominant feature of that ring, Billy?"

"Without referring to my notes, I seem to recall it was a human skull."

"Right you are. The shape of the victim's bruise is quite distinctive because there is so little soft tissue between the right temple's epidermis, or skin, and the relatively fragile bone at that point on his skull. Care to guess the *shape* of the contusion—the bruise—on Mr. Grant's right temple?"

"The hell, you say!"

"I do, indeed. What's more, over time, such injuries that comprise water, blood and other fluids beneath the skin will migrate to lower areas like the eyelids. Or in Mr. Grant's case, the bruise's fluids would have descended to his cheek. They did not have time to do so. This tells me this skull-shaped bruise was incurred shortly before your deputy shot him.

"By the way, your clown was punched on the side of his forehead in a particularly vulnerable spot with sufficient force to fracture the underlying skull bones. That caused an intracranial hematoma on the temporal lobe of his brain. His brain was bleeding, Billy.

"This also means that even if Mr. Grant had survived your deputy's three bullets, his, ah, brain bleed would have killed him within minutes, anyway. Someone dispensed a great deal of anger to your clown moments before your deputies arrived on the scene. That most probably contributed to his already-drug-induced state of mania, as well as to his ultimate demise. He was already dying."

Billy said it again. "The hell, you say!" He and Dwight looked at each other, then hurried to put their ears back to the phone's earpiece.

Billy continued, "Let me get this straight. An old circus guy wearing a weird ring goes crazy and does himself in with a circus truck. Another guy breaks into your morgue, steals that same weird-ass ring, uses it to clobber *yet another* circus guy who *also* goes crazy and forces my deputy to shoot him? But he's already dead? Just doesn't know it? That about it, Doc?"

"Like I said, gentlemen, this is interesting. I thought you should hear about all of this post haste."

"Thanks, Doc. This links the two deaths—numbers one and three —and makes it a lot more likely that our truck driver was a murder victim. *And* this clinches that the murderer is still hangin' around inside Madame's show. Say, Doc?"

"Yes, Billy?"

"Thanks for throwin' our young Deputy Jimmy a lifeline here. He ain't a killer."

"That's what you should tell him, Sheriff. And you're welcome."

Dwight hung up the earpiece. He had yet to set the phone down on his desk when Billy shot both of his arms up in the air and let out a *whoop!* His deputy smiled.

Billy said, "I gotta call Jimmy right now! Yessir! I got me a call to make!"

59

Dwight looked forward to meeting Justina again at the diner in Rock Rapids. But something was wrong as he watched her body language. She rushed in, distracted and distressed.

Justina sat down, and with a flourish, adjusted the stiff fabric of her ruffled skirt before she spoke a word. She didn't even wait for Dwight to hold her chair for her.

"Dwight, what is it with these circus devils? They kill each other. But are they practicing before they come for us? Why aren't you and the sheriff doing something about this? How bad does it need to get before something is done?"

"Whoa, there, Justy. What's whipped you into such a lather?"

"I just came from a civic league meeting and that's all they're talking about."

"Justy, we're doing everything we can to solve these crimes, so we can let the show move on."

She grew more agitated by the moment, wringing her gloved hands like she was washing them, until in exasperation she stripped off her gloves to better strangle them.

"Wait. *Let* it move on? You mean that, that circus *wants* to leave town, leave Lyon County, and you won't let them? Does that mean what Laticia has been saying is *true?*"

Now Dwight grew agitated. "Look, you know the law doesn't allow criminals to leave the scene of a crime, right? That's not how the law works."

"But what about the safety of our community? What are you and the sheriff doing about *that?* I'm sorry, Dwight. I shouldn't have come in my current state of mind." And just like that, with another flourish, Justina Ringwall, junior church lady, rose and swept from the room.

Dwight sat there, stunned. Ordered a piece of pie. And coffee.

Black.

No sugar.

STILL REELING FROM THE FIGHT WITH JUSTINA, IF HE COULD EVEN call it that, Dwight reminisced over his coffee. He'd already demolished a huge slice of strawberry-rhubarb pie.

He enjoyed being a detective on a big city force back in the day. Before the war. It had always been his dream, and it came true.

The Minneapolis Police Department legitimately claimed to be every bit as sophisticated in their methods as Chicago or New York or LA, but he had always called the metro area home. By 1916, he'd been a beat cop for three years when he earned his gold shield at the tender age of twenty-two.

Dwight's seventeen-year-old brother, Ned, was small for his age at five years younger. He depended on Dwight for almost everything. Ned had a smart mouth, and expected his big brother to get him out of one scrape after another. Most often this happened after he insulted or took advantage of someone else, usually someone bigger than he.

Their parents worked all the time. They had little time or money to spare for family because they prioritized food and a roof. But Dwight took pride in being a good big brother—maybe too good. Then he joined the force while Ned still lived at home and sent money by mail. That way, they wouldn't have to face him when they took his cash. Didn't seem to make much difference, except Ned got more out of control, even with a brother as a cop.

IT WAS AUGUST 1916. A TRAVELING CIRCUS CALLED HEBERHOFF'S Big Show came to the Scott County Fairgrounds in Shakopee, a south-western suburb of Minneapolis. The Spooner family's home was less than a mile away. Heberhoff's little show was more of a carnival than a circus, but the local folks didn't care. It was almost as if they didn't mind getting cheated out of their scarce nickels and dimes as long as they felt entertained, morally outraged at being cheated, or both. If only for a few hours, it jerked them out of their mediocre lives.

Dwight could never forgive himself for what happened at the hands of those carnies. He learned later that Ned and a few of his ruffian friends swaggered down Heberhoff's little midway one Saturday night, picking pockets or hassling smaller kids. Normal stuff. For them. Then they hassled the wrong person—a barker at a gaming concession.

The guy was a pro—a grifter. He picked the kids out of the crowd, drew them in and provoked them. Ned took the bait. Smooth as silk, the carny made it look like he was being attacked by a young hoodlum. He stuffed a knife and a few small bills into Ned's pocket, and screamed bloody murder that he was being robbed. The carny and a couple of his accomplices grabbed three witnesses—locals—and wouldn't let them or Ned leave. They all got interviewed by the Shakopee cops. A clear-cut case of armed robbery gone wrong, the cops concluded.

"Justice" had been swift. But the carny, supported by Heberhoff himself during the police interviews, was disappointed that the well-dressed kid that "attacked" him came from a poor family, not a rich one. Any hope of working a variation of the badger confidence game for a sizable score evaporated.

Such a con involved setting up a mark like Ned for a serious offense, and then blackmailing the affluent family to entice the grifter —in this case, the barker—to drop the charges. Not only did the Spooner family have no money, the kid's older brother was an MPD police dick. They dropped the charges against Ned and walked away from the con.

Now that would have been the end of it, but Ned could not let it go. He went back to find the barker and tried to stab him with the guy's own knife. The barker turned the knife on him, stabbed him in the stomach, and then, in the presence of a host of witnesses, tried to save the kid's life. He held an improvised compression bandage on Ned's fatal wound, hollered for an ambulance, and made himself out to be a Good Samaritan. Made little Ned out to be a vengeful stalker.

Ned died. The barker walked. The show left town.

It wasn't until Heberhoff's Big Show was long gone that Dwight pieced together what happened by grilling Ned's hoodlum friends. He sweated answers out of the little pricks. Ned had told them the outcome of the initial con and his plans to go back and confront the carny.

EVER SINCE THEN, DWIGHT'S LACK OF CLOSURE AND HIS DISTRUST OF all show people knew no bounds. His little brother may have been a big prick, but he didn't deserve to die at the hands of a lying, cheating carny.

If he were to take off his uniform and badge, he sort of agreed with Justina and the church ladies. But he neither would nor could take off the badge.

Not now.

60

Sister Shipton's mother had been a recent immigrant and Italian circus performer. She shared with Sister at an early age—as soon as she could understand—the origin of her unusual name. That name had a rich heritage in the magical world of sixteenth-century England.

Sister's mother told her, "I named you after the amazing Ursula Southeil, who, even though very young, they called her *Mother* Shipton.

"Like you, she was deformed, with a hunched back, twisted legs, a large deformed head, and sunken cheeks. This was how most of the old stories described witches, thanks to the cuss-ed white Christian men of the day. And like you, dearie, she had been born so ug—different— that villagers believed she came from the Devil's loins, and suspected her of witchcraft.

"Mother Shipton lived in a place called Yorkshire. Her reputation spread because of the strange things that happened around her. That started as a child, like flying objects and other sorcery."

Sister remembered this conversation at a remarkable three years old. "You named me after a witch?"

"This is a compliment, dear. Even though she lived as an outcast, she had exceptional talent. She read people—like you—and she even predicted future events, many of which came true. She attended mass, but also practiced the magical arts, and extended her field of expertise from palm reading to selling love potions, among other skills. And you, little Sister, possess exceptional talent too. You just don't know it yet."

That was Mother's *pep talk*. You're ugly like a witch, and you have talent. You're just ignorant.

She had to have been a better aerialist than a mother, but I suppose she did what she was able.

Sister huddled in the solitude of her wagon. Despite the painful cramping in her fingers, she clutched the pendant that now dangled from a slender bronze chain around her elongated neck. The chain, along with her neck, had earned the hint of a green patina.

That chain's length allowed her to hold the pendant to her face. She contemplated its symbolism. The left eye, brow, and tears crafted from heavy bronze wire represented the moon god Horus from Egyptian mythology. The sizable turquoise eyeball symbolized a secret society's watchful protection from the shadows—behind the scenes—often concealed under a veil of sorrow.

Madame had recruited Sister into this ancient international sorority not long after she first observed and admired Sister's formidable intellect and insight in action. Sister still remembered that night as if it were last evening....

⬥

THE TWO OF THEM HAD HUNCHED IN SISTER'S WAGON, CLOSE TO THE stove and to each other against the pre-dawn chill. Several triple-wick candles illuminated their faces and their mood.

A solemn expression adorned Madame's angelic face, as if about to bestow a great honor. "Little Sister, I am of the sisterhood of *Ha"u-*

Wil'uk." She pronounced it with precision—HA-oo-WHEEL-ook—with four crisp syllables, the beginning of each enunciated with a slight puff of her breath. "The very name itself is an invocation of immense but subtle power.

"We influence events anywhere that exists the evils of man, or the misfortunes of nature. We do not make such events happen, nor do we prevent them from happening. That is not our calling. But we influence affairs everywhere. We have for more than a thousand years.

"It may seem strange to you that those of us who *seem* to exert such little influence should be recruited. The range of our diverse membership around the world would surprise you—from peasantry to royalty.

"Simply, we nurture the natural balance in nature, our Mother. Often, we are twice or thrice removed from direct action, which makes us even more formidable and reservado—invisible. We can only be effective when the degree of our influence goes undetected."

"Madame, is this witchcraft?"

After a thoughtful pause and the tiniest of enigmatic smiles, Madame said, "Call it what you will, hermanita. An hombre's heart, while seeking happiness or fulfillment, often travels through darkness —or ignorance—to get there. It is our task to give the path through the light a chance. Comprende?"

"And how do we achieve this, Madame?"

We? Madame smiled. Just by telling Sister of this, she had invited her in. And the deformed little seer already included herself. "We achieve our sacred mission by sharing the goodness in our own hearts. By helping others seek justice. And by shedding light on that which is often counter to conventional wisdom, even to our personal safety. Sometimes, we must be clever at how we accomplish this, and survive."

THIS HAD TESTED MADAME'S CREDIBILITY WITH HER, SO SHE sounded more cynical than she intended. "And what has this sistership achieved in a thousand years?"

"More than you might imagine, caro. We have exerted influence throughout the ages. Most of that influence has taken the form of paquetes pequeños—small packets—of wisdom and guidance offered to others. When done properly, we vanish back into the shadows with no one the wiser. We are the reason there is the saying, 'Behind every strong man whispers an even stronger woman,' even if that woman is never drawn from behind the veil into the light."

HOW MANY YEARS AGO WAS THAT NOW? FOUR? FIVE? AT FOURTEEN, Sister had already been wise to the ways of a cruel world when Madame came to America and recruited her as she first pulled together Perlatelli's Oddities and Wonders and passed through the Northeast.

She would have joined Madame's show anyway. That's where her brother Babbo wanted to work at the time. Madame had offered him his own Single-O, that is, his own single-act show. That's how she poached him away from one of the big shows where he was only part of a Ten-in-One.

Had Madame known Babbo was her brother all along? If she did, she never let on, as if she knew that would be an important secret some day.

Now, she herself used the principles of *Ha"u-Wil'uk* to not only seek justice for little Babbo, but to bring balance back to her little piece of the world. Un paquete pequeño, as Madame would say. One small packet at a time. A great woman not afraid to think small. And probably practicing a few of her own paquetes pequeños.

Sister now wondered about the demise of Happy Grant, and whether Madame had influenced events in some way to stop that monster. As Madame would say, 'if we perform the spirit of *Ha"u-Wil'uk,* no one will ever know.'

61

Mayor Harold Deemers failed to explain it, nor would he try.

He had always taken a certain perverse pleasure at the discomfort of others. He found no shame in exercising such power. It was not a bad thing to leverage one's advantages through clever machinations. After all, one would be foolish not to press one's strengths. At least that's the lie he convinced himself to be the gospel truth.

Take today. Good old Billy suffered, the pathetic country hick. Three weeks downrange of two murders in their peaceful little community, and now a third death out at that wretched circus lot. A clown, no less, shot by one of Billy's own deputies. The shit sure rolled down his chute, alright. Too bad. Worth a private grin, and a rubbing-in. Lord knows he'd been on the receiving end of such admonitions all his life—a victim of unachievable expectations. Yes, he was a victim. And misery loves company.

"Velma, get me Sheriff Kershaw on the phone for me, would you, dear?"

"Certainly, Mr. Mayor."

Instead of calling Billy himself, he enjoyed using his secretary to announce him. More official. Also, it reminded Billy of his official capacity as mayor of the whole damn town.

"Billy, have you solved these murders yet? We need this matter resolved, and it would be nice to get it done *today,* so we can get this awful circus out of my town."

"Harold—"

"That's *Mr. Mayor* to you, Sheriff."

The delicious pause that followed lasted long enough for the mayor to wonder if they'd been disconnected. Finally, "Mr. Mayor, we're winding up our investigation. You'll be the first to know."

"Yes, well, that's just fine, Sheriff. But we need results, not more investigating. Do you understand?"

"Sure thing, *Mister* Mayor." Click.

Did that impertinent prick just hang up on me?

HE HAD LEARNED THE CIRCUS PLAYED SEVERAL TOWNS ON THEIR WAY north from Florida, and that they planned to play Rock Rapids in early April.

As clear as a bell, he remembered the day he drove down to Sioux City, where the silly little circus appeared at the time. Almost a hundred miles south meant a long drive, but he needed to know, and not just for himself....

THE SUN HAD ALREADY SET BY THE TIME HE FOUND PERLATELLI'S Oddities and Wonders at the local fairground outside Sioux City that night. Tried to look casual and stay out of sight all at the same time. Kept his hat drawn down low over his face. Nobody saw him. After about an hour, he spotted the little freak. Hard to miss. Walking the midway, like an inspection tour or something.

He'd needed to confirm whether this was a one-time deal or a habit. He returned late the next night. Waited for a couple of hours. *Bingo! Okay, so around midnight each night, the little freak walks the midway and visits the animal cages to feed 'em scraps.*

He drove all night to be back before anybody missed him. Piece a cake.

⚜ 62 ⚜

❦

Sophie was running out of suspects and time. They needed a break. And she just wanted to get home to Jake, little Leo, and even cousin Walt. Wanted to bake some of her mile-high loaves of bread the boys always swooned over. She wanted to collect and wash her eggs and feed the chickens. Even that feisty rooster who never learned he was only supposed to crow at sunrise. And she was tired of all the questions. But they needed answers—for Sister. And for the three victims.

She would step up her interview technique a notch. The last interview Sister arranged was with the show's ringmaster, Aloysius Cogholdt. He greeted her at the entrance to his small but elaborate tent. Sophie wasn't sure what to think of this guy, other than he was not old. That surprised her. And he was devastatingly handsome, with razor-sharp features that advertised annoyance.

"Please, do come in. Sister says I am to grant you an audience. There is that. What can I do for you, miss?" A broad wave of his right arm and a shallow bow invited her through his door flap.

Cogholdt thought a great deal of himself. But according to Sister, he was now little more than a glorified barker in the center of the show's single ring, and just a dirt-rimmed ring at that. Sister said he even was expected to help the rousters shovel up that rim of dirt on setup day. Yet he seemed to *live* back in his glory days with the big shows. He remained in denial that he was past his prime, even though he was still a young man.

"My name is Sophie, a friend of Sister's. I understand you're the show's ringmaster. That must be quite an honor—"

"Indeed, it is. I am the face of Perlatelli's Oddities and Wonders." Expansive arm sweeps with multiple flourishes, palms turned upward, chin thrust skyward... he took a bow for some yet-to-be-seen performance. The little man with the big voice basked in his own glow.

Since Cogholdt's ringmaster duties only required his full attention during big top performances—a few hours each show day, at most—he squandered a great deal of free time. According to Sister, Madame also assigned him the job of boss canvas man, what little canvas there was, which was in poor shape. All their colors faded to near gray tones and seams rotted from exposure went un-repaired. Sister said that thankfully, the rousters who set up the canvas for the big top did their job in spite of Cogholdt's meddling as "the boss."

He was also a janitor, which consumed most of his time. That, and complaining about cleaning up animal dung, dirty straw and the trash strewn by the rubes each night, as if it was beneath him. Sister thought little of this dandy. Not that she'd say that. Sophie was told by others, however, that *whining* seemed to consume him these days.

Sophie already observed for herself that this popinjay possessed wild delusions of grandeur. He was pompous, boisterous, pretentious... a malcontent. But he professed to love the circus life.

Though leery of speaking to any outsider, he also seemed eager to dispense his personal plight to anyone who would listen. He said, "It's not like it used to be, miss. Madame wishes to differentiate her show from all the other ragbag shows. Let's face it. Few can afford the big acts anymore. Why? Because they *think* small. And they *become* small. Do you have any idea what it costs to feed just one elephant? And who wants to see just one? That frightens off small thinkers. We must go big, but we can't afford it, so we go small, and the gate receipts reflect that."

"Then, what's her solution? Doesn't sound like you're too happy about it, or that it meets your career expectations."

"She says to keep it simple based on how tough it is just to make the nut—"

"The nut?"

"Yes, well, every show spends money each day, just to keep it together and touring. That daily break-even cost is called the nut. We all must live and breathe the nut. Not like it used to be.

"Anyway, this show is, and has been for a while, more oddities than wondrous acts. A trained dog act as our headliner? Instead, our audiences now must be drawn to our wondrous sense of the macabre, the odd, the weirdness lacking in their humdrum lives. In the big cities, small towns, anywhere."

"So, what's the problem?"

"Well, not as much a problem as, ah, artistic differences. Madame wants a ringmaster to set the tone for the entire show, including the sides—"

"Sides?"

"Yes, you know, the sideshows. And the midway with the concessions, grab joints, where the chumps—the customers—can grab some victuals so they don't need to leave the lot to eat. The ringmaster, that's me, sets the tone.

"Foremost, I am a salesman. I sell our little dog act, and a few clowns beating the stuffing out of each other. And maybe I offer the chumps a quick peek at a couple of the freaks. You want more? Get your asses out of the big top and hit the sides. Spend your dimes. Meet a few of the freaks up close for a dime. Even talk to them. Check out the wondrous displays in the dime museum. Get your fortune told for a dime. Check out Crocodile Boy for a dime. And by all means, do ogle his bride, the beautiful but bizarre two-headed girl, for another dime. That's a lot of dimes, miss. I move them from the big top to the sides where we rake in the dimes. And that puts food on the table in the commissary tent, fuel in the generators and trucks, plus greases the wagons' axles.

"We used to travel by train, but who can afford *that* anymore? Anyway, now we go where there *are* no tracks. Our route is a bunch of short hops. The show stretches out like a snake as it slithers down country roads—the horses pulling wagons lag the trucks, sometimes by miles and miles."

All the while he spoke, Cogholdt practiced his diction, posture, facial, hand and arm gestures. He kept his slender ramrod body in constant motion, pacing in a small pattern in the center of his tent, no doubt performing to the attention given to him by an imagined coal-oil spotlight. Sophie perched on the edge of his bed. Followed him with her eyes while she inspected his abode without being too obvious about it. The tent lacked any other furniture. Not even a chair. No personal memorabilia, although she had learned that wasn't uncommon —less stuff to pack, move and unpack at the next lot.

"So I repeat. What's the problem, Mr. Cogholdt?"

"I made my bones as a ringmaster in several of the big shows. I earned quite a name as a showman. My *brand* expects a certain style. Madame says I need to be half cheery and half scary. You know, don't scare the little shits too badly, but just enough to fascinate their bored parents. All without robbing too much focus from the acts. Well, that isn't what I do. But if I wanna eat, guess what? Madame's the boss."

"I see."

"*Do you?* All this might not seem a big deal to you, sitting in your nice comfortable home, but out here on the lot, I don't truck with freaks, and these performers aren't much better. Now, for *me* to get painted up every show like I'm on the gaff—you know, a fake freak or a clown, or something else—well, like I said, artistic differences."

"You really don't like the show's freaks very much, do you, Mr. Cogholdt? Because it seems you *do* truck with freaks, at least when you're moving from town to town. You choose to stay with the show. What is it that makes you hate freaks so much?" She knew she was now pushing hard.

"Well, for the truth to be known, they don't produce the revenue like they used to, much like the lame acts Madame books these days. I say we need to be more traditional. Go after the old acts that *always* produced: high-wires, big cats that do more than sleep and shit, trained horse acts with attractive trick riders in scant costumes, the works."

"But aren't those acts expensive?"

"Sure, but they also more than pay their own way. On this, Madame and I will never agree. But like I said, I must eat."

"Why did you leave the big shows you obviously admire? Creative differences there, too?" It was the way Sophie said it that ruffled the ringmaster's hackles. He stopped his incessant gesturing long enough to stare down at Sophie, still sitting on his bed. She propped herself up with stiff arms on the bed frame near her hips. Her back and hip burned like the blazes.

Aloysius Cogholdt, ringmaster and showman extraordinaire, suddenly lost some of his polish. "Look, lady. This is a rough business. It isn't like any other, and that means you make employment decisions every single day—for yourself and for others. No show has it all, but this show, well, it's only a few steps up from a damn Hooverville. And if you tell Madame I said that, I'll deny it. Yeah, I care little for most of the freaks around here. But I didn't harm Babbo, if that's what you're getting at. Barely knew him. Most folks liked him okay, I guess. You should talk to Tom Smalley, or Croc Boy. They both either hated that pinhead, got serious anger issues, or both."

"Mr. Cogholdt, I have to ask this. Where were you Friday the 6th between midnight and, say, five AM?"

"Ah. Alibi time. Inevitable. Very well. I was sleeping. Here. Like most normal folks. With a hootch girl named Lola. Ask her. She has *nothing* to hide." He tossed a sleazy wink toward Sophie.

She thought she might vomit, but swallowed her pride and smiled. Almost. Well, more of a naked smirk of disgust.

"Mr. Cogholdt, do you practice the dark magic?" He was facing away from her at that moment, but wheeled around—too fast. He studied Sophie with a cocked head to see if she was making a joke. She was not.

"What have you heard?"

"It's a simple question with a complex answer, isn't it, sir?"

"This interview is over." He placed his hands in the pockets of his high-waisted trousers behind their impeccable creases. Gestured toward his tent's entrance with a dismissive nod, all the while holding Sophie's quizzical gaze. He was done performing.

"Thank you for your time, Mr. Cogholdt. Good luck with your career."

"Hmmm...."

❦ 63 ❦

❦

Josh had grown fond of this rube. Miss Sophie didn't judge anyone, and she listened with an open mind. In his experience, that was rare, especially in the smaller towns. Now that they were off the show's customary route—he wasn't sure why—it was especially meaningful to find someone like Miss Sophie.

He escorted her back from one of the last interviews Sister arranged for her—Aloysius Cogholdt, the cocky ringmaster who was too good for Madame's little show. Another "performer" whose only skill was his mouth and his looks—a different sort a natural freak, if you asked Josh. Sophie's expression said a lot about her view of Mr. Fancy Pants as she exited his tent.

They strolled, arm in arm, through the back lot crowd from Cogholdt's small tent toward her car out front. Josh spotted Jed marching in their direction. He lowered his eyes, hid under the rim of his fedora to avoid eye contact. But Jed raised a fist as he passed close by Sophie. Josh released Sophie's arm, threw up both of his own arms wide, and placed himself between Jed and Sophie. Instead of clobbering them with that fist, Jed just sneezed into it.

As a reflex, Sophie chirped, "Gesundheit!"

Jed met Josh's eyes for a momentary glare—up close. Confused, Josh grabbed Sophie's arm once more. They kept walking, now at a quicker pace, away from Jed. Sophie could hardly keep up, even with Josh holding onto her right arm and dragging her along. Josh whipped the knife out of its sheath. He always carried that knife strapped to his right leg. He raised it, struck, and blood flowed. It seemed the only thing possible. No choice. None at all. Sophie wondered what had happened, but then didn't seem to care.

❧

THEY PASSED CLOSE BY THE TENT OF CM, TAM & TARE. NOW dragging Sophie who had lost her feet, Josh rushed in without warning. Left a trail of blood. CM and his wives sat across from each other at a small table, sipping something. The last ninety seconds terrified and confused Sophie. Now, the pain overwhelmed her, the burning, something else. Josh dragged her to the center of the tent.

CM held one of his wives' hands. At the confusing and bloody intrusion, he jumped up so fast his chair tipped over. All three short glasses and their contents tumbled from the flimsy folding table to the rug that covered their dirt floor. He bunched both fists, flexed his battering-ram arms, and stood ready to defend their home. He screamed, *"What the Hell?"*

Josh planted Sophie onto their bed, turned to face CM with his arms raised, palms out, fingers spread wide. He had dropped his knife. He croaked, "Help...." Fell to his knees. Squeezed out two words. "Devil's Breath." Settled back onto his haunches. Fell silent with glazed eyes, head sagging, his breathing ragged.

Recognition dawned on CM's scarred face. He kneeled in front of the kid. Blood had drenched Josh's hands and the front of his dungarees where he'd stabbed the front of his own right thigh to retain focus, at least for a few precious seconds. Grabbed his chin and pulled it up. Josh's constricted pupils confirmed he'd been dosed. CM threw a terrified glance toward Sophie. Then back to Josh.

"Son-of-a-bitch! Who?"

It took Josh several moments and a few shallow puppy breaths to respond. Then the boy wheezed, "Jed." Dragged one bloody hand across his confused face, smearing crimson on his brow and right cheek.

CM shook with rage. Tam and Tare heard it all, rushed over to sit by Sophie on the bed, who looked like she would cry. She was looking at her bloody hands, staring down at little Josh, then looked wide-eyed at Tam and Tare, shaking her head. Sagged forward. She would have slid onto the floor if they hadn't embraced her.

SOPHIE'S LEFT HIP BURNED, LIKE SOMEONE HAD JABBED A HOT POKER into it. Her back was on fire, too. Why was she sitting on a bed in a tent? *Where am I? Haven't I been here before? Someone stole my spit! Who would do that? I'm all red, too.*

She flapped her flattened lips with exaggeration. She was sure she needed to be somewhere, doing something, but what? Was she being hugged by someone with two heads? Confused, she said, "You are exquisite, but which one are you?"

Tam said, "Dear, lit's not your blood. Lie down for a while."

"But I'm sure I have chores. Little Leo. We're short on breast milk at home. I need to—"

"You will lie down now, Miss Sophie. Do as you're told."

She sing-songed, "Okaaay." Her eyelids succumbed to the numbing force of gravity, as did her upper torso. She flopped over to her right onto a stack of colorful pillows. Dead weight.

The girls arose and stood back with terror in their eyes. Tare bit her lip. Tam looked pissed. CM left Josh kneeling in the center of the tent on their rug in a small pool of blood. Came over to lift Sophie's limp legs and her blocky orthopedic shoes onto the bed.

That's when he heard the voice behind him that dripped with accusation.

"WHAT THE HELL IS *SHE* DOING HERE?" JED STRAIN SLANTWISE nodded toward Sophie, who was now out cold. Josh had collapsed in on himself in the middle of the floor. The bleeding had slowed, maybe even stopped.

"Jed, you get your uninvited ass right out a here before I kick it and your balls all the way to the Kentucky state line."

Jed then realized he needed to be careful. This huge freak had a short fuse jammed into a load of explosive anger. He simply said, "Madame will hear about this." He turned to leave.

Before he got half-way out of the tent's flap, CM bolted forward, grabbed his shoulder, spun him around with vicious intent. Said under his breath, "Be sure to also tell her how you dosed a rouster *and* a rube, you motherfucker. And don't you *ever* come into my home again without an invitation, or you'll regret it, you shit-bastard."

Jed recognized the threat was real, made even more believable in its almost-whispered fury at close range, and clenched in the big man's iron grip. He smelled whiskey on CM's breath.

"I have no idea what you're talking about." He shook loose. Took three tries. The freak let him go on the third try, accompanied by a throaty growl.

No, he might not say anything to Madame—just yet.

❦

Billy twisted the wall switch until he heard the satisfying *clack*. The LEC's overhead lights blossomed into a warm yellow bath. Lengthening shadows from the dying dusk slanting in from the front windows disappeared like magic.

How'd we ever get along without electricity?

He plopped into his desk chair with a grin. Sophie's progress on the case landed him in a decent mood. Just then, two clumsy figures banged and clattered through the front door. A huge dark man in a below-the-knee hooded robe was... *barefoot?* He darn-near carried a semi-conscious little woman under one protective arm like a rolled-up carpet.

What in thee hell?

Then... he'd recognize those clunky black shoes anywhere.

Is that... **Sophie** *bundled under that blanket? Is that...* **blood?**

Shit-balls!

He jumped up. Rounded his desk like a madman. Accidentally swept a third of its contents onto the floor as he thundered around it.

His arms flailed like he was a salmon swimming upstream. Charged the pair of figures before the man even closed the front door.

"What the fu—? Who're you?"

"Don't matter, man. Miss Sophie needs help. She told me to bring her here."

"What's wrong with her?"

"Drugged, Sheriff. You gotta help her. She's good people."

"Shut the hell up. Let go. I got her. You sit. There. We'll talk. Is she... bleeding?" He choked out this last word with bile rising in his throat that he didn't bother swallowing. Just spit sideways like a salivating wolf on the scent.

"Not hers. The rouster who brought her into my tent stabbed himself in the thigh to keep focus long enough to get her out of harm's way. Brave kid, that little shit, Josh."

With a noisy sigh of relief, Billy guided Sophie down into his guest chair. Looked into her eyes. Pin-prick pupils. Dazed. He gripped her shoulders as he kneeled in front of her. He whispered, "What's the matter, Soph? What happened?"

"He sneethed. I jus' said, 'Geshundheith!' But he said nothing after. Jus' walked away. Billy? *Billy!* You were always a handsome man. Poor Alice. Sorry.... My hip. My back. Burning. I just love your hair, Billy...." She reached up to touch his cheek. He backed away, guiding her hand back down to her lap. Pushed the blanket back to see if there was any blood or visible signs of injury.

CM TOWERED OVER BILLY, AND OUTWEIGHED HIM BY AT LEAST thirty pounds of grizzle, but when the sheriff came at him, CM feared for his life.

"What the fuck have you done to her? You'd better talk right now, mister, or *I will beat you to a bloody pulp with the butt of my gun right here, right now. You feel me, you fuckin' freak?*"

CM realized this hick sheriff cared a great deal for Miss Sophie. He let the guy shake him by his cinched robe. Looked down into those ferocious eyes. He understood this kind of madness. Respected it.

Kept his arms raised and hands open. Waited for the worst of the adrenaline-fueled delirium to pass before rumbling in a quiet voice.

"Sheriff, it wasn't me. But I can tell you who did this. To Miss Sophie *and* to one of my *other* friends, too. If I'm right, she's in no danger," he nodded toward Sophie, "just groggy, and open to suggestion. Seems my little friend caught the worst of it by throwing his body in front of hers. I'll tell you everything. But first, you let go of me. Right now." He suppressed his own rage, not as much at this guy who also cared for Miss Sophie, but at the brilliant flame that *needed* to burn that asshole, Jed Strain, to ashes.

The sheriff let go of CM's robe with a jerk. He planted his right hand on the butt of his service weapon as he stepped back, pointed to a chair, waited for CM to sit down before he returned to Miss Sophie. Never took his eyes off of CM as he huffed through his flaring nostrils.

Sophie's head had sagged. She was falling asleep in the hard chair, heading toward an unpleasant encounter with the even harder floor. Billy kept one eye on CM as he carried her into cell number one. He laid her with care onto its cot, and tugged down on the hem of her dress that had ridden up. Covered her with a wool blanket. Returned to his suspect.

Billy sat on his desk. He needed to keep his gun hand free. He said, "Okay, talk."

⬥

AFTER CM TOLD HIM WHO HE WAS AND SUMMARIZED THE CHAIN OF events as he knew them, Billy softened. "Okay, let's say I'm inclined to believe you. I've met Jed, and didn't much cotton ta him from the get-go. If what you say is true, Mr. CM—"

"Just CM, Sheriff,"

"Fine. If what you say is true, I am in your debt for taking care of Sophie. She told me you've been helpful in our investigation. We appreciate that. Now why would this son-of-a-motherless-goat drug Sophie and your friend?"

"Ya gotta understand, Sheriff. We're all takin' a risk just talkin' to an outsider like Sophie, and you. Jed is kind of our own sheriff, and we got different rules than out here. He pulls a lot of sway with Madame. But seein' as most of us cared for Babbo, and Miss Sophie is a friend of Sister's, we took a chance when folks started turnin' up dead. But now this...," silent tears started to roll down this big lug's scarred cheeks, "I just don't give a shit no more. Attackin' Miss Sophie? And little Josh? Fuck the job and all the rest. I just can't risk Jed now takin' it out on my wives. And if he finds out Sister's been helpin' y'all? She's in danger too. Maybe he already knows. How can you help, Sheriff?"

Sophie had explained how this guy was married to a two-headed girl, as unbelievable as that was. The man cared for his... wives. And his friends. He thought of Sophie as one, too. And he and this other fella *had* rescued her. Billy didn't know what this visit might cost this guy, but it was sure to be a lot.

"Where can I find this prick, CM?"

"I'll show you. But keep your distance. You get close, this asshole's got tricks." He glanced over at unconscious Sophie in cell number one.

BILLY CALLED DWIGHT OFF PATROL TO WATCH OVER SOPHIE. GAVE him the short version. She'd been drugged, and he was to let her sleep in her cell. Told him to call Doc Gus to check her out ASAP. Explained that he had show business to attend to. Dwight demanded to come along. But Billy wasn't sure he even trusted himself at that moment.

"Damn it, Dwight, I need somebody I trust to watch over Sophie and to get the doc over here. No tellin' what else could happen if they think she's some kind a threat. You read me, soldier?"

"Okay, Billy. But you call if you need help. I'm two minutes out. I'll call the doc."

LESS THAN A MINUTE LATER AT THE LEC'S FRONT DOOR, DWIGHT met his boss flying out with a big circus freak in tow. He panicked when he saw Billy's eyes—twitching, glaring, not focused. Not since the Argonne had he seen that crazy-eyed mania, not even last summer when they were locked in mortal combat with that small army of Chicago mobsters.

With those thoughts muddying his thinking, Dwight got on the phone to Doc Gus in Spencer, who asked a few questions about Sophie's condition. Said he'd come right over.

They'd call her husband, Jake, once things settled down. That was sure to be exciting.

❧ 65 ❧

❧

Even though they were only seven blocks from that gypsy circus at the county fairgrounds, Billy stuffed the half-naked crocodile man into his cruiser. The huge lug had to hunch over. His head still rubbed against the cruiser's headliner.

Right now, Billy wanted some metal and glass around the both of them. Besides, walking down Main Street on a cold Iowa night toting a shotgun with a barefoot negro freak in tow? Sounded too much like the opening line for a terrible joke headed for a disastrous punch line.

BASED ON CM'S INSTRUCTIONS, BILLY DROVE TO THE SIDE OF THE fairgrounds opposite the show's main gate on an "authorized use only" access road. Only five hundred yards south of where Tama Street intersected Main. A plowed-under field of corn stalks lay on their left. And the only obstacle between them and the rear edge of the back lot to their right was a sagging four-foot lath-and-wire fence. It was loose from years of weather and neglect.

After Billy retrieved his twelve-gauge and a belt of shells from his cruiser's trunk, he closed its lid. A few steps later, they shoved that fence flat enough to step over it with little effort. So much for security. CM led him to the back of Jed's tent. Distracted by the sound of muffled voices coming from inside, there was no mistaking the louder voice they heard from behind. "Hands up, assholes, or I ventilate your spines."

Billy recognized the subdued snick of two hammers being thumbed back on a double-barrel. They did as they were told after Billy laid his own shotgun and ammo belt in the knee-high weeds without being asked. He felt a hand unsnap his holster strap and lift out his thirty-eight as the double-barrel pressed harder into his lower back.

"Walk." They were being guided to Jed's tent entrance. Four men stood inside talking in a crowded cluster—Jed and three huge rousters.

Jed turned on his good heel and said, "Well, looky here. An outsider and a freak. What're you two love birds doin' skulkin' around my back lot? Boys, what are we to do with a couple of interlopers like this?" A few snide chuckles suggested grim prospects for their near future.

Billy stood there, glaring at Jed, the low-down bastard that drugged *his* Sophie. If he lost control of his emotions now, this would not end well for anybody. He let CM take the lead.

❧

CM SAID, "BOYS, OLE JED HERE DOSED LITTLE JOSH *AND A RUBE* with the breath tonight. That what you call stupid, or what? Bringing outside law down on all of us?" He nodded toward Billy. "And they know we're here. Cuz this man *is* the law, and more of 'em are on the way. What the hell were you thinkin', you dumb shit?" He crinkled his eyes toward Jed like he couldn't believe the man would do something that idiotic. At the same time, his bluster felt forced.

Jed snickered. "The freak speaks. What he didn't tell ya, boys, was that CM here and a few other freaks been talkin' to *outsiders* behind Madame's back."

CM trembled with outrage. "And what you been doin', Jed? You also dose brother Garth, you fuckin' snake. He wasn't no freak. Did you also have somethin' to do with little Babbo's killin' too." CM glanced with deliberation at the other three boys in front of him. Ignored the bruiser behind him. Babbo played cards and cut jackies with most of these boys. Mention of Babbo caught their attention. They stopped smiling.

One bruiser named Strike stood to Jed's right. He crinkled his nose, looked down, flicked a wooden match clamped in his teeth from one corner of his mouth to the other with the tip of his deft tongue. He glanced sideways over at Jed. "That true, Jed?"

"A course not. Garth got his own self in trouble with a curse that backfired. Everybody knows that. But there ain't *no* excuse for—"

Strike would not let this go. "Nightshade's kind a your thing, though, ain't it, Jed? Would explain ole Garth runnin' hisself right off the road in broad daylight. Why he was runnin' scared. That shit makes ya scared a most everything, don't it? Now ya did another rouster with that shit tonight with little Josh? Did ya dose little Josh, Jed? Did ya do little Babbo, too?" Strike and the man standing to *his* right both turned away from CM and Billy to square off with Jed to await his answer.

"Boys, we're here to deal with this outsider and this here freak. Now—"

"I didn't hear no answer there, Jed. *Did ya dose Josh?*"

"Well, yeah, I did, but—"

"Did you dose Garth?"

"Already told ya. I din't do that."

"Well, who did, goddammit?" The huge man called Strike who towered over Jed had become agitated with creeping doubt. Spit out his perfectly good match, and stared Jed down. "Now don't give me any a that curse bullshit. And I don't care how close you are to the boss lady. We're family. You answer me, Jed."

"Strike, you can kiss my ass. Now, are we gonna deal with the business at hand, or—"

It happened in a blur. Strike's slab of a right cross slammed into Jed's jaw. He went down like a sloppy-wet side of beef thrown onto the steel saw conveyor in a slaughterhouse. Back-flopped onto a folding table that crumpled. On the way down, the back of Jed's head struck the only light in the tent, a coal-oil lantern that hung low overhead. It now swung wildly, flinging bizarre shadows in every direction. The lantern started smoking from the commotion. It stunk.

Strike looked the other two rousters in the eye. Then he glanced toward the rouster who held the shotgun pointed at CM and Billy. "Lower your blunderbuss there, Jax. We gotta sort this out, and we ain't goin' ta war with the local law over this. Not just yet, anyway. Give the man back his piece. Sheriff, what do you know about all this?"

❧

BILLY WATCHED THIS ARTFUL DE-ESCALATION. TOOK HIS GUN BACK. Nodded at the man called Jax, holstered his piece and snapped its retaining strap. Sent the signal he wasn't planning to draw it any time soon. Jed still sprawled on the ground on top of the collapsed table.

The sheriff said, "First, Jed, you stay down til I say otherwise." He noticed Jed wore a skull ring on the hand that he now rubbed his jaw with—*his left hand.* "Mister Strike, I was the one following Mister Nitstone when he rolled his truck. He was drivin' real crazy and crashed hard, like he was real drunk or drugged up. I come up on his body right after he crashed. But I din't smell no booze on him or in his truck. He had to be drugged. Tonight, one of my dear friends—a *lady* —was drugged by *him,* along with your friend."

Billy spit out the accusation as he bobbed his chin down toward Jed. Though the lamp swung less, it still tossed smoky shadows around. Jed still rubbed his chin and nursed his now-bleeding nose. "CM here brought her to my office at her request. She's a friend of your seer—"

"A friend a little Sister's?" Strike turned from staring down at Jed to look surprised at Billy.

"That's right. CM, tell these boys what you saw tonight."

"Well, me and Tam and Tare was mindin' our own business in our tent when Josh and Sister's friend come stumblin' in. Josh said Jed dosed 'em both with the breath. Stabbed himself in the damn leg to stay straight long enough to escape. And Strike, the sheriff's friend done been touched by the polio, just like our little Sister. Ain't right, man. Ain't right a'tall—outsider or not."

Billy added, "By the way, boys, just so's you know, Happy Grant was also actin' crazy enough to attack my deputies with a weapon before one of 'em shot him defending themselves. Now, whatever you thought a old Happy, our doc thinks he might a been dosed with the same kind a drug.

"And here's a real kicker for ya. See that ring on Jed's left hand, right there?" Billy pointed at Jed's hand, still rubbing his jaw with it. "Garth was wearin' a ring *just like that one* when I come up on him dead after his so-called accident. Our medical examiner found a small skull-shaped bruise on Happy's forehead same as that ring. Probably what killed him—made the inside a his brain bleed real bad. My deputy's bullets just sped up the dyin' process, I'm told. Doc also says the killer was likely left-handed. Jed's left-handed. Now what does that tell ya, boys?"

One of the other men knelt down and grabbed Jed's hand to check out that ring. "Hey, this here *is* Garth's ring! Bent up some. He made somethin' of a big deal of it a time or two. Called it his *Death's Head ring*. Part a his magic schtick, he said." Now all eyes cast unspoken accusations toward old Jed whose eyes now darted with fury and fear. He looked nobody in the eye.

Billy said, "Just so's ya also know, somebody broke into the morgue over ta Spencer the day after Garth's "accident" and stole that ring. Not too smart takin' a trophy like that, Jed. Not too smart at all. What'd ya do? Follow me chasin' Garth, and then follow the ambulance over ta the morgue? I got a witness says ya did."

Strike scratched his chin, rubbed the top of his stubbled head with the same hand, snarled down at Jed, looked at the other three boys. All of 'em gave him a subtle nod.

"Sheriff, what you wanna do, man?"

Billy didn't tell these rough men what he *wanted* to do. He told them what he was *going* to do. "I'm takin' Jed here into custody for assault, and possibly for two counts of attempted murder, maybe murder, too. I'll overlook what I could call kidnappin' of me and CM here at gun point in the interest a servin' justice. You alright with that, boys?" He already knew it was based on the nods, but maybe more cooperation would be forthcoming with a little give-and-take.

Strike spoke for the group. "Sure 'nuff, Sheriff. Meanwhile, I'm fixin' to have a sit-down with Madame. This shit's gone on long enough." Then he surprised Billy and his fellow rousters by wheeling around to face Jed, still on his back, now propped up on his elbows. He spit at the man's bloody face—explosively. Said to Jed, "Josh is a good shit, you asshole. I didn't much care for Garth, but he was one of us. And if you also done that asshole clown, well, he was still part of Madame Purgatory's family. But if you done little Babbo too, ain't no hole dark enough. We done put up with your bullshit long enough. Adios, *amigo*. Hope you rot in a Hell a yer own makin', you weasel." He turned away from Jed.

As an afterthought, he turned back and booted Jed between his spread-out legs.

A surprised Billy hauled a now-howling and bleeding Jed up vertical enough to slap on a pair of cuffs behind his back. CM offered a small nod to Strike, who didn't respond. He followed Billy out to escort him and Jed back to his cruiser.

Just in case.

66

Both Jake Hardt and his cousin Walt Weller drove like demons chased them up to Rock Rapids to fetch Sophie. Both were fit to be tied. They wanted blood. Might as well be Billy's for allowing her to get hurt.

When they arrived at the LEC, they parked the farm truck right out front, one tire up on the boardwalk, and charged through the door like an invading army.

BILLY AND DWIGHT STOOD CHATTING IN THE CENTER OF THE SQUAD room. They both turned at the sudden ruckus, both reaching for their holsters, until they recognized Sophie's husband and his cousin. But then Billy grew concerned by their crimson expressions—blood lust. He held his arms out straight in front of them to slow them down.

"Now, boys, she's sleeping just fine. I suggest you keep your voices low, okay?"

Jake walked with a swift pace up to within three inches of Billy's face and seethed, "How *dare* you put my Sophie at risk, Billy? There is no excuse on God's green earth that justifies what happened to that poor girl. Now what do you have to say for yourself before I force you to put me in the cell next to her, mister?"

"Jake, you are one-hundred percent right. There ain't no excuse. You wanna take a swing at me? You get a free one if—"

Jake backed off a step. Rounded a hay-maker that cracked off the left side of Billy's jaw like a two-by-four slapping the rump of a hog. Billy's head jerked, and his torso wobbled, but he kept his feet. Cousin Walt was about to join the fracas. With his eyes wide, Billy held his arm out straight toward his deputy—stopped Dwight from charging in to tackle Jake. Walt froze.

Billy rubbed his jaw, steadied himself, wiped a dribble of blood from the left corner of his mouth, his teeth tinged pink. Smacked his lips to assess the damage. Said, "I guess I deserved that. No more free shots, though. That one hurt. Now let me ask you somethin', Jake. Why didn't you keep your wife at home during this whole affair?"

Now nursing his knuckles, bruised and raising blood welts, Jake had cooled down and said, "Cuz Sophie's got a mind of her own."

Billy grinned—pink teeth and all—despite shifting his jaw back and forth to make sure nothing was broken, and said, "Exactly. I'm thinkin' maybe you owe some a that energy toward your bride, pardner. Now, you wanna check on your wife, or not?"

"Aw, shit, Billy, I couldn't see nothin' but red when I heard somebody attacked Sophie."

"It's okay, Jake. Now go tend to your wife. I already shipped out the man who attacked her down to Fort Madison. Turns out he'll face federal charges too. Plus, no way I wanted him here when you came to pick up your bride."

Billy grinned again. Slapped Jake on the shoulder. "C'mon, pardner. Doc Gus says she just needs to sleep it off. But I'll warn ya right now. The stuff that circus creep blew into her face? She got a low dose, but it was enough to act like a truth drug. She's bein' real honest when she ain't dozin'. I suggest ya don't ask her no questions you don't want the answers to."

"No shit?"

"No shit, Jake."

"Golly. Okay, I'll try to keep her home."

"Good luck with that, son."

AFTER JAKE AND COUSIN WALT TRUNDLED SOPHIE OFF DOWN MAIN in their truck with her wedged between them, Billy looked at Dwight and nodded. Dwight went out the LEC's alley door. A minute later, he and Jimmy ushered Jed Strain in and deposited him back in the cell just vacated by Sophie. They had anticipated the boys' visit to pick up Sophie.

Billy said, "Better 'n Jake and Walt goin' off on this criminal, right? And the bus to Fort Madison won't get here til midday tomorrow."

"Nope, good call, boss."

Jimmy said with pride, "And he didn't give me any trouble at all, Sheriff."

Smiles all around. Except for Jed.

***

67

CM had passed a message to Josh at Billy's request, asking him to head over to the LEC for a chat the morning after Jed's attack. They now sat facing each other across the desk in the fish tank.

Billy said, "You sleep that shit off, okay, pardner?"

"Yeah, no problem. Headache and Hellish dry mouth is all, Sheriff."

Josh looked like a cat perched on the sharp rim of a bucket of ice water. A bandage wrapped his right thigh over his dungarees, like he never took them off. He glanced over his right shoulder at Jed curled up on the bunk facing the back wall of cell number one. The cell farthest from where they sat was still in full view. Billy made a mental note to get some blinds installed in the fish tank windows.

"Josh, you want our doc to peek at the front of your leg?"

"Naw, it's fine." To reinforce his claim, he slapped the *side* of his leg, and almost didn't wince at all.

"Say, I need to ask you myself about Jed's attack, but first, I wanted to thank you face-to-face for takin' care a our Miss Sophie. She means a lot to folks around here, including me."

"Hey, Sheriff, I get it. Haven't known her very long. She's a nice lady, and I like her, too. But she don't take no shit from nobody."

"Yeah. Anyway, I wanted to check your version of what happened when Jed first approached the two of you in the back lot. Already talked with CM. Can you help me, Josh?"

"Sure. I was walkin' Miss Sophie back to her car from the ringmaster's bunk tent. She done talked ta him about what happened to Babbo. Had my left arm hooked into Miss Sophie's right arm. The one with her bad hand."

"Yeah, Josh, I know."

"Okay, well, I seen Jed comin' toward us, but I didn't want to get into it with him, me walkin' close-like with an outsider. He looked to pass us a good ten feet distant, off to our left. Had me head lowered enough to hide me face with the brim of me hat. Then he made a bee-line for us.

"Raised his left fist, Sheriff. Thought he aimed to punch Miss Sophie. She woulda been between us. I jumped in front of her, to take a blow. Then I saw the dust comin' at us. Kind of a white puff. Had a pretty good idea what it was. And Jed said real loud, 'Run—' and I hollered right back at him, swung my arms down.

"I missed him, but I think I shook him up some cuz he walked away. I started gettin' real confused. The breath'll do that, they say, but that was the first time I...." He fell silent, remembering. Started to glance toward Jed's cell, but then didn't.

Billy said, "That's real good rememberin', Josh. And that jibes with what Jed said. Once we got him in here," Billy nodded over to cell number one, "he cracked like a rotten melon. Said he was gonna command you to 'Run from the fire! It's everywhere!' If he'd a gotten that out, might a put you both in real danger with the power a that suggestion, maybe with y'all hallucinatin'? Dunno. Our doc says that stuff makes ya *suggestible*. Instead, you got the both a you to safety, Josh. You're a hero, son."

The kid blushed, and just said, "Not sure about that, but man, did I have the strongest urge to run—anywhere—after gettin' a snoot full a that powder. Glad Miss Sophie's okay. Sheriff, can I go now? Sittin' this long in a cop's office? Startin' to break out in the hives!" He smiled. Got up and left without another word. Billy just smiled after him.

᠌᠍⚜᠍

JED STRAIN WOULD SOON BE PLACED IN CUSTODY AT THE FBI FIELD office in Omaha, courtesy of Agents Sam Ellis and Lang Eubanks. But for now, they would keep him in the Iowa State Penitentiary in Fort Madison, awaiting arraignment on current charges.

Dwight and Jimmy found a potted flower in Jed's tent called an "Angel's Trumpet." He had it surrounded by two coal-oil lanterns to keep this deadly tropical plant alive and thriving, even in the chilly Iowa air.

Doc Gus's research found this plant to be the source of a substance called scopolamine, from which the drug burandanga, or devil's breath, is derived. Jed claimed he used it to treat his asthma. While Doc confirmed scopolamine is used for that purpose—with *very* low doses, among other uses—when the prison physician examined Jed, he found no evidence of asthma.

Due to the circumstantial nature of the evidence against Jed for the murder of Garth Nitstone, the county attorney was less optimistic for a conviction. But the two assault charges for drugging Josh and Sophie with a dangerous substance? Plus, the evidentiary proof placing him on the scene of Happy Grant's death? And the probability of Jed having delivered the death blow to his head?

Together, all this would send him away for quite a few years, if not life. Possibly even to the noose, even before the feds got their hooks into him for what they said were *undisclosed offenses in other states.*

68

If only Babbo's murder were as clear-cut a case. Madame Perlatelli cooperated fully and ensured all within the show would, as well. Much of the fear of Madame's reputation within the troupe had been churned up by proxy—by Jed—not by her.

But they found no compelling motive for Jed Strain to have killed Babbo. A very different kind of crime, Babbo's murder presented a different method, murder weapon, and body disposal.

Also, Jed's alibi for the night of Friday, April 6 through early the next morning held solid. Several roustabouts either played cards most of the night with him, or he was in view of them in his bunk. There was also no circus transportation unaccounted for and available to move Babbo's body.

Billy, Dwight and Sophie all agreed this just had to be a different killer based on the evidence. But who? CM and his wives were each other's alibis. Now, both Sophie and Billy found it impossible believe they were killers, despite CM's anger issues. And the money CM owed Babbo was not enough to be an obvious motive for this brutal murder.

Besides, it had been too... personal. Happy Grant was now dead, and the guy was a sexual predator, not a murderer.

While a psychopath, Milo Vladinov, the other clown from the show, was on a suicide watch due to excessive self-medication the Friday night Babbo's murder took place. According to his bunkmate, the man was in an opiate stupor from eight PM until at least six the next morning. Even then he could barely lift his head off his pillow. No way he could have hoisted a hundred-pound corpse into a vehicle and driven a forty-mile round trip to dispose of it, at night, no less. Even if he had access to a vehicle, which he did not. Milo didn't even have a driver's license. Madame said he tried to drive a show truck once and failed miserably. He was not their man, either.

While Sophie had not interviewed every possible suspect, their best suspect for Babbo's murder—Garth Nitstone—had the best alibi of all. He was already dead.

⊗⊰⊗

IT WAS TIME TO CAST A WIDER NET. COULD BABBO'S KILLER BE someone from the local community, as Madame had already suggested? But who? And why?

Dwight recommended they search for any and all possible connections. He said, "Babbo's body was dumped in the same place as your deputy a year ago. That suggests local knowledge from that time, not a member of the circus, even though we still have no idea *why* he was dumped there."

Billy scratched his head as he tapped a pencil on his desk with his other hand. "Could be a coincidence, but not likely. Okay, what else?" His insistent tapping continued.

"You said the snake lady admitted they were off their normal seasonal route, that they don't play towns this small. Not enough customers. Then, why Lyon County? Why Rock Rapids? And why now?"

"Let's go ask her." Not that Billy was looking for an excuse to be in the snake lady's presence again. Much.

Once more, they crowded into Madame's office wagon. She sat

behind her desk in a slinky white tunic and skin-tight trousers (trousers!) under knee-high riding boots. Dwight and Billy crowded together onto the small sofa. They both craned their necks to their right, to where she sat. Billy was once more distracted by everything about the lady, as if under a spell. Dwight asked the questions.

"So, Madame, why did you come to our town? You told the sheriff you decided to hit smaller towns like Rock Rapids, but why?"

"That is no mystery, Diputado." She pronounced it *DEE-poo-TAH-doe*. "Times, they are muy difícil—very difficult. The few shows still touring have had to go to the more, ah, under-served areas, the smaller communities."

"But *specifically,* why Rock Rapids?"

"Well, we need the space and structure of a county fairground. In your county, that is here." She tapped her slender index finger on her desktop, not with impatience, but to emphasize her point. Dwight had never seen a woman who wore one or more rings on every single finger, *and* both thumbs.

"But again, *why Lyon County?*"

"Oh, well, let me see. Ah, yes, I had more than one discussion with little Babbo about our route. He was very clever about such things. Although I now find I regret giving his suggestion as much weight as I did."

A light bulb slowly illuminated in Dwight's mind. "So you came here because Babbo thought it was a good idea?"

"Sí. Boy's Town, Sioux City and here, to begin our Midwest season. He can be quite convincing. And I saw no reason to disagree, given our, ah, circumstances."

"Did Babbo know somebody here?"

"This I cannot say, Diputado, but when he talked of your village, a dreamy look captured his face, as if... no sé—I do not know. It seemed like he was... coming home."

"Billy, that's gotta be it. Babbo was here in Rock Rapids because he knows somebody here. Odds are that's where we find our next clue, and that could lead us to a motive. Thanks, Madame.

"Let's go, Billy.... Billy!"

"Ah, yep, let's go. Thanks, Madame."

69

B ack at the LEC, Dwight needed to say something as they walked in, side by side. "Man, you got it bad, Billy. You were damn near drooling over that snake lady. What *is* the deal?"

"Look, brother, we'll get the job done, between the two of us, anyway. For the first time in sixteen years, I'm feeling, well, different. I know that's corny, and it ain't no excuse, but let me have this without bustin' my chops over it. Now, dad-blame-it, let's move on, *okay?*"

Dwight busted out in a crazy grin, chortled, and slapped his brother-in-arms hard enough on the shoulder to cause him a wince in pain, or embarrassment. Then Dwight said, "Look, if you feel that way, you need to say something to the lady, sooner or later. And since she personally has a rock-solid alibi for the little guy's death window, she's no longer a suspect. But your chances of doing something about your feelings are gonna evaporate pretty soon. Just saying."

"Thanks, pardner. Now, the case, if ya please." They sauntered over to Billy's desk. Both plopped down, more from frustration than fatigue. But now they had something to go on.

Billy's excitement grew. "Didn't Sophie say she learned from that seer that Babbo was from New Jersey? Let's dig into that. Anyone in Rock Rapids from there? Or spent time there? Hey! Wait a minute! Didn't our esteemed mayor go to Princeton? Ain't that in New Jersey?"

All of a sudden, Dwight looked a little peaked. "Shit, man, we're not saying the mayor is our killer, are we? Good gravy...."

"Yeah, I reckon that would be a barrel a booger snot, alright." They both fell silent, lost in a dangerous reverie. Billy continued, "But that would make a whole lotta sense. He's a public figure. Name's in the paper more often than not. He spent a few years in Jersey about twenty years ago. Sumbitch! Babbo was about twenty... you don't think —D, could the mayor be Babbo's daddy? Cripes, just pursuin' that *possibility's* gonna suck rotten eggs. This might be a wild goose chase, and could really hurt the mayor's reputation, even if it ain't true. Okay, we gotta be real careful here. Agree?"

"So how do we go about this, Billy?" Dwight looked worried, not for himself, but for his friend. This was dynamite with a short fuse close to a flame. What he wasn't saying—if they screw this up, Billy'd be voted out of a job, for sure. Or worse.

Dwight said, "How about we first verify from public records the exact time that Deemers was at Princeton. I can study his bio. I gotta imagine he's pretty proud of that part of his life. Good school, right?"

Billy said, "So what are we sayin'? That somehow, Babbo finds out who his real daddy is, comes to town, confronts the mayor, who decides to make an embarrassin' episode from his past disappear? That would be especially bad since the kid is a carny freak. Wait! Sister told Sophie that she is Babbo's twin. That makes her part of the problem, too."

"Only if Deemers knows that." Dwight referred to his notes. "Remember, Sister also said... yeah, here it is. She said, 'Yes, he is—was —my twin brother. I do not believe even he knew that.' Now, if Babbo didn't know she was his sister, maybe Deemers—or whoever—doesn't either. All the same, we should recommend Madame assign somebody to keep a close eye on Sister until we figure this out."

They shared hopeful looks, but then both faces fell again. Billy knew this was a long shot, but it was their only lead. He said, "Lots a folks live in New Jersey. How do we put Deemers and Babbo's momma in the same place twenty years ago, for cryin' out loud?"

Dwight had worked a few cold cases in Minneapolis Homicide. He said, "First things first. Let's verify the dates Deemers was in Princeton, New Jersey. Then we ask Madame if she knows of any birth records for Babbo or Sister. If not, and I hate to say this, we may need Sophie to talk to her friend, the fortune teller, at least one more time. Jake's gonna toot crapola. But if we got a murderer living in our town...."

Billy started tapping his pencil again. "Listen, I might take a hit for this, but, well, it's part of the cotton-pickin' job."

The next afternoon, Dwight and Billy reconvened. Dwight reported first. "Okay, I found Deemers' detailed biography on file with the elections office. He attended Princeton from September 1914 to June 1918, which was just five months before the end of the war.

"The guy was a damn saint, if you believe his bio, even though he didn't enlist. Didn't say why. Even stayed in the town of Princeton over summer breaks, volunteering at soup kitchens and homeless shelters in the area. If Babbo was between the ages of fifteen and twenty, that's our window of coincidence."

Billy's eyes brightened. "Turns out that Sister says she and her brother are nineteen. Now that's a solid start, Deputy.'

70

❧

J ake allowed Sophie to talk to Sister one more time, but only if he could help her walk—she was in some pain—and stand guard outside the seer's tent. And that's exactly what he did.

Sophie learned that through all of Sister's travels, one of her most treasured possessions stayed with her—a birth certificate. She didn't have Babbo's, though. New Jersey issues one for each twin, but she had no idea what happened to her brother's.

❧

BACK AT THE LEC, DWIGHT SOUNDED HOPEFUL. "WE NOW KNOW three more things. First, the twins' actual date of birth was December 13, 1915. Second, the father's name on their birth certificate was listed as 'unknown.'"

Dwight smiled. "Cold case rule: we use research to confirm our hypothesis until it no longer fits. Guess what? Nothing we've discovered relative to our working hypothesis eliminates it as a genuine possibility. The twins' ages fit our mayor's timeline at Princeton. The father is officially unknown which does not eliminate the mayor. And Sister's birth certificate confirms the kids were born in the same city as the mayor's place of residence at the time of their birth. Still not proof, but—"

Billy interrupted, "Yes, we need something more solid. What's next?"

Dwight said, "Well, let's see if the mayor has an alibi for our murder window."

Jimmy Lenert sauntered in from his patrol shift. "Hi, guys. What're you workin' on?"

Billy looked just a little startled at his appearance. "Oh, just chewin' the fat." The sheriff was still worried about Jimmy's state of mind. The shooting less than a week ago just had to be on Jimmy's mind even though Doc Gus said Grant was already dying from a lethal blow to the head minutes earlier. Because he remained concerned, and to deflect the conversation away from their treating the mayor like a murder suspect, Billy asked, "Jimmy, you doin' okay?"

Dwight chimed in. "Yeah, man, any time you wanna talk, we're here for you, brother."

"Thanks, guys. I *am* thinking a lot about that, but this is part of the job, and I really like being a deputy. Appreciate the offer. I'm good for now. End of shift. Okay if I head home, boss?"

Billy smiled and said, "You betcha, little brother. See ya in the mornin'."

Yeah, the kid would be okay.

He hoped.

May 2, 1934

THE FOLLOWING MORNING, DWIGHT AND BILLY PUT THEIR HEADS together again over Billy's desk at the LEC. His tabletop lamp with its green glass shade thrust the front of their faces into a bright pool of hooded yellow light. Overhead lights burned too, but could not compete with that desk lamp. Jimmy walked in at sunrise. He had requested a double shift, and Billy would not object, budget be damned.

Jimmy hooked his thumbs in his equipment belt and strolled over. "You guys didn't pull an all-nighter, did ya?"

Billy croaked, "Nah," with his best casual expression as he straightened a short stack of papers like he was just tidying up. But Jimmy's nose twitched.

He said, "Okay, you guys are working on something, and you don't want me involved. That's fine. Don't worry. I'm not gonna to butt in. Want some coffee?"

Dwight said, "Sure, kid. Just don't burn it this time, okay?" That was a joke. It wasn't cop coffee *until* it was burned.

As Jimmy backed away to build the morning brew, an unsolicited visit to the LEC by Madame Antonia Perlatelli startled all three men. As the early morning's gauzy rays cast her in an unmistakable silhouette—a slender woman in tight trousers—she made what the boys all felt was a theatrical entrance. Billy assumed that was an occupational hazard. She filled the LEC with not only her presence, but her scent. What *was* that? It telegraphed *exotic allure*.

Dwight observed Billy's now-expected transformation from an efficient law enforcement officer to a near-bumbling boy infatuated with a playground schoolmate. He took the lead. "Madame, an unexpected pleasure. To what do we owe—"

"I'd like to speak in private," she cast her eyes around the squad room, "with the sheriff, por favór." She slapped a set of thin leather gloves in her right hand against her left palm. Even though she wore a long-sleeved tunic, Dwight spotted colorful body art peeking out around her wrists.

Billy stood. He rounded his desk and said, "Of course. Please. The fish tank. That's what we, um, call that glass-walled office over yonder." He waved toward the back corner enclosure they seldom used. Except for private conversations. Next to the two bolt-in cells, the fish tank was also where Doc Gus roosted when they needed an in-house medical or forensic consultation.

She led the way. Dwight looked over at Jimmy, whose jaw had dropped, and glanced back toward Dwight just in time to catch him wink.

෧෯෨

BILLY SAT ON THE CORNER OF THE SMALL DESK, SWINGING ONE LEG. She remained standing. He said, "How can I help?"

Madame wore a contrite expression. "It is awkward, Billy," (his name still came out BEE-lee), "but a witness to little Babbo's murder has just come forward."

Billy snapped out of his fantasizing with a full-body spasm and said, "What? Now? Who?"

"First, I have offered assurances to this person that I will protect them."

Now Billy's dander bristled. "Look, it's been more 'n three weeks since Babbo's murder. Why didn't this... person... come forward sooner? And what makes you think you should make promises you can't keep?"

Maybe this is the witness Sophie said would—must—come forward on their own.

"Billy, do you wish to hear this or not? This person feared for their life when they thought Babbo's killer was Jed. Now that bastardo is in custody for his other crimes. That danger is gone. You see?"

"Okay, fine. Who is this person, and what did *they* witness?" Billy's shoulders slumped as if he had been out-maneuvered by this damnable woman yet again—head of the snake. He needed a clue!

Why can't she just be what she appears to be?

"You know of her. She was Babbo's ser querido—the love of his young life. Lilith Smalley knew of Babbo's habits. That he walked the midway most midnights. To clear his complex mind. She was to surprise him. But when she approached, she saw a man."

Bingo! "Tall, handsome, distinguished?"

"No, Billy. This man was short and dressed like a laborer, like one of my roustabouts, but not of our show."

This news crushed Billy. He thought for sure he'd just placed Mayor Harold Deemers at the scene of the crime. By now, they knew Babbo had been killed near the big cat cages in the animal menagerie not far from the show's front gate. Dwight had spotted an almost-invisible blood spatter on the under-carriage of the old lion's wagon when he followed his smelly-dung hunch.

Billy needed this witness. He shut up and listened. *Egad, this woman is a distraction. I bet the church ladies'd have words about them trousers. Yessir. And that perfume, or whatever in thee hell it is!*

"So, where did Lilith see this man?"

"Hiding behind the cage of our lion. We call him King. Before little Lilith could approach Babbo, this man, he crept out from behind

King's cage and struck poor Babbo from behind. He fell. Knowing she could do nothing, she kept as quiet as her sudden grief allowed. At least the monkeys chattering and the wind whistling were louder than her sobbing.

"She watched the man hoist Babbo over his shoulder and carry him through the gate. To a truck. That is all she told me, Billy. Can you protect her?"

"I can only promise that we can take her into protective custody, or have someone keep an eye on her for a few days. Good enough?"

"Sí. That is good. I wish this matter to be resolved as soon as possible. Can you assign one of your deputies to protect the Lilith and Tom Smalley?"

"Yes, but I need to talk to this Lilith."

"Of course. She waits in my truck outside. With Josh. He will also protect her. We will take no chances."

72

L ilith Smalley was *way* out of her element. Her fear almost paralyzed her. But despite her acute anxiety, she remained resolute, even from within her despair. She would seek justice for her dear Babbo. With Madame's help.

Not even three feet tall, the giant's world presented countless challenges. Kind Josh lifted her into the sheriff's guest chair. Josh would never allow her to suffer the indignity of crawling up like a child.

Her short stature could not diminish her youthful beauty and grace. Almost hypnotic, like a perfect little lady. Her tasteful dress, all her clothes and accessories, were of the highest fashion of the day.

"MISS SMALLEY, MAY I CALL YOU LILITH?" BILLY COULDN'T HELP BUT imagine how unlikely a couple she and Babbo must have been.

"Of course. I will do *anything* to help capture my poor, brave Babbo's killer." Her lower lip quivered. She crossed her perfect legs. They dangled as she perched upright on the forward edge of the massive chair. She straightened the fabric of her dress. Removed her white gloves and clutched them in pink-knuckled fists.

Billy wanted to get right to it, but first, he needed to establish this young woman's relationship with his victim. "You and Babbo were close." Not a question.

"As unlikely as you might imagine, Sheriff Kershaw, and as much as it distressed my father, Babbo was the love of my life. He was brave and clever. He worshipped me, and I adored his humanity, despite his many disadvantages. Babbo was a survivor, against *all* the odds. Yet, he was always gentle, even with those who would speak ill of him, or even do him harm. He possessed a marvelous sense of dry humor, and he was ever loyal to the show, to Madame, to me. Yes, Sheriff, I loved Babbo, with all of my heart."

"That kind of love is rare." And he meant it. He thought of Alice, and cast a meaningful glance toward Madame, who now sat perched in elegance on Dwight's guest chair that Josh had pulled over. Dwight now stood behind the two ladies. Billy got to the meat of the matter. "Madame tells me you saw who attacked Babbo. Can you tell me about that, Lilith?"

She crossed and re-crossed her shapely legs, encased in shiny silk stockings, and pointed downward her open-toed shoes as women of fashion often did to display their fancy painted toenails. Billy had seen pictures in Life Magazine at the barbershop.

Lilith retrieved a folded and pressed handkerchief from inside her left sleeve, but then did nothing with it, other than to wring it between her hands. Her now-wrinkled gloves lay ignored in her lap. She dropped her head and sobbed. As an afterthought, she retrieved the hanky, capturing her tears with dainty dabs.

Billy waited. He imagined the depth of her grief. It seemed genuine, despite her orchestrated body language. Madame placed a gentle hand on her tiny shoulder, and gave it a gentle squeeze. Madame whispered, "It's okay, Lilith. You do this for your Babbo. Justice must be served, no?"

Her eyes remained downcast, but she forged ahead in a soft voice. "Yes, of course. Um, from what I could see from the far side of Man Eater's cage—"

GK JURRENS

"Man Eater?"

"Oh, yes, he is our ancient tiger. His cage sat less than fifteen feet from King's cage—our lion. I hid around the corner of the closest concession stand. A small and very ordinary man in some sort of uniform... attacked... Babbo, from behind. He struck him on the head very hard. Babbo just fell straight down."

She paused. Billy waited. Then, she continued with a voice quivering in a sing-song cadence. Her words took on a life of their own as they gushed out—faster and faster.

"He carried my Babbo over his shoulder through the main gate to a truck just beyond. There were letters on the door. I only saw the top word—'City'—and then I ran and hid, Sheriff. I said nothing! Did nothing!"

She began sobbing again. "I am such a coward!" Her tiny frame shook with her sobs.

Madame said, "You feared for your life, caro. There was nothing to be done."

Billy scratched his chin, furrowed his brow. "Lilith, Madame said you were afraid to say anything until after I apprehended Jed. Did you think it was Jed that attacked Babbo?"

"Oh, no, but Jed has a great deal of influence over others. I was not sure what to think. But once you arrested Jed, there is now such a different attitude within Madame's show. Most of the troupe loved, or at least respected my Babbo, with a few exceptions. But with Garth, Jed and Happy gone, well, it is now different. I found my lost courage. Do you understand, Sheriff?"

"I think I do. Would you recognize this man if you saw him again?"

"Yes, I am certain of it."

"Lilith, did Babbo say or do anything to help us understand why he'd suggest Madame bring the show to Rock Rapids?"

"Um, sorry?"

"Did he, ah, seem different in any old way after the show got here?"

Lilith's eyes darted up toward Madame's, who offered an encouraging nod. She then brushed the fabric in her lap again before answering. But once again, she kept her now-puffy eyes downcast. "Well, he seemed both more nervous and more excited. As if he expected something to happen. But something good. What, he would not say." She then raised her eyes to meet Billy's.

He sensed she knew more, but would not press it, especially since Madame had started fidgeting.

Billy directed his next remarks to the rouster standing there, delivered with a warm smile. "Josh, I will ask my deputy, Jimmy, to help you watch over our star witness here for the next few days."

"No problem, Sheriff. Thanks." Josh was here now against his baser instincts, but Madame had told Billy he wanted justice as much as anyone. Wherever his troubled young life had led him to this point, he had a strong sense of right and wrong. And of justice.

"Lilith, I'd like to collect some photographs for you to look at in the next day or two. Maybe identify Babbo's attacker from one a them. Is that okay with you, young lady?"

The miniature woman glanced over at Madame and got an approving nod. She said, "I guess. It was dark, but I got a very good impression."

"That's all we ask, Lilith. That's all for now. Thank you for coming forward."

Josh rushed around to the front of her chair. She raised her arms to accept his help down to the floor. Even such a gesture showed her elegance in motion in a world foreign to her stature, and too often lacking in grace. An amazing girl. *They grow up fast in the circus.*

Madame followed them out of the LEC. She glanced just once over her shoulder to catch Billy's eye, and to deliver a warm smile.

His heart thundered.

73

B illy and Dwight were once again alone in the LEC. They resumed their brainstorming position around the sheriff's desk and its pool of yellow light. Now it was only somewhat brighter than the still-illuminated overhead lights mixed with the shafts of dusty sunlight invading the LEC through the large windows facing the street. It was to be a brilliant if hazy morning.

Billy said, "How are we gonna put together photos for Lilith to examine?"

"Well, she said she read the word 'City' above some other words on the door of the perpetrator's truck. What say we scour the phone book and see what businesses in the area use that word?"

Dwight waited and watched Billy, just to see if his puppy-love brain still worked like a cop's. Then... "And let's not overlook the obvious. Public works runs a couple of trucks that say 'City of Rock Rapids' on the doors, right? But I recall only one a them is an open truck, like the one Lilith described."

"Bingo. First we collect pictures of city employees with access to that truck, given our suspicions of the mayor, also a city employee, and we start there. But we look at other businesses to be thorough. Yup, that's a plan right there. I'll start with the business list. You get the city employee list, okay, Billy?"

"Sure thing. This is gonna get real sticky real fast, ain't it?"

"That it is, boss. Like one of those fly-catching strips you hang from the ceiling."

DWIGHT SCOURED THE WHITE AND YELLOW PAGES OF ALL THE towns in Lyon County. But he found only one business in their small jurisdiction that used the somewhat pretentious word 'City' in their business name, given the rural nature of their community. That was *City Delivery,* and they used no open-bed trucks like the one Lilith reported. They only owned one panel van.

Billy performed a similar search in the government pages. The only town in Lyon County that used open trucks with the word 'City' on the door was the *City of Rock Rapids Public Works.* He confirmed they operated just one such truck as part of the city's maintenance fleet.

Of the three public works employees in Rock Rapids, only one had free access to that truck on April 6th. Billy recognized the name— Clayton Moore. He had applied for the deputy's job late the previous year, but he came across as bigoted and interested in the job for all the wrong reasons. Plus, he had a felony record.

The township required photos to be on file for every town and county employee. He signed out Moore's photo, along with five others at random.

It seemed easier for Billy and Dwight to visit Lilith rather than her visiting them again. They drove to the fairgrounds and stopped first at Madame's wagon to invite her along. She dropped the unpaid bills she agonized over and happily agreed. Led the way—in those tight trousers.

TOM SMALLEY WAS AN ARROGANT PRIG. BILLY LEAPED STRAIGHT TO that conclusion when the little man answered their hail from their two-room tent's entrance. Madame knocked on the front peak pole and announced their presence. Smalley drew aside the heavy flap. He arched his short back to the extent he was able to peer up at the trio of giants about to invade his domain. Madame took custody of holding open the flap.

Smalley said, "Madame, as always, I am pleased to see you. But why have you brought *these* with you? Almost imperceptibly, he issued the tiniest of dismissive waves in Billy's and Dwight's general direction with the stubby little fingers he couldn't bother to even raise above his hip. He sneered at them, shot the cuffs on his impeccable vested suit, tugged his tailored vest smooth, and shifted back to a brilliant grin with his too-white teeth at Madame. Transparent little shit smoked his little cigar like a stack at a rendering plant.

Billy thought he must be a moneymaker as Madame addressed him with some deference. They needed to speak with Lilith. Billy could see Smalley hated the idea as his grin disappeared. He shifted his weight from one size two shoe to the other, but since it was Madame, he re-pasted on his smug little smile and said, "Of course. Please come in. *All* of you. You must forgive the low overhead." His voice lacked any sense of sincerity.

The tent contained no suitable furniture for giants, although they could not see into the rear partitions. They all remained standing, stooped and hunched over, except for Billy. Lilith reposed in her chair with her legs crossed just so. The sheriff got down on one knee in front of her. Still, he scooched down to meet her at eye level. Mr. Smalley raised one eyebrow and puffed on his miniature cigar—had to be custom-rolled.

Billy opened a folder he'd had tucked under his left arm and used it as a platform to spread out six photos at random. "Hello again, Lilith. Do you recognize any of these men from the night of April 6th? Take your time."

In an instant, after one brief glance, she shivered and pulled away, sitting back in her chair. She clamped her eyes shut—the skin on her temples wrinkled and whitened. She crossed her arms to hug herself as she scrunched her lips.

Her father said, "Madame—"

Billy swiveled a stern gaze toward the little man who still stood, almost at eye level from where he kneeled, not three feet away. He said with an abrupt tone, "Sir, please remain silent while your daughter thinks. That is not a request." Billy could tell the man was unaccustomed to being commanded. He grunted.

Billy turned back to Lilith, whose eyes were still closed, shutting out the horror of the night in question. Despite her facial powder, her forehead now glistened. She opened her eyes, and unfolded her arms with deliberation. She pointed without saying a word and without leaning forward, as if to distance herself, but still perform her duty. She identified Clayton Moore.

"You're sure?" She closed her eyes again and just nodded. The girl had not spoken a word, but her body language spoke volumes.

Mr. Smalley said, "Alright, that's quite enough. Out you get. Now. Madame, please. She's been through a great ordeal."

"Of course. Thank you, Tom. Sheriff, if you please."

Dwight looked like he was about to blow a fuse, or dance a jig, or both. Madame observed his body language and said, "Diputado, will you take my arm, please? This irregular ground, you know." She snatched his left arm with her right, pressed her right bosom into it, and sweet-smiled up at him.

Billy spotted the maneuver and added, "Yes, let's go. Sir, Lilith, we very much appreciate your cooperation." They all hunched to exit the low tent.

As they put some distance between them and the Smalley home, Billy hooked his right arm into Madame's left and whispered into her ear, "Thanks, Antonia."

Now with a cop on each arm, she purred, "Oh, Billy, the pleasure was *all* mine." Another sweet smile, like this was just another day at the office for her.

A tough nut—this one—for sure. What else?

❦ 74 ❧

༺✦༻

T hey got lucky.

Billy dug into Clayton Moore's record while Dwight searched the county maintenance garage. As a matter of expediency, they shared that cavernous structure with the city of Rock Rapids.

Billy reviewed Moore's record and background check still on file from his interview for the deputy's job. Several arrests, most minor, many associated with violence and assault, but many more that were never prosecuted over the years—curious. *No* known associates—also curious. And one felony—involuntary manslaughter—time served. Attended high school right here in Rock Rapids. A local boy.

Billy remembered the man's eyes.

On a hunch, he also searched the stacks at the municipal library. They kept a complete collection of RRHS yearbooks. Clay Moore was a senior in 1914—a ruffian.

Well, looky here! Same time Harry Deemers attended Rock Rapids High.

They didn't travel in the same circles, though, at least not on the surface. Billy found a small picture of a scared Harry Deemers riding

252

on the back of a motorcycle driven by none other than Clay Moore. *They knew each other.* This got Billy to think they might still be connected to this day, but how to prove that?

❦

MEANWHILE, INSIDE THE SPACIOUS COUNTY/CITY MAINTENANCE garage on the backside periphery of the fairgrounds, Dwight located the truck that little Lilith had seen. They had cleaned it up—too clean. Following his gut, Dwight risked getting mud on his crisp uniform by crawling under the recently washed and detailed truck. Found a heavy old canvas tarpaulin in a pile nearby, and spread it under the truck. Shimmied under the rear end on his back.

Said to nobody, "Yes! Forgot to clean the top of the axle, you dummy. *That* has to be dried blood!"

Dwight got up, rushed to his cruiser, and called Jimmy. "Hey, Deputy, where you at?" He was always surprised when that new-fangled radio in the car actually worked. Sometimes it didn't.

"Just leaving the LEC for my first shift patrol."

"Nope, you're not. I need you to secure vital evidence in our murder investigation. Meet me at the county maintenance garage. Now. Out."

"Roger. Out."

Ninety seconds later, Dwight heard Jimmy's siren. Gotta love that kid. Roared right into the open garage door with lights too. Before his siren had even wound down, the kid *ran* up to Dwight with an expectant look, his head on an inquiring swivel, thumbs hooked into his belt - like the big dogs.

"Okay, Jimmy, *nobody* comes near this truck. We're gonna need Doc Gus to go over it with his fine-tooth comb. Got it?"

"Got it!" The kid grinned from ear-to-ear. Dwight understood. He was a part of the *big investigation* at last!

Dwight rushed out to his own cruiser and high-tailed it back to the LEC where he found Billy at his desk. As he galloped through the door, both men shouted at each other in unison, "I broke the case!" They both chuckled.

"You first, boss."

"Seems Harry Deemers and Clay Moore were more than casual acquaintances in high school right here in town. But I had to dig, like they kept their relationship very low profile for some reason. I interviewed a few classmates still in town.

"They attended a lot of the same parties, even dated the same girl. Maybe even at the same time. That girl, Milly Hill, was killed in an automobile accident in their senior year. Both Harry and Clay were in the car when it happened. The police report says Clay was driving—drunk. He served four years for involuntary manslaughter down in Fort Madison. Harry skated. Makes ya wonder, don't it? What you got, D?"

"Nice, boss! Well, more in the category of current affairs, I found *the* truck in the county maintenance garage. And Billy, looks like it was cleaned up pretty good, but I think there's blood on top of the rear axle. What if that's Babbo's blood? Jimmy's standing guard over it. We need Doc to scour that truck for evidence. "

Silence descended. They both hoisted celebratory smiles, and at the same time, they sang out, "We broke the case!" They celebrated with a few moments of silence before Billy took on a grim expression.

"Bring in Clay Moore for questioning, Dwight. Let's call him a person of interest."

"Yessir!"

🦋 75 🦋

❦

Dwight rounded up Clay Moore. He planted him in one of their cells to stew in his own juices for a spell. Billy went for a mid-morning drive to clear his head. Besides, he figured he owed Jake Hardt a little more crow. And he wanted to update Sophie on their progress.

Billy kicked the dirt in the yard outside the Hardt's mudroom door. Dust coated his already dull boots. "Hi, Jake. The farm looks good. How's Sophie doin'?"

Jake's flat expression gave away nothing but resentment. "Hey, Billy. Fine. No thanks to you. S'pose ya wanna come in." Jake watched him kick more dirt. They weren't looking each other in the eye just yet.

"Jake, I get that you're still pissed. You got every right to be. And I'm not here tryin' to convince ya otherwise, or to ask for Sophie's help. I just owe her catch-me-up. She made some friends among them circus folk. And I got good news for her, okay, pardner?"

He then looked Billy in the eye. "Okay, Billy. Say, I know you got a job to do, and we appreciate it. I was just *pissed* Sophie got attacked. I keep thinkin' what I'd do if—"

255

"I get it, Jake. And I am truly sorry we placed her in danger. I care a lot about Sophie, too."

"Alright. C'mon into the front room. She's propped up on the couch with a bunch of pillows." Billy started to ask, but Jake headed him off. "Got her back and hip tweaked when that young fella dragged her to safety. She's in some pain.

"The hell, you say!" Billy thought he'd vomit, but pasted on his best smile.

WHEN HE SAW HER IN HER HOUSE COAT AND BARE FEET, ONE ALL gnarled up, and all of her propped up against the obvious pain, he knew the lump in his throat was not from bad coffee trying to come back up. *Holy Hell! What have I done?*

Sophie smiled at her visitor, but before she said anything, she caught Jake's eye, then nodded toward her feet. He quickly threw a blanket over them. Almost too cheerfully, Sophie chirped, "Hi, Billy. Did I hear you have news? You could have called—*should* have called."

"Hi, Soph. Not for this." Jake was about to give them some privacy to discuss *police business,* but Billy said, "Why don't you stick around for this, Jake? I'll need you to keep a lid on this as it's pretty sensitive, but you deserve to hear this, too."

"Uh, okay." He watched Jake watching his reaction to seeing Sophie like this. Seemed like they all could use a distraction.

"Soph, I suspected you'd be on pins 'n needles wantin' to hear what's happenin'. Now you keep this quiet for now, cuz we're sneakin' up on a couple of suspects for Babbo's murder," he looked at Jake and said, "the little circus freak that got killed."

"Yeah, Sophie told me."

"Well, the good news is it don't involve any a your circus friends, Soph, with one possible exception."

"Who do you suspect was involved? Somebody other than Jed?"

"Your friend, Sister... maybe."

"*What?* Oh, no, Billy, why would you even think that? She's been the one helping us from the very beginning."

"See, this drug Jed used on you? It's called Nightshade. They also call it the Devil's Breath. Doc's research with a gal he knows over in Des Moines says this drug is real popular with circus and carny fortune tellers. They dose their customers with a small amount a this stuff. Makes 'em more suggestible or somethin'. I questioned Sister, real nice-like, mind you, and she admitted she knew about this stuff. Claims she doesn't use it cuz she don't need to cuz a her 'sight,' whatever that means. Also, she admitted she didn't mention this to you—on purpose."

"Oh, my goodness. Did she say why?"

"She didn't want to give us another reason to *only* look for suspects inside the show. But here's the thing, Sophie. I'm inclined to believe her. She was right that we should look outside. Remember, I said I got good news? That we now have pretty strong evidence that nobody from the circus killed Babbo? Well, the bad news is it might be our favorite mayor right up there in Rock Rapids, along with one a his flunkies."

"*What?*"

"Yeah, him and an old high school friend, Clay Moore. Know him?"

"Ah, no. Golly. I didn't expect that."

Jake was shaking his head, looking at his feet. Said under his breath with disgust, "Politicians."

"We're still looking into this, mind you, and nobody can find out about this just yet, but the mayor might be Babbo's and Sister's biological daddy."

Sophie jerked in surprise. She winced at having put just the wrong pressure on her back. Maybe her hip, too. "Oh, Lord save us. And you think Mayor Deemers had Babbo killed to cover that up? Wait! Does that mean Sister's in danger? Billy, this is bad!"

"Hold on, now. Remember, you said even Babbo didn't know they was related. No reason to go after her. All the same, we got her covered, just in case. By the way, now Madame and the whole show, they's cooperatin' with us, thanks to you and your friend, Sister. Turns out it wasn't Madame fightin' us at all. It was Jed Strain who spoke for her. Now he's in custody for attacking you and that rouster, Josh.

"That kid's okay, by the way, and is helpin' us out. Plus, we're pretty sure Jed's good for dosin' that Garth Nitstone fella too. Not only that, but we like him a lot for causin' the death a that clown, Happy Grant. Soph, he's a bad man, a serial killer, we think, and we couldn't a cracked this rotten egg without you."

"Well, I'm glad to have helped, but for the truth be told, I'm even more glad to be back here with Jake, Leo, and Walt. Besides, that whole episode with Josh, Jed and that Devil's Breath, somewhere there I, well, now my dear husband is nursing me back to health." She reached over the back of the sofa and squeezed Jake's hand.

Billy looked up at Jake's stern expression, expecting another tongue-lashing, but some body language from Sophie stifled that. Maybe a preemptive hand squeeze.

"Oh, Soph. I feel like sh—ah, crap over this." He looked at how she made every move with great care, wincing all the while.

"It's okay, Billy. Like some of my wonderful new friends at the circus say, every day offers challenges for folks like me... and Sister... and CM... and his adorable wives. Even little Josh. The Good Lord has a plan for all of us."

"Well, kiddo, not sure about that. But I'm glad to call you a friend, Mrs. Hardt. You're a hell of an investigator. Holler if I can do *anything* for you and your little family."

Billy looked up at Jake in time to see him smear a tear away with his free sleeve. Billy said with more cheer than he felt, "Now where's that pint-size shaver? I'd like to hold little Leo for a bit. That okay, Jake?"

⚜️

JAKE SMIRKED. IT WAS HARD TO HOLD A GRUDGE AGAINST A COP who invites you to slug him after he's put your wife in danger. "C'mon, Billy, let's go find Walt. He and Leo are as one these days. You can fight with him to hold our little farmhand."

❧ 76 ❧

L
ate afternoon, around sunset, a call came into the LEC. Dwight answered. It was Justina. He tried to apologize for being brusque with her at the diner earlier in the week, but she interrupted him. She sounded frantic. Said an unruly crowd of locals was about to descend on the circus lot—with guns. Laticia had invited her to join them. The church ladies and a group of local men were out for blood.

Justina said, "Dwight, this is getting out of hand. Lionel Johns from the Lyon County News is riling up anyone who will listen. He's saying the circus is protecting a gang of serial killers who are also devil worshippers and defilers of children, and they are coming for the town's children next.

"Somehow, he found out that clown who died had a record for being a child molester. And the other fellow in the truck rollover, that he worshipped Satan. And now you and the sheriff have arrested a Rock Rapids man, Clay Moore for those killings—*not* the murdering Satan worshippers from the show.

"Dwight, he's got Laticia and the rest of the church ladies, along with a bunch of local men, all lathered up. Saying it's time for 'concerned citizens to rid their town of this den of child molesters and Satan worshippers once and for all.' They have guns, Dwight!

"Lionel's talking about capturing the head of the snake and cutting it off, as doing that would send the rest of these subhumans scurrying for their burrows elsewhere. Something like that. Says they need to make sure of it.

"Dwight, I've never seen folks worked up like this. It's... crazy!"

He heard her almost sobbing out her final words, and then huffing, like she was out of breath.

"Justina—breathe—you do *not* go to the fairgrounds. You'll be in danger, and I can't have you in danger."

"You can't?"

"Aw, hell, Justy, I just care about you too darn much. I couldn't bear it if anything happened to you."

"Dwight, I am *really* scared. Laticia and the ladies mean well, but—"

"We'll be careful with them, m'dear. Now I gotta go to work." He hung up and turned to Billy, who had just returned from the Hardt farm.

"Billy, there's a situation. We gotta get to the fairgrounds, pronto, or we'll be mopping up more blood. We got a mob in the making."

"The hell, you say! To the cars. Now. Show a force."

Once they had both hopped into their cruisers and got underway, Billy radio'd both Dwight and Jimmy who was still patrolling. "Guys, let's get in between this mob and the show's main gate. Lights, but no sirens, okay?"

"Copy, Sheriff."

"Copy." Jimmy's excitement was hard to hide... mostly because the darn car radio contraption actually worked. Again.

77

B illy and Dwight arrived at the fairgrounds just outside the circus gate—lights, no sirens on both their cruisers. Jimmy followed right behind them. They came up on a large semi-circle of a dozen cars, their headlights all shining toward the center, the open side of which faced the show's gate just twenty yards distant. More than a dozen local men had shown up, including a half-dozen church ladies, led by Laticia Morgenstern. Some men even toted shot-guns. Dwight spotted a few handguns in old western-style holsters strapped to a few hips.

Lionel Johns, the rabble-rousing reporter from the Lyon County News, carried no visible weapon, but had grabbed the crowd's atten-tion and was pronouncing some wild claims as facts. The three police cruisers faced the open end of the semi-circle in a straight line toward the other cars. Lionel stood in the middle, like the ringmaster of his own little show. A prairie wind had kicked up, casting the entire scene into a dusty cloud of grit which gave all the headlight beams substance, as if in a snow storm.

After interrupting the reporter's little show and settling the bois-terous crowd down in order to be heard, Billy addressed them from in front of his cruiser that was positioned between Dwight's and Jimmy's. He boomed, "What in God's green acre is goin' on here, folks?"

Lionel turned from "his" crowd to face Billy and his two deputies. He said, "Sheriff, my sources tell me you have one of our own in custody for the murder of that circus freak. Is that true? Have you arrested Clay Moore, one of our township's loyal employees? How in God's name can you justify turning against your own community to defend these... *circus people?*" He spat out the last two words as if they were poison.

Billy responded, but addressed the crowd at large in a loud, clear voice that the rising wind and dust tried to dissipate. "Mr. Johns, first, let me be clear. It is *not* department policy to discuss the details of an ongoin' investigation. And you and I, sir, are goin' to have words about where you got your information. But I will share with you that we have not arrested Mr. Moore. He has been detained as a person of interest in our investigation, as supported by physical evidence and eyewitness testimony. Now, if you believe you have concrete evidence that will contribute to the case, I invite you to the law enforcement center to offer up such evidence. That is how our city, county, state and national system of justice works. Not based on wild claims made in a parkin' lot in the middle of the night."

Lionel looked like he was itching for a fight—a rhetorical one, anyway, but lost some momentum as Billy spoke. At that point, Laticia Morgenstern, the very vocal leader of the church ladies of Lyon County and the chair of the county's civic league, spoke up loud and clear. "So how do you explain a string of deaths that only started after this, this, den of iniquity, showed up in our county, Sheriff?"

"Laticia, we always appreciate your staunch sense of civic duty. That's one thing that makes our community strong. And this string of deaths is what you elected me to deal with on your behalf. I will repeat for you what I just told Mr. Johns here. This is an ongoin' inves-tigation—"

"Yes, Sheriff. Ongoing for how long? This nightmare has lasted for over three weeks, with no end in sight. How many more people must die before you do your job?"

A smattering of muttering issued from the crowd now clustered close behind Laticia and the reporter who both fancied themselves voices of the community.

Billy thought it transparent as hell that Johns was just trying to drum up sales for the paper. And something else given what he had just learned, but could not share with this mob. But he wasn't sure of Laticia's motivations.

The crowd pressed in.

A new voice from behind the sheriff and off to his left shouted, "Excuse me, excuse me, might I share a word with you all?" The silhouette of a well-dressed young man marched toward the crowd, now gathered at the center of the headlight circle.

Lionel said, "And who the hell are *you?*"

The man displayed his open wallet containing official credentials that nobody could read. But he held it out like a badge. The young man said, "I am Federal Agent Samuel Ellis. I represent the United States Department of Justice in this matter. Several of you might recognize the name of Senior Supervisory Agent Lang Eubanks, my boss. Our agency came to your community's aid last summer, working with Sheriff Kershaw here."

Lionel and Laticia, both further deflated by the unexpected and timely show of big guns at their little soirée, shared an awkward moment of silence. Or at least as much as the escalating wind allowed. Folks leaned into the wind, grabbing or losing their hats. Then Lionel said, "And what is your role here, Agent Ellis?"

For a little man, Agent Ellis boasted a hell of a voice when he spoke up. "I am at liberty to share with you we have arrested a circus employee in this case. And we are very close to concluding the investigation into *all* the recent unfortunate casualties. Now, do you wish me to charge every one of you with obstruction of justice for interfering with a *federal* investigation being spearheaded by Sheriff Kershaw and his department? He has our full confidence, by the way."

Nobody said anything more, not even the sheriff who wore a surprised expression.

Agent Ellis continued. "Alright, then. I assume you do not wish to face arrest and detention at this time; therefore, I urge you to disperse and let law enforcement do its job. Objections? No? Then please return to your homes. I'm sure Sheriff Kershaw will share all the news at the appropriate time. Thank you for your cooperation."

With that, Ellis placed his hands on his hips and waited for the now-milling crowd to return to their cars. Lionel looked conflicted. Laticia appeared... what? Impressed? Most everyone else used the escalating weather as an excuse to seek shelter without losing too much face.

Billy thought, *Yessir! Ole Lang knows how to pick his agents, alright!* He walked up to Agent Ellis, who had distanced himself from him and his deputies standing off to his left during the conflagration and said, "Where'd you come from, Sam?"

"I'm staying at the Marietta Hotel here in town. Was listening to one of the bureau's latest toys, a portable radio receiver that I tuned to monitor all your local law enforcement frequencies. I overheard your terse discussions over the air waves with your deputies. Thought I might join the party. Okay by you, Sheriff?" He hoisted a boyish grin, already knowing the answer.

"Nicely done, son. Thanks for backin' our play, and maybe savin' me a few votes come election time." Dwight walked up and slapped Agent Ellis on the back hard enough to cause him a stumble-step forward. The kid was about to draw his weapon until he realized he was being congratulated, not attacked.

Dwight laughed. "Kid, you gotta loosen up a tad. Thanks for having our backs there, Agent Ellis."

Jimmy stood nearby, but was *way* out of his depth. He just stood and watched. They all ducked against the now-howling wind.

Sam raised his voice to be heard. "Right. Now who is this Clay Moore you have in custody, and how is it this reporter knows about that before I do?"

After he watched Dwight *attack* Agent Sam Ellis with amusement, Billy's face transformed into a mask of granite. "That is an excellent question, Sam. And we're gonna find out. Dwight, let's dig into this reporter's life. He's been snipin' at the circus and our investigation from the get-go. I wanna know why. And let's find out what biscuit eater's been shootin' off their mouth?"

"You got it, boss."

"Meanwhile, Sam, why don't you join me back at my office? Catch ya up over a cup. Get out a this weather."

78

Once inside the LEC, both men used their hats to slap some dust off their clothes as best they could near the front door. They meandered back to the fish tank with Billy leading the way.

Billy's little-used desk in the fish tank supported two cups of yard mud, Sophie's special farm coffee recipe. Except *she* served it hot.

It had been a while since either man slept, as witnessed by bags under Billy's eyes and the uncharacteristic not-so-dapper appearance of the young ATF agent. *Welcome to the country, big city!* Billy grinned at that notion.

"Sam, we have strong physical evidence and an eyewitness placin' this Clay Moore at the scene of the circus freak's murder, committin' the crime, and movin' the body. He's a city employee, and an old high school buddy of our esteemed mayor, Harold Deemers."

Billy also told Sam about the auto accident back in the day. That both the mayor and Moore had been in the car. And the involuntary manslaughter beef that Moore took on and did the time.

Sam looked over his right shoulder at the cell not very far on the other side of the fish tank's waist-to-ceiling windows. Looked like the prisoner was sleeping, or pretending.

"Most interesting." The kid scratched his chin. "Are you wondering if this Moore was acting on behalf of Deemers?"

"Maybe. We need proof."

"Sensitive. Did you break this mook?"

"Not yet. Wanna crack at him, kid?"

Sam grinned. Right then, Billy thought this "kid" looked more like a hungry wolf than a junior agent.

❦

CLAY MOORE HAD BUNCHED HIMSELF UP INTO A FETAL POSITION ON the cot in cell number one. Just for this occasion, Billy dug his night-stick out of the same filing cabinet as the department's Christmas decorations. Seconds later, He roused Clay from a sound sleep by clacking that nightstick against the bars.

Billy led him the twenty feet from his cell to the fish tank with a firm grip on the guy's sloppy shoulder. He now felt frail. Closed the door behind them. Plopped him down, none too gently. Sam was about to sit in Billy's desk chair, and their suspect occupied the chair Sam sat in earlier. It was close to midnight.

Billy stood behind Clay, facing Sam, who straightened his tie. Then, as an afterthought, silently removed his dusty suitcoat and hung it over the back of "his" chair. Brushed more dust off his vest and gave it a tug. Then he sat and slowly opened a folder on the desk in front of him with a solemn motion long before he uttered a single syllable.

"Mr. Moore, my name is Federal Agent Sam Ellis. I represent both the ATF and the FBI in this investigation. Be aware that the full force of the United States Department of Justice is backing Sheriff Kershaw on this case. We suspect these circus murders are all connected. We have clear evidence and an eyewitness that makes you good for one of these murders, and we'll find evidence on the others as well. Do you understand? A serial killer with interstate implications?"

"I ain't no serial killer."

"That means we can hang you by the neck until you are dead. Ever see a hanging, Clay? I've seen my share. The idea is to break your neck, making your demise quick. But sometimes, things don't go right—more often than we'd like. Sometimes, your neck won't snap, and you just hang there, suffocating, for several long minutes. But no air can get past that hangman's noose. Your face swells into one big purple blister. Your eyes might even bug out of their sockets. All the way out, just hanging there by some stringy nerves and veins. That happens too. Your tongue swells up, fills your mouth and throat. With your hands tied behind your back, you can't swing your arms, much less clutch at your strangling throat. But you do what you can, which isn't much, by jerking your shoulders. Later, your legs stop swinging. They'll twitch, though. And all the while, your brain keeps telling you everything, while it's happening. By that point, you'll be wishing you would have done *whatever* you could to have avoided this awful death."

Through this entire gruesome description, Sam leaned forward on the desk. Stared into Clay's eyes, never wavering. At first, Clay just looked down at his twiddling thumbs. But then he got caught up in the vivid imagery, no doubt imagining this happening to him. His initial expression was that of defiance. But that transformed into one of anxiety and... fear? Even got misty eyes.

"Might you want to consider what you can do right now to avoid this awful fate?" Sam fell silent. He waited. A full minute. Just staring. Then....

"Um, what could I do?"

"Clay, killing all these people wasn't your idea, was it?"

"Told ya. I ain't no serial killer."

"Well, that would make a difference now, wouldn't it, Billy?" He looked over Clay's right shoulder, up at the sheriff still standing behind Clay, guarding the fish tank's half-glass door.

The sheriff grinned. This kid could interrogate. "Sure would make a difference, Agent Ellis."

"So you did the three circus folk? Nitstone the roustabout, Grant the clown and Babbo the freak? Hey, Sheriff, that sounds like a really bad joke, doesn't it?"

"Sure does, Agent Ellis, except the punch line here is that ole Clay's neck's gonna get stretched and throttled in the bargain."

A battle raged within Clay Moore. Again, Sam stared and waited. After another agonizing minute, Clay blurted, "Hey, I delivered the little freak, okay? Scoped out his habits down in Sioux City. Saw he walked the midway every night around midnight. Found him. Tapped him. Dropped him off. That was it. You gotta believe me. I didn't do nobody. The man said we gotta search him, make sure he din't have nothin' connectin' him to anybody from town. Plus, dumpin' him out in the county made damn sure he'd get found. Otherwise, no tellin' what those circus jerks would cover up. Thought this'd pin the deed on one a them, and get that bunch booted out a town real fast—over and done. Now what's that mean fer me?"

Sam tugged on his tie. Loosened it some more. Sat back in the chair behind that small desk. The agent said, "Still could be a capital crime—murder's a hanging offense in the state of Iowa. Especially if you acted on your own. Right, Sheriff?"

"Yup."

"But if this truly wasn't your idea, well, that might shine a different light on it. I'm sure the sheriff would be glad to share your cooperation with the county attorney for some leniency. Maybe even take the rope off the table. Is that a possibility, Sheriff?"

"Sure thing, but we gotta have some cooperation from Clay here, Agent Ellis."

"So what's it going to be, Clay? You willing to work with us here so we can help you? Or—"

"Listen, none a this was my idea. I was only doin' a favor for a friend. Ya gotta believe me."

"And what is this friend's name?"

"I ain't takin' the noose—not for *no* friend. Not alone, anyway. It was Harry. Harry Deemers. Somethin' about that freak bein' his kid or somethin'. Dunno. Harry's a great man. Made a mistake, is all. Way back when. I ain't never done nothin' like this before. That's gotta count fer somethin', right?"

"Sheriff?"

"Sure. But you gotta write all this down. You'll do that for us, to show you're cooperatin', workin' *with* us, right, Clay?"

"Yeah, okay. But you guys gotta tell 'em I'm cooperatin'. Almost like a deputy. Right, Sheriff?" And the bastard turned around to half-grin at Billy, who worked mighty hard to keep a flat smile pasted on his disgusted face.

Sam saw Billy's expression, and quickly added, "Look at me, Clay. Hey, that's why we need you to write it all down. Here's a pad of paper and a couple of pencils. This will help you help yourself. Sheriff, let's give Clay some time to think and write, okay?"

Billy said with fake enthusiasm that Clay couldn't see. In a sing-song voice he said, "Yeah, good idea. Clay, we'll be right outside if you need anything. Hey, how about a glass of water? Or a mug a coffee?" Sam wasn't sure if Billy'd set it in front of the prisoner or hit him over the head with it.

"Sure, Sheriff, coffee'd be great. Black."

"You got it, pardner." Billy grit his teeth so hard on the way out of the fish tank, he thought he might have chipped a couple.

79

S aturday,
    May 5, 1934

୧୬୨୬

BILLY ADMITTED TO HIMSELF THAT HE WOULD ENJOY *THIS* VISIT TO City Hall. He even put on a uniform shirt under his badge for the occasion, the collar discolored with a dust line from neglect, and from hanging for years—untouched—in his closet. Dwight suggested Billy lose the smile, though. Not professional. Yup, he would enjoy this, even if he couldn't grin like a cowpoke stretched out in his bunk after a three-day ride and a two-day drunk.

Velma, the mayor's assistant, jumped up from behind her desk when she saw Billy and Dwight marching toward the mayor's grand office doors. "I'm sorry, Sheriff. The mayor is in a meeting—"

"Not anymore, he ain't." He and Dwight charged into the mayor's office, swinging both doors open hard enough to bang them against their stops. They found not only the mayor, but Laticia Morgenstern, and... Lionel Johns? The *reporter?* They were sharing a good belly laugh. He'd fix that.

Laticia and Lionel stiffened where they sat side-by-side on a small couch across from the mayor who was in a stuffed armchair off to their right. Mayor Deemers aborted his revelry in mid-chortle, and looked startled. "Sheriff, what is the meaning of this rude interruption?"

Billy couldn't help himself. "Mr. Mayor, I may be rude, but I ain't no murderer."

"What did you just say to me?"

"Harold, please stand up." As Billy spoke, he crossed the expansive office with hard purpose. Early morning sunlight—almost no dusty haze in the air—streamed through the windows behind the mayor's desk off to his left, oblivious of the high emotions flooding the room. A nice day for a change.

Dwight remained at the door. Like a prison guard.

"What? I'm—"

Meanwhile, Laticia and the reporter remained seated on the sofa with their jaws about to drop to the floor in front of them. The reporter started to get up. Laticia placed a protective hand across Lionel's chest to stop him. Like you'd protect a child sitting next to you in a car making a sudden and unexpected stop. They both stared up as this ominous drama played out in front of them.

"Harold Deemers, you are under arrest for conspiracy to commit murder. Now, how's that for rude?" He gently pulled the man's wrists together behind his back and placed the hand cuffs on him, working around those elegant French cuffs and diamond links.

Billy hustled him out with only a nod in Laticia's direction and a suspicious glance toward the reporter. He didn't like what he saw. Something....

DWIGHT NOTICED THAT EXCHANGE. HE'D TALK WITH BILLY ABOUT that once they were alone. That reporter not only knew confidential information, he had been tampering with the court of public opinion since this investigation began. Something else, too....

He also noticed Billy took the law enforcement equivalent of a victory lap, shame be damned. Why not? It's not every day you get to arrest your election opponent who is also likely a stone-cold killer. If it weren't for the iron-clad confession from the mayor's flunky, and the pile of evidence they'd collected....

There would still be fallout, but that didn't seem to bother his boss. Justice would be served. He was proud to work with a guy like Billy, even if they hadn't shared the same foxholes back in the day.

⊛

HAVING THE HIGHEST-LEVEL CITY OFFICIAL SITTING IN A CELL twenty feet away might have made their entire day in the open floor plan of the LEC awkward. Worse, his co-conspirator who just ratted on him sat in the cell right next to his. None of that had fazed Billy. Not one lick.

But now, Billy could not believe what he was hearing.

The sun set and Dwight turned on the overhead lights when Billy started squinting at the sheave of papers in front of him. Deemers' attorney had planted himself in front of Billy's desk. He lobbied for a change of venue. Said he feared the mayor had shit where he ate. He and Laticia Morgenstern had been the loudest rabble-rousers in town about the circus being such a "den of iniquity," yet *this asshole commissioned the murder of his own handicapped son.* No small wonder he wanted to get the heck out of town for the trial.

They would ship both Moore and Deemers down to Fort Madison, where they'd remain awaiting arraignment. Unlike here, they had plenty of cells at the pen. *Those boys don't play nice down there, either. Serves 'em right.*

At that moment, however, Mayor Harold Deemers' attorney dropped yet another bombshell in Billy's lap. After three minutes of listening to this guy—the high-priced lawyer the mayor had imported from Des Moines a couple of hours earlier—Billy scratched his head. Then he wrinkled his nose and shot a lopsided gaze of disbelief at the mayor's mouthpiece, then at the mayor.

Sumbitch!

The last piece of the puzzle fell into place, or so he thought. Billy motioned to Dwight, who had been sitting on the corner of his own desk, the one he almost never used. Billy whispered into his ear. Dwight nodded, tossed his boss a casual salute, and said, "Be back shortly."

Things were about to get even more interesting. A breeze followed a small group of folks in through the front door as Dwight rushed out. The circus rouster, Josh, pushed a wheel chair. A long hooded robe hid its occupant from view. Madame followed them, appearing as spectacular as ever, but she had concealed her magnificent body art under a floor-length caped cloak. Billy frowned.

Besides, his head still spun from the grenade the mayor's lawyer had just lobbed in his general direction.

❦

Madame's cloak flowed behind her as she took the lead, crossing the squad room in a graceful glide to interrupt Billy's discussion. She looked down at the dapper attorney, said to him, "Lo siento, señor." She turned back to Billy and while speaking to him, projected a proclamation to the entire LEC, as if she were introducing royalty. She ensured Mayor Harold Deemers behind her heard every word.

"Sheriff, I would like to introduce to you Sister Deemers, Babbo Deemers' twin." She peered with pleasure over her right shoulder to cell number two, just in time to see the mayor leap to his feet.

At that same moment, Josh wheeled Sister to the side of Billy's desk, her back toward the cells. Billy stood and waited expectantly. A pale hand with spindly fingers appeared from within the robe's folds, extending it toward him.

After the slightest hesitation, he stooped forward to grasp Sister's hand with both of his own and said, "Sister, it is a pleasure to meet you at last. I wish Sophie was here too. You've helped us seek justice for your brother. I am truly very sorry for your loss."

The thin haunting voice could only be heard by Billy, Josh, Madame, and the wide-eyed attorney now to Sister's immediate left. He stared at that incredible hand. Like everyone else in the room, he must wonder what was under that lop-sided hood and oddly proportioned robe.

Sister said, "I will always treasure my new friends in Rock Rapids. Dear Sophie risked much to seek the truth. Despite your own distractions, and the holes in your soul, Sheriff, you found our truth. Now, may I be allowed to witness what will happen next?" She raised her head just enough. Billy saw her face. Still partially in shadow, her asymmetrical eyes and a rope-like smile slanted down and to the left. Her other hand then appeared and engulfed both of Billy's in a firm grip.

Billy stared at that strange, yet compassionate face. For a moment, Sister's eyes hypnotized him. He stood there, still stooped forward. Four hands clasped, almost as if in an embrace that transcended anything physical.

Billy wondered, *What is happening here? My own distractions? Holes in my soul? Who **is** this woman? Girl? She knows what's coming next?*

After ten seconds of interrogating himself, Billy smiled, as if peace had descended over him, like a warm blanket on a crisp Iowa morning. He looked up at Madame, who, at that moment, appeared downright angelic. A distraction? Billy said, "I wouldn't dream of having it any other way, little Sister." He shook those hands, just a little, exercising care not to harm this frail creature who oozed strength—as if to emphasize the depths of his feelings for her at that magical moment.

Their hands parted and Sister's once again disappeared into the folds of her robes as a ruckus at the LEC's front door turned everyone's head—except Sister's. Madame nodded to Josh who maneuvered Sister's wheelchair around. He positioned her beside Billy's desk with a perfect view of the squad room, including the front door to her right and the two cells to her left.

The outraged voice captured everyone's attention. "Do you have any idea who I am? I'll have your badge for this!"

Dwight said, "Shut up, mister, before I gag you." The deputy smiled.

"This is outrageous!"

Then, as they burst through the front door, Dwight's prisoner got an eyeful that shut him right up. He spotted Mayor Deemers in one cell at the back of the LEC, and Clay Moore in the other. Both looked as guilty as the occupants of Hell itself. At that moment, Lionel Johns, the Lyon County News reporter, realized he was screwed. He had witnessed the mayor's arrest, but to see Clay there visibly disturbed him. Billy waved them over. Dwight hustled the reporter toward the sheriff's desk, and toward Sister.

Billy took over. With Johns' hands cuffed behind his back, he steered him to stand in front of Sister. From behind, Billy bucked both of the reporter's knees with his own. Johns dropped to the ground, now eye level with Sister. Out came her frail right hand and those long spindly fingers, but with only her index finger extended.

The man tried to lean back, away from that frightening finger, but ran into the sheriff behind him. Sister touched the tip of that skeletal digit to the man's forehead. She whispered, "I will pray for your black soul, sir, but I fear it will only deepen your regret for murdering my dear brother. I will also pray that Babbo not curse you from his grave. He is quite capable, you know."

Before she removed her finger, she increased the pressure to bobble his head back an inch. And the hand disappeared into her robe once again with lightning speed.

Billy understood that everyone grieved differently. This was closure for Sister. She deserved it. But it wasn't quite over yet, was it? *Wait! How did she know....?*

❦

BILLY LOOKED JOSH IN THE EYE. "MAY I?"

Josh glanced over at Madame. She had yet to say anything since introducing Sister to Billy. She nodded with just one lazy little bob of her head.

With slow deliberation, Billy pushed Sister over to the mayor's cell, to within three feet of the bars. Sister looked up into the mayor's frightened face and said, "Hello, Father. I will pray for your blackened soul, too. I won't ask why you had your own son killed. Your aura reveals all. Your ambition has morally blinded and bankrupted you. I am sorry. You are to be pitied."

"My... *daughter?*" All pretense in the mayor's face had evaporated. He just stood there with his manicured hands dangling like useless ropes next to his costly trousers. But there was something in his eyes that made him look very un-mayor-like.

"Yes, Father. Babbo and I were twins. Would you have had me killed too, had you known? Or is having a female freak for a child less horrific? No?" And if that didn't give this wretched excuse for a human being enough to think about, she'd give him something else to contemplate while sitting alone in his cell. She struggled to reach the rim of her hood and laid it back onto her shoulders. Her distorted hands trembled with the effort.

The mayor stumbled back in shock, tripped over the cot behind him. He fell onto that cot and took a nasty bump to the back of his head from banging it against the cell's rear wall. Billy wondered whether the tears that now ran down his cheeks were from the painful bump? Or from regret? Or fear of his new future? Maybe something darker. More closure for Sister.

She then tried to raise her hood, but failed to reach it. When she tried, however, the sleeves of her robe fell back to reveal crooked forearms of pale gray flesh draped over bones. Every eye cast in her direction widened. Some gasped. Madame rushed forward to help her, then turned to face Billy, who stood almost too close, and too concerned.

She said, "Billy," (BEE-lee), "so these three conspired to kill our Babbo? Madre de Dios! Why?"

 She crossed herself with some strange eye-shaped bronze charm clutched in her fingers as if warding off the evil that surrounded her.

"**M**adame, we have a full confession from Clay, here." He nodded toward cell one. "Turns out he didn't kill Babbo, he only knocked him unconscious, and hauled him to the city maintenance garage based on instructions from the mayor." He tossed a glance toward the reporter, still on his knees by Billy's desk. "That's where Lionel over there beat poor Babbo to death with his bare hands, and used the city's truck to move the body. See those bruises on his knuckles, It was real personal for him. Hates freaks *and* is loyal to the mayor.

"Ya see, the mayor was coverin' up a steamy relationship he had with an unemployed circus performer while at college out east. He took advantage of this young lady who worked in a soup kitchen. Eight months later, Babbo and Sister were born. Harold abandoned her when he learned she was pregnant.

"Babbo influenced your decision to bring your show to Rock Rapids as he aimed to reconcile with his daddy. We're still not sure how the kid learned who that was." A nod toward cell two. "Called him

279

up. Said he planned to come to town with your show. And that's when this all started."

"But what about *that* hombre, Billy?" She pointed an accusative finger at the end of her outstretched arm toward the reporter.

"Well, now, we just learned more from the mayor's lawyer over yonder—yeah, that fancy suit. He offered the mayor's cooperation in return for leniency. Harold here don't wanna get sent to Fort Madison with the real bad boys. Aims to deal for one a them lower security prisons. Nicer cell mates, they say, 'n better food. Could be even one a them talkies to listen to the news or Amos 'n Andy.

"The real deal maker here ain't Clay, but it ain't the mayor either. This here's where it gets real interestin'. Our reporter here, Lionel Johns, is really Richard Dinkley. His legal name back at Rock Rapids High before goin' off to journalism school. Looked real different too. That's why we didn't connect him right off with the mayor or with Clay. Ricky here was also a friend a Clay's and the mayor's. Changed his name before comin' back to town. *He's* the one that put Clay up to coppin' to involuntary manslaughter back then.

"The *three* of them were in a car with a girl named Milly Hill. Back in 'fourteen, Milly was a freshman, just sixteen years old. Ricky here," another nod toward the reporter, "along with Harold and Clay, were all eighteen-year-old seniors. They had been drinkin' and got in a nasty accident. Milly died. Turns out Harold was driving, but the three of them agreed Clay would say he was. He'd take the heat. Why Clay? Because both Ricky and Harold had bright futures. Clay just didn't give a damn. Went to prison for four years.

"But Harold here, our illustrious mayor, he came from serious money. His family owned several businesses in Northwest Iowa, including our very own Lyon County News, the biggest newspaper in this part of the state. Plus, Harold was a strong student and a good lookin' kid. He was ambitious, had that natural smooth nature—the "complete package," as they say. Ricky 'n Clay were both convinced Harry here would go far. Plus, he made all kinds of promises 'n backed 'em up with his family's money. But even that's not the complete story.

"See, that wasn't just a car accident what killed Milly. After gettin' drunked up at a party, them three boys gang-raped little Milly in

Harold's car—Daddy's big Buick. She threatened to scream bloody murder after they were done with her 'n beat her up some. There was an accident, alright, but they staged it.

"The boys made their deal, but Milly, she was goin' to ruin everything, screw up all their lives. They couldn't have that. Their solution was to run Daddy Deemers' Buick into a tree on a country road. Harold drove, cuz he figured he was safest with an iron grip on the wheel. Then, after they slammed into that tree, Ricky here bashed little Milly's head into the dashboard hard enough to snap her neck.

"Ricky was an ambitious prick too, could be the most ambitious of the three back in high school. But he didn't have the pedigree or the money or the looks like Harold. But he was damn smart and knew how to bide his time. It was the long con, as you might say, Madame.

"Ricky—now Lionel—made a side deal with Harold, unbeknownst to even Clay there. As far as Clay knew, these days, Ricky dangled that high school scam to eventually land the editor-in-chief job at Harold's newspaper. Clay must a respected that in his own twisted way. Lionel knew Harold was goin' to be governor some day, maybe even president. He wanted to ride along as his chief of staff, once they both "escaped" Rock Rapids. That's where all our evidence, confessions and deals have led us, Madame. We got it all in writing, too."

Madame Antonia Perlatelli just shook her head. Sister's head had sagged down onto her chest. Her asymmetrical shoulders appeared narrower than ever and looked to be heaving up and down. They thought she might be sobbing at the sorrow of it all. The three conspirators all hung their heads, maybe in shame, more likely in embarrassment, or regret at getting caught.

Madame said to the room at large, "And your town accuses my troupe of being un guarida de iniquidad—a den of iniquity. These... hombres... represent more concentrated... evil... than my entire show could ever imagine."

To Billy's surprise, she sauntered over to Lionel Johns, still on his knees with his hands cuffed behind his back, as if she hadn't a care in the world. When her face came to within a foot above his, she hissed, "Two murders, señor? For what? Money? Ego? Tu eres la puta del diablo!" With an expression dripping with disgust, she spat into

Lionel's upturned mouth, pivoted, and returned to Josh and Sister. Placed a gentle hand on her shoulder.

As she alternated her gaze between the three prisoners, she said, "You may think some of my people are ugly because they are different on the *outside*." She glanced down at Sister beside her. "But *nothing* can compare to the ugliness *inside* you three monsters. Get justice, Sheriff Billy." She squeezed the upper part of his left arm as she passed him without taking her eyes off the back of Sister's bowed head. And they made for the door.

⊗⅏⊗

Dwight sidled up to Billy. He whispered, "What did she say to that reporter? My Spanish isn't too good."

"I think she called him the devil's whore before she launched that loogie. Quite a lady, that."

"Yup. That she is, boss." Slapped the sheriff on the back. Walked back to figure out how to fit three back-stabbing lizards into two cells so they'd all survive the night until they shipped out the next day.

Dwight figured he'd be babysitting demons tonight.

❧ 82 ❧

T he late afternoon shadows painted Main Street in subdued colors, blanched even more by the dusty haze. The prairie winds had kicked up again. It would be worse out in the county. Usually was.

Billy crossed the street from the LEC, took a right, and walked down the block to Laticia Morgenstern's house. He glanced back across the street to peer at Mayor Deemers' big house with the wall and gate near the sidewalk. Knocked on Laticia's front door. Her husband, Ralph, a thin wisp of a man a full foot shorter than him, answered the door with a quizzical expression. Invited Billy in.

"Ralph, I gotta talk to Laticia."

He hollered for her, and she came into the front room where they entertained, probably where Laticia held her prayer meetings. Billy didn't care. She wore an apron from baking something. Smelled all yeasty.

"Laticia, might we have a word in private?" She was shocked to see the sheriff standing in her front room and traded some scathing comment for one with less fire behind it when she saw his dead-serious expression.

"Ralph, give us a minute. Why don't you go out to your garage for a while?"

When they were alone, Laticia said, "What's this all about, Sheriff? Have you kicked that awful circus out of town yet?"

"Laticia, don't you worry about that circus just now. You need to worry about yourself. I'm doing you the courtesy of questioning you here instead of hauling you across the street in the back of my cruiser."

"What?"

"I'm here to decide whether to charge you with conspiracy to commit murder or not."

"*What?*" Her knees buckled. She plopped into a very proper chair upholstered in very proper fabric across from the sheriff. He seated himself on a fancy little sofa with a matching pattern below a bunch of proper pictures hanging on the wall to his right. He leaned forward with his elbows on his knees and peered with the most serious intent into Laticia's wide eyes.

"I've locked up Clay Moore, Lionel Johns and Mayor Deemers for conspiring to kill Babbo Deemers. You remember, Laticia. He was that gentle little circus freak who was loved by everyone close to him. Those three also gang-raped a sixteen-year-old girl when they were in high school, murdered her, and staged an automobile accident to cover up their crimes. Talk about your den of iniquity."

Laticia sat and stared, processing what she'd just heard. She began wringing her hands in her flour-spotted apron as if they were soiled and she was trying to cleanse them. Finally she said, "This is some sort of cruel joke, Sheriff. Please tell me you're jesting."

"Fraid not, Laticia. I'm dead serious. Now the burning question in my mind is how much of all this did you take part in?"

"Wait, did you say the victim's name was Babbo *Deemers?*"

"Yup. He and his twin sister, the fortune teller over at the circus, who is also Sophie Hardt's new friend, by the way. They were the fruit of one of Harold's trysts with a circus performer when he was at that fancy college over in New Jersey back in 'fifteen. Little Babbo was only nineteen when he was beaten to death three weeks ago. He found out a few months back that Harold was his daddy. Contacted him and convinced the circus owner to bring the show to town so as to connect with his only living family. And that sumbitch Harold had the kid—his own son—murdered because it wouldn't look good to have a freak in the family. Nice crowd ya hang with, Laticia. Now what was your part in all a this?"

"Sheriff! You can't think I had anything to do—"

"Can't I? You, Harold and that reporter have done nothing but point accusing fingers at the circus ever since it hit town. Even the day before yesterday when I came to arrest Harold, there you were yukkin' it up with two of the three conspirators. And remember when the reporter who done the actual deed to little Babbo, by the way, started to object to me arrestin' Harold? It was *you*, Laticia, *you* who put a protective hand on his chest to hold him back."

"I—"

"And what's more, Harold has always been your boy, ever since he was the good little neighborhood kid across the street, warn't he? He's been close under your wing. He shared with you his burnin' desire to become governor, or even more. You've been his biggest supporter all along. Haven't you, Laticia?"

"Well, yes, but that has nothing to do with—"

"We found the letters, Laticia."

Her face had already grown pasty. Now, though, beads of sweat popped out all over her forehead, just beneath her well-coifed hairdo. She muttered, "Letters?" But it was obvious she grasped what this meant.

"You orchestrated the whole deal, Laticia. It was you, wasn't it? You wanted your very own mayor, or governor, in your pocket. Hell, Harold had it all—money, looks, what folks call charisma and such, whatever the hell that is, but Harold had it. He figured out how such games were played, and you had the dirt. You figured out what happened with Milly Hill and the boys. Maybe Harold told you all about it, asked for your help. You even knew who else was in the car. With Daddy Deemers' nod and his dough, you bribed the sheriff at the time to cover it all up even though he found the circumstances around Milly's death mighty suspicious, didn't he, Laticia?

"Yup, *you* were the one pullin' the damn strings. You even promised Harold's friend, Lionel, that he'd ride the same gravy train if he just hung in there with y'all. But you didn't care about Clay Moore none. He had nothin' to offer you and your little train ride to glory, did he? Other than he was useful muscle. And he just didn't give a damn, did he? Jesus, Laticia, this is some twisted shit."

The woman's expression hardened. "So what is it you think you have, Sheriff? Some twenty-year-old correspondence? Good luck with that."

Billy smiled. "Well, we have a little more than that. Ya see, Harold fancies himself a writer. He thought someday he'd publish his memoir —edited, a course. But what is it they say about them writers? Until they whittle their chicken scratchin's down, there's some pretty raw stuff at first. We executed a search warrant of his house across the street over there. Guess what we found, and right next door to my law enforcement center. Twenty years worth a journals, Laticia. Life and times of a future president, right up to and includin' the murder and cover-up of a little circus freak that nobody shoulda given a shit about. But this conspiracy would hide a mistake that'd be a career-ending scandal, wouldn't it?

"Harold gives you a lot of credit, Laticia. He says you arranged all the details of the kidnappin', killin' and dumpin' gentle little Babbo out in a county ditch, right about where they found my deputy last Winter. That way, he'd be sure to be found. After all, you know how clever them show people can be. They might just conceal the killin' and you couldn't have that, now could ya?

"Harold also documented your *coordinated court of public opinion campaign* against the circus—get 'em kicked out a town before we could investigate the killin'. Your civic league outrage, the reporter's negative publicity campaign, your little riot at the fairgrounds, gettin' Harold to put the full force a his newspaper behind slanderin' the circus? I believe that's what they call complicity. Oh, and not so's you'd notice, most a them circus people are pretty good folks. Not that you'd know that because they don't serve your selfish needs. Right, Laticia?"

Her already hard expression turned to stone. "I wish to speak to an attorney. Now."

"Sure thing, Laticia. You should ask Harold if he'll share his with you. That Des Moines suit already cut a deal for the mayor. Maybe there's still a few scraps left over for you. Now if you'd please stand up and turn around...."

"Is this necessary, Billy?"

"Nope. Not at all. Turn around. Laticia Morgenstern, you are under arrest for conspiracy to commit two murders—of Milly Hill and Babbo Deemers. We might be talking more than a few counts for obstruction of justice, too, among a list of other offenses. But this'll do for starters. Let's go." He hustled her toward the front door with her apron still smelling like fresh-baked bread and her hands cuffed behind her back.

Laticia's husband had not gone out to his garage. He had been listening from the kitchen. He said, "Laticia, is this true?"

She called out over her shoulder, "Shut up, Ralph. Call Jacob. Have him meet me at the sheriff's office."

Ralph stood there slack-jawed.

She said, "<u>Now</u>, you idiot!"

83

Ralph headed for the telephone in the front room. Billy heard rapid footsteps coming up behind him from the kitchen. Before he turned around, the knife penetrated his upper back with tremendous force. Propelled him forward. He fell on top of Laticia near the front door.

As Billy dropped, though he was thrown into instant shock by the attack, he spun as he fell. Spotted the knife descending again, now toward his chest. Got his hands up. The knife sliced into the underside of his right forearm through the sleeve of his shirt before he grabbed the wrist wielding the knife. Somehow, he hung onto that wrist. His attacker wasn't very strong, but he was losing blood from the wound on his back and now from his arm at an alarming rate. He felt it saturating the back of his shirt. Warm, almost hot. And he could smell it, like a wet penny.

Then Laticia screamed, "Justina, no! Ralph, help!"

The animal-like voice from his attacker pierced his semi-conscious haze, the voice of... *Justina Ringwall?* She screamed, "You leave her alone!"

Blackness crept over Billy. The knife came closer, now an inch from his left eye. Billy thought, *I survived a damn war in Europe, murderous mobsters with Tommy guns down-county, and now I'm gonna to die across the street from my own damn office at the hands of a crazy girl? Now that's funny right there.* And then everything faded.

All grew quiet, the blackness complete.

🍂

84

Billy opened his eyes. And there was Sophie. He croaked, "Am I in Heaven?"

Sophie held his hand below the bandages on his right arm and chuckled. "Silly, you're in the hospital in Spencer. Nice room, too, courtesy of the Lyon County taxpayers."

"How long?" Then he noticed Jake behind Sophie, and Dwight, too. Dwight stepped up to the edge of his bed. "Darnedest thing, boss. Justina attacked you with a butcher knife yesterday at Laticia Morgenstern's house. Her husband, Ralph, pulled Justina off of you. Held her while he called me." Dwight looked embarrassed. He fell silent.

Billy collected his thoughts. At least he tried.

This is.... "Why in God's green acre would she attack... me? You— What's—?

The effort of speaking made him dizzy. Faint. Closed his eyes.

A nap would be good.

He heard another more official voice echoing off the walls, "He needs to rest now. Later."

THE THREE OF THEM SAT IN THE SECOND-FLOOR WAITING ROOM. THE whole place reeked of antiseptic and sorrow and hope.

Sophie was furious. "What is going on, Dwight? Why did your girl-friend attack Billy, for Heaven's sake?"

Dwight slumped, elbows on his knees. He spun the stiff rim of his official deputy's hat in his hands, as if he'd been practicing. He barely brought himself to speak, but Sophie wouldn't let him off the hook. "Deputy!"

That startled him. He looked up and met Sophie's eyes. Jake stood behind her. His hands rested on her shoulders, massaging them a little. She rested a cane between her knees. Dwight spoke so nobody else overheard, even though they were the only ones in the room.

"When I arrived at the Morgenstern's, Billy was unconscious, but he had a strong pulse. Ralph applied pressure on the wound to Billy's back. There was blood everywhere."

Dwight stopped, swallowed, kept turning his hat. Then, "Ralph had already wrapped Billy's arm up with a dish towel to slow the bleeding there, too. Laticia still had Billy's handcuffs on, and was slumped on the floor with her back against the entryway wall, maybe three feet from Billy and Ralph. Justina had curled up on the parlor sofa, sucking her thumb. Ralph had already called the hospital. The ambulance got there a while after I did.

"After they hauled Billy away, I took Ralph, Laticia and Justina to the LEC. I kept saying to myself, 'we're gonna need a bigger jail.' Until I sorted things out, I threw 'em all into cells—Ralph and Laticia in one, Justina in the other. Good thing the bus from Fort Madison had already picked up the mayor, Clay and that reporter."

Sophie grew impatient. "Alright, Dwight, but *why did Justina attack Billy?*"

"I questioned Laticia on the spot. After what Justina did to Billy, she spilled her guts. Turns out Justina is Laticia's *daughter* with one of the teenage neighborhood boys—none other than Harold Deemers, now our damned mayor twenty years later."

"Oh, for pity's sake." Sophie imagined there were no more surprises left. She was wrong. "That's disgusting. The man can't keep to himself!"

Dwight droned on as if describing a dream. "With that scandal brewing, the Deemers family took action. Laticia conspired with Harold's father to cover up their nasty affair. He also had one of his fancy doctors diagnose Laticia with consumption. She scooted off to a fancy sanatorium the last few months of her pregnancy to deliver and then miraculously recover.

"Laticia said all of this happened without her husband's knowledge. The man must either be a complete idiot, or is blindly in love with his wife and buried his head in the dirt. Right now, though, he is devastated. Says he heard this whole story for the first time tonight."

Sophie scratched, then rubbed her neck. Her brow wrinkled. Shook her head—more like a nervous tick. Dwight fell silent. She said, "So how did Justina end up a Ringwall?" She winced. Her back still stung like a hornet's nest from Josh dragging her all over at the circus.

"Well, again, courtesy of old man Deemers—Harold's daddy—he arranged for an adoption out of state before she even came home from the sanatorium. But Laticia insisted Justina be placed somewhere within the county. She ended up in George with the Ringwalls. I guess Laticia wanted to keep track of her. In case you hadn't noticed, Laticia gets her way. And since she and Ralph were incapable of having children of their own, she needed to get Justina placed."

Sophie's brow furrowed less as Dwight laid out the facts. She pointed a rhetorical finger. "She tucked Justina under her wing in her church group to be close to her only daughter." She popped up another finger. "And to keep close her strong connection to a future mayor, governor, or even president. Has Justina always known, Dwight?"

"No. In fact, once she settled down in her cell, Justy told me she always wondered why Laticia was always close to the mayor, spending so much time with him. She started snooping. She overheard Laticia and the mayor talking in the church office one day a few weeks ago—the only place they could talk, she guessed. Justina figured it out from there. She then grew protective of her. She said she was a far better mother to her than Mrs. Ringwall, despite her best efforts and a derelict husband. That's why Justina warned me about the mob at the fairgrounds. She was afraid for Laticia's safety if they went through with their plan to assault the circus."

"Dwight, did you find out if Justina knew about Babbo's murder, or Laticia's relationship with that weasel Lionel Johns?"

"No, I don't think she did, but we'll have to determine that from the evidence. I sure hope not. She's unstable, but I'd like to believe she's not capable of that. Aw, what the hell do I know? Even though my cop sense was screaming at me, I fell for her anyway."

"I'm really sorry, Dwight."

"Thanks, Soph. And here I thought circus folk were the snakes. Deemers, Moore, Johns, Laticia, and now Justina? The circus has its own problems, and was kind of the trigger for all of this, but—"

"Dwight, we're all human. We all have our frailties. The Bible teaches us we need to have faith in the Lord, and in each other."

"Yeah, I get that. Sometimes, it's harder to see the good in people, especially in my line of work. But you're right, Soph, we can't ever stop trying. Justina grew up hard, under confusing circumstances. But she tried to kill Billy! I guess we just need to get her the help she needs, huh? I think I also need to revise my opinion of *show people*, especially compared to everyone else. We have our own brand of performers, freaks and rousters here in our own community, don't we?"

Sophie just smiled. Dwight had grown since she'd met him. For that, she was grateful.

85

The Iowa Department of Corrections had picked up Mayor Harold Deemers, the reporter Lionel Johns, a.k.a. Ricky Dinkley, and city sanitation worker, Clayton Moore. Laticia Morgenstern was picked up by the ICIW - The Iowa Correctional Institution for Women, the minimum/medium security prison, also located at the state penitentiary in a separate block.

The bus carried the men ever closer to the dark hole Harold feared above all—the state penitentiary in Fort Madison where they'd await their arraignments. His lawyer advised him of no viable alternative, but only for the moment.

With only three prisoners on the bus, they each sat in a different row, but not too far from each other.

The rapid chain of events that led to this dismal moment in Harold's otherwise spectacular and well-orchestrated life astounded him. More than anything, after all the scandalous events in his past, now to be held accountable delivered a most profound shock. He got caught.

Remorse and regret plagued lesser mortals, not him. He remained confident that his money and contacts would extract him from this legal swamp; however, there was no doubt he would not escape unscathed. *Unless* he flipped this into a campaign for championing the rights of victims who fall prey to an unjust legal system. Yes, that might bear fruit.

"HARRY, WHAT ARE WE GONNA DO? YOU'LL BE ABLE TO GET ME MY job back as sanitation chief for the city, right?"

"Shut up, Clay."

Lionel sat two rows behind the mayor, one row behind Clay and across the aisle. He muttered, "Aren't we a fine trio of felons?"

"You can shut up too, *Ricky!*"

LIONEL JOHNS, THE REPORTER, A.K.A. RICKY DINKLEY WAS DONE with this arrogant prick. They'd been covering up his messes his entire life. "Us? You got balls, Harry. Who threw his own baby momma over to get assigned to a sweeter cell, you fucking hypocrite? Yup, you are right. We *are* on our own. Clay and me always have been. But you, you sorry spoiled brat, have always depended on somebody else to clean up your messes: your daddy, your neighbor lady-slash-whore, Clay, me.... Shit, man. You, my ex-friend, are on *your* own, maybe for the first time in your entitled life. Go fuck yourself, Harry."

The guard in the first row of seats that faced aft, toward his prisoners, shouted, "Hey, put a lid on it, or I'll gag every one a yer sorry asses!"

Lionel turned toward the window. He had said what was on his mind for a very long time. He was done, anyway.

Poor Clay just sat between them, not knowing what to say or do. His world collapsed. Again.

Harold shivered.

Commoners. They have no idea. This Phoenix will rise from these ashes. But not them.

May you two rot in whatever Hell of your choosing.

❧ 86 ❧

❧

Strike Bastian—nobody knew his real name—stepped in as Madame's lead rouster once they hauled Jed away in cuffs.

That asshole's betrayal of trust crushed Madame. Broke his heart. She had given him a job when nobody else would. He offered to do whatever it took to make it right, although he didn't have a clue what that might mean.

"Strike, that is awfully good of you. I do have an idea if you are, como se dice, *game?*"

"Name it, Madame." He wanted to say much more, but he'd shut up and listen.

THEY CRAFTED A PLAN—A CON—AND HOPPED INTO A CIRCUS TRUCK on a Tuesday morning after Madame made several telephone calls from the Post Office in town. The show was closed down, anyway. And they would move on soon now that they had solved the murders.

They aimed the truck south toward the opposite corner of the state, over four-hundred miles away, with enough provisions for several days. Their target: a particular resident of the small town near the state penitentiary in Fort Madison. It would take a day or two each way. Neither Madame nor Strike were strangers to living off the land. They'd spell each other driving. She seemed possessed. He understood and respected her reason.

LATE WEDNESDAY AFTERNOON, THEY ARRIVED IN FORT MADISON. They sought a local watering hole called *Racks,* a public house that served beer, strong drink, smoked ribs and slaw. As agreed, Strike waited in the truck.

❧

MADAME SAUNTERED INTO THE SMOKY BAR, TURNING EVERY HEAD, even in the joint's dim haze. Southeastern Iowa women didn't look anything like Antonia Perlatelli. A gorgeous woman in tight trousers that barely contained her hourglass figure? A blouse that almost failed to restrain what threatened to bust out all over? *And* thigh-high leather boots with cuffs and buckles? Even the few women in the place stared with admiration.

She sauntered up to the bar, shrugged off her crimson cape and laid it across her lap as she roosted on a stool and modestly crossed her slender legs. She noticed the burly man sitting next to her wore a uniform. In her most alluring accent, she purred, "Pardona, señor, are you policía? I *adore* men in uniform."

"Uh, well, ma'am, I work at the prison. I'm a guard supervisor—a, uh, pretty important job out there."

"Oh, sí, you must be muy importante. Buy me a drink, señor?"

"Uh, sure thing." He looked around, as if to make sure she was talking to *him*. Like his luck had changed. She picked *him* out of all the other men in the bar. "Beer?"

"¿Por qué no? Why not?" She giggled like a schoolgirl, as if this was all new to her. "You wear the ring. Will that be a problem?"

The oaf followed her eyes down to peer at the dull wedding band on his left hand, and that's when he caught her implication. "Uh, no.

No problem. She's, uh, out of town, anyway. Some foo-foo women's thing. Nope, no problem at all, Miss—"

"I would be honored if you would call me Maria, señor. And you are..."

"Sure, Maria. I'm Charlie. You sure are a looker."

Of course, she already knew who he was. "Do you have el automóvil, Carlos?"

"Carlos? Oh, yeah, I like that. Mexican for Charles, right? Yup, got a real fancy car outside. Wanna check it out, Maria?"

"Only with you, Carlos!" She giggled again.

Do men fall for this? Stupido!

They sauntered outside, arm-in-arm, with Antonia's left bosom pressed into Charlie's right arm. He stared down at where it made contact. The idiot was on the verge of drooling on both of them.

"Here it is. A gen-u-wine 1933 Master Sedan. Jet black, a course."

"Oooh, she is very beautiful. Does it have a soft back seat, Carlos? Oh, show me, please. *Please?*" A little girl asking daddy for a big favor.

"You got it, darlin'." He opened the rear door with a flourish. She spun him around so his back was to the bench seat, pushed him in, and fell in on top of him. Ripped open his coarse but limp uniform shirt and started rubbing his hairy chest with her rust-red nails. Reached down to unbuckle his trousers, but had some difficulty. He helped himself. Charlie didn't seem to worry about the rear passenger's side door still swung wide in the poorly lit parking lot with their legs hanging out, toe to toe.

With his trousers now shoved down almost to his knees, and only dirty white boxers covering his privates, Madame covered his face with her hair. Lost in her scent, he heard a voice outside the car rumble, "What the hell are you doing to my wife, ass-hat? Maria! Get your tail out a there, and I mean right fuckin' now! You go get in the truck, or I'll whip you 'n your boyfriend's ass right here!"

She gasped and scrambled backwards out of the car, feigning fear. With *her* clothes still intact, she managed a brief squeak and a sniffle before she made her escape. With Charlie now behind her, she winked at Strike as she swept past him.

"Sir, she didn't tell me she was married. I meant no harm."

"No harm, the man says with his pants down around his knock-knees. And is that a wedding ring on your hand there, pardner? For the love a—"

"Listen, mister, let me make it up to ya. Lemme buy you a drink."

"I don't want no damn drink. How about I follow you home and tell the little woman about you attackin' my wife? Yeah, that can work. That'd even things out, a'right." Strike stood close enough to the open car door that Charlie couldn't get up and out. He struggled to even pull his uniform trousers back up. He succeeded, but still lay on his own back seat with nowhere to go.

"No! We don't need to do that."

"Say, you a cop or somethin'?"

"I'm a guard out at the prison."

Strike paused, as if this was news to him. "Yeah? Well, maybe you could square us up another way, and then we wouldn't have to bother the little woman on the home front."

Charlie looked concerned. "Like what?"

"I just wanna visit an old friend there. Cut through the red tape. No big deal. I'd like to get him a letter, is all. You do that, *Carlos?*"

"Oh, you heard that, huh? Well, nothin' but an envelope and a sheet a paper inside?"

"That's it. We got a deal? Or are we goin' home together to visit the wife?"

"Okay, look. You be at the main gate tomorrow at nine sharp, and I'll get you in. No problem. What's the inmate's name?"

"Clayton Moore. I think he's waitin' on his arraignment."

"Yeah, okay, that should be easy. This mean you ain't gonna say nothin' about this, right?"

"You just get me in to see my buddy, and the rest'll be between you, me and that bitch I got for a wife."

"Alright, then. What's your name so's I can get it into the log?"

"Bennie. Bennie Arnold. And Charlie? You wanna be a hero? If anything happens to my buddy, God forbid, look at a detainee named Jed Strain. They got a thing."

"Okay, Bennie. Thanks, Tomorrow. Nine AM."

◌

87

The next day, a prison guard logged in Clay Moore's visitor, a stranger named Bennie Arnold. His boss had vouched for him. The visitor carried an envelope for a detainee. The guard grabbed it, looked it over, and handed it back to the visitor.

Bennie—a.k.a. Strike—sat across a scarred table from Clay Moore in the small visitor's room at the state pen. He said, "Clay, the mayor says he'll take care a ya, man. Like always. Said to hand you this note, but it don't mean nothin."

He passed the envelope across the table under the watchful eye of the guard. Clay read just three words: *Circus was fun*. He was about to ask *Bennie* what it meant when his visitor said, "Like I said. Don't mean nothin'. My excuse to get in to see ya, Clay. I'm here for you and Harry."

"So all the yelling on the bus?"

"The yelling? Oh, ah, that was just a misunderstanding. You can imagine he and Lionel were both stressed out, just like you, I'm sure. You understand."

"Uh, yeah, a course. Who are you?"

"Like I said, a friend of Harry's. Here's the deal. He needs you to do him a favor. There's this asshole from the circus in here. He's the reason you and the other boys got caught and is a dangerous witness against y'all. Name's Jed. Jed Strain." Strike looked over at the guard who was watching from a distance, but couldn't hear what they were saying.

Clay understood, and it scared him. "Oh, man. I ain't never done nobody before."

"Don't worry. You don't have to. When I leave, I'll shake your hand. That's when I'll pass you a small packet of powder. You get close to Jed with the powder in the palm of your hand. Make like you're gonna sneeze. Blow a puff of that shit into his face. But ya gotta be close. Tell him he needs to fly. Got that? You say, *'You need to fly.'* Now, remember, when you got that powder in your hand, you exhale. You do not inhale. That's important. Clay, Harry needs you to do this. Afterwards, you wash your hands. Can he count on you?"

"So I don't have to stick no knife into him or nothin'?"

"Nope. But remember. Sneeze this powder into his face, and—"

"And I tell him he needs to fly. And Harry needs me to do this?"

"Yup. For all y'all. He just can't get to you on account a where they got him locked up. You can do this, Clay, and y'all just might get out a this scrape."

"Okay, Bennie." And then Clay said too loud with too much enthusiasm, "Thanks for comin'. Nice to see you again, Bennie."

Strike thought the guard might get suspicious witnessing the world's worst acting job, but he didn't give a damn. "Alright, Clay. Put 'er there, amigo." He'd already palmed the packet of Devil's Breath and passed it to Clay with his right hand while patting him on the shoulder with his left. Logged out and met Madame waiting in the truck outside the gate in the small visitor's lot.

"Well?"

"In play, Madame. Now if the idiot can just do his part."

"And the second packet?"

"Under his collar. Let's go home."

"Thank you, Strike."

"For you, Madame, anything." And he meant it.

She muttered, *"Ha"u-Wil'uk...."* Fingered her bronze and turquoise pendant.

"I'm sorry?"

"Nothing, Strike. Nothing at all."

88

The Deemers Foundation made a hefty donation to the judge's favorite charity. He had served Harold's family for two generations. Got Harold released on bail while he awaited trial. He would be out by morning.

The mayor's legal team also hired a private detective agency to amass overwhelming evidence to convince any sane jury that one Clayton Moore became obsessed with the honorable mayor, as he followed Harold everywhere. This agency possessed considerable resources and the mayor could afford them. At the same time, they built the case to annihilate Moore's credibility.

Team Deemers planned a similar playbook for Lionel Johns—a.k.a. Richard (Ricky) Dinkley. They would prove, beyond a shadow of a doubt, the Milly Hill coverup turned out to be all Dinkley's idea who had tried to curry favor with his wealthy and influential friend. And that Harold had remained unconscious throughout the entire high school incident, by the way. They had drugged Harold and set him up.

Likewise, they amassed solid evidence to show the killing of the circus freak had been all Dinkley's brainstorm. Forensic evidence would demonstrate that Dinkley was indeed the killer. They also solidified the mayor's alibi, and documented—ad nauseam—a diabolical and twisted plot to curry the mayor's favor. In fact, their case would show, also beyond a reasonable doubt, that the mayor had become the victim of two devious high school friends. They attempted scheme after scheme over the years to weasel their way into the Deemers' family fortune. Desperate men, unscrupulous men, who had victimized the mayor—the innocent victim—his entire adult life.

His legal team also assured Harold the letters and journals recovered from his home would never see the light of day. They would be suppressed. He didn't need details.

They would also make a motion to declare one Laticia Morgenstern criminally insane so she would be assigned to a minimum-security wing at the ICIW—the Iowa Correctional Institution for Women. As such, any testimony she might offer would be discredited.

Harold grew optimistic about his prospects after a lengthy strategy meeting with his legal team in a private conference room reserved for such purposes at the prison. A guard escorted him back to his cell where he relaxed on his uncomfortable bunk and contemplated the public spin he'd place on this unfortunate affair. And how he'd take a temporary detour to achieve his political objectives. He stretched. Almost time for lights out. Freedom tomorrow! He drifted off.

It was pitch black. A powerful hand clamped down over his nose and mouth.

I must be dreaming. Yes, of course.

He only saw the hulk's silhouette by the sliver of moonlight penetrating the cell block via overhead skylights just outside his... *open cell door?* A gruff voice rumbled, "*Ha"u-Wil'uk,* motherfucker."

The blade penetrated Harold's lower abdomen. It was incredibly sharp. He didn't even know he'd been stabbed until his attacker jerked upward at the hilt toward his chest and twisted. Harold's eyes remained wide from the shock of the attack. He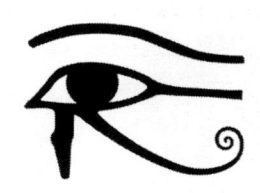

wondered how this could have happened, and at how little pain there was—at first, at least. Became aware of how hot his blood and other fluids were.

But most of all, Harold Deemers was appalled at the unfairness of it all.

89

They had released Billy from the hospital Wednesday morning. He rested in his apartment on Thursday, bored silly. Friday morning came and went. The wounds in his back and arm caused him to wince occasionally, but he was glad little Justina Ringwall didn't know jack about anatomy, and wasn't all that strong. His wounds were almost superficial. At least, that's what he told himself.

Billy realized his older arm injury from last summer's beating with a razor-blade-infested bat didn't hurt as much anymore. Doc said he should rest longer. He figured sitting on his butt was rest enough. The paperwork piled up while he was in the hospital. Then he got the call at his desk that would confound him, perhaps for the rest of his life.

"SHERIFF KERSHAW, THIS IS WARDEN SETH OLIVER DOWN HERE AT the Fort Madison State Penitentiary. I have some bad news about folks you have here awaiting arraignment. Not sure how to tell you this."

"Spit it out, Warden. What's going on? Did somebody escape?"

"No. Well, detainee Jed Strain committed suicide early this morning. Took a dive head-first off a second story causeway in one of our cell blocks. Killed him instantly. Damn strange. It appears the person responsible is another one of yours—Clayton Moore. He was holding a suspicious substance. Our medical team is in the process of identifying it, but it matches traces we found on the body. That might explain Strain's suicidal behavior,"

"The hell, you say! Well thanks, Warden."

"Sheriff, that's not the worst of it. Someone murdered another one of your detainees, Harold Deemers, in his cell in the wee hours of this morning—at about the same time as detainee Strain's suicide. And we found the murder weapon—a knife—along with copious traces of Deemers' blood and viscera in the cell of detainee Lionel Johns. Any idea what's going on here, Sheriff?"

Billy was stunned. He had no words, but he wondered.... *No, not possible.* "What about Laticia Morgenstern?"

"Another unusual development. We're holding her in our minimum-security women's block. She appears to have suffered some sort of psychotic break. Damn strange, Sheriff."

With no response forthcoming, the warden continued. "We're launching a full-scale investigation, of course, but the men seem to have turned on one another, with some outside help. In my forty years in the penal system, never have I seen anything like this!"

"Warden, that's, that's, ah, well, shit. Please keep me informed of your investigation. Thank you."

How...? No!

"**A**ntonia, you look tired." She sat behind the petite desk in her wagon. She looked ragged, but content. He stood. She smiled at the sheriff using her first name, and his obvious concern for her.

"Billy," ('BEE-lee'), "there is a great deal of work to prepare our show for travel. It has been a long few days. What may I do for you this day?"

"I wanted to tell you myself. Jed Strain committed suicide in prison this morning. Took a two-story nose-dive onto a concrete floor." He judged her reaction.

She stared at him, jerked her head from side to side twice, dropped her jaw. The pencil in her hand fell. He waited and watched. Then....

"Madre de Dios!" She looked down, fingered a bronze eye-shaped pendant with a turquoise inset that hung around her neck. But she met Billy's gaze with a most unusual expression. "Well, I cannot say that I am sorry. It seems justice is served. It is a shame, I suppose, that he will not stand trial for his crimes."

"They suspect Clay Moore, our city sanitation worker, dosed Jed

309

with what could be Devil's Breath." Once more, he studied her reaction.

She seemed perplexed. She shook her head. Looked at him. "Un momento—*your* city employee poisoned *my* Jed? That.... Wait, what else, Billy?"

"Someone killed Mayor Deemers in his bunk last night—early this morning—around the same time."

At this news, she splayed her fingers on the desktop with sufficient pressure to crumple pages. Her eyes widened, then she started blinking rapidly, and she shook her head again as if to clear the cobwebs, to process this latest nugget of news.

"How can this be? Is that prison *so* dangerous? This is not justice! This is too... easy! They deserved to live with their demons for a very long time!" Her shouting pierced his good ear. He winced. She threw a pencil hard enough to shatter it when it hit the wagon wall.

She throws like a man!

"Well, they're investigatin', but it *is* a dangerous place. Also, they suspect the reporter, Lionel Johns, killed the mayor. It appears they came down on each other. Not surprising after Clay informed on the mayor, and the mayor did the same to the reporter. Plus it was no secret that Clay and the others hated all circus people, including Jed. And, get this, Laticia Morgenstern, the church lady who looks to have orchestrated both the murders and the cover-up, suffered some sort a mental breakdown. They got her in a damn straight-jacket. Anyway, looks like both Clay Moore and Lionel Johns will be charged with first-degree murder now if the evidence bears out."

It was as if she had stopped trying to process this chain of events. She sat dazed, eyes glazed. Rested her forehead in the palms of her hands, elbows on her roughed-up desktop.

No, there is no way she could have orchestrated this. Those rat-bastards just turned on each other.

At last, she broke her stunned silence. Was it dismissal? Denial? He understood. That's exactly the way he felt at hearing of all this.

She sighed, "Gracias, Billy." She stood, paced, rubbed her forehead, tugged at her necklace, and sat back down in her desk chair. No sooner had she settled in, though, than she got up again and moved over to the small sofa, having settled something in her mind. Like she had put something behind her. Forever.

Her voice, her face, everything... changed. "Well, ah, I say good riddance. Monsters all." She reached down to open a small chest next to the sofa. As she closed the lid to use it as an end table, she set a fanciful bottle, two small glasses, a bowl of sugar cubes, four small wooden skewers and a box of matches on the chest's lid.

She said, "May I offer you a drink, Billy? I have a small bottle of some most excellent French absinthe that will settle our nerves. We may not see each other again, and it will be good for the pain and the confusion—both outside and inside. Will you join me?"

Billy wasn't sure this was a good idea, and he didn't really know what she meant, but what the hell? He couldn't believe he now trusted her.

"Sure, why not?"

Madame just smiled and muttered something strange under her breath.

"What was that, Antonia? Did you say *'how we look?'*"

"No, Billy. It is just an ancient expression that does not translate well. But it is some-thing like, 'Nature's balance will not be denied.'"

Billy just returned her smile.

Gypsy women!

❦

The circus tore down, packed up, and prepared for their move. The show did not leave the same day to travel all night. That was their routine. Instead, Madame had given the order they would get a fresh start early the next morning. There were rumors about her, the sheriff, and a bottle of absinthe.

Jake drove Sophie to the fairgrounds in time to witness the tail-end of the tear-down. Despite her back and hip pain, she was insistent. An overwhelming sadness consumed Sophie as she viewed the remnants of the midway and back lot.

They parked at the edge of the vehicle and wagon assembly area as they lined up for their journey. Sophie spotted Josh who led them to Sister's wagon. They needed to say their goodbyes. This also enabled Jake to slap Josh on the shoulder and shake his hand for saving Sophie's life. Then they made their way up Sister's steps and into her wagon.

"Jake, this is my friend, Sister. And Sister, my beloved husband, Jake. I wanted you—*needed* you—to meet each other."

"Sister, we meet, finally. It is truly a pleasure." He stared at her array of deformities, not in horror, but in *wonder*. Sophie had shared with Jake the lifelong courage demonstrated by this young girl.

"And you as well, dear Jake. Your Sophie is a treasure. You two complete each other. Yes, Jake, am I not *wondrous* to behold?"

They weren't sure, but the sound from Sister might have been a shallow chuckle, even a thin laugh. "Sophie, it is rare the man who looks at me with wonder and not horror. I am renewed in that there are still people in this world who seek inner beauty despite external unseemliness."

Jake looked at her in shock. "You read minds, Sister?"

She offered that lopsided ropy grin under her droopy nose and said, "Don't be silly. I just read people." Now a wider lop-sided grin aimed at Sophie. "Remember, dearie?"

But she had grown tired and sagged in her wheelchair. Sophie sensed it was time.

Sister croaked, "I must say goodbye now, my dearest of new friends."

They each embraced her, even as she sagged further.

"Goodbye, Sister. Tell the others how much—"

"I will, dearie. Tell Josh—"

Sophie said with a smile, "Of course, *dearie*." They walked out, closing the door behind them with a certain reverence. Josh waited outside. "Josh, dear, Sister—"

"Thanks be to ya, Miss Sophie, and blessings be upon ya." He saluted by dragging his hat off his head and used it to offer her a sweeping bow. Off he went to prepare Sister for the short trip to their next lot.

Jake said, "It seems like I'm listening through a keyhole and missed most of a conversation. I felt—"

"Yes, dear. That is Sister's way. We'll talk at home."

Later, Sophie would discover a letter had appeared in her pocket. She would read it many times over the years:

MY DEAR SOPHIE,

Josh wrote this out for me so that I could leave you a final word. He is clever and kind, as I am sure you noticed (he was reluctant to write these words —I gave him no choice).

Dearie, I will treasure our brief time together, seeking justice for someone I loved and someone you never met. I will never forget. And neither will the many friends you made within our troubled little troupe.

Eternally your friend,
Sister

As Jake and Sophie made their way back to the car, a beautiful and exotic woman blocked their path. Sophie recognized the magnificent Madame Antonia Perlatelli in an instant. She stood with her hands on her hips, all business, every bit the boss lady of a rough-and-tumble traveling show. But the warm smile that appeared on her face told Sophie she already trusted her at this, their first meeting. As they drew close, Madame threw open her arms and said, "Is it not time we met, Miss Sophie?"

◈◈◈

Jake looked confounded and more than a little mesmerized by this woman's natural beauty and unusual appearance. What with those trousers and rings and tattoos and white-blonde hair.... He stood aside as Sophie and Madame embraced. He recognized this was a significant moment.

◈◈◈

Madame whispered into Sophie's right ear as they hugged, "I am happy I asked Sister to recruit your assistance. Please forgive our little ruse."

Sophie pulled away enough to peer into Madame's twinkling eyes. "What?"

"Yes, she was my agent in this matter the entire time. You see, I did not know who I could trust. I see things, but my sight is limited. Does that not sound familiar to you, *dearie?*"

"What? But how—"

"My dear, it is a matter of survival for me to understand a community before we arrive. As much as *is* knowable. Call this... intuition. And more than a little research. Or shall we just label it *magic?*"

Madame smiled enigmatically at Sophie's confused expression that turned into one of amazement.

"Unbelievable."

"And that, mi hermana, is why I am in *this* business, and you are very good at what *you* do. Always protect that wonderful open-minded and caring intellect of yours, caro. Now I must attend to business. Your new friends, including me, are forever in your debt, Miss Sophie Hardt. Adios, mi amiga."

And with a quick squeeze and shake of both shoulders, with one final loving look, Madame Antonia Perlatelli swept away with a flourish to issue a series of rapid-fire commands.

JAKE HADN'T HEARD WHAT THE WOMEN SAID, BUT SAW HIS BRIDE standing there like she'd just seen a ghost. "What the hell was that all about?"

"Dear, I'll tell you later, even though you won't believe it. I'm not sure I do."

"Show people. And politicians. Eh?"

He chuckled at his cursory dismissal of the two most important things in Sophie's life during the past month, except for her husband, his cousin, and especially five-month-old Leo.

Her family. And his Sophie.

And she didn't even scold him for swearing!

✦ 9 2 ✦

❦

In an emergency meeting of the Rock Rapids city council, they unanimously named county attorney Clint Grossman, acting mayor. And nobody else threw their hat in the ring for the permanent job in the upcoming November election. While Clint had no political aspirations, he was an excellent administrator, and most agreed he would make a fine mayor.

Chief Dan Rustywire and his fiancée-in-perpetuity, Edie Everniss, along with Jake and Sophie Hardt, along with their live-in cousin, Walt Weller, would continue as fast friends and communal parents for little Leo, their "papoose." Sophie swore her days as an amateur sleuth were now behind her.

THE DEEMERS FAMILY ESTATE ADJACENT TO THE LYON COUNTY LAW Enforcement Center in Rock Rapids went up for auction. As the now-deceased sole heir, Harold Deemers neglected to leave a last will and testament. Apparently, he never found the time for such finery, and had convinced himself he would live forever. Acting Mayor Grossman found a way for the county to purchase the Deemers estate—those in the know said it was a real bargain.

The Lyon County Civic League transformed the Deemers property into what would become a sanctuary for unwed mothers and the handicapped. It would be called the *Babbo & Sister Sanctuary* in honor of the little man who finally found his way home, and the larger-than-life little woman who ensured somebody cared. They extended an open invitation to Sister should she ever need a home off the road among friends. The community felt this was the least they could do.

Once staffed, one of the Sanctuary's first transfers in was a distressed and confused Justina Ringwall. Doc Gustavsen volunteered his time there, along with a few of his colleagues from the hospital in Spencer. From that humble beginning, several substantial endowments found their way into the Sanctuary's coffers. The idea caught on, especially with the Lyon County church ladies who felt compelled to make amends for one of their prominent members. From there, a small full-time staff came on board. News of the Sanctuary in Lyon County spread far and wide. Its reputation as a fine institution blossomed.

Sheriff Billy Rhett Kershaw would run unopposed in the November election for sheriff. Deputy Dwight Spooner and Deputy Jimmy Lenert would continue on with the department. Dwight volunteered his every spare moment at the Sanctuary. It was time he did more than his job for his community. Maybe he could help Justina Ringwall as one of their first residents.

Billy thought about running away to the circus, but if he got re-elected in November, that would be a problem. Just for a visit, now and then? To one lady in one show in particular?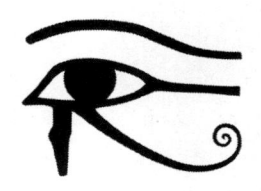

Yup. That could work.

APPENDIX A - CAST

Cast of Major Characters (in alphabetical order):

- **Babbo (the Manimal):** Born a "pinhead" (a medical condition called microcephaly). One of Madame's featured sideshow "freaks."
- **Strike Bastian:** A roustabout for Madame Perlatelli's show.
- **Aloysius Cogholdt:** Ringmaster for Madame Perlatelli's show.
- **Crocodile Man (a.k.a. CM or Charles Macklin):** A "made freak" and husband to the two-headed girl, Tamra and Tara.
- **Harold Deemers:** Mayor of Rock Rapids, Iowa.
- **Samuel Ellis:** Junior ATF agent working for Lang Eubanks.
- **Josh (no last name):** A young roustabout and Miss Sophie's protector while on the circus lot.

- **Milford Langford (a.k.a. Lang) Eubanks:** Senior Supervisory Agent for Alcohol, Tobacco & Firearms (ATF); a "G-man" (government man) from the US Department of Justice.
- **Edith Everniss:** Sophie's friend from George, Iowa, four years her junior.
- **Fenton (a.k.a. Happy) Grant:** A clown for Madame Perlatelli's show.
- **Jacob (a.k.a. Jake) Hardt:** farmer; inventor, and Sophie's husband.
- **Leo Hardt**: Sophie and Jake's infant son.
- **Sophie Hardt:** Jake Hardt's wife and reluctant amateur sleuth.
- **Silas Hummel:** A farmer and neighbor to the Hardt farm.
- **Lionel Johns (a.k.a. Ricky Dinkley):** Lyon County News reporter.
- **Billy Rhett Kershaw:** Lyon County sheriff.
- **Deputy Jimmy Lenert :** Junior Lyon County deputy.
- **Linus (no last name):** Dog trainer for the act, Linus and his Magnificent Hounds.
- **Clayton (Clay) Moore:** City of Rock Rapids sanitation worker.
- **Laticia Morgenstern:** Chairperson of the Lyon County Civic League and lead "church lady" from Rock Rapids, Iowa.
- **Antonia Perlatelli (a.k.a. Madame, or Madame Purgatory):** Owner and general manager of Perlatelli's Oddities and Wonders circus/carnival.
- **Justina Ringwall:** A young "church lady" from George, Iowa.
- **Dan (aka Chief) Rustywire:** Jake's friend and boss at Red Chief Dirigibles, Inc.
- **Sister Shipton (aka Sister):** Seer, twin to Babbo the Manimal. Madame has kept them together.
- **Lilith Smalley:** Midget performer for Madame Perlatelli's show and in love with Babbo the Manimal.

- **Tom Smalley:** Lilith's father and single parent, also a midget.
- **Dwight Spooner:** Ex-Minneapolis homicide detective & friend of Sheriff Billy; now his senior deputy.
- **Jed Strain:** Big cat trainer & Madame's head of security.
- **Milo Vladinov:** A clown for Madame Perlatelli's show.
- **Walter (a.k.a. Walt) Weller:** Jake Hardt's cousin and little Leo's godfather.

APPENDIX B - GLOSSARY

❧

Glossary of terms from circus & carnival history & tradition:

- **Back Lot:** That area of a circus lot not open to the public, where the cast of a show eats, sleeps and relaxes when not in the public's eye.
- **Bally or Ballyhoo:** A free show given outside a side show to attract a crowd of potential patrons. The word came into being at the 1893 Columbian Exposition in Chicago. Fakirs, gun spinners and dancing girls from the Middle East spoke no English, only Arabic. Interpreters used the expression "Dehalla Hoon" to call performers outside to the show fronts. Western ears of the talkers translated it as 'ballyhoo' and so used it when the interpreters were away for lunch.
- **Banner:** Pictorials on canvas hung in front of circus sideshows and carnival midway shows, depicting the wonders to be found inside.
- **Barkers:** Carnival workers whose job it is to draw in passersby with an appealing pitch.

- **Big top:** The large tent that houses the main performances of a circus.
- **Bill:** A piece of advertising paper, or the act of placing advertising paper on, or in selected locations in and around the town to be played by the show. They also use the term in other ways, as in, "How was he billed?" meaning "How was his act advertised?" and "Was she on the bill?" meaning, "Was she in the show?"
- **Blowdown:** When one or more tents or riding devices are leveled to the ground by a windstorm.
- **Boss Canvasman:** Literally, what it says. He's the man in charge of making sure the canvas goes up properly and doesn't come down on the show short of a major blowdown.
- **Cabinets of Wonder:** The English translation of kunstkammer and wunderkammer, the cabinets of curiosities and wonders that evolved into the dime museums of the 19th century. They were private collections of odd, bizarre, unusual, exotic and—by today's standards—relatively mundane objects, many of which might be found in any Museum of Natural History.
- **Carnival:** A cooperative business arrangement between independent showmen, ride owners and concessioners to present outdoor amusement for the public.
- **Carny:** Someone who works at a carnival. The term is also applied to the carnival itself. It's a term used by some in the business and disliked by others.
- **Chumps:** Local customers. Also called rubes or marks.
- **Cons:** Confidence games are designed to win the mark's (target's) confidence for the purpose of bilking them out of their money.
- **Cutting Up Jackpots (Jackies):** Telling tall tales about previous circus/carnival jobs with co-workers in the show, often distorted in the telling among showmen.
- **Dime Museum (a.k.a. Odditorium):** A collection of specimens, exotic objects and live acts and performances, usually set up in its own building or tent. They were most

popular primarily in the 19th and early 20th century. Present day road-side museums are their descendants.

- **Do-gooders:** Individuals who believe in the innate evil of the amusement business, focusing generally on the notion that it exploits or demeans those who work in it. The do-gooders are generally despised by the same supposedly exploited individuals: the carnival and circus workers. The common terminology today is "PC" or "politically correct."
- **Freak:** A human oddity on exhibition in a museum or in a circus or carnival side show. Early day circuses also displayed some featured freaks in their menageries.
- **Freak Show:** A show where human oddities and freakish working acts performed. The term applies to both circus and carnival. In practice, these shows were often ten-in-one shows and usually had a high percentage of working acts, like sword swallowers and fire eaters or 'made freaks' like tattooed people.
- **Gaffs:** In the broadest sense, anything controlled or faked. In the case of freak animals (and human oddities as well, on occasion), for example, a gaff wouldn't be a genuine freak of nature, regardless of how convincing it looked, but a specimen manufactured to look freakish.
- **Grab Joints:** An eating concession (with circuses, a hamburger or sandwich stand). The customer is served directly over the counter from the griddle, juice bowl, etc. Circus grab joints had no seating of any kind for customers. The only seating for them was in the big top.
- **Grift:** The crooked games, short-change artist, clothes-line robbers, merchandise boosters, pick-pockets and all other types of skullduggery carried by some of the "fireball shows" —those who left towns in their wake ruined (flamed) for future shows. The opposite of a fireball show was a "Sunday school show."
- **Heat:** Problems, arguments or battles between the show, or its people, and town's people. Most heat was caused by illegal activities of a show, but not always by the show

involved. A "burn em up" outfit in ahead of a real "Sunday schooler" could and did leave a lot of heat for the latter.

- **Hooverville:** Similar to a refugee camp, its residents fell victim to living in poverty. Called Hoovervilles after the president most blamed for their economic plight.
- **Lot:** The show grounds.
- **Marks:** A carnival term for townspeople. Particularly, the ones who 'go up against the games.'
- **Midway:** In its broadest sense, the location where all the concessions, rides and shows are located in a circus, fair or carnival. In a circus, the midway is just that: the midway between the 'front door' to the circus lot itself and the 'big top' where the circus performers do their acts.
- **Parade:** The procession which announces the arrival of the circus to town. Traditionally, circuses would make them as glorious and spectacular as possible and they'd wind through the middle of town all the way to the lot where the big show was to occur.
- **Pickled Punks:** A carnival term for human fetuses. Two-headed human babies, joined together twins, also normal specimens from one to eight months. Found in the Dime Museum in most shows. Not India rubber, as many believed. These specimens were repulsive to some, but highly educational for millions of others.
- **Pinhead:** Human oddity afflicted with microcephaly. The under-developed head came to a point, a fact which was often further emphasized by leaving a top knot of hair to emphasize the head shape.
- **Pitchman:** Sells merchandise by lecturing and demonstrating.
- **Ragbag:** What they call some carny shows, especially those smaller and less reputable.
- **Roustabouts (a.k.a. rousters):** Circus working men on the lot, particularly the big top crew. Men in each department had designations from the job they performed (in the larger shows): dog boys, pony punks, property men,

skinners, bull men, cage hands, front door men, lead bar detective, honey bucket man, coffee boy, pastry cook....

- **Route:** List of towns and events played each week, month, or year (season).
- **Rubes:** A not very affectionate term for the towners or townies.
- **Russian Swing:** A large, floor-mounted swing which is sometimes used in circus performances to make impressive high acrobatic jumps. It has steel bars instead of ropes, and its swinging platform is able to rotate 360 degrees around the horizontal bar from which it is suspended. Two or more acrobats stand on the swing platform, pumping it back and forth until it is swinging in high arcs.
- **Siamese Twins:** The medical and more politically correct term is conjoined twins, that is, any twins who were joined at birth. The configurations are many and varied, from joining at the breast, the hips, top of the head, etc. The term originated with the "original" twins, Chang and Eng, who were from Siam.
- **Side or sideshow:** Any show that plays the midway, though the now more common application is to the freak shows or ten-in-one shows. Technically, however, even a menagerie on the midway of a circus is a sideshow.
- **Single-O:** A show consisting of a single attraction.
- **Spiel:** The speech made on a show front by the talker or pitchman to the gathering crowd.
- **Spot:** Where the show plays; its location. For example, "We played that spot." Also applies to placement of the show itself as in "When we got to the lot, our show was already spotted for us." May also apply to the location of a particular act within the show.
- **Ten-in-One:** A carnival midway show with ten attractions inside. It is usually an "illusion" show or some other "string show." Can be either a "pit" or a "platform" show. Most of them worked on ground level, though. Also '10-in-1.'

- **The Nut:** The operating expenses of a show (daily, weekly, or yearly). The story is that the word came into usage after a creditor came onto a circus grounds and took the nuts off the wagon wheels. "I will keep them until I get my money," he announced. He was paid. The nuts went back on the wheels and the show moved that night. "So a show always sought to 'make the nut' and start making money above its expenses. A show that hadn't yet 'made the nut' was said to be 'on the nut' and one that had been said to be 'off the nut'."
- **Trouper:** A person who has spent at least one full season on some type of traveling amusement organization. By then, they are usually hooked.

DISCLAIMER

This is a work of fiction. Any similarity to actual persons, behaviors, places or events should be considered coincidental and fictional.

No part of this publication may be stored in a retrieval system, transmitted, or reproduced in any way, including, but not limited to, digital copying and printing without prior agreement and written permission of the publisher, UpLife Press.

Research of this manuscript's period and its theme mandated judicious use of ethnic pejoratives and mild profanity, and are not meant to offend the reader. Quite the contrary, the use of these literary devices is intended to demonstrate the authentic commitment to a higher set of moral standards and to the strength of each character's faith, or lack thereof.

DEDICATION

For Mom, who had dreams of her own, and made most of them come true.

ACKNOWLEDGMENTS

- Many thanks to my treasured beta readers, and to *all* my readers!
- Zara Altair, thanks for turning me onto the incredibly robust genre of mystery fiction.
- I must credit Troy Lambert for his "Sleuth's Journey" story structure which breathed life into the mystery you are about to experience.
- The wonderful online research resources are just too many to list. But I gained many insights from visits to circus museums like The Ringling Museum in Sarasota, Florida, and Circus World in Baraboo, Wisconsin.
- I'd also acknowledge inspiration gained from visiting the Circus Arts Conservatory and a Circus Sarasota performance in Sarasota, Florida. Most useful were discussions with performers after the show!
- And finally, I hungered for information *way* outside of my wheelhouse on the topics of nature religions, witchcraft and the occult in order to add realism to belief systems held by those outside my own social milieu, but important to my story and characters. Again, I explored too many sources to cite, but all told, informative and fascinating!

BEFORE YOU GO

Please write and post a brief review on Amazon. Or email your thoughts to gjurrens@yahoo.com.
Remember, other readers and I need to know what you think. **I read every single review with gratitude. Thank you.**
Also, feel free to browse or subscribe at GKJurrens.com for announcements and giveaways.

- GK Jurrens

AUTHOR'S NOTE

I built this story on the foundation of "Black Blizzard." Many of the same social issues exemplify what the characters in that book faced. Some overcame them, some succumbed to them.

Physical and mental handicaps, social prejudices, and pointing fingers at others without admitting to their own weaknesses or biases in the 1930s are not unlike our real world today. The more things change, the more they remain the same.

I felt this little corner of the world reflected issues we see today on an interpersonal, local, national, and international scale. I keep asking myself, why do we keep making the same mistakes when we superficially look at those not like ourselves? Why do we jump to conclusions based on personal biases? And why are we so prepared to condemn the weaknesses and frailties of others while ignoring or overlooking our own?

I have no answers, my friends, other than having written this book for these reasons. For you. And for me.

OTHER BOOKS BY GK JURRENS

<u>Contemporary Fiction (Thrillers)</u>

- Dangerous Dreams: Dream Runners: Book 1
- Fractured Dreams: Dream Runners: Book 2

<u>Historical Fiction (Great Depression Era Crime)</u>

- Black Blizzard: A Lyon County Adventure
- Murder in Purgatory: A Lyon County Mystery

<u>Futuristic Fiction (Paranormal Mystery Thrillers)</u>

- Underground, Mayhem: Book 1
- Mean Streets, Mayhem: Book 2
- Post Earth, Mayhem: Book 3
- A Glimpse of Mayhem: Companion Guide to the Mayhem Trilogy

<u>Non-fiction</u>

- Why Write? Why Publish? Passion? Profit? Both?
- Moving a Boat and Her Crew
- Restoring a Boat and Her Crew

ABOUT THE AUTHOR

🙚✶🙜

GK Jurrens writes with undiluted passion. He also teaches writing and publishing on the road. More often than not, GK and his wife live and travel in a motorhome when they're not spending time at their condo in Southwest Florida. They wander their beloved North America as a source of endless inspiration.

After studying Liberal Arts and Electronics Engineering Technology, GK earned a Bachelor of Science degree in Business and a Master of Science degree in Management of Technology from the University of Minnesota, USA. He is the proud father of two adult children and the equally proud grandfather of three almost-adult grandchildren.

Six years of government service and a successful three-decade career in global high-technology preceded more than a few years of sailing America's waterways, the Florida Keys, and the Eastern Caribbean from the British Virgin Islands to Granada, near the coasts of Venezuela and Trinidad, with a brief foray sailing around the Greek Cyclades Islands in the Aegean Sea.

GK now pursues his life-long penchant for the creative arts: prose and poetry, painting (watercolor), traveling (North America), playing guitar (acoustic-electric) and playing his growing collection of Native American flutes, some of which he crafted while living in the Arizona desert.

He enjoys quiet evenings reading and exploring movies, when not writing or sitting by a campfire alongside his copilot and soulmate of over half a century—Admiral Kay.

If you'd care to offer the author feedback, for which he'd be grateful, consider emailing **gjurrens@yahoo.com** or visit **GKJurrens.com**.

- facebook.com/genejurrens
- x.com/gjurrensı
- instagram.com/gjurrens
- linkedin.com/in/gkjurrens

Made in the USA
Middletown, DE
20 June 2024

55602292R00205